Please return or renew this item by its due date to
avoid fines. You can renew items on loan
by phone or internet:

023 9281 9311
www.portsmouth.gov.uk

Portsmouth
CITY COUNCIL
Library Service

THE
RED CHAMBER

Pauline Chen

virago

VIRAGO

First published in Great Britain in 2012 as a paperback
original by Virago Press

First published in the United States of America
in 2012 by Alfred A. Knopf

A CIP catalogue record for this book
is available from the British Library.

ISBN 978-1-84408-796-9

Printed and bound in Great Britain by
Clays Ltd, St Ives plc

Papers used by Virago are from well-managed forests
and other responsible sources.

MIX
Paper from
responsible sources
FSC
www.fsc.org
FSC® C104740

Virago Press
An imprint of
Little, Brown Book Group
100 Victoria Embankment
London EC4Y 0DY

An Hachette UK Company
www.hachette.co.uk

www.virago.co.uk

And that was when, faced with a real death, and with this new wonder about men, I laid aside my drafts and hesitations and began to write very fast about Jack and his garden.

V. S. Naipaul, *The Enigma of Arrival*

In loving memory of
BIH-JAU CHEN
6 OCTOBER 1939, TAIPEI, TAIWAN
10 JUNE 2008, PORT JEFFERSON, NEW YORK

Author's Note

The Red Chamber is inspired by Cao Xueqin's *Dream of the Red Chamber*, the eighteenth-century novel widely considered the most important work of fiction in the Chinese literary tradition. However, Cao's masterpiece is largely unknown to western audiences, perhaps due to its daunting length (2,500 pages) and complex cast of characters (more than 400). My book, *The Red Chamber*, makes little attempt to remain faithful to the original plot, but is a reimagining of the inner lives and motivations of the three major female characters. In a world where women lacked power and were pitted against one another by the system of concubinage, these characters are strong and unforgettable, forging bonds with each other that far transcend sexual rivalry. In addition, like many readers, I was haunted by a sense of incompletion: Cao's original ending has been lost, and a new ending was written by another hand after his death. What follows is my attempt to finish the story for myself, while paying homage to this beloved masterpiece and sharing it with a wider audience.

Major Characters

THE LINS
LIN DAIYU, the daughter of an official in Suzhou
JIA MIN, her mother
LIN RUHAI, her father

THE JIAS
JIA BAOYU, pampered heir of the Jia family in the Capital, cousin of Daiyu
JIA ZHENG, his father
LADY JIA, his grandmother
JIA ZHU, Baoyu's older brother, dead at the beginning of the novel
JIA LIAN, Baoyu's cousin
JIA HUAN, Baoyu's half brother
WANG XIFENG (pronounced "Shee-feng"), Jia Lian's wife
PING'ER, Wang Xifeng's body servant
"THE TWO SPRINGS": JIA TANCHUN, Baoyu's half sister, and
JIA XICHUN (pronounced "Shee-chun"), Baoyu's cousin
JIA YUCUN, a rising official and distant relative of the Jia family

THE XUES
MRS. XUE (pronounced "Shreh"), a widowed sister-in-law of Jia Zheng's, living with the Jias
XUE BAOCHAI, her daugher
XUE PAN, her profligate son
XIA JINGUI (pronounced "Shah Jin-gway"), wife of Xue Pan

THE ZHENS
SNOWGOOSE, Lady Jia's body servant
ZHEN SHIYIN, her brother, a blacksmith

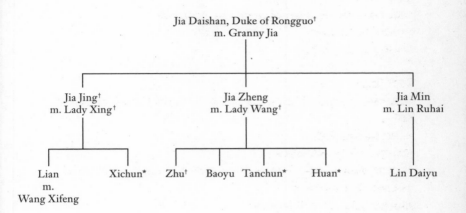

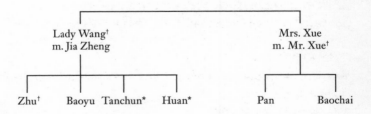

*Child by a concubine
†Dead at the beginning of the novel

PART ONE

Fifth Month, 1721

In the Garden of the Five Senses
Let Delight know no bounds.

Inscription on a tablet in the garden
at Rongguo Mansion

1

Lin Daiyu crushes apricot kernels and black sesame seeds in a marble mortar. She scrapes the medicine into a bowl of stewed bird's nests and stirs it with a porcelain spoon. She brings the bowl to her mother's bed near the window. Propped against her bolsters, Daiyu's mother sips the dose, grimacing a little. Daiyu watches every mouthful, as if by her vigilance she can somehow will the medicine to work.

Mrs. Lin lies back, exhausted even by the act of drinking. "Daiyu," she says, her voice a reedy thread.

"Yes?"

"I want to show you something."

"What is it?"

"Go and look in the bottom of my old trunk."

Daiyu kneels before the wardrobe and opens the battered chest where the family keeps their winter clothes. She rummages beneath the piles of bulky padded trousers and quilted jackets, and finds a flat bundle in a crimson brocade wrapping cloth.

"Yes, that's it. Bring it here."

Her mother's thin fingers struggle with the knot, and Daiyu leans over to help. Inside are two flat boxes. Mrs. Lin opens one to reveal a necklace of reddish gold in the form of a coiling dragon. In the other is a tiara of flying golden phoenixes, a string of pearls arching from each beak.

"These are from your dowry, aren't they?"

Mrs. Lin does not seem to hear the question. "Help me up," she says.

Daiyu climbs onto the bed and adjusts the pillows so that her mother is sitting upright. Her mother places the tiara on her uncombed hair. "Bring me a mirror."

Reluctantly, Daiyu gets the one on the dressing table. Leaning against the cushions, her mother tilts the tiny bronze hand-mirror back and forth, catching little glimpses of herself on the polished surface. "What a fine young lady I was back then, looking down my nose at everything. Why, I'd never even touched, let alone worn, silks like these, made by common weavers." Her fingers pluck at the worn honey-colored material of her robe. "Everything we wore was made in the Palace by the Imperial Weavers. Even our maids didn't wear such stuff!"

Daiyu's mother laughs a little, as if marveling at her younger self.

"I was fond of fine things in those days, and my parents spoiled me by giving me anything I wanted. My eldest brother, Jing, didn't mind, but my second brother, Zheng, was always jealous."

Daiyu sits by her mother's feet, watching the play of expression on her face.

"I remember one New Year's, when our grandfather—the first Duke of Rongguo—was still alive. He asked us to write lantern riddles in verse. When he read what the three of us had written, he said it was a pity I hadn't been born a boy, for I would have been sure to win the Jias glory if I had been allowed to take the Civil Service Exams."

Daiyu nods. Her mother loved poetry, and had taught Daiyu the rules of meter and rhyme as soon as she could read.

"As it was, Zheng had to take the Exams I don't know how many times until he passed. Your father passed the first time, of course. But in the end, Zheng did pretty well for himself." To Daiyu, her mother's voice sounds slightly grudging. "Under-Secretary in the Ministry of Works. Zheng always was a hard worker."

"What about your eldest brother?"

"Jing never did pass. All he did was fritter away my father's money on concubines and gambling." The reminiscent smile fades from Mrs. Lin's face, and her expression grows somber. She hands Daiyu the mirror and plucks the tiara off her hair. "And now Zheng is the only one of us who is still alive, and living at Rongguo Mansion with my mother."

"Do I have any cousins there?" Daiyu says.

"Well, there's the famous Baoyu, of course."

"Why is he famous?"

"Haven't I told you about him?" Her mother's delicate eyebrows arch in surprise. "He's Zheng's son. He was the one born with the jade in his mouth. That's why your grandmother named him 'Baoyu,' 'Precious Jade.'"

"How could a person be born with a jade in his mouth?"

"Who knows?" Mrs. Lin shrugs. "All I know is that my mother—your grandmother—thinks it's a miracle, and spoils him to death. His own mother died when he was barely twelve or thirteen, and from all I've heard he's turned into a rare handful. He skips school every other day, and runs around with his girl cousins in the Women's Quarters instead of studying."

"How old is he?" Daiyu asks.

"Eighteen—more than old enough to take the Exams. Your other male cousin, Lian, is more than twenty-five, but they gave up on his passing years ago. He's Jing's son. Like father, like son, I suppose. I don't know how the Jias are going to keep up their prestige if they don't have more sons entering the Civil Service. If Baoyu doesn't pass—" Mrs. Lin pauses, coughing, then leans back against the pillows with her eyes shut, trying to catch her breath.

"Help me lie down."

Daiyu climbs onto the bed and eases her mother into a lying position. She wipes her mother's lips.

After Mrs. Lin's breath has slowed, she says, still with her eyes closed, "You'll have to go live with them, you know, after I die."

"You won't die," Daiyu says quickly, but even to her own ears her voice lacks conviction.

"Yes, I will. And when I do, you'll have to go to the Jias."

"I'll stay with Father."

"I want you to go to the Capital."

"Why?" Daiyu starts to cry.

"You'll be able to make a good match there—someone from one of the big families. The Jias will see to that."

"What does that matter?" Daiyu cries. "You didn't have a match like that." Though her father comes from an old and educated family, he had been the sole offspring of an only child; and now only distant members of the clan, whom she has never met, are still alive. "Why can't I stay here?"

Her mother lies silent for a long time, staring at the ceiling. At last she says, "When I was young, I didn't think anything mattered as long as I was with your father. Now, since I've gotten sick, I've realized how hard it is to be without any family." Her eyes turn to Daiyu, and Daiyu sees they are full of tears. "I'm worried about what will happen to you when I'm gone. I don't want you to have to struggle like I did ... "

Her words fill Daiyu with something akin to panic. "But— but you've been happy with Father, haven't you?"

Mrs. Lin doesn't answer. Her eyes move past Daiyu to the phoenix tiara on the dressing table. "We should never have raised you like this."

"Like what?"

"Keeping so much to ourselves. You've never met people of your own age and background." She looks back at Daiyu and her eyes are almost challenging. "Well, you'll have to learn how to get along with other people at Rongguo. You'll need to learn to think before you speak." She puts out her hand, and Daiyu takes it, feeling how cool her fingers are. "Still, you mustn't let them cow you. You're strong enough to stand up to them."

Daiyu wants to ask more questions, but her mother starts to cough again. This time she coughs so long and hard that Daiyu rushes to get a spittoon. Mrs. Lin spits out a mouthful of phlegm scarlet with fresh blood. When her mother finally stops coughing, Daiyu does not say anything more, just climbs into bed beside her. She feels how small and frail her mother has grown over the last six months, her limbs like twigs against her own strong, warm body; yet her mind shrinks from picturing a future without her. She nestles her face deeper in the crook of her mother's neck, and sniffs for the last lingering scent of her skin not yet obscured by medicine and sickness.

Towards the end of the Forty-Nine Days mourning, a strange man appears at the temple where Daiyu and her father are keeping vigil beside her mother's coffin. Like them, he wears mourning robes of undyed hemp. Daiyu's father stares at the man unrecognizingly. Then he starts to his feet with a cry of surprise.

"Why, it's Zheng, isn't it?"

"Ruhai, old fellow. It's been a long time!"

Daiyu scrambles from the floor, startled by her uncle's unexpected arrival. She searches his careworn face and stocky figure for something of her mother. The only resemblance she can find is about the eyes: there is a little thickness to the eyelids, giving her uncle the same dreamy, slightly sleepy look as her mother, and as Daiyu herself.

Daiyu's father tries to kowtow, but his brother-in-law catches him by the elbows. "I set out as soon as I got her letter," Jia Zheng says. "When did she die?"

"More than a month ago."

Jia Zheng's eyes begin to water. "That's probably just after she sent the letter. Did she suffer at the end?"

"Not too much. It was quicker than we expected."

Daiyu turns away to hide her tears. Her father manages to control himself. He clasps her uncle's hand. "I'm glad you've come. Will you stay the rest of mourning?"

"I'm afraid I can't. I have some business in Nanjing. My barge is waiting for me at the dock."

"You'll come for dinner at least?"

"Yes, of course."

For the rest of the day, Jia Zheng stays at the temple with them, kneeling before the spirit tablet. For the past six weeks, Daiyu and her father have come to the temple every morning, the mourning rituals and funeral arrangements drawing them together and organizing their days. Now, the presence of her uncle disrupts their silent rapport, making her self-conscious. She watches him mopping his streaming eyes, finding it odd that a stranger is sharing their grief.

Before dinner, her father accompanies Jia Zheng to his barge. Back in the kitchen at Bottle-Gourd Street, Daiyu distracts herself with her daily tasks. She makes up the fire, washes the rice, and chops the vegetables. The wooden handle of the cleaver, smoothed by years of use, fits effortlessly in her hand, and her eyes are soothed by the familiarity of the room: the blue and white dishes, the faded picture of the Kitchen God on the wall, the sound of neighbors' voices through the open window. She sees that the bucket is almost empty and goes to the well to draw water. It had rained earlier in the afternoon, one of those late summer showers, and the stone bridges and canals are dark and slick. The air is so heavy that it feels as if the least disturbance would bring on the rain again. The byways are nearly empty at this time of day, but on the other side of the canal a woman stoops beside the water with a basket of winter clothes. The hollow sound of the woman pounding the laundry with a wooden block reminds Daiyu that, despite the heat, summer is drawing to a close.

As she slips back into the kitchen, she hears voices in the front room.

"Daiyu, is that you?" her father calls.

She is surprised to see two tall, elegantly dressed women standing near the front door. She remembers her mother's words about how even the maids at Rongguo didn't wear ordinary silks.

"I want to introduce you to Nanny Li and Nanny Ma," Uncle Zheng says, rising from his chair. "They'll be taking care of you on our trip north."

"North?" Daiyu shakes her head. She backs away from the women instinctively. "I'm not going north."

"Min wrote that you were coming. Everyone at Rongguo is making preparations for your arrival." Uncle Zheng smiles at her, stooping his head and rubbing his hands together. "You'll like it there. You'll have many cousins to play with. There's another girl staying with us, too, Xue Baochai. She's the daughter of my wife's sister. She's eighteen, just one year older than you."

"I don't 'play,'" Daiyu says, irritated that he is speaking to her like a child.

Ignoring her interruption, he continues, "And Wang Xifeng, your cousin Lian's wife, will take good care of you. She's only twenty-three, but runs the household like a little general."

She looks towards her father for support, but to her amazement, he is nodding as if in agreement with her uncle.

"I'm not going!"

With a muttered apology to Uncle Zheng, her father leads her out through the kitchen to the back stoop so they can speak privately.

"I can't leave you here alone," she says.

"Before she died, your mother made me promise that you would go north to stay with her family."

She feels a surge of outrage, as if her parents have been colluding against her. "But what about you? You can't stay here on your own." The picture of her father eating alone every evening pierces through her own grief.

"Of course I can. I'll have 'Granny' Liu down the street cook and clean for me. I'll be fine."

"But—"

"You must go. It's what your mother wanted."

She can hear the finality in his voice. She looks at him in the light filtering through the paper panes of the kitchen window. His face looks tired, and a little irritated. He is too exhausted to argue with her.

"It's just a visit," he says.

"How long do I have to go for?"

"Just a few months. You can come back in time for New Year's."

She calculates quickly. It is now the Seventh Month. To be back for the New Year she will have to leave the Capital by the end of the Eleventh Month.

Thus it was decided that she would go north to her mother's family.

2

Wang Xifeng opens her eyes. The gray light of dawn is already filtering through the windows, and she can hear the twitter of a thrush somewhere in the courtyard. She lies there, listening. Only now, in the early morning, when Rongguo Mansion is silent, is it possible for her to hear the noise of the street all the way here in the Women's Quarters. Dimly she catches the rumble of traffic, the braying of donkeys and the raucous crowing of cocks, all the exciting sounds of the city she so rarely gets to see, cooped up here in the Inner Quarters with the other women of the Jia family.

Lian is still snoring beside her, a trickle of saliva running from the corner of his open mouth to make a damp, darker patch on the crimson pillow. Gingerly, she raises his arm flung carelessly over her bare breasts, and eases herself from beneath its weight. She rolls off the *kang* and feels for her slippers with her bare feet, aware of the slight tackiness of Lian's semen between her legs. Her slippers aren't there. Balancing with one foot on the cold floor, she reaches for a robe. She pads out to the front room. Ping'er is already up, squatting before the stove to blow on the fire.

"Get me some warm water," Xifeng says. She gestures at the area between her legs with a grimace. "And find me my slippers, will you?"

The maid nods, an expression of sympathetic comprehension overspreading her pink-cheeked face. She pours a jet of steaming water from the kettle into a basin, uses a hollow gourd to scoop in cold well water from the bucket, and brings the basin over to Xifeng. She fetches Xifeng a washcloth and soap, but looks away as Xifeng squats over the basin and sponges herself off. After Xifeng dries herself, Ping'er hands her the clothes that Xifeng laid out the night before: underclothes of silk so fine that it clings to her damp skin, her turquoise underskirt of imported silk crepe embroidered with flowers. She buttons up the frogs on the fitted bodice of her red brocade gown, patterned with butterflies in raised gold thread. Even though she has worn clothes like this every day of her life, she still feels a shiver of pleasure at the weight of the heavy damask against her skin.

Then she seats herself before her dressing table, and Ping'er, as she has done since both were little girls at the Wang mansion in Chang'an, begins to do her hair. When she was betrothed to Jia Lian more than three years ago, her mother, worried at how far away she would live, sent four maids to accompany her to the Capital. Of the four, only Ping'er remained. One had gotten sick and died; Xifeng had married the other two off when they were twenty. Like Xifeng herself, Ping'er is twenty-three, but Xifeng would sooner cut off one of her own arms than give her up.

Ping'er loosens Xifeng's hair from the "lazy knot" that Xifeng has slept in. Then she gathers Xifeng's hair like a skein of silk and begins to comb it, catching it in her hand between each stroke. When at last the comb slides through Xifeng's hair without the least resistance, Ping'er scoops up a handful of hairpins.

"Allowances are due today. Did you remember?" Xifeng asks, looking at Ping'er in the large West Ocean glass mirror mounted on the dressing table. Ever since her mother-in-law, Lady Xing, died three years ago, Xifeng has run the household.

"Mmm," Ping'er grunts. She has put the hairpins in her mouth, and plucks them out, one by one, as she coils Xifeng's hair into a knot. She jerks her chin at the cloth-wrapped packets lined up neatly on a side table, and Xifeng counts them to make sure they are all there: two large ones for Baoyu's and Lady Jia's apartments; two small ones for the Two Springs; and then three even smaller ones: one for Uncle Zheng's concubine Auntie Zhao, and two for Baochai and her mother, Mrs. Xue. Mrs. Xue is, of course, more than rich enough to pay the salaries of both her own and her daughter Baochai's maids. The allowances they receive are purely symbolic, meant to indicate that they remain at Rongguo as honored guests, and are thus considered part of the household.

"See that the allowances are delivered this morning," Xifeng says. "And did you hear? A messenger from Uncle Zheng came last night. Their boat is only twenty *li* from the Capital. He and Miss Lin Daiyu should be here by this evening. Have a room prepared."

"Which one?"

"How about that little room behind Granny Jia's?"

Xifeng sits back and looks at herself in the mirror. She catches up a loose tendril with a turquoise-blue kingfisher pin, and then reaches for her carved ivory box of face cream. With practiced fingers she smooths it over her face, working it over her eyelids and into the creases beside her nostrils, before dusting her whole face with a fine layer of jasmine-scented powder. Then she pulls the outer corner of her eyelid taut with her left index finger, and begins to line her eyes with sure, confident strokes. It is the shape of her eyes more than any other feature, she knows, that distinguishes her face, giving her the reputation for beauty. They are rounded at the inner corner, but long and tapered near her temples, like a teardrop, or a tadpole: "phoenix eyes," they are called. Now that she has become a matron and it is permissible to wear heavy makeup, she always exaggerates their shape by lining them boldly with kohl and extending their outer corners into long points reaching nearly to her temples.

Ping'er reappears at her elbow. She holds a steaming cup of the medicine Dr. Wang had prescribed to help Xifeng conceive.

"But it's been barely a week since my period."

"It can't hurt to start taking it early, especially since you and he ... you know ... last night."

"Oh, all right." Xifeng begins to sip it. When she is halfway through, the West Ocean clock on the wall bongs six times. Breakfast is served at seven, but if the table is not set by the time Granny Jia emerges from her bedroom, Xifeng will be blamed. She gulps the rest of the bitter-tasting brew down, and hurries towards the door.

"Wait. Have a few mouthfuls," says Ping'er, intercepting her with a small bowl of rice porridge. "It isn't too hot."

"I don't have time." Xifeng waves it aside.

Ping'er blocks her path. "Dr. Wang said you have to take better care of yourself. You can't stand for hours on an empty stomach. No wonder you miscarried last time—"

To stop Ping'er from saying more, Xifeng takes the bowl. There is a sleepy shout from the bedroom. Lian must be waking up.

"I'll go see what he wants," Ping'er offers, hurrying down the hallway.

After Xifeng has eaten half the bowl, she notices that there is no sound from the bedroom. Even though she knows she should go to Lady Jia's, she slips down the hallway and pushes aside the door curtain. Ping'er is standing next to where Lian is still lying near the edge of the *kang*. He is smiling and reaching up a sinewy brown arm to grasp her by the hand, as if to pull her down to the bed. Ping'er blushes and pulls away, giggling. Xifeng is suddenly struck by how pretty Ping'er is, the tail of hair hanging down her back glossy and black, her fair skin set off by her apricot gown.

"Excuse me for disturbing you," she says in a brittle voice she can hardly recognize as her own.

Lian and Ping'er jerk apart, Ping'er turning a stricken face to her mistress.

"What dirty business you get up to while I'm not here is none of my affair," she tells Ping'er. "But you'd better watch out, or he'll give you some nasty disease he's picked up at a whore-house."

"Be quiet!" Lian says threateningly, but of course, he can't think of a retort. What could he say? What she says is true, after all. He started staying out all night within three months of their wedding.

He gets up out of the bed, raising his hand. Though he has never hit her, she moves instinctively towards the door. Then he lets his arm drop, looking sullen and defeated. "It's not like that—" he begins.

"I don't want to hear it," she says, and turns on her heel to go to Lady Jia's.

3

"What do you think?" Oriole asks.

Xue Baochai looks at her reflection in the West Ocean mirror, trying to hide her disappointment. Oriole had promised that doing Baochai's hair in the newest style would be far more becoming, but the two heavy buns on either side of her head make her face look broader and flatter than ever. Her small, single-lidded eyes, lacking in any expressivity, stare back at her in the mirror. She turns away from her reflection.

"Don't you like it?" the maid says. "Or, I can do it with the front combed up and—"

"Do it the usual way. I'm in a hurry. My mother had a headache last night and I have to go see how she is," Baochai says curtly. She waits impatiently as Oriole re-dresses her hair. It is always the same each time she tries a new gown or hairstyle. The promised transformation never occurs, and she is forced yet again to confront the disappointment of her appearance: the plain uninflected expanse of her face, the solid, almost matronly figure, even though she is not yet nineteen.

After Oriole is done, Baochai hurries from her apartments across the Garden to see her mother. Like Baoyu and her unmarried female cousins at Rongguo, Baochai lives in one of the apartments clustered around the lake in the Garden, while the matrons—her mother, Granny, Xifeng—live in more imposing and formal apartments in the front part of the Inner Quarters. Skirting the lower end of the lake, she makes her way to her mother's apartments and goes straight to the bedroom. She finds Mrs. Xue sitting before the dressing table while her maid Sunset combs her hair. There are heavy bags under her mother's eyes.

"You don't feel any better?" she asks.

Mrs. Xue shakes her head, putting a hand to her temple. "I had a bad night. I can't find my pills. Do you know where I put them?"

"Perhaps you left them at Granny's last night at dinner. Why don't I go check?"

She hurries to the principal apartment of the Inner Quarters, occupied by Lady Jia. As she passes through the small reception hall into the large courtyard, she sees Jia Huan using a straw to tease a cockatiel in one of the cages hanging along the verandah. She tries to slip by unnoticed. Jia Huan is Baoyu's half brother, born to Uncle Zheng by his concubine Auntie Zhao. Though almost seventeen, he has not outgrown his fondness for tormenting his sister and cousins.

He catches sight of her. "What are you doing here so early?"

"I came to look for my mother's pills. Why don't you help me?"

He follows her into Granny's front room, empty at this hour. She climbs onto the *kang*, rummaging beneath pillows and bolsters.

A moment later he holds up an embroidered drawstring purse from the other side of the *kang*. "Is this it?"

"Yes," she says, relieved. She crawls towards him, putting out her hand. "Thank you."

He puts it behind his back. "What will you give me for it?"

She hates how he always tries to take advantage of another person's weakness. She looks at his receding chin, his rodent-like eyes, so unlike Baoyu's. Her temper rises, but she says pleasantly, "Please, Huan. My mother has a headache."

"All the more reason you should be willing to give me something for it."

"Come on, Huan," she says, more sharply. She usually makes a special effort to be kind to him, to show that she does not hold his birth against him, but today she has no patience for his teasing.

Baoyu comes in, with his light step. Huan tries to conceal the purse in his sleeve.

Seeing the situation at a glance, Baoyu puts out his hand. "Give it to me, Huan."

"Why should I?"

"Because I'll make you if you don't." Baoyu probably outweighs Huan by six or seven *jin*, and is as graceful as Huan is awkward.

After a moment, Huan flings the purse at Baoyu and slinks out of the room.

She tries to hide her rush of pleasure at being alone with Baoyu. She notices that, unlike Huan, he is wearing stay-at-home clothes, a slightly worn blue gown, and thick-soled red slippers instead of boots. "Aren't you going to school today?"

"I asked Granny to let me stay home so I could greet our new cousin."

"Huan is going."

He gives her a look, which clearly says that if Huan is too stupid to get out of going to school, it isn't his fault. He climbs onto the *kang* to give her the purse.

"Thank you." She reaches out her hand, but just as she is about to take the purse, he puts it behind his back.

She laughs. "Now don't you start!"

His brilliant black eyes are alight with mischief.

She lunges at him. Quickly, he transfers the purse to the other hand. She tries to grab it from the other side, and he switches it back. As she tussles with him for possession of it, sometimes her hand or shoulder brushes against his chest. This kind of contact, even between cousins, is highly improper. She glances nervously towards the door to make sure no one is coming. She lunges again, laughing and out of breath, more and more wildly. Finally, rather than dodging her, he lets her crash full into his chest, and puts his arms around her.

She cannot breathe. She feels a hot blush rising to her face, and lowers her eyes. She feels his arms around her, his chest against hers. She knows she should push him away. She has known him ever since she and her mother would visit from Nanjing when she was a little girl. But when she and her mother moved to the Capital for good last year, he was no longer the naughty bright-eyed little boy she remembered. He had grown so handsome and poised that it made her catch her breath.

"Let me go," she says, but he only holds her tighter. "Give me the purse." She glances shyly up at him. His face, with its bold, laughing eyes, is only inches from hers.

"What will you give me for it?" he whispers.

"You're as bad as Huan!"

"What will you give me for it?" he repeats.

"Nothing," she whispers back.

He holds her tighter, lowers his head. Is he going to kiss her?

There is the scuffle of feet on the verandah outside the door curtain. They jump apart.

Xifeng comes in, and Baochai can tell from the mockery in her brilliant eyes that she has guessed, if not seen, what was going on.

"Now, Baoyu, what have you been doing to make your cousin blush like that?" Xifeng says, stooping to unlock the heavy *tansu* in the corner. She begins to take out the silver ladles and bundles of ivory chopsticks for serving breakfast. Baochai has always feared Xifeng's sharp tongue, for which she is notorious in the household. Today she detects an added note of malice.

Baoyu gives Baochai the purse. Not daring to glance at him in Xifeng's presence, Baochai hurries out. She is halfway to her mother's rooms before she recovers her complexion. Beneath her shame at being caught in such a predicament by Xifeng, of all people, she feels an unfamiliar euphoria. Baoyu has always been good-natured and charming to her, but this was the first time he had ever shown that he might regard her with more than cousinly affection. She feels herself blushing again at the thought of how he had held her and looked at her. When Baochai was a baby, Mrs. Xue had joked with her sister, Baoyu's mother, that they should make a match between Baochai and Baoyu, just six months younger. Whenever Baochai heard this story, she was secretly pleased, and hoped that it would come to pass. However, while she is aware that her birth and fortune make her an excellent match, she has never dared to hope that she could attract Baoyu's attention.

When she enters her mother's room with the pills, she is pulled up short by the sight of her older brother, Xue Pan, slouched on the edge of the *kang*. "What is it?" she asks, her eyes going swiftly from her mother, whose hair is still only half done, to her brother, who looks shamefaced.

Her mother waves the pills away, looking at Pan. "Go ahead. Tell your sister the mess that you've gotten us into this time."

"Don't, Mama. It isn't that bad—" Pan protests.

Baochai cuts him off. "Let Mama take one of her pills before we talk any further." As Mrs. Xue swallows her medicine, Baochai steels herself. "Now, why don't you tell me what happened, Pan?"

"Two days ago I bought a beautiful girl, barely sixteen years old, at the slave market. I paid three hundred *taels*, and had her sent to my place that afternoon," Pan begins in an aggrieved tone. "Barely an hour later a man called Zhang Hua turned up claiming that *he* had already bought her, and had not taken her home because he was arranging a wedding for the following day. A fight broke out." Avoiding Baochai's eyes, Pan admits that

Zhang had been beaten pretty badly. "And then, early this morning, Zhang's family went to the magistrate to ask about bringing charges for assault and battery."

"How badly did you hurt him?"

"I told you it wasn't me. It was the pages."

"But still, they were under your orders. How badly was he hurt?"

Pan looks down. "Two of his teeth were knocked out, and I think he may have broken his arm—"

Her composure breaks. "A broken arm! How can you stand there telling me—" She cuts herself off, drawing a deep breath. "You must send the girl to Zhang's house—"

"What would he want with her? He's injured. I haven't even had a chance to touch her—"

"All the better. Don't you understand you must show you are sorry for what happened?"

"But I don't want to give her up."

"You can find another girl easily enough! It's not worth all this trouble to keep this one."

"I'll keep the girl and give him some money."

"It's too late for that. They have already gone to the magistrate. If they bring a charge, you could be clapped into jail at any moment!"

Pan looks stricken, as if this has not occurred to him. "All right," he says sulkily.

"And then," she continues, "you must send money, saying that it is for Zhang's medical expenses. What sort of man is he, anyway?"

"He's the son of a small landowner, I think."

Pan speaks dismissively, but Baochai is alarmed. As a landowner, Zhang is probably both literate and possessed of significant financial resources.

"If they are educated, we can't try to fob them off with some token amount, and expect them to be satisfied." She looks at her mother, biting her lip. "How much should we send, then? Three hundred?"

Her mother thinks for a moment, then nods. "We can't afford not to be generous."

"Let's make it four hundred, to be safe." Baochai turns back to her brother. "Now go home and attend to this right away. I don't want to see you until you have returned the girl and sent over the money."

Pan looks chastened and a little frightened, as if the severity of the matter has at last sunk in. After he leaves, Baochai feels her mother's gaze on her, but neither of them speaks. They are all too familiar with Pan's impulsiveness and ungovernable temper. Thrown out of school when he was ten for fighting, he had since been educated by a tutor at home. He had been so backward that despite all her father's beatings, there had never been any hope of his passing the Exams. Seven years later, when Mr. Xue died and Pan inherited his position as Imperial Court Purveyor, he had taken to drinking and cockfighting, gambling and chasing women, without any thought of the future. It was, in fact, Pan's wildness that had forced the Xues to leave Nanjing a year and a half ago and come north to take refuge with the Jias, who were after all only relatives by marriage. Nevertheless, Baochai has thought of her brother as foolish and lacking in self-control, never as violent.

Her mother, breaking the silence, seems to put Baochai's thoughts into words. "Somehow, I never thought that Pan would ever really hurt anyone."

It suddenly strikes Baochai how old her mother looks. "Maybe he got carried away." She tries to make light of the affair.

"He always gets carried away. But maybe even he feels that he went too far this time, and will finally learn a lesson."

Mrs. Xue breaks off, as Lady Jia's body servant Snowgoose comes in.

"Lady Jia sent me to tell you that breakfast is about to be served."

"Oh, yes. We'll be right over." Baochai helps her mother to her feet, smiling brightly to conceal her anxiety that Snowgoose has overheard their conversation.

4

Even before Daiyu steps off the barge onto the dock of the Grand Canal, the hot wind hits her: dry and dusty, full of grit and sand from the Gobi desert more than a hundred *li* north of the Capital. The sun even has a different look here in the Capital, glaring and yellow, its light undiffused by shade or greenery. Squinting, she sees a dozen servants with sedan chairs and a wagon waiting on the dock for their arrival. She wonders how long they have been waiting there in the hot afternoon sun. She cranes her neck and sees the Capital in the distance, its gatehouses and towers piercing the sky, its walls stretching as far as she can see. All above the city hangs a faint black cloud, like a smudge in the sky.

She has barely taken her seat beside Uncle Zheng when the bearers heave the sedan chair to their shoulders and set off at a brisk trot. She clutches the windowsill, pressing her nose to the gauze window. There is nothing to see here, just a few large buildings that look like storehouses and a jumble of ramshackle houses along the canal banks. However, as the sedan crosses the dusty, empty stretch before the city walls, she becomes aware of an unfamiliar stench, compounded of coal smoke, cooking oil, manure, and rotting garbage, all stewing together in the late summer heat. They pass through a massive gatehouse, flanked by a few dozen uniformed guards, the walls more than five paces thick.

Then they are in the city, the sedan surrounded by a jostling throng of human and animal traffic. There are palanquins, ox carts and donkey carts, peddlers balancing their wares from wooden yokes across their shoulders. The wide avenues, so different from

Suzhou, are laid out at right angles, like a chessboard. Her ears are filled with the spine-tingling shriek of a knife sharpener's whetstone, the clang and hiss of cooking pots, the scrape of wheels and the jangling of harnesses, and above all the clamor of a hundred voices raised in argument and bargaining and gossip. The northern dialect, with its harsh, barking gutturals, grates on her ears. Like a child learning to speak, she silently mouths the new sounds, her teeth and tongue trying out the unfamiliar positions.

As the sedan slows to get out of the way of a richly dressed man clattering by on horseback, Daiyu looks down the side street towards a lively marketplace. There is a butcher in a bloody apron, cages of squawking fowl, pyramids of peaches and apricots. At the edge of the crowd she notices a woman holding the hand of a little girl, standing as if mesmerized before a pile of gooseneck gourds. The woman, with her sloping shoulders and silky black hair, reminds her of her mother, and as the sedan pulls away she turns and watches the woman as long as she can.

After about five minutes, she feels the sedan bearers slow to a walk. Uncle Zheng, who has been dozing in the corner of the sedan, opens his eyes. "There's Rongguo Mansion."

She presses her nose against the window in time to see a towering triple gate with crimson pillars, flanked by two massive stone lions. The huge central gate is shut, but the smaller ones on either side are open. Above the central gate hangs a tablet reading:

RONGGUO MANSION
FOUNDED AND CONSTRUCTED BY IMPERIAL COMMAND

She makes out the inscription before they sweep through the left gate. They shoot through a narrow corridor enclosed by high, whitewashed walls, the bearers' feet jogging in perfect unison on the stone pavement.

"It's a strange household," Uncle Zheng says.

Daiyu turns away from the window to look at him curiously. All through the long barge journey up the Grand Canal, he had seemed distant and preoccupied, his head buried in stacks of official documents. "What do you mean?"

He gives a short laugh. "Most people think that Granny Jia runs Rongguo Mansion, but it's your cousin Baoyu that rules the roost here." He does not look at her, continuing to gaze out the window, although there is nothing to be seen but high blank walls. "It's all on account of that jade of his."

"He couldn't help being born with it."

"Maybe not. But the way he chooses to flaunt it, the way that he uses it to lord over gullible people ... "

Even though she can tell that her uncle does not relish the topic, she cannot help asking, "Will I get to see him? Will I get to see the jade?"

"See him? You won't be able to move without tripping over him. He lives in the Women's Quarters!"

Given how strict her uncle appears to be about matters of propriety, it surprises her that a boy, almost a grown-up, is allowed to live among unmarried girls.

Now he is staring out the window again. "Things would be different if Zhu were still alive."

"Zhu?"

"My eldest son. He died seven years ago, right after passing the Exams."

She is about to ask more when she feels the sedan being lowered to the ground. The sedan bearers disappear, and in their place appear four handsome young page boys, only fifteen or sixteen years old. They must be entering the Women's Quarters, where no full-grown male servants are permitted. The pages carry the sedan through a gatehouse with a hump-backed roof of half-cylinder tiles. As they pass beyond the latticework gates she sees a green mountain springing steeply out of the ground before her, covered with flowering shrubs and mossy crags. It is so tall that she cannot even see its peak. "How can there be a mountain like this right in the middle of a city?"

"That?" Uncle Zheng says, his gravity momentarily lightened by amusement at her surprise. "We had that built ten years ago for the Imperial Visitation."

"How can you build a mountain? And what's an Imperial Visitation?"

"We had the dirt and rocks and plants carted here, basket by basket. Your great-aunt—may she rest in peace—was an Imperial Concubine. One year His Highness decreed that all the Palace Ladies might pay a visit to their families at New Year's. We built the Garden for her."

Something about the way her uncle says "the Garden" strikes her, as if it were something known to everyone, like "the Great Wall" or "the Emperor."

"What's the Garden?"

Uncle Zheng shouts out the window to the bearers. "Go the long way around the mountain, so Miss Lin can see the Garden!"

The sedan veers onto a path lined with low trees. She catches glimpses of ripening plums amid glossy dark leaves, and hears the rush of water. She looks up to see a small waterfall foaming down a wet black rock face. On her other side is a lake, purplish in the setting sun, with a nine-angled bridge leading to a pavilion. Near a grove of spotted bamboo, a snowy egret balances on one spindly leg and dips its beak into the water. "It's beautiful, like a fairy kingdom!" she cries.

Uncle Zheng points to a terracotta roof amid pine trees along the shore of the lake. "That's Baochai's place. That one near the arched bridge is Tanchun's—"

"My cousins live here?"

"The Imperial Concubine decreed after her Visitation that the girls be allowed to live here so it wouldn't lie empty. The girls and Baoyu, of course." His mouth twists wryly. He looks at Daiyu kindly. "Who knows? Perhaps you'll get to stay here as well. Wouldn't you like that?"

She does not answer. Her initial amazement is giving way to a sense of the strangeness of the place. She has visited the famous gardens in Suzhou: exquisite spaces, in which mounds of rock suggest mountains, mossy pools represent lakes, by their art evoking the broader sweep of nature. But this garden, in its attempt to duplicate natural wonders in their true scale, seems incongruous, as if a child's toy has been enlarged to human size.

Now the bearers lower the sedan again. This time her uncle steps out and leads her to a small gate with a roof curving upwards at the corners like water buffalo horns. Following him around a white marble screen, she passes into a spacious court-yard. At the far end is a large five-frame building with enameled red pillars. Her attention is caught by the birds. They hang in tiny bamboo cages along all four sides of the courtyard, dozens of them: parrots in every tropical color, cockatoos, "painted eye-brows," thrushes, and finches. Some sit on perches, others cling to the bars of their cages. She wants to stop and look at them, but her uncle is already hurrying ahead.

As they cross the courtyard towards the main apartment, a young woman darts out of a side door and intercepts them.

"Here you are at last! We've been expecting you for the last hour. Welcome home, Uncle!" The young woman clasps her hands and bends the upper half of her body in a kowtow, but with a roguish smile, as if no one could seriously expect such formality from her.

Daiyu stares at her. She has never in her life seen a person so exquisitely dressed, in silks as delicate and fluttering as a butterfly's wings. She turns to Daiyu, her rouged lips parting in a smile.

"And here's my new little cousin." She puts a beringed hand on Daiyu's hair. "I'm Wang Xifeng. I'm married to your cousin Lian." She pulls Daiyu up the steps into the main apartment. "Come in. Everyone is dying to see you."

Daiyu's first impression is of a large, opulently furnished room filled with people, some of them sitting on the *kang*, some of them standing along the walls, all of them as beautifully dressed as Wang Xifeng. She is wearing her rose-sprigged gown, the last thing her mother made for her before she fell ill. It is her favorite gown, but now she is conscious of how rumpled and stained it is from her journey.

Her eyes fall first on a boy, about her own age, standing before the *kang* while an elderly woman adjusts the set of a magnificent cape on his shoulders. The cape is of a type she has never seen before, woven of some sort of silky black feather, shot through with gleams of bronzy green iridescence. The boy's head, with its sleek braid and brilliant black eyes, rises like the crest of some exotic bird from the collar encrusted with golden embroidery. Three girls on the *kang* are looking critically at him. The oldest one is holding up a basin-sized West Ocean mirror, and the boy is craning his neck to see his reflection.

"What do you think?" he says.

"Very elegant," the old woman approves.

The oldest girl puts down the mirror and climbs down from the *kang* to rub the fabric between her fingers. "It will keep him warm and dry, at any rate."

But the youngest girl, who looks to be about fourteen, pipes up. "I think boys look perfectly silly in feathers. Better something simple in red camlet or fur-lined felt, *I* say."

"That shows how much you know, young lady," the old

woman retorts sharply. "This is the best quality 'peacock gold,' given to the Prince of Nan'an by the Russian ambassador. It's what fine gentlemen there wear in the winter. This cape is worth a thousand *taels* if it's worth a penny. It's far more valuable than camlet or fur."

The boy appears to be much struck by the youngest girl's opinion. He stares at her face for a moment, before casting the cape onto the *kang*. "Xichun's right. It's too showy. Give it to someone else," he says carelessly.

Before the old woman can remonstrate, Xifeng tugs Daiyu up to her. "Look, Granny. She's here!"

The room falls silent as everyone turns to stare at Daiyu. She is seized by shyness, but thinking of her mother's injunctions, she remembers her manners and falls to her knees. "Grandmother," she says, pressing her forehead to the floor.

"Raise her up, Xifeng," the old woman says. Xifeng tugs Daiyu, not gently, to her feet.

"So this is Min's daughter. Let me have a look at you." Lady Jia pulls Daiyu closer. Daiyu expects her grandmother to ask about her mother, or perhaps embrace her. Instead, Lady Jia simply stares at her. Daiyu stares back, trying unsuccessfully to find some resemblance to her own mother. Whatever pretensions Lady Jia ever had to beauty are long gone. Her iron-gray hair is pulled into a tight knob, and her snub nose and broad jaw give her face a pugnacious look.

"You look like your father," Lady Jia says. Her tone leaves no doubt that she does not consider this a merit.

"I can see something of Min in her," says Uncle Zheng. He has seated himself on one of the chairs near the door and is drinking a cup of tea.

"Let me see your hand," Granny says.

Unable to think of a reason for refusing, Daiyu puts out her right hand.

Granny clutches it in her hard, dry grip and draws it a few inches from her eyes. "Hmm, very pretty. Fingers as slender as scallions. Even prettier than yours, eh, Baochai?"

The oldest girl on the *kang*, the one who had been holding the mirror, looks up and smiles. "Yes, Granny." Daiyu is afraid that she will be offended by the comparison, but her placid face shows no sign of displeasure. Unlike Daiyu and the other girls, Baochai's figure is womanly, with full hips and breasts. Her honey-colored gown, though clearly costly, is drabber than the pinks and greens the other girls wear. Her complexion is beautiful: almost poreless, with the flush of a peach on her rounded cheeks. She gives the impression of distinction, but on closer scrutiny her face is not really pretty. Her mouth is rather tight and thin-lipped for her broad face, and her smallish, single-lidded eyes make her face look expressionless.

"How's your father's health?" Lady Jia asks.

"Good."

"How old is he?"

"Forty-four."

"Your mother gave birth to a son some years ago, didn't she?"

"Yes, but he died when he was only three." Daiyu still winces at the memory of the sweet, delicate little boy.

"Your father's getting on. Why didn't he get himself a concubine then, when your brother died? Now he has no heir, and the Lins are about to die out."

Daiyu jerks her hand away. "My father would never have gotten a concubine."

"Maybe he'll get one now."

Daiyu is jolted from her shyness by anger. "My father has no intention of remarrying. He loved my mother—"

Lady Jia gives a bark of laughter. "That shows how much you know about men."

Xifeng intervenes swiftly, taking Daiyu's hand with a smile. "Why don't we introduce you to everyone?"

Baochai comes up to make her bow, followed by the other two girls on the *kang*. "We call these two the 'Two Springs,'" Xifeng says. Even though their gowns are of different colors, the cut and design of their clothes, and the jewelry and ornaments they wear, are nearly identical. The elder, who is tall with sloping shoulders and a pretty oval face, looks to be about Daiyu's age. The younger one, who had criticized the cape, is shorter and plumper, with an upturned nose like a kitten's.

The older girl, who closely resembles the boy in the "peacock gold" cape, smiles at Daiyu. "I'm Tanchun, 'Exploring Spring.'" She points at the other girl. "She's Xichun, 'Cherishing Spring.'"

"They were named for our great-aunt Her Highness the Imperial Concubine," Baochai explains. "*Her* name was Yuanchun, because she was born on the first day of spring."

And now the boy who was trying on the cloak comes up. He cannot be anyone but Baoyu. He is so handsome that all the light in the room seems to shine on him. Low over his brow he wears a gold headband shaped like two dragons playing with a large pearl. He is dressed in a jacket of slate-blue silk with tasseled borders and medallions down the front, over a pair of ivy-colored embroidered trousers. He does not kowtow, but looks at her as if he and she are the only two people in the world.

"Haven't I met you before?" he says. She expects him to be arrogant, but the tone in which he addresses her is gentle, almost courtly.

"No, I've lived in the south for my whole life." Although she has almost never spoken to a boy her own age before, she does not feel shy with him.

"That's odd. I feel as if I've seen you before. What are the characters in your name?"

"The 'yu' is jade, like in your name, and the 'Dai' is the kohl that women use to darken their eyebrows."

She senses him staring at her long, straight eyebrows, without the hint of an arch, something that the neighborhood children back in Suzhou teased her about.

He laughs. "It suits you. Do you have a nickname?"

She shakes her head.

"Then I've got one for you: Pinpin." It is a diminutive form of the word for "frown." Baoyu continues teasingly, "Your given name refers to a kohl that women put on their brows. And your own brows are puckered together in a little frown. It's a perfect name."

She feels her cheeks start to redden, half in embarrassment, half in annoyance.

"It's the first time you've met and already you're giving her a nickname," Baochai murmurs. "Don't you think you're being a little too familiar?"

"Baoyu, where are your manners?" Uncle Zheng says, but the boy ignores him.

"Can you read?" he asks.

"Yes."

"Do you mean girls' reading, like *The Classic for Women*," he speaks scornfully, "or real books?"

She draws herself up. "I've read the Four Books. That is, I've read Confucius, and Mencius, and the Great Learning, but I'm still in the middle of the Doctrine of the Mean. My father taught me himself."

"What poets do you like?"

Daiyu hears Lady Jia click her tongue disapprovingly. "Isn't it enough that girls receive a basic education, enough for them to be able to run the household? It's a waste of time for them to be educated like men."

Ignoring her grandmother, Daiyu says, "I like Li Qingzhao's

song lyrics. I used to like Li Shangyin when I was younger, but now I find him rather vulgar—"

"Li Shangyin?" Baoyu interrupts her. "But most people consider his poems very difficult. They're filled with references to lots of obscure ancient texts. Are you sure you understand them?"

"What do you know about ancient texts, Baoyu?" Jia Zheng interrupts dryly.

"I read what interests me," Baoyu replies. Now it was time for his cheeks to redden.

"Let's see how far that gets you on the Civil Service Exams." Uncle Zheng sets down his cup of tea. "I was under the impression that before I left we agreed you wouldn't miss any school while I was gone. Yet I find you quite at your leisure."

"I said he could stay home to meet his cousin," Granny Jia puts in. "Besides, he wasn't feeling well these last few days."

"Well, Baoyu, are you fully recovered now?" Uncle Zheng's tone is sardonic. "Would it be reasonable to expect you to go back to school tomorrow?"

"Yes, sir."

"And if I speak to the schoolmaster in a few months and find that you haven't made any progress, I'll beat you. Actually, I feel I owe him an apology for sending him such a hopeless case."

"How can you talk like that?" Lady Jia says. "Baoyu is exceptionally talented."

"Is he? I have yet to see evidence of any extraordinary talents, except for laziness and obstinacy."

"I don't understand you, Zheng," Lady Jia says. "So eager to put down your own son. It's almost as if you were jealous."

"Jealous! What could I possibly be jealous of?" Uncle Zheng's incredulity strikes Daiyu's ears as overdone. She remembers her mother's words: Uncle Zheng had been jealous of her as well.

"I'm sure I don't know, but I seem to recall the schoolmaster beating you for not learning your lessons when you were Baoyu's age."

Her uncle's face flushes with anger.

Once again, Xifeng is swift to intervene. "Surely our cousin is tired after her long journey." She pats Daiyu's hand fondly. "Why don't I take her to wash up so we can all have dinner?"

The dinner is as extravagant as Daiyu could have imagined. A procession of maids brings an endless supply of dishes, while others stand at attention holding fly whisks and napkins. Often she cannot tell what she is eating. Even ordinary ingredients are prepared in elaborate, unfamiliar ways, like the eggplant, which seems to have been cut into thread-fine strips, before being fried and smothered in a sauce with minced chicken. She is unused to such rich food, and would have liked to fill up on rice, but even the rice is of an exotic sort, lacking the comforting blandness she craves, the grains such a dark purple that they are almost black. She tastes and nibbles, hoping no one will notice how little she eats.

Two new young men are present at dinner. The older one introduces himself as her Cousin Lian before taking his seat. He is good-looking, somewhat more thickset than Baoyu, and carries himself with an easygoing air. The other one, a skinny boy about her own age, sidles in as if he half expects to be thrown out. He does not say a word but stares fixedly at her from his seat on the other side of the long table. She hears the others call him "Huan." She herself is seated between Tanchun and Xichun, across from Baoyu and Baochai. Uncle Zheng and Lady Jia sit at the head of the table.

Uncle Zheng is telling his mother about the flooding on the Jia estates he had visited during his trip south. "The damage was worse than I expected. They say the water reached all the way to Hankou."

He proceeds to describe the necessary repairs, but Lady Jia hardly looks up from her dinner. Daiyu is surprised by the greedy way she attacks a drumstick of roast duck.

Xifeng, as the *xifu*, or daughter-in-law, does not eat with the others, supervising the serving of the meal from behind Lady Jia. "That piece looks tough for you, Granny." She chooses a breast piece, cutting the meat off the bone.

Around Daiyu, Baochai and the Two Springs chatter about how they have spent the afternoon copying sutras.

"Ow," Tanchun says. "My hand is so sore that I couldn't write another word."

Baochai turns to Daiyu. "Granny wanted us to do it so the family would accumulate merit," she explains.

"I liked copying the sutras," Xichun says, her small face serious. "I never understood them so well before. Have you read any sutras, Cousin Daiyu?"

"Only the Heart Sutra," Daiyu says, pleased to be included in the conversation.

On the other side of the table, Jia Lian asks Baoyu, "What are you doing tonight?"

Baoyu sighs. "I suppose I have to go to the Prince of Beijing's birthday party. I'd rather stay home and spend time with our cousin."

"What is the Prince doing for his birthday?"

"The usual. An opera troupe, some singing girls."

"Watch out that Uncle doesn't get angry," Lian warns him, shooting a glance up the table towards Jia Zheng.

Baoyu shrugs. "He can't expect me to stay home and study every night. It would offend the Prince if I didn't come."

"You don't have to convince *me*. I'm just telling you to watch yourself now that Uncle is back."

At long last the meal is over. When the table is cleared, the maids pour tea into cups of celadon crackle glaze. Daiyu reaches for her cup and drinks thirstily, eager to wash away the greasiness in her mouth.

A ripple of laughter fills the room. The maids cover their mouths to stifle their giggles. The boy called Huan guffaws. At the head of the table, Lady Jia takes her cup, sips the tea, and gargles with it. Deliberately she spits it into a *Ding*-ware bowl that a maid holds before her.

Daiyu has drunk the tea meant for gargling. She feels herself grow hot with embarrassment. Across the table, Baochai, her gaze tactfully averted, daintily gargles and spits out her tea.

"Hey, Frowner," Baoyu says. He picks up his tea and downs it to the last drop.

5

On his second day back at Rongguo, Jia Zheng goes to his mother's bedroom, where she has retired after breakfast, to tell her that he is returning to work at the Ministry, and will not come home until evening. She is half reclining on the *kang* while Silver, one of her senior maids, massages her legs. Even though they finished breakfast barely half an hour ago, Snowgoose is bringing her two little yam cakes with date stuffing on a small lotus-shaped platter. That is an aspect of his mother that never fails to irritate him: despite her sensitive stomach, she refuses to exercise the least restraint over her diet. Lady Jia opens her eyes as Snowgoose offers her the cakes.

She takes a cake and leans back, shutting her eyes again. "I hope Min's funeral wasn't too much of a disgrace."

He pauses, uncertain what to say. For twenty years his mother has grown angry at the mention of his younger sister. When Jia Zheng received Min's letter saying that she was dying and that she wished for her daughter to know her family, his mother said little, but had agreed to his suggestion that he go south to fetch Daiyu. He had hoped his mother was at last repenting of the long estrangement. Now he is surprised by her spiteful tone.

"It was a little modest, but—"

"Modest! I know what that means." She begins to eat the cake, her jaws moving busily. "What sort of place did they live in?"

"They had a small apartment—"

She snorts. "Any servants?"

"A maid, I believe."

"No wonder Min died. And Lin Ruhai expects to raise a young girl in conditions like that."

"He seems a devoted father."

"He hasn't done a very good job with her manners." She pops the second cake in her mouth and hands the plate back to Snowgoose.

He pauses. While Daiyu is shy and a little gauche, he does not find her ill-mannered. Unable to contradict his mother directly, he changes the subject. "I'm going to the Ministry today and won't be home for lunch."

"The Ministry? But you've barely been home one day."

"I have been gone for over three months. There are sure to be questions they wish to consult me on . . . "

"Surely they can do without you for a few more days."

It is typical of his mother to belittle his role at the Ministry; this reminds him of his annoyance that she let Baoyu stay home from school yesterday. "How many days of school did Baoyu miss while I was away?"

She stares at him, as if offended by the question. "How should I know?"

"I'm simply asking for a rough estimate."

"I have no idea."

He takes a deep breath, trying to control his anger. "I told Baoyu before I left that he must stop missing school. The Exams are barely six months away."

"What a fuss about missing a few days of school! Didn't the schoolmaster tell us that when Baoyu sets his mind to it, not one of the boys in the whole school can match him in quickness?"

"He told us that years ago, and Baoyu has apparently still not seen fit to 'set his mind to it.'"

"He still has all of the fall and winter to study."

"I'm afraid you don't understand, Mother. It takes years of

hard work to prepare for the Exams. He can't just cram for a few months. Don't you remember how hard Zhu studied before he passed—"

He sees that she is not even looking at him, apparently absorbed in thought, and breaks off.

After a moment, she says, "There is something about Baoyu I want to talk to *you* about. You know Baoyu's body servant Pearl?"

"Yes, but—"

"She's a good girl, and very devoted to him. I've been thinking of making her his chamber wife."

"Chamber wife! What does he need a chamber wife for?" He raises his voice despite himself.

"He is nearly nineteen. He has natural desires, like any other man. Why not give him a chamber wife, so he can—"

"We can betrothe him after he passes the Exams, like we did for Zhu." Unfortunately Zhu died of a sudden illness before the wedding could take place.

"Zhu passed when he was sixteen. Baoyu is already a grown man. It's wrong to expect him not to feel attracted to girls, especially living in the Inner Quarters with them—"

He pounces on this, interrupting her. "I've never thought that he should continue to live inside. It's improper, and people are beginning to gossip about it—"

"It's just like you, to want to deprive me of the company of my favorite grandson, just because of what people say. He's the only one who keeps me amused now that I'm too old to be of use to anyone."

The West Ocean clock in the outer room bongs, giving him an excuse to cut off the familiar argument. "I must go. I said that I would drop Baoyu off at school on the way to the Ministry. We'll talk of this another time."

When he arrives at the stable yard, his already frayed temper is tried further when he finds Baoyu is not there. He sends a page to call him, and waits in the carriage for several minutes before Baoyu appears.

"Hurry up! You'll be late for school!" he cries, as Baoyu climbs in beside him. It is the first time since he arrived home that he has been alone with his son. "What did you study while I was gone?" he asks, as the coachman whips up the horses and the carriage finally trundles out through a side gate into the streets.

"Mencius."

"Tell me what Mencius says about dutifulness and self-preservation."

"*Fish is what I want; bear's paw is what I want,*" Baoyu begins. "*If I cannot have both, I would rather take bear's paw than fish. Life is what I want; dutifulness is also what I want. If I cannot have both, I would rather take dutifulness than life. On the one hand, though life is what I want, there is something I want more than life ...*"

The glibness with which Baoyu rattles off the passage nettles him. Even he cannot deny that Baoyu's memory is exceptional, enabling him to recite a poem after one or two readings; but the boy takes excessive pride in his aptitude. He interrupts, "You're not taking your studies seriously."

Baoyu breaks off with an innocent face. "But I am, Father. I know the Mencius passage backwards and forwards—"

"You promised me you wouldn't miss school."

"I only missed it a few times—"

"You should be setting an example for the other boys, not making excuses." Again he tries to explain the special responsibility he feels as an Imperial Bondsman, the same responsibility that he wants Baoyu to feel. "My grandfather, your great-grandfather, was one of the first settlers in Mukden. He was captured by the Manchus when they conquered Mukden, and made a Bondsman—"

"A slave to the Manchus! You act as if that were something to be proud of," Baoyu mutters.

He ignores the interruption, continuing, "Then, when the Manchus conquered China, your great-grandfather, and all the other Bondservants of the Plain White Banner, were made into the Imperial Household.

"So our family has always had a special tie with the Imperial family. My father—your grandfather—was practically raised in the Palace. His mother was His Majesty's wet nurse. My father was five or six at the time, and he would tell stories of being allowed to hold His Majesty's rattle when he was an infant."

Baoyu makes an impatient movement, but Jia Zheng goes on, "All through the years, my father served His Imperial Highness with a singular devotion. You must understand we are not like most people who become officials just because they have passed the Exams. We owe His Highness not just the ordinary duty of an official, but a—a personal loyalty." He struggles to find the right words to express the deep-held convictions that give him his sense of purpose. "For as long as the Manchus have ruled China, we have been the ones His Highness turns to when he needs someone he trusts."

Baoyu's eyes shift away. "Most people don't even want the Manchus in China in the first place. Besides, the Bondsmen don't have any real power these days. The eunuchs control what goes on in the Palace."

"Who told you that?" Jia Zheng thunders.

"They don't say it in public, of course, but everyone thinks so."

"Like who?"

Baoyu shrugs. "The Prince of Beijing, for one."

Jia Zheng stops himself from saying something cutting about the Prince of Beijing. The Prince is a very upstanding young man, one of the few of Baoyu's friends that he approves of. Of course, the younger generation has a different conception of matters. Jia Zheng remembers all the times he had been taken to the Palace as a child. Now that Emperor Kangxi is well over seventy—may he live for ten thousand years—he rarely appears at Court. It is no wonder that he seems a mere figurehead to the younger men, and seems closer to the eunuchs than to his ministers and Bondsmen.

"His Imperial Highness would never depend on the eunuchs," he tells Baoyu. "He knows that was what brought down even such a glorious dynasty as the Ming."

"What makes you think his successor will feel the same way?"

Jia Zheng flinches at the allusion to Emperor Kangxi's eventual death. He has been fortunate enough to live his entire life under Emperor Kangxi's wise and peaceful rule, and does not like to be reminded of its inevitable end. "Prince Yinti has always been close to the Bondservants, just like his father."

"Why do you think Prince Yinti will succeed to the throne?"

Jia Zheng smiles at Baoyu's ignorance. "Surely you, with all your Court connections, know that Prince Yinti has always been His Highness's favorite."

Baoyu ignores Jia Zheng's sarcasm. "Then why doesn't he make Prince Yinti Heir Apparent? What if something happens while Prince Yinti is still away at the Tibetan front?"

Jia Zheng is taken aback. Usually, Baoyu listens to him in sullen silence. This is the first time he has dared to challenge Jia Zheng directly. A memory of his older son, Zhu, flashes into his mind: Zhu asking Jia Zheng to read his practice essays for the Exams, fidgeting in suspense while waiting to hear his father's judgment.

The carriage comes to a stop before Baoyu's school. The forecourt is deserted, and the schoolroom doors are shut.

He thrusts Baoyu out of the carriage. "Hurry! You're late." To his fury, Baoyu saunters across the courtyard as if he has not a care in the world.

6

Baochai has never seen her brother so frightened. He has come to their mother's apartment before dinner, his ruddy face haggard. "The usher from the district magistrate's office came to me this afternoon. He said Zhang Hua died late last night, and his father wrote out a complaint for murder. What am I going to do? I could be arrested at any moment. And the sentence for murder is execution!"

"We'll have to send Zhang Hua's family more money. Perhaps they will withdraw the charge," Mrs. Xue cries.

"No!" Baochai cuts sharply through their voices. "We can't send any more money. It will look as if we have something to hide."

Both of them turn to look at her. "Then what should we do?"

She must distance herself from her mother's and brother's agitation, trying to stay calm so she can think clearly. "Is there any evidence of what Zhang Hua died of, Pan? Could it have been from something else?"

"The usher said he'd been coughing up blood, so they suspected internal injuries."

"We must find the doctor and raise the possibility that it could have been something else. And we must find a good scrivener, someone who knows all the legal terminology, to help us write a petition. We'll argue it was an accidental death. Pan, you must find one this afternoon."

"All right," he says, scared into submission.

"And whatever you do, don't go home. Tell your servants to say you're out of town, and go stay in an inn somewhere. In the meantime someone must speak to the district magistrate on Pan's behalf."

Her mother turns to her with a worried frown. "Do you mean offer him a bribe? If we were to be caught, that would be a serious offense."

Baochai shakes her head. "If someone with sufficient influence vouches for Pan, he may simply drop the charges as a favor. That would be far better than offering money."

"Should we send down to Nanjing to your father's brother?"

"There isn't time to send to Nanjing. I think we must ask Uncle Zheng."

"Jia Zheng?" her mother exclaims. "He's only a relative by marriage."

"Yes, but the Jias are one of the most prominent families in the Capital. Uncle Zheng knows everyone from all his years in the Civil Service."

Her mother demurs. "I don't like to ask him. It's not as if he's a close relation."

Pan cuts in, "But you've been staying with the Jias for nearly two years." His expression is hopeful, as if he, too, realizes that asking the Jias for help is his best chance to escape his predicament.

"But I've never spoken to them about—" Mrs. Xue breaks off.

Baochai understands. Her mother shrinks from the shame of revealing Pan's troubles to the Jias. "Mother, we must act as quickly as possible, before the lawsuit goes any further."

Still her mother hesitates. "But we will be so beholden to the Jias. I don't know how we will ever repay Zheng for this."

"Surely he can't want his own nephew to go to prison, or worse."

So it is settled that her mother will speak to Uncle Zheng that evening. Pan leaves to look for a scrivener. Instead of staying and comforting her mother, Baochai goes to her own apartment in the Garden. She wants to be alone, to wash her hands and change her clothes. She feels dirty, sullied by the fact that she is the one instructing Pan and her mother how to make sure he is not convicted. She is ashamed of her knowledge of the court system, which years of dealing with Pan's scrapes have given her. What do other girls, locked away in the Inner Quarters, know of scriveners and magistrates? She would give anything for the luxury of ignorance.

When Daiyu asks her grandmother where her mother slept as a child, Lady Jia, barely looking at her, waves her hand towards the northeastern corner of the apartments. At naptime, she walks down the hallway to the room that Granny Jia had pointed out, pushing aside the crimson door curtain. The stark impersonality of the room startles her. It is merely another of the large, opulently furnished rooms that seem to fill the mansion, with a row of locust-wood chairs along the wall, an elaborately carved armoire. Nothing reveals the taste of its former inhabitant: there are no dog-eared rhyming manuals or calligraphy books on the shelves, no brushes or inkstone on the desk.

On an impulse, she goes to the dressing table and pulls open a drawer. It is empty. She opens another. She doesn't know what she hopes to find.

"Miss Lin, what are you doing here?" It is Snowgoose, Granny Jia's body servant, carrying a duster.

Daiyu shuts the drawer and jumps back guiltily. "I was just looking. Lady Jia told me this was my mother's bedroom."

Snowgoose nods. Daiyu thinks that she sees sympathy on the maid's face. "Don't let me disturb you. I was just making sure the junior maids had dusted properly."

"Is it the same as when my mother was here?" Daiyu asks shyly. Of all the maids, she finds Snowgoose, with her air of quiet authority, especially intimidating.

"I'm afraid I don't know. That was before I came here. Why don't you ask Lady Jia?"

"I did, but she said she couldn't remember." Daiyu watches Snowgoose dust the shelves, carefully lifting the vases and screens, and feels awkward about standing there idly while the maid works.

Snowgoose pauses. "How do you like it here at Rongguo?"

Daiyu wonders whether Snowgoose will be offended or report to Granny if she tells the truth. She shakes her head. "It seems strange to me."

"How do you mean?"

"It doesn't seem like a family at all. Everyone lives in their own apartments, and never sees each other except at meals." She doesn't know how to describe the endless pomp, the atmosphere of stultifying formality.

Snowgoose gives a little laugh, beginning to dust the dressing table and chairs. "It *is* strange, I suppose. But you should visit the others at their apartments. I suppose it's easy for you to be left out, since they all live in the Garden, and you are here."

"I feel shy going to see them when they haven't invited me, and they never come see me."

"You must overcome your shyness. It isn't personal, you know." Snowgoose hesitates. "I suppose Miss Tanchun and Miss Xichun aren't the type to take the initiative, having been 'born in the wrong bed,' as the saying goes."

"'Born in the wrong bed'?" Daiyu echoes, afraid that she is revealing her ignorance.

"It means that they were born to concubines."

"Does it matter so much?"

Snowgoose considers. "Yes and no. Huan is a concubine's son. He is only Baoyu's half brother, and you see how differently he is treated. He's hardly ever allowed in the Inner Quarters, and no one pays much heed to him when he comes. Everyone knows Lady Jia doesn't care for him."

"Who is his mother?"

"Lord Jia's concubine Auntie Zhao, a very disagreeable woman. She is Miss Tanchun's mother as well. Everyone hates her, so Miss Tanchun avoids her as much as possible, but Huan is always going to her for attention." Snowgoose breaks off abruptly with a laugh. "But enough gossiping. There's too much gossiping around here, anyway. I only told you because you are new to the household. The important thing is to overcome your shyness and visit your cousins." Snowgoose nods at her in a friendly fashion, before moving towards the door. "I know you must miss your mother and home, but you should try to enjoy your time here."

She follows the maid to the door, wanting to talk longer. "How about you, Snowgoose? Where is your family?" She suddenly recalls that many girls who become maids have been orphaned, or sold by their families as little girls, and regrets her question; but Snowgoose seems pleased at her interest.

"I grew up here in the Capital, and was sold when I was twelve. My mother is a cook in another household, and my father is a groom. But my older brother is a blacksmith. He finished his apprenticeship last year, and just opened his own shop, in Flowers Street."

Daiyu sees the pride and happiness glowing on Snowgoose's face, and envies Snowgoose for having a brother. "Do you ever get to see them?"

"Lady Jia lets me visit them on holidays sometimes, if she can spare me. Sometimes my brother comes to the back gate and sends a message, and I go out to meet him. But I'm afraid I must

go now. Lady Jia will be waking up soon, and will want me."
With another friendly nod, she leaves the room.

Daiyu feels a pang of loneliness. In this household full of
people she spends far more time alone than she did at home.
Her talk with Snowgoose is the first real conversation she has
had since coming to Rongguo.

7

The district magistrate's office is a small airless room off a dusty courtyard. When Jia Zheng passes through the doorway, he sees a young man in shabby official's robes sitting behind the desk editing a closely written document with a writing brush. Because the magistrate is younger than he expects, probably only in his early twenties, Jia Zheng asks in some surprise, "Excuse me, am I addressing Jia Yucun?"

The young man finishes drawing a neat line through a column of text before he looks up. His face is fine-boned, with clever, almond-shaped eyes, but his hairless cheeks are marred by a few pockmarks.

"Yes, I'm Jia Yucun," the young man says, but he neither offers a greeting nor rises from his seat, continuing to look coolly at Jia Zheng.

Taken aback, Jia Zheng says, "I beg pardon for intruding on you. I am Jia Zheng, Duke of Rongguo, and Under-Secretary of the Ministry of Works. I wrote you a note yesterday that I would be coming to see you."

"Ah, yes." Jia Yucun leans back in his chair, putting his fingertips together meditatively, still without offering his visitor a seat. "Who doesn't know the Rongguo Jias? As a matter of fact, I am a kinsman of yours."

"Is that so? I wondered, when I heard your surname."

"Only a very distant one. Our grandfathers were second cousins, I believe."

"What was your grandfather's name?"

"Jia Dairui, of Huzhou."

"Oh, yes. I've heard the name." Jia Zheng feigns recognition.

"I doubt it," the district magistrate says, with a shrug.

Jia Zheng forces himself to say, with an assumption of pleasure, "I had no idea we had another kinsman in the Capital. We must have you over to Rongguo sometime."

Jia Yucun's smile is unmistakeably malicious. "The Rongguo Jias have ignored the Huzhou Jias for more than thirty years. Are you sure you wish to change that?"

Jia Zheng grows flustered. If the young man feels snubbed by the Jias, he is unlikely to help Xue Pan. He vaguely remembers hearing his father complain years ago about a distant branch of the family in Huzhou. "We never hear from them unless they want money," his father would say.

"Really, I had no idea you were in the Capital," he says, flushing. "Otherwise, I would have—"

The young man bursts into laughter, as if delighted by Jia Zheng's discomfiture. "Don't worry! I'm not offended." He rises from his seat and walks around the desk to Jia Zheng. "I'm not so thin-skinned! I would never have gotten this far if I were. My father died when I was two, and my mother died ten years later. She took in sewing to support the two of us. Now, what brings you here?"

Caught off balance by the direct question, Jia Zheng stammers, "Perhaps you remember among your cases one involving a young man named Xue Pan."

"Xue Pan? Yes, I'm hardly likely to forget a murder case."

"Well, it so happens that Xue Pan is the son of my widowed sister-in-law—"

"Your nephew, is he?" Jia Yucun interrupts. "I wondered to what I owed this unexpected honor."

At Jia Yucun's sarcasm, Jia Zheng falls silent. But Jia Yucun looks at him expectantly, and he forces himself to speak the words he had rehearsed before coming. "I have come to ask for leniency on Xue Pan's behalf. He is an upstanding young man, and has never been in trouble with the law before. While he did lose his temper and try to throw Zhang Hua out of his house, he had no intention of inflicting serious injury. In fact, he was so shocked when he heard Zhang Hua had died that he could not speak." He sees the incredulity on the magistrate's face, and breaks off, feeling foolish.

Jia Yucun seats himself behind the desk again and looks through a sheaf of papers. "Yes, he has already submitted a petition asking that the charge be reduced from 'intentional homicide' to 'fatal bodily harm by mischance.' Although I issued a warrant for his arrest, he is nowhere to be found."

Though Jia Yucun's expression is openly contemptuous, Jia Zheng forces himself to continue. "I came to ask if there is anything you can do to help my nephew. He is truly contrite. That is why, when he heard how seriously Zhang Hua was injured, he returned the girl at once, and even paid for the medical expenses—"

"Tried to pay him off, you mean," Jia Yucun cuts in. "The case looks serious. Look at the list of injuries that Zhang Hua sustained: a broken arm, teeth knocked out, several serious cuts on his face. I find it hard to believe that his death was accidental."

"I see," Jia Zheng says slowly. "In any case, I thank you for taking the time to speak to me." Secretly he is relieved that his mission has been unsuccessful. When Mrs. Xue came to him, his first impulse was to have nothing to do with the matter. However, when she begged and pleaded, and said that Xue Pan was in danger of his life, he had agreed to help, in part because he feared the scandal would redound upon the Jias, and also because he could not stand by coldheartedly while his nephew ran the risk of execution. He is a man who has always followed rules to the letter. He had slept badly the night before, hounded by a sense of wrongdoing and also by a fear that his misdeed would somehow be discovered and punished.

"Just a minute," Jia Yucun says as he reaches the door.

He stops and turns. The magistrate is leaning back and putting his fingertips together, just as he was doing when Jia Zheng introduced himself. "I said it was a serious case, but not that it was hopeless."

Jia Zheng takes a step back, wondering whether Jia Yucun has been feigning reluctance to fish for a bribe. "What do you mean?"

Jia Yucun shuffles through his papers again. "The testimony is far from conclusive. I can see some potential weaknesses in the prosecution's case. Over the next few days, I will be calling witnesses in for questioning: those who were present at the fight—"

"The only people there were my nephew's servants," Jia Zheng says.

Jia Yucun continues as if he had not spoken, "I will question the eyewitnesses as to who struck the first blow—there may be some question as to whether your nephew acted in self-defense. I'll ask for an examination of Zhang Hua's body and a coroner's report. Finally, I'll question Zhang's doctor about his injuries, and his general state of health." He looks up from the papers. "I'll let you know if something comes up. Why don't you come back in a few days?"

Not knowing what to make of the magistrate's about-face, Jia Zheng hesitates. "You are taking so much trouble on our behalf. Surely there is something we can do for you—"

Jia Yucun cuts him off sharply, drawing himself up. "I am simply doing my duty. There is absolutely no need to offer me anything. I should not accept it in any case."

While no one would accept a bribe outright, Jia Yucun's response seems unequivocal enough to be a true refusal. Jia

Zheng gives him credit for being sufficiently shrewd not to risk his career for a few thousand *taels*.

Jia Yucun returns to the examination of the documents before him. He nods dismissal to Jia Zheng. "Remember what I said. Come back in a few days."

8

When Xifeng falls behind on household tasks, she works without resting through the period after lunch when everyone else naps. Even Ping'er, who has a headache, is lying down in her small bedroom behind Xifeng's apartments. Xifeng sits at her desk, piled high with cloth-covered ledgers, adding up household expenditures on coal for the last month, her fingers swiftly clicking the wooden beads of her abacus. There is a cough at the door. She looks up.

It is Mrs. Lai, one of the head stewardesses. "The gatewomen told me you would be here giving out tallies."

"What do you need?"

Mrs. Lai hands her a sheet of paper requesting permission to order paper for the windows of Baoyu's study in the outer part of the mansion. Xifeng checks the amount of paper requested before copying down the quantity in one of the ledgers. She opens a locked box on the desk and takes out a tally.

"Go ahead and order it." She hands the small wooden tally to Mrs. Lai. "But remember, I won't give you the tally to authorize payment until the goods have been received."

"Of course. I'll bring you the receipt when the paper comes."

"One more thing. Could you send Autumn to me?"

When Mrs. Lai returns with Autumn, one of the junior maids in the apartments, a single glance confirms Xifeng's suspicions. Autumn does not dare to meet her eyes, her expression at once fearful and defiant.

Xifeng leans back in her chair, watching the maid. "This is the second time something has gone missing after your shift."

She catches a twitch of fear in the maid's thin body, hastily suppressed.

"First, it was two dozen candles," Xifeng continues. "Now it's more than a pound of soap. Perhaps you think that because there are so many costly things lying around, no one will notice if some of them disappear."

"Oh, no, Mrs. Lian. Truly, I have no idea where those things went. Maybe somebody else took them."

"Somebody else indeed!" Mrs. Lai snorts. "All the other maids have been here more than two or three years. Things only started disappearing after you came!"

It is true. They never had problems of this sort until four or five months ago, when Granny Jia had given Autumn to Xifeng. Granny had imagined that Autumn would be a good maid—she is unusually pretty, and quick-witted, and well-spoken. Xifeng has always disliked her long, sideways-glancing eyes, but because she was Lady Jia's gift, it is impossible to dismiss her.

Lian walks in. He almost never comes home to the apartments before dinner. "What's the matter?" she says, jumping up.

"Nothing. I'm just tired. I'm going to take a nap."

He disappears down the hallway to their bedroom.

Xifeng turns back to Autumn. "I told you the last time what would happen if something disappeared again." She looks at Mrs. Lai. "Give her twenty strokes of the bamboo, and stop a month of her wages."

Autumn falls to her knees and starts to beg and weep.

"If you make such a fuss about it, I'll make it thirty. Now take her away."

Mrs. Lai leads Autumn away. Xifeng notes the deduction in Autumn's salary in one of the ledgers, scrupulously adding the amount back into the operating expenses for the month. She knows many people in her place would simply pocket the two *taels* as their own, but she would scorn to stoop to such dishonesty. She shuts the ledger and hurries to the bedroom.

Lian is sitting on the edge of the *kang* untying his sash and shrugging off his robe. She kneels to take off his shoes and his socks. "Aren't you feeling all right?"

"I'm fine. What was happening out there?"

"This is the second time that maid has been caught stealing. I was just teaching her a lesson."

"You don't have to be so harsh with the servants."

His tone is mild enough, but still his criticism irritates her. "You have no idea how hard it is to maintain order and respect in this household," she tells him. "I'm only a *xifu*, a daughter-in-law." She does not mention that her failure to bear the family a child makes her status even lower. "If I showed the least weakness, everyone would be upon me like a school of sharks. It's a good thing everyone knows that Lady Jia likes me. Otherwise, I'd never have survived this long."

He shrugs, not deigning to reply. When she helps him strip down to his tunic she sees a few patches of rough red skin on his arms. "Your eczema is flaring up again. Do you want me to put some rose-orris on it?"

"All right."

She takes off his tunic, and sprinkles some rose-orris powder onto her palms. She kneels behind him on the *kang* and rubs the powder into his smooth, hairless back and broad shoulders. When Lian was in his early teens, he had loved all sports: archery, horseback riding, swordsmanship. He had been forced to give them up in order to study for the Exams. She remembers how good-looking she thought him the first time she saw him, when she had lifted a corner of her wedding veil and peeked out at him from under the blind of her wedding sedan. Now he has become too lazy for exercise, preferring to spend his spare time gambling and drinking. Even though he has kept his athletic build, a spreading slackness has developed around his belly, which jiggles a little as she rubs his shoulders.

Usually, when she rubs the rose-orris into his chest and belly, she can feel his body relaxing beneath her fingers. Today his muscles remain tensed.

"What's the matter?"

"Nothing."

"Really?" Now she bends down to smooth the powder on his thighs and calves.

After a moment, he says grudgingly, "Well, if you must know, now that Uncle Zheng is back he'll want to go through the accounts with me."

She nods, understanding why he is tense. When Lian could not pass the Exams, he was given the job of managing the family's farming properties in the south. He is supposed to keep track of the rents, harvests, operating expenses, taxes, and salaries. But he has neither a head for numbers nor the patience to sort through receipts and records every month. Every time Uncle Zheng thinks to ask for the accounts, Lian's neglect and confusion are exposed. Uncle Zheng shouts at him and calls him lazy. But in the end nothing changes, because, Xifeng suspects, Uncle Zheng himself has as little idea how to run the estates.

"I could help you," she says timidly. She has always been quick at figures, and has perfected a system of recording income and expenditures. Even though running a household is women's work, she suspects managing a farm involves similar principles.

"No, thank you," he says sharply.

She should not have offered, of course. He has never been able to accept that she is cleverer than he is. When Lady Jia praises her for running the household, she always notices him chafing, jealous that he himself cannot merit such praise.

He seems to regret his sharpness, and changes the subject. "What do you think of Lin Daiyu?"

"If she is going to survive here, she had better learn to stay on Granny's good side."

"Baoyu seemed quite taken with her. I've always heard that girls from the south had a special sort of languorous grace—"

She feels a prick of jealousy. "Don't be ridiculous. She isn't really a southerner. Her mother was your Aunt Min, after all. They only moved south for her father's posting."

"Still, there's something about her. Uncle Lin is a southerner, isn't he?"

She wipes the rose-orris off her hands, and rolls out the bedding for him. "Why don't you lie down now?"

He stretches out in his underclothes, but instead of shutting his eyes he looks at her.

"What is it?" she says, with a sense of foreboding.

He looks away from her. "How long has it been since your miscarriage?" he asks abruptly.

The mention of her miscarriage makes her wince. She knows what is coming and is filled with a dread bordering on panic. "A year and four months."

"It's been longer than that, hasn't it? I'd say it was almost two years."

"No, it happened last spring. I remember because Baoyu was thinking about taking the Exams, and then he got sick—"

He puts up his hand as if he does not have patience to hear the details. "I think I should get a concubine."

She puts her arms around his neck and buries her head in his chest. "No, please. Give me just a little bit longer. Dr. Wang gave me some medicine, and I'm taking it every month—"

"No, listen." He grips her shoulders so she is forced to look him in the face. "You always act like it's an attack against you, for me to get another wife, but it's not. If she has a child, it will still be considered *our* child, yours and mine. You'll still be called 'Mother' and—"

She wrenches herself away, shaking her head. Having grown up in the Wang mansion, she knows what happens when a principal wife cannot bear children. The husband marries again, and favors the concubines who bear him sons. The sons grow older, and make every effort to promote their birth mothers, while resenting the principal wife, whom they are forced to call "Mother." Meanwhile, everyone sneers at her barrenness behind her back. The fact that she retains the trappings and title of motherhood only makes things worse.

She clings to Lian's arm. "Please, give me just a little longer. Two years—"

He pulls his arm away. "Then what? I promised you one year already, and now you're begging for another. It is not as if you won't be able to have a child even if I marry again—"

She shakes her head vehemently, grabbing his arm again. She knows that if he gets a concubine, she will have to compete with a younger, fresher girl. If she cannot conceive now, how much harder will it be when he sleeps with her only occasionally? The tears are starting to stream down her face, even though she hates to cry in front of him.

He pulls away from her again. "And then what?" he repeats. "How much longer do I have to wait?"

She feels all the old grief welling up inside her. "You never cared that I lost the baby," she says. She remembers the way he had gone to look at the small, bloody creature in the basin. He used his forefinger to part its legs, and had walked away without a word when he saw that it was a girl. She has never forgiven him.

He does not bother to respond to her accusation. "It's no use pleading. I've made up my mind." He dresses quickly and walks out of the room.

After he has gone, she sits for a long time, trying to stop herself from crying. When she looks at her watch, she sees that it is already past three o'clock. Granny should be up from her nap by now. She feels a ray of hope. Surely Granny will side with her favorite. Without washing her face or fixing her makeup, Xifeng hurries to Lady Jia's bedroom. Lady Jia is sitting up in bed with her iron-gray hair still down, while Snowgoose massages her legs. Xifeng climbs onto the *kang*, kneeling before Granny.

"Granny." It occurs to her that Lady Jia will not be able to see the tearstains on her face, so she starts to sob again.

"Whatever is the matter, Xifeng?"

She continues to cry.

Granny puts a gnarled hand on Xifeng's shoulder. "Tell Granny what's wrong. Snowgoose, can't you see how upset Mrs. Lian is? Get her some tea. Now tell me what's the matter."

"Lian is tired of me. He wants to get some new girl to replace me." She puts her hands over her face. "Granny, you don't know how hard I try to serve him and please him. Everything I do is to make him happy ... "

Peering through her fingers, Xifeng sees that Granny Jia's expression is shrewd rather than sympathetic. She tries a different tack. "It isn't that I think he should never marry again. It's just—why does it have to be so soon? We've only been married a few years."

"It has to be so soon because you haven't given him an heir yet." Lady Jia's voice is as dry as the rustling of autumn leaves. "I'm surprised someone as intelligent as you isn't being more reasonable. You can't expect to be the only wife in a family like this. If you wanted to be the only wife, you should have married into a lesser family."

"*You* were the only wife."

"I bore my husband three children, including two sons," Lady Jia says, even more dryly. "I am only speaking for your own good. You don't want people saying you're a jealous shrew, do you?"

"They say that anyway."

"All the more reason not to give them grounds to say anything more. I've wanted to talk to you about this for some time. Why don't I send for Lian, so we can settle the matter?"

"But he doesn't know that I've come to you—" Xifeng says, beginning to feel that the situation is slipping out of her control.

Ignoring her, Lady Jia sends Snowgoose to find Lian. "Come on, help me out to the front room."

Xifeng has no choice but to support Granny off the *kang*. When they get to the front room, Xifeng sees that there are four maids sweeping and dusting. She understands. Granny knows that if they discuss the matter in front of servants, Xifeng will not object, for fear of losing face.

When Lian arrives, Lady Jia begins, "Xifeng tells me you have finally decided to get a concubine. It's about time."

An expression of triumph crosses Lian's face as he realizes that Granny is on his side. "Yes, it's our wish to give you another heir soon."

Aware of the maids listening avidly, Xifeng forces herself to smile and nod.

"How much do you think it will cost?" Granny asks.

"That's the only problem," Xifeng says quickly, grasping the faint chance of escape. "It should cost at least two or three hundred *taels*. I'm afraid we don't have that kind of cash just now. Maybe we'd better put it off for a few months."

"I'll pay for it myself," Lady Jia says. "Snowgoose, go get three hundred *taels* from my room." Xifeng knows that Granny's room is filled with money and treasures that she has squirreled away over the years, hidden in all the wardrobes and trunks that line the walls. Snowgoose is indispensable because only she remembers where everything is.

"Just a minute," Lian says. He looks so sheepish and ill at ease that Xifeng wonders what more he can possibly want.

"Yes?" Granny says.

"Actually," he stammers. "I have someone in mind."

"Who is it?"

Lian looks at the floor. "I want Ping'er."

Xifeng is dumbstruck. She feels sick, remembering how she had caught them flirting two weeks ago.

Granny, after the first moment of surprise, seems pleased. "That's a wonderful idea! Ping'er is such a lovely girl. I've always said it was a pity she was born a maid." She laughs. "And there's no danger of her not getting along with Xifeng!"

A wave of sourness washes over her. It has something of the heat of jealousy, yet is not jealousy—at least if it is, she is not sure whom she is jealous of. She doesn't know which she resents more, sharing Lian with Ping'er, or sharing Ping'er with Lian. Can't Granny see that letting Lian have Ping'er is to rob her of her peace? Ping'er is the only one in the household that Xifeng trusts.

With a desperate effort of self-control, she manages to speak calmly. "You've forgotten one thing. Ping'er is my personal body servant. I can't possibly do without her."

"That's no problem." Lian is cocky and relaxed now that he has Granny's support. "Why don't you take the three hundred *taels*? That's more than enough to buy half a dozen maids."

"You think it's so easy? Ping'er is no ordinary maid. I have been training her to help me run the household for years."

"I have an idea," Lian says, as if he is being very generous. "Even after we're married, she can keep on helping you."

"She can't do everything I need while she has to worry about serving you—"

"Why don't I give you Suncloud?" Lady Jia interrupts. "That way you'll be able to spare Ping'er."

Because Granny seems to be granting her a great boon—Suncloud is one of her senior maids—refusing seems impossible.

Granny takes her silence as assent. "That's settled. Snow-goose, why don't you call Ping'er so we can tell her of her good fortune?"

Xifeng is beginning to feel desperate, as if she is scrabbling up a mountainside of crumbling rock. Her only hope is that Ping'er will refuse.

Ping'er appears quickly, looking scared. She kowtows to Granny.

"Now, Ping'er, you've received a very fine opportunity."

Ping'er says nothing, twisting her hands nervously.

"Master Lian has taken a fancy to you. He is planning on making you his Number Two. What do you think of that?"

Ping'er darts a beseeching glance at Xifeng. Even to Xifeng's suspicious eyes, Ping'er does not evince the least sign of triumph or pleasure. She looks wretched.

"Come now, Ping'er," Lady Jia prompts her again. "Why don't you give Master Lian a kowtow to thank him for the great honor he is paying you?"

Finally Ping'er whispers, "Only if my mistress agrees."

"You don't have to worry about that," Lady Jia says. "Your mistress agrees. Master Lian has agreed to let you continue serving her, so you don't have to feel like you're abandoning her."

"But—" Still Ping'er hesitates. She looks at Xifeng again. "Are you sure?"

Ping'er is giving her another chance, yet Xifeng cannot bring herself to admit her weakness. She is too conscious of the maids moving around her, trying to do their work as silently as possible so they can catch every word. No matter how hard she works running the household, everyone hates her for her strictness. They cannot wait for her to show her vulnerability so they can attack.

She shrugs, feigning indifference. "I don't mind," she says. She turns to Lian. "I should think you could get someone a lot prettier and younger than Ping'er. But if that's what you want, suit yourself."

Lian smiles at Ping'er, ignoring Xifeng's jibe. "You heard her. She doesn't mind." He takes Ping'er's hand. "I'll go and consult an astrologer about a lucky date for the wedding."

"Why didn't you tell him that you didn't want to?" Xifeng says, when she and Ping'er are alone in their own apartment.

Ping'er stares at her. "How could I? I'm only a slave."

Xifeng knows she is being unfair, expecting Ping'er to stand up to Lian and Granny when she couldn't do so herself. "I suppose it was too good for you to pass up. From maid to mistress—what a promotion!"

Ping'er starts to cry. "That isn't fair. Why couldn't you have just told them 'no'?"

She cannot explain how Granny had cornered her into discussing Lian's marriage in front of everyone, offering her money and her own maid to make it impossible for Xifeng to refuse. "How could I?"

"If you had just told them 'no,' it would have been the end of the matter—"

"I did say 'no' at first, but then—"

"You should have stood your ground." Ping'er speaks as tauntingly as Xifeng had a few moments before. "But, no, you wanted to seem like the perfect daughter-in-law, Lady Jia's favorite, whom no one can criticize—"

She slaps Ping'er.

9

"Baochai, good news," Mrs. Xue cries, when Baochai walks into her apartment after breakfast. "Zheng just told me that Pan's case is settled!"

"Settled? What happened?"

"All the witnesses said Zhang Hua struck the first blow, so Pan was justified in defending himself. And the doctor said Zhang had suffered from a chronic heart condition, which may have caused his death rather than the beating. So the magistrate decided there was insufficient evidence, and dropped the charges."

"That's wonderful!" Baochai says. Underneath the first flood of relief, she is aware of a feeling of disappointment. Is that it? Pan had killed someone. Could he actually escape scot-free? She tries to suppress the feeling, shocked at herself.

"Yes, and all thanks to Zheng," Mrs. Xue says. "We can never be sufficiently grateful to him."

She is tired, tired of living in the shadow of Pan's endless crises and alarms. Surely her mother is, too. "Mother," she says abruptly.

"Yes?"

"Does it ever occur to you that when other people help Pan get out of these messes, he never faces the consequences of what he does?"

"Why, what do you mean?"

"Maybe if he really believed that he would go to jail, he wouldn't have beaten Zhang Hua up."

"For shame, Baochai. Do you actually want to see your brother punished? To see him suffer?"

Abashed by her mother's shocked expression, Baochai wishes that she had not spoken.

In silence, Mrs. Xue settles herself on the *kang* and takes up her sewing. Baochai notices that she is mending one of Pan's jackets. Baochai slowly gets her workbasket and begins sewing as well.

"I don't think you understand, Baochai," her mother says at last. "A person's nature is inborn. Even when Pan was a baby, he was always in trouble. As soon as he could crawl, he would pull down everything: books, furniture, tablecloths. Once a pot of hot tea tipped on him and he got horribly scalded—that was how he got that scar on his arm. I thought, finally he would learn his lesson. But as soon as he got better, he kept doing the same thing.

"Then, when he was older, your father would beat him for bullying, or not doing his homework. Pan would cry and promise to reform, but even before the welts healed, he would be back to his old tricks." Mrs. Xue laughs a little, and Baochai is surprised by the tenderness on her face. "After your father died, I didn't have the heart to beat him myself. Besides, I knew it wouldn't be of any use."

She seems to notice Baochai's disapproving expression. She smiles, and reaches for Baochai's hand. "It was just the same with you. Even as a baby, you were just as you are now. I'd never seen or imagined a baby who cried so little. Nothing ever bothered you.

"And then, when you were older, you picked up everything so quickly: sewing, weaving, housework. Your father taught you to read and write, just for fun, and you could read whole passages of the *Three-Word Classic* by the time you were four. How proud and happy your father was!" Mrs. Xue smiles reminiscently. "Pan was already eight or nine, and was still struggling to write his name. Your father and I used to joke about it: how we had one child who would never give us a moment's peace, and another who would never give us a moment's trouble."

Her mother squeezes her hand fondly, and Baochai forces herself to squeeze back. She feels oppressed by the weight of being the perfect daughter. She is almost nineteen, and cannot help but wonder how her own prospects will be affected by Pan's troubles.

"I've been thinking about what to do about Pan," she says. "It isn't good for him to be kicking his heels around the Capital with nothing to do. He'll just get into more trouble."

"What else can we do?"

"Why don't we have one of Father's old clerks take him south this autumn to buy supplies? Old Feng would know how to keep him in line."

Mrs. Xue looks dubious. "Would he go?"

"He might try to refuse, but surely you can make him go, after all the trouble he has caused."

"You're right. Besides, after all this, it might be better for him to be out of the Capital for a while."

Someone calls from outside the door curtain. "Auntie! Cousin!" Daiyu pokes her head in. "Can I come in and sit with you?" she says, her face wistful.

Baochai laughs at the way that Daiyu is poised there, as if unsure of her welcome. "Come in. What are you afraid of?"

"I didn't know if you were busy."

Baochai and her mother climb off the *kang* to greet her. "Of course not," Mrs. Xue says. "And even if we were, we should be glad to have you visit. Sunset!" she calls.

Sunset appears from one of the back rooms.

"Make Miss Lin some tea. And put out those little cakes the Countess of Zhenguo sent us."

They draw Daiyu onto the *kang*. Baochai is glad Daiyu has come. She has liked Daiyu from the first. Even though she seems quiet and self-conscious at mealtimes, Baochai senses some quickness, some spark, in her that the other girls lack.

"I am sure you must find the weather here terribly dry and dusty, after being in the south," Mrs. Xue says.

Daiyu looks curiously at her. "Have you lived in the south before?"

"We're from Nanjing. We moved to the Capital a few years ago."

"Nanjing! My parents took me there when I was a little girl. I remember playing near the stone animals at Mingxiao Ling."

"Mingxiao Ling," says Baochai. "I remember wanting to play there, too, when I was little." She turns to her mother, laughing. "But you wouldn't let me. You said it wasn't proper to play near an Imperial Mausoleum."

Daiyu laughs too. "My mother probably told me to stop, too, only I didn't listen to her. Why did you leave Nanjing to come here?"

Not wanting to explain that they had left because of Pan's scandals, Baochai casts about for an excuse. Fortunately, her mother says, "After my husband died, we always spent a lot of time here so that I could be with my sister, Lady Wang. She was Baoyu's mother."

"I see." Daiyu smiles at Baochai. "So you are Baoyu's cousin as well. That means we are cousins, too." She looks back at Mrs. Xue. "But Baoyu's mother died years ago, didn't she?"

"Yes." Mrs. Xue sighs. "Things were very different here when my sister was alive. When she died, the whole atmosphere of the house changed. Both of Lian's parents are dead as well. Usually, it's the mothers who hold a family together."

At Mrs. Xue's remark, Daiyu's eyes fill with tears. Mrs. Xue sees them and puts her arm around Daiyu's shoulders. "You must miss your mother terribly."

"I dream of her all the time. I dream that she is still alive, and that we are at home in Suzhou together, washing the dishes or feeding the chickens—and then I wake up and realize she is gone." Daiyu looks up into Mrs. Xue's face. "Did you know my mother when she was younger? What was she like?"

"I saw her for the first time when my sister married Zheng. She was wearing a green gown, and was as graceful as a rush swaying in the wind. My sister grew very fond of her before she went south with your father. She always said that Min was so warm and lighthearted ... "

Sunset comes in carrying tea and food boxes on a tray. Daiyu stops crying and wipes her face on her sleeve.

"These are marzipan cakes made of ground lotus root and sugared cassia flowers," Mrs. Xue says, opening the food boxes. "Why don't you have some? I'm afraid you've lost weight since you've come here."

"I doubt that very much. The food here is so rich that I won't be able to fit into my clothes by the time I go home."

"You don't have to worry about that! You're too thin to begin with," Baochai says, laughing. "It's people like me who have to worry!"

"I had hoped it would be easier for you here at Rongguo," Mrs. Xue says. "That being in a new place would help you think of other things. How do you like having all these new cousins to play with?"

"The truth is, I hardly see them."

"How can that be?"

"Everyone else lives in the Garden, while I am at Lady Jia's. I don't even know what they do all day."

Baochai realizes that she has been too preoccupied with Pan's troubles to notice how Daiyu has been excluded. "I have an idea. Why don't you come live with me?"

A smile crosses Daiyu's still tear-stained face, as if she cannot believe her good fortune. "Really?"

"Why not?" Baochai is flattered by Daiyu's eagerness. "I have plenty of room. There is an extra bedroom right down the hall."

"That's a wonderful idea," Mrs. Xue exclaims warmly. "The two of you can be company for each other. Baochai has always longed for a sister."

"Yes, it's true," Baochai says. "Because my brother Pan was so much older, I always wanted a little girl to play with."

"I would love to!" Daiyu says. "But will I be allowed?"

"We'll have to ask Xifeng. But I don't see any reason why she would object—"

At that moment they hear a laughing voice in the courtyard. Xifeng comes in carrying a bundle.

Daiyu looks at Baochai. "'*As soon as you speak of General Cao, General Cao appears!*'" she quotes with a laugh.

As Mrs. Xue orders Sunset to serve more tea and cakes, Baochai says, "We wanted to ask you whether Cousin Lin could move into my apartments in the Garden with me."

Xifeng thinks a moment. "I don't see why not. The only problem is that, since Cousin Lin doesn't have a maid of her own, Snowgoose has been helping her. If she moves over here, that will hardly be feasible."

"That's all right. I have two body servants," Baochai says. "I'll let her use one of mine."

"I wouldn't think of depriving you of your maid," Daiyu demurs.

"Nonsense. I don't need two body servants. There, that's settled!" Impulsively, Baochai takes Daiyu's hand and squeezes it.

Xifeng opens her bundle. "These are some clothes I had made for you, Cousin Lin," she says, smiling. Inside are two jackets, one pomegranate satin lined with ermine, the other leek-green silk lined with gray squirrel. In addition there are a couple of padded skirts, one in slate blue, the other black sprigged with various colored flowers. "It will begin to get cooler in just a few weeks, and I was afraid that your things wouldn't be warm enough."

Baochai waits for Daiyu to exclaim at the beauty of the clothes, to make effusive thanks. Instead Daiyu makes no move to touch the clothes, fingering the material of her own rose-sprigged gown. "I brought warmer clothes with me," she says coldly. "I just haven't taken them out yet." Baochai realizes she is offended, taking the gift as a suggestion that her own clothing is inadequate. She has an urge to nudge Daiyu, to whisper to her to take the clothes. Doesn't she realize how unwise it is to offend someone like Xifeng?

At last Daiyu musters a smile and manages to thank Xifeng quite prettily. But it is too late for her to erase the poor impression she has already created.

10

"Look at this!" Tanchun bursts into laughter, unrolling a scroll from the box that Xifeng has sent over.

Daiyu gazes at the painting, of a fleshy woman in what appears to be a metal gown. She has staring blue eyes and two braids of yellow hair hanging to her waist. "Who is that?"

Baochai comes over, with Xichun behind her. "It's a picture of a westerner, I think," Baochai says. "My father saw one once, a girl, when he was visiting the port near Shen. He said that he tried to speak to her in Chinese, and she was actually able to answer."

"Why is she carrying a sword?" Daiyu asks.

"I think she must be a warrior," Baochai says. "That's why her clothes are metal. It's some sort of armor."

"Look how pale her eyes are," Xichun giggles.

"How on earth did Xifeng get hold of something like this?" Baochai says.

"Somebody must have given it to Grandfather," Tanchun says. "Why don't you put it up?" she asks Daiyu teasingly.

Daiyu laughs. "No, thank you. I prefer calligraphy."

Her new bedroom at Baochai's apartments is littered with furniture and carpets and bedding that Xifeng has sent over. Her girl cousins are helping her set up the room. Freed from the adults' presence, they are gay and carefree as the girls Daiyu knew in Bottle-Gourd Street. That morning she tried on the clothes Xifeng had given her, unable to take her eyes off the fashionable stranger in the mirror. Among her chattering cousins, she feels like one of them for the first time.

"Come, everyone." Baochai claps her hands. "We want to

finish before dinnertime. Why don't we put these shelves next to the door, and the desk by the window?"

The room is nearly as big as the Lins' whole apartment in Suzhou; Daiyu has no idea how to arrange it. "That's a good idea."

Xichun kneels on the floor helping her choose a tea set. "Here's a nice one," she says, opening a silk-lined case. "It's 'sweet white' eggshell china. See how adorable these covers are. When I get married I'm going to get a set like this."

"Who would marry you?" Huan comes in suddenly.

Tanchun says, "What are you doing here? Aren't you supposed to be at school?"

"The schoolmaster let us out early," Huan says, bristling at his sister's officious tone. "I came to see our mother."

Tanchun's brows draw together. "How many times do I have to tell you not to call her my mother? Lady Wang was my mother."

"All right. *My* mother, then." Huan looks at Daiyu and speaks to her for the first time. "So you're moving in here, too. You're lucky. I wish I could live here."

No one else echoes his wish. Daiyu thinks how it must pain him, to see Baoyu lavished with privileges he is denied.

Huan says, "Could I have some tea?"

Baochai tells Oriole, "Make some of that Old Man's Eyebrows tea."

"Why don't you make yourself useful?" Tanchun tells her brother. "Can't you see we're in the middle of arranging the furniture?"

As the maids move the shelves, Oriole returns with a cup of tea. Jia Huan sips a little, then bends to look at the rolled-up carpets on the floor.

"Which one are you going to put on the *kang*?" he asks Daiyu.

"I like that red one."

"The Kashmiri one? That's nice. Or how about this green one? It's Persian. It's even nicer." As he unrolls it, his elbow knocks against the teacup he has placed on the edge of the desk. It falls and breaks into half a dozen pieces.

"I'm sorry," he begins, but Tanchun cuts him off, "You clumsy oaf."

"I said I'm sorry—"

"That's a nice *Ru*-ware cup, too. You'd better kowtow to Cousin Baochai for breaking it."

Huan's apologetic demeanor vanishes in the face of Tanchun's hectoring. "It's not like Miss Golden here can't afford a new one," he snickers.

Struck by the strange nickname, Daiyu asks Baochai, "What did he call you?"

Baochai avoids her eyes, but Huan repeats, "Miss Golden."

"Why does he call you that?" Daiyu asks, eager to be initiated into the intimate histories of her cousins' relationships.

Baochai still does not answer.

"Why don't you ask to see her gold pendant?" Huan says tauntingly.

Baochai looks annoyed, but at Daiyu's inquiring look, she undoes the top buttons of her dark blue gown and draws out a cloud-shaped golden pendant edged with sparkling gems.

"There is something written on it." Daiyu squints to make out the tiny words.

"It says, 'Never leave me, never abandon me; and you'll enjoy a rich old age,'" Baochai says. "I was very sickly when I was little. My parents asked a wandering monk to tell my fortune. He gave me these words, and said they must be carved on something gold, since of the five elements, I had too little metal. He said I must wear it every day." She tucks it back inside her gown. "To tell you the truth, I would never wear it if not for that. It's so heavy that it's always banging against me."

Since she almost never feels jealous of the opulence around her, Daiyu is startled by a sharp twinge of envy. "What a strange household this is. It seems like everyone here has something special to wear around their necks. I feel quite left out."

Baochai looks at her with a sudden intensity. "You mean Baoyu?"

"Of course."

"It's not the same thing at all," Baochai says quickly. "He was born with his jade. I was just given this."

Yet her air is self-conscious. Daiyu suspects that Baochai feels a special link with Baoyu on account of the pendants they both wear. What was that old saying? *Gold and jade make a perfect pair.* She tries to discern emotion on Baochai's perfectly complected face, but, as always, it is composed, inscrutable. Perhaps she was too quick to read feelings for Baoyu in Baochai's manner—or rather, she tells herself, probably there isn't a single girl, maid or mistress, within the walls of Rongguo who doesn't cherish secret dreams of him.

At that moment Baoyu himself enters the room.

"Oh, good. You're back. We had your favorite pudding for lunch today," Tanchun tells him. "I got Snowgoose to put some aside for you."

"You mean that almond custard?" Baoyu puts a careless arm around his half sister's shoulders. "That was sweet of you." He is wearing tall black boots and a camlet cape, as if he has just ridden home.

As Baochai sends Oriole to fetch some more tea and snacks, Baoyu flings himself into a chair and looks around the room. "It doesn't look like you've made much progress," he says to Daiyu.

"We've just decided where to put the furniture," she tells him.

Sighing, he pushes himself up from his chair by its arms, as if exhausted. "What can I do?"

"You're going to help? You're still in your 'going-out' clothes."

"Sure." He notices the half-unrolled red Kashmiri rug, and heaves it to his shoulder. "You want this on the *kang*?"

"How about that green one?" Huan says.

Baoyu glances at it over his shoulder. "This one is much better quality."

He unrolls it on the *kang*, and then throws himself down on it, pillowing his head on his hands. "I'm resting from my labors." As Oriole comes in with food boxes, he calls out, "Bring them over here, that's a good girl. Set them right next to me."

Giggling, the maid sets a small table on the *kang* next to him, and places the food boxes on it.

"Mmm! Bean curd dumplings!" He reaches for one with his fingers.

The maid gives his hand a playful slap. "Eat properly, Master Baoyu! Wait till I bring you a plate and chopsticks."

In a moment she comes back with a full tray. "Here you are, Sir Baoyu." She hands him a plate, chopsticks, and a napkin. "And here's a candle, too, so you can see better!"

"It really is getting dark," Baochai says, glancing out into the back courtyard. "We'd better hurry up if we are going to be done before dinner." She orders the maids to put Daiyu's clothing in the wardrobe, and tells Daiyu to choose a set of bed hangings.

Tanchun says, "I'll put your books on the shelves for you."

Daiyu has just chosen some pale green bed hangings when Tanchun exclaims, "It's getting so dark I can't read the titles to arrange them. Bring me that candle, Huan." She points to the one next to Baoyu.

Huan climbs onto the *kang* to get it. He has to crawl around Baoyu, who is still lolling on his back eating a dumpling and chatting with Xichun next to him. As Huan walks on his knees

around Baoyu with the candleholder in one hand, Daiyu notices
a strange expression on his face in the yellow glow. The candle
topples over onto Baoyu. He gives a hoarse cry, throwing his
arms over his face. Someone screams. Daiyu cannot move,
thinking of Jia Huan's expression. He did it on purpose. She
scrambles onto the *kang* after the others.

"Are you hurt?" Baochai cries, leaning over Baoyu.

Slowly, Baoyu removes his arms from his face. The right side
of his face, from his forehead to his cheek, is covered with wax,
hardening on his skin. Horrified, she looks away. Some of the
maids start to cry.

"It's all right," he says. She is startled by how calm his voice
is.

"Oriole, get some almond oil," Baochai says. She has
regained control of herself, and though she speaks more quickly
than usual, her voice is equally calm.

When Oriole brings the oil, Baochai pours the whole vial
onto her handkerchief. Daiyu forces herself to watch as Baochai
massages the oil into the wax. The wax softens and breaks up,
revealing skin bubbled with red blisters. Baoyu opens his right
eye slowly, and blinks the swollen lid.

"Can you see?" Baochai says.

"Yes, it's fine."

"Thank Heaven! If that eye hadn't been shut you would have
been blinded!" Tanchun says, trembling. She climbs off the *kang*
down to where Jia Huan is standing. "What happened?"

Huan looks flustered. "I don't know. It just slipped out of my
hand."

"Xichun, you were right there," Tanchun says. "Tell us what
happened."

Xichun looks scared. She shakes her head. "I don't know. I
wasn't paying attention. We were talking and the next thing I
knew Baoyu was screaming—"

"I bumped against him, and he lost his balance," Baoyu interrupts. His eyes are shut. Baochai is still dabbing at his face.

How can he cover up for Huan? Daiyu thinks indignantly. Doesn't he know the truth? She is about to speak, then realizes Baoyu might want her to remain silent in front of so many people.

"What's going on here?" Xifeng, followed by Snowgoose, comes in. Her voice sharpens. "What's happened to your face?"

Baoyu pushes himself to a seated position and starts to explain. Xifeng bends over to examine his face. "Save your explanations for Granny." She glances over her shoulder at the others. "I wonder when someone would have been good enough to inform me of Baoyu's injury."

"We didn't have time. It just happened," Tanchun protests.

"Let's take you to Lady Jia's. Come here!" she barks at a couple of maids. "Help me support him! Lady Jia will want to send for the doctor. And I'm sure she will have something to say to you, Huan," she adds unpleasantly.

"It was an accident," Huan says, looking frightened.

"It wasn't his fault," Baoyu says. "And there's no need for a doctor."

"You're being ridiculous. Have you seen your face?"

Xifeng supports him off the *kang* with the help of the maids and leads him away. Everyone follows until Daiyu is left alone with Snowgoose, who, Daiyu now notices, carries a box full of objects for her toilet: soap, a hair string, coarse salt for cleaning her teeth.

As Snowgoose stows the items in the dressing table, she pauses and looks up. "What exactly happened just then?"

Daiyu pours out the story, including the queer expression on Huan's face. "I'm sure he did it on purpose!"

"Yes, I imagine he did."

"Why didn't Baoyu tell on him?"

Snowgoose stoops to put hand towels in a lower drawer. "Who knows why Baoyu acts as he does?"

"It's noble of him to protect his younger brother like that. Don't you think so?"

Instead of answering, Snowgoose says, "Huan wouldn't be so bad if he weren't constantly being overshadowed by Baoyu. In another family, he would probably be considered a promising boy." She sighs. "But Lady Jia doesn't care what he does. As for Lord Jia, even though he is so strict with Baoyu, he never seems to pay Huan any attention at all." Snowgoose pushes the drawer shut. "But why are you so worried about other people? The person you should worry about is yourself."

"I? What should I worry about?"

"Why don't you try to spend more time with Lady Jia? You're here to get to know your mother's family, after all. Try to get on her good side."

Daiyu laughs. "What does it matter? I'm going home in a month or two, anyway."

11

"Your eyebrows are still a little messy," Xifeng tells Ping'er, looking at her critically. She cuts another length of white thread, loops it around a fine black hair above Ping'er's brow bone, and jerks the two ends.

"Ouch!" Ping'er winces.

"Hold on. I see a few more hairs."

Ping'er's eyes turn nervously towards the clock. "But it's almost—"

"Hold still. Don't you want to look perfect on your wedding day?" Xifeng yanks out another few tiny bristles. "There. That'll do."

She steps back to observe the effect. She can hardly recognize Ping'er, her eyes downcast in her red wedding gown on the chair before Xifeng's dressing table. All that is left of her brows are two high, faint crescents, as delicate as moth antennae, giving her a slightly startled expression. Her skin, covered with a powder made of crushed garden-jalap seeds, instead of the usual lead, glows with a lustrous pallor, accented by the blood-red carmine on her lips. Her head rises like a beautiful flower above the high, stiff collar of her dress. Her hair, which she has worn all her life in the maid's style, with one bun on either side, like horns, and a long tail down the back, is gathered for the first time in a sleek knot at the back of her head. Only she seems ill at ease with the reversal in their roles, sitting passively before her reflection while Xifeng attends to her.

Xifeng senses a tensing in the muscles of Ping'er's face. "They're coming. Can't you hear them?" Ping'er says.

Xifeng has to listen a moment before she hears it herself, the distant clanging of the gongs in the silence of the clear autumn morning.

Ping'er kicks off her old slippers, thrusting her feet into red high-heeled shoes. Now Xifeng can hear the wailing of the *suonas* above the gongs. Ping'er grabs a handkerchief from the dressing table, and presses it to her nose. Only now does Xifeng see that her eyes are filling with tears.

"Don't cry. You'll ruin your makeup."

Ping'er nods. She presses the handkerchief to the inner corners of her eyes to absorb the tears before they escape down her face.

With a shrill blast and the rattle of gongs, the wedding procession comes through the front gate.

"Hurry. Blow your nose," Xifeng says.

While Ping'er buries her nose in the handkerchief, Xifeng runs to get the red silk square. She flings it over Ping'er's head. Her last glimpse of Ping'er's face is of her staring blindly ahead, biting her bottom lip. Her front teeth are stained with rouge.

The wedding party fills the room with cacophony. Two old women take Ping'er's hands and escort her out the door. Unable to see under the veil, she stumbles on the threshold. She steps into the wedding sedan, festooned with garlands and ribbons. The red curtain is let down behind her. As the bearers heave the sedan to their shoulders, the musicians re-form into a little procession. Striking up a different tune, they lead the sedan out of the courtyard. And then Ping'er is gone.

Daiyu slips into Lady Jia's apartments. The front room is empty, the chairs lined up neatly against the wall, all evidence of the lunchtime meal cleared away. She tiptoes down the hallway to

Lady Jia's bedroom. Snowgoose comes out through the door curtain. When she sees Daiyu, she puts a finger to her lips. "Shh. I've just gotten Lady Jia to fall asleep," she mouths.

She leads Daiyu back to the front room. "What is it?"

"Nothing. I was just coming to see you. I never see you now that I live with my cousin Baochai."

"Really? That's nice of you," is all that Snowgoose says, but Daiyu can tell that she is pleased. "Unfortunately, I can't stay. Lady Jia wanted me to bring this over to Master Baoyu's. It's an ointment for his burn that the Abbess of the Water Moon Priory sent over"—she takes a small parcel out of the cupboard—"and then I have to come back and sit with her. Why don't you come with me?"

"Is Baoyu well enough to see people?" she asks, following Snowgoose out of the courtyard.

Snowgoose nods. "He was in a great deal of pain the first few days, but he is much better now."

"Was the burn very serious?"

"It looked terrible, covered with blisters and pus. Then a lot of the skin sloughed off, and it doesn't look too bad now. Lady Jia wants to keep him home from school until the skin is healed."

"Was Huan punished?"

"Yes. Lady Jia said he wasn't allowed in the Garden anymore. He can come into the Inner Quarters to see his mother at Lord Jia's place, but he isn't to go anywhere else. She was furious. It was lucky for him she didn't have him beaten."

They are walking in the Garden now, amid the leafless trees that fringe the banks of the pond. Instead of the clear azure of the summer, the water is now a fathomless green. On the far side of the lake a gardener in a punt skims dead leaves off the surface with a net.

"Have you heard from your father yet?" Snowgoose asks.

Daiyu shakes her head. "I haven't gotten anything but that short letter after I arrived. I'm starting to worry."

"You told me you are going back before New Year's. Perhaps he isn't writing because he knows he will see you soon enough."

"Yes, but I should be getting ready to leave in less than six weeks. I still haven't heard from him about how I'll travel, or whether he'll send someone here to fetch me. It's not like him to leave such details to the last minute."

Now they have arrived at Baoyu's apartments, across the lake from Baochai's. She has seen them only from the outside. They must walk through a circular opening in a bamboo trellis before they reach the whitewashed walls of the compound, surrounded by weeping willows, now leafless. They pass through the front gate into a forecourt planted with broad-leafed plantains on one side, and Sichuan weeping crab apple on the other. Snowgoose leads her up the verandah and through the front door.

They enter a room of a design that she has never seen before. Some of the walls are paneled with exquisite carvings in the shapes of bats, and clouds, and sunflowers, or the "three friends of winter"—pines, plums, and bamboos—all inlaid with gold and mother-of-pearl and gems. Other walls are pierced with window-like perforations in the shapes of zithers, swords, vases, or screens, through which you could peep into the adjoining rooms. Lying on the *kang* under a gold-embroidered quilt, with his head and shoulders propped up by cushions, is Baoyu. The top right third of his face is covered with a patch of blotchy, scaly skin. He looks pale, and seems to have lost weight, but his eyes are bright, and he speaks in the same lively way.

Jia Lian is sitting on a chair drawn up to the *kang*, talking about a party that Baoyu had missed. "The Prince of Beijing was there. He asked how you were. Shang Pingren sent his regards, too."

Baoyu grimaces. "Shang Pingren! If ever a person deserved to be called a career worm ... "

"A career worm?" Her attention is caught by the unfamiliar phrase. "What's that?"

"Don't tell me that you've lived in the household for over a month without learning what a career worm is!" says Snowgoose playfully. "It's what Master Baoyu calls people who study hard for the Exams!"

Daiyu looks at Baoyu, curious. "What else do you expect them to do?"

"What do you mean?"

"I mean, what else can they do to make a living? Your family is rich and powerful—"

"I never asked for any of that," he says quickly.

"You are the beneficiary of it, just the same," she points out, surprised at his thoughtlessness. "You'll inherit a position, or your father will buy you one. Who are you to criticize people who aren't so fortunate, who have to work hard to get ahead?"

"Getting ahead!" he cries, seizing on the phrase. "That's what it's all about, isn't it? They go on and on about 'civic duty' and 'moral cultivation' and the 'love of wisdom,' when all they want to do is get ahead."

"It's on the Exams; that's why they study it. I don't think there's any secret about that."

"But it's so hypocritical—"

Lian laughingly intercedes. "Don't get him started!" he tells Daiyu. "He isn't supposed to get excited." He urges Baoyu to rest, and leaves. Snowgoose steps forward with the parcel. "This is from Lady Jia."

"What is it?"

"It's supposed to prevent scarring. You're to put it on twice a day."

As Snowgoose places the medicine on a table already crowded with ointments and dressings, Baoyu smiles at Daiyu. "So you have finally come to see me."

She says nothing, embarrassed by his suggestion that he has been eager for her to visit.

"Sit down." He pats the *kang*.

Instead, she takes the seat Lian has vacated. "How are you feeling?"

"Pretty well. Mostly I'm bored."

"Can't you get out of bed?"

"The doctor says I have to stay in bed the rest of the week."

"I'm afraid I have to go back to Lady Jia's," Snowgoose says.

Daiyu rises. "I'll go with you."

"No, don't go," Baoyu says. "You've hardly stayed for five minutes."

"You've just been tired out by another visitor. Why don't you get some rest?"

"I'll be so bored and lonely after you go."

She hesitates. She wants to stay and talk to him, yet feels shy about being alone with him.

He stretches out his hand beseechingly. "Please stay."

Daiyu looks at Snowgoose, who gives a tiny shrug.

"Oh, all right," she says, sitting back down. "I'll stay for a little while."

There is a brief silence after Snowgoose leaves. Then she asks, "Why did you defend Huan? You know he dropped that candle on you on purpose."

She half expects him to contradict her, to insist it was an accident, but his eyes meet hers directly, seeming to acknowledge the truth of her words. "Why should I make things harder for him?"

"You know he hates you. Don't you want to protect yourself against him?"

He seems to consider the question. Then he smiles, and shrugs. "He can't hurt me."

"He did hurt you. He burned you."

"Don't say that in front of anyone else, will you?"

"Why not?"

"Because he'll get in even worse trouble. What do you do to amuse yourself all day?"

"Don't try to change the subject."

He sighs. "What do you want me to say?"

What does she want him to say? She understands. He follows his own particular code of honor: knowing that the others treat his brother unfairly, he tries to protect him, without necessarily liking Huan or being nice to Huan himself.

"What do you do to amuse yourself?" he repeats, smiling.

"I read a lot. Sometimes I talk to Baochai."

"What are you reading?"

"*Strange Stories from a Do-Nothing Studio*, by Pu Songling."

"What stories do you like best?" He pushes himself off his pillows and sits upright, drawing up his knees and clasping his elbows over them, as if settling in for a long talk.

"I like the one about the man who was a connoisseur of stone."

"Which one is that?"

"There was a man who was a collector of rocks, who finds a rare and beautiful stone entangled in his fishing net. It was shaped like a small mountain, with all sorts of tunnels and crannies, and had magical powers: whenever it was going to rain, it would emit puffs of mist, just like a real mountain."

Baoyu wrinkles his brow. "That sounds familiar. I think I read it a long time ago. Then what happens?"

"A powerful official covets it, and accuses the man of a crime he didn't commit. Then the stone is confiscated and the man is thrown in jail."

"Oh, yes! I remember! Then the stone comes to the man in a dream, and tells him that it can only belong to one who truly loves it, and that one day it will somehow return to him."

"Yes, that's right."

"That's a good story. I'd almost forgotten it. I really should read it again sometime."

The story reminds her. "You know, I still haven't seen that famous jade of yours."

He says nothing, looking at her gravely over his clasped knees.

"Never mind," she says quickly, afraid that she has assumed an intimacy that does not exist.

"It's really not so special."

"I said I didn't need to see it. I'm sorry I asked."

"Everyone who sees it is disappointed," he continues, as if she had not spoken.

She fidgets uncomfortably, not knowing whether she is supposed to contradict him. He is acting like a spoiled child: pushing people away and demanding reassurance at the same time.

"I hate it," he adds. "It always makes people think that I'm very special."

She has to stop herself from smiling, for it is obvious from the way he talks and carries himself that he is fully convinced of his own specialness.

"What are you laughing at?" he demands suspiciously.

"Nothing. You don't have to show me if you don't want to."

But he slips his fingers inside his collar and loops a black and gold silk cord over his head. "Here."

She stares at it in the palm of her hand, still warm from his skin. It is about the size and shape of a sparrow's egg, with the suppressed, milky radiance of a sunlit cloud and veined with iridescent streaks of color. Somehow, she had expected a jade found in a person's mouth to be rough, unpolished; but this is satin-smooth to her touch. He is right: the stone itself is not special. You might find something similar in any jewelry stall for thirty or forty *taels*.

"I hate it," he says again. "I hate the things people imagine about me because of it."

"It's all just stories, you know."

"What do you mean?"

"People make up stories to explain things they don't understand."

He looks doubtful. "I suppose so."

"You should make up your own story, too."

"Like what?"

She hands the stone back. "Oh, I don't know. Like ... once upon a time, up in the Heavens, by the banks of the River of Immortality, there was a stone who wanted to come down to earth to taste the pleasures of human life. He begged and pleaded with the gods, and finally they granted his wish. They agreed to let him be born into the world of men in the mouth of an infant boy, Jia Baoyu of Rongguo Mansion ... "

He laughs, slipping the jade back on. "I like that. What happened to him on earth?"

"How should I know? Perhaps he fell in love with a human girl."

"And?"

"Well, maybe they got married and lived happily ever after."

"But the girl would die, wouldn't she?" he points out. "Because she was only human, whereas he was immortal."

"Then his heart would break."

"Then maybe he would ask the gods to turn him back into a stone."

"Why would he do that?"

"Because it would be better to be a stone than to feel the pain of human suffering," he explains.

"Do you really think so?" she says, thinking about her mother.

"Yes," he says. "Because he would always be missing her, and the pain would never stop." He speaks as though the thought of such emotional pain is unbearable to him, even though he has endured the physical pain of his burn without a murmur.

"I don't think so," she tells him. "If I lost someone I loved, I would never want to forget them, even if it gave me pain until the end of my days."

By the time Xifeng returns to her apartment after overseeing dinner at Lady Jia's, it is after ten o'clock. For the first time since she can remember, Ping'er is not waiting for her, to rub her aching feet or to fix her a snack. As she stands there in the gloom of the empty front room, she hears the talking and laughing and clink of dishes from down the hall. The new couple is celebrating their wedding night in the new bedroom that has been prepared for Ping'er. She hears Lian's voice, his braying laugh punctuating his stories about the horses he has bought and the wagers he has won. Occasionally she catches Ping'er's voice, bleating a reply, or giving a self-conscious titter.

She advances slowly into the room and lights the lamps. Ping'er's clothes lie in a tangle on the *kang*. The dressing table is littered with hairpins and face powder. She cannot stand to leave the room like this. She folds Ping'er's clothes. She thinks of calling for one of the junior maids, but decides not to. She does not want anyone else to be a witness to this scene that is so humiliating to her.

She puts Ping'er's clothes away. Autumn comes in from the courtyard holding a kettle of wine in one hand and a stack of food boxes in the other. She seems surprised to see Xifeng there and gives a nervous little bow.

"Why didn't you clean up this mess?" Xifeng says.

"I've been busy fetching food and wine for Master Lian and Mistress Ping'er. I'll do it as soon as I've delivered these dishes."

Nevertheless, after Autumn has scuttled down the hallway to Ping'er's room, Xifeng lingers there instead of going to her own bedroom, both dreading what she will overhear and unable to tear herself away. She hears Lian joking with Autumn as she serves them the food. She gets a broom and sweeps the floor.

Autumn reappears, this time with a stack of dirty dishes. "I can clean the room now, if you like," she says. "Master Lian said they won't be needing anything more."

"Never mind. I'll do it myself. Why don't you take that stuff back to the kitchens?"

Alone now, Xifeng arranges the hairpins and cosmetics neatly in the drawers. She sweeps the spilled powder onto a sheet of paper, and folds the paper in half to pour the powder back into its little jade box. She can no longer hear talking from Ping'er's room. She tells herself she should go to bed, but she cannot bear to face the emptiness of her bedroom. She has never, for as long as she can remember, gone to bed alone. When she was a little girl in Chang'an, Ping'er had slept beside her every night. Then, when she was married, she slept with Lian. If he was out late, Ping'er would come in to make up her bed and blow out the lamp.

She shuts the front door and shoots the bolt into place, looking around for another task. Her eyes fall on her loom in the corner, long unused since she became responsible for running the household. She takes a lamp from the desk and carries it to the loom. When she removes the dust cover, she sees that she had been working on a pillowcase with a pattern of a pair of mandarin ducks drifting among lotuses. She had completed the top third, the ducks shading off into nothingness below their crested heads and arched necks.

After staring at the pattern, she sits down before the loom. As if about to begin a difficult piece on the zither, she flexes her fingers, then flicks back her sleeves. With her left hand she takes up the shuttle wound with silver thread. She places her right hand below the weft, and she begins to pass the shuttle back and forth between her two hands, working it over and under the threads. Her fingers are clumsy at first, but after a minute or two they regain their old rhythm, the shuttle becoming a blur between her hands. Even in her concentration, she listens for sounds from Ping'er's rooms. She cannot hear anything now, just random murmurs and rustlings. Sometimes she imagines that she hears the sound of heavy breathing, but perhaps that is only the rush of blood in her own ears.

She reaches the end of the row. Her fingers slow as she works the shuttle through the last few threads of the weft. She hears a moan. She kicks the treadle hard. The brake releases and falls with a thump. She packs the row she has just woven against the edge of the finished cloth, then shoves the beater bar violently away. She begins a new row. It is pointless to try to sleep. Seized by a perverse inspiration, she tells herself she will weave all night: the thumping of the loom telling Lian and Ping'er that she is still there, still alive, still awake.

She turns her head, distracted by a movement at the corner of her vision. A moth has blundered into the glass cover of the lamp. It crawls a dozen steps, turns a half circle, then flutters helplessly against the hot glass, the yellowish eyespots on its tufted brown wings pulsing uneasily. She takes off the cover and reaches out her hands to capture the moth. She feels its furry, surprisingly strong wings beat against her cupped hands. She opens the catch of the window with her elbow, and pushes open the paper-covered wooden frame. She leans out and releases it, breathing the coolness of the night deep into her lungs.

12

Jia Zheng ushers Jia Yucun into a reception hall in the outer mansion. "I wish that my nephew Xue Pan were here to thank you for your help, but I am afraid my sister-in-law has sent him south to learn about the family business."

"No doubt it is wise of him to leave the Capital," the magistrate says dryly.

"Won't you sit down and have some tea?"

Instead of sitting down, Jia Yucun stands in front of the antique bronze tripod on the side table. "Where did you get this?" Though he keeps his hands clasped behind his back, as if to show that he does not presume to touch anything, he looks so closely at the tripod that his nose is only an inch or two away. Like a shopkeeper, Jia Zheng thinks disgustedly.

"That was given to my grandfather by His Late Majesty Shunzhi," he says.

Jia Yucun's attention drifts towards the two ebony boards inlaid with gold characters on either side of the door. "'*May the jewel of learning shine in this house more brightly than the sun and moon*,'" he reads aloud. "'*May the insignia of honor glitter in these halls more brilliantly than the starry sky.*' What's this?"

"His Highness Prince Yinti gave them to me when my son Jia Zhu passed the Exams."

"Jia Zhu? I didn't know you already had a son in the Civil Service."

"He died eight years ago."

Jia Yucun finally takes the cup of tea that Jia Zheng has poured for him. He gives Jia Zheng a knowing smile, as if he has discovered something to Jia Zheng's discredit. "Naturally an old Bondsman family like yours would be close to Prince Yinti."

"What do you mean by that?" Jia Zheng bristles at his tone.

"Why, only that it doesn't surprise me that you would support Yinti. He is one of the few Princes who have any use for the Imperial Bondsmen."

"Everyone knows His Highness has always favored Prince Yinti—"

"Then why doesn't His Highness appoint him Heir Apparent? Otherwise, what can the Princes do but fight it out? And who knows how long and bloody that will be? As for who will succeed in the end, I'm betting on Prince Yongzheng—"

"Yongzheng!" Jia Zheng cannot stop himself from breaking into laughter. "That—that dolt!"

"You are wrong. I have spoken to him, and on the contrary I found him very intelligent."

"I would have said out of the twenty princes, he would be the *least* likely to succeed. His Highness has never cared for him. He is so—so common, with such abrupt manners, and that slow, halting way of speaking, almost a stutter—"

Jia Yucun smiles maliciously. "Well, I can see how you wouldn't like it if he became Emperor. He's made no secret of how he hates the Bondsmen."

To Jia Zheng's relief, Baoyu, accompanied by Lian and Huan, comes in to meet his new kinsman. He hurries forward to make the introductions. Lian and Huan kowtow to the magistrate.

"I've already had the pleasure," Baoyu drawls.

Jia Zheng catches the insolent edge to Baoyu's voice, surprised. "You didn't tell me you'd already met," he says to the magistrate.

Jia Yucun says nothing.

"It was last month, at the Duke of Nan'an's party," Baoyu says. "He was there with 'Daddy' Xia."

"Daddy" Xia is the Eunuch Chamberlain's nickname. For the first time, Jia Yucun seems ill at ease, probably because he knows that most officials hold the eunuchs in disdain and do not willingly associate with them. Unlike the officials, the eunuchs are poor and uneducated men whose parents had taken the shameful step of castrating them so they could serve in the Imperial Palace.

"You spent the whole evening at his side," Baoyu continues. "How did you meet him?"

Jia Yucun shrugs, his cheeks flushing.

Aware that it is dangerous to let Baoyu offend the magistrate, Jia Zheng attempts to deflect the barbs. "Baoyu, Magistrate Jia passed the Exams last year, high on the lists. Perhaps he can help you with your essays."

"Yes." Yucun tries to recover his footing. "Many people find Eight-Legged essays very difficult. I would be happy to help you."

"That is very kind of you," Baoyu says. "But Academician Mei said he would read my practice essays whenever I liked."

Academician Mei is a high-ranking official known for his Eight-Legged essays. Baoyu is being so rude that Jia Zheng wonders whether he should apologize for his behavior. Looking at the two young men, he is struck by the contrast between them. Despite the patch of roughened skin from his burn, Baoyu, sleek with the best care and food, is like a pampered cat; whereas Jia Yucun is like a stray dog, ready to growl and snap over the meanest scraps. He wonders whether his own distaste for the district magistrate's lack of polish has blinded him to Yucun's good qualities.

"Cousin Yucun would like to see the Garden," he says. "Why don't the three of you take him around?" He bows to Yucun. "Please excuse me. I would go with you, too, but my rheumatism is bothering me."

Baoyu darts a look at his father, in which Jia Zheng can read Baoyu's outrage that this distant kinsman, almost a stranger, should be allowed into the sanctum of the Garden.

"I'd be delighted to," Lian says. "Only it isn't as nice in the fall as in spring. You'll have to come back again then." He is friendly to the magistrate, striking up a conversation and offering to take Yucun to his favorite haunts in the Capital. Huan also is eager for the excursion; since the burning, he has not been allowed into the Garden.

Only Baoyu refuses, offering a perfunctory excuse. "You go without me. I have a headache today."

When the others leave the room, he says, "You ought to send a servant to warn the girls to stay in their apartments. It might frighten them to see a stranger in the Garden."

Jia Zheng finds Baoyu's reproof disrespectful. "You're making a fuss about nothing," he says.

"I don't understand why you're having anything to do with someone like him, let alone inviting him into the Garden."

Jia Zheng does not want to tell Baoyu about Yucun's help in Xue Pan's case. He wishes to protect his son from such unpleasant realities, he tells himself. Underlying his reticence is also shame at his own involvement. "How dare you treat a guest in our house like that?"

Baoyu wipes his fingers on his gown as if he has been soiled by mere contact with the magistrate. "I've never met anyone so vulgar."

The theatricality of Baoyu's gesture nettles Jia Zheng. "I don't know what you have against him."

"You should have seen him at the Duke's party, trying to ingratiate himself with all the right people—"

"You look down on him just because he isn't as well connected as you—"

"Flattering and fawning on everyone in sight, and then telling that sob story about his father dying when he was a little boy, and expecting everyone to pity and admire him for it . . . "

He smiles at seeing Baoyu shaken out of his usual complacency. No doubt Baoyu is threatened by a young man who has succeeded entirely by his own wits, without any of the advantages Baoyu himself enjoys. His initial dislike of Yucun fades. He thinks of ways he can serve as a patron to the young man, who is after all a relative. "You're being small-minded. You should learn from him, instead of trying to belittle him."

Baoyu stares at him, as if he has sensed the shift in Jia Zheng's sentiments. "He is using you to get in with the right people, to meet the higher-ups—"

Half amused, half offended, Jia Zheng waves off Baoyu's accusations. After all, he is Under-Secretary of the Ministry of Works. Isn't his own position sufficiently high that he would be worth knowing for his own sake?

"Mark my words. He's a dangerous man."

"Dangerous!" Jia Zheng laughs outright. "What a child you are, for all your airs. You condemn a man as a villain, just because he has bad manners. Perhaps after you've passed the Exams and been in the Civil Service for a few years, you'll be wiser."

Baoyu opens his mouth, then shuts it. He turns on his heel and stalks out in a huff.

13

Baochai, sitting alone sewing, is startled by a loud banging on the door. She rushes to open it. A band of men in elaborately embroidered yellow jackets are standing there.

"Who are you? What do you want?" she cries in a voice she can hardly recognize as her own.

"We are looking for Xue Pan."

With a throb of horror, she realizes who they are: the Embroidered Jackets, the Emperor's Secret Police. Her heart starts to hammer. "There must be some mistake. My brother hasn't done anything wrong. Can you tell me the charge against him?"

They try to push past her.

"You mustn't come in!" she cries, trying to shut the door. "My mother isn't well. Pan isn't here. He went south last week."

"Nevertheless, we must search the apartment."

As they force the door open, she rushes to their leader, clinging to his arm. "No, no. You mustn't! I tell you he isn't here. And you will just upset my mother!"

Pan himself comes through the door.

"Pan! What are you doing here?"

Before he can understand what is happening, the Embroidered Jackets descend on him. "That's Xue Pan! You're under arrest!"

"Run, Pan! Run!" she hears herself scream.

As the Embroidered Jackets surround him, he begins to fight with a ferocity that terrifies her. He punches one, kicks another in the stomach. Baochai catches a glimpse of his face. His lips are curled back into a fierce and desperate expression that makes him look like a stranger.

"Baochai! Baochai!" She hears someone calling her name.

She turns to see who it is and finds herself staring into darkness. Her heart pounds, and her body is soaked with sweat.

"Baochai!" Someone is gently shaking her shoulder.

She realizes that she has been dreaming, and that she is lying in bed in her own room.

"Baochai, are you all right?"

She sees a glimpse of a pale face through the darkness, and realizes it is Daiyu. She struggles to raise herself to her elbow. "Yes, I'm all right," she gasps. "I was having the most terrible dream." Even now the images of the yellow-coated police, and of Pan's savage expression, are vivid before her.

"I heard you crying out in your sleep." Daiyu is kneeling on the *kang* beside her. She reaches for Baochai's hands. "You're shaking. Your hands are freezing. Do you want me to get you some water?"

"No, no," Baochai says, instinctively gripping Daiyu's hand, as Daiyu pulls away to fetch the water. "Stay here with me."

"Of course. What were you dreaming about? You seemed so frightened."

"I—I—It was about my brother, Pan."

Daiyu sneezes. Baochai realizes she is dressed in only a sleeveless tunic and undertrousers. "You'd better come under the covers, too, or else you'll catch cold."

Daiyu slips under the quilt beside Baochai, and snuggles against her. Daiyu's skin is warm, and her hair, falling against Baochai's cheek, is soft and smells faintly of sweat mingled with sandalwood soap. "What were you dreaming about Pan?"

Baochai lies there silently.

"Are you worried that he'll get sick or hurt on his trip?" Daiyu prompts.

"No, it's not that at all. It's not what you, and everyone else, thinks."

"Then what is it?"

Shaken out of her usual reserve, she blurts out the truth about Pan: his drinking and gambling and wildness. As she speaks, she is conscious of a queer relief in at last sharing what she and her mother have so long kept hidden. In the darkness, when she cannot see anything of Daiyu's expression, just the pale shadow of her face, it is easier to speak; yet she is also aware that it is something about Daiyu that elicits this openness. She is some-one who has grown up outside the complicated web of extended family that hampers Baochai's movements. She is as curious and observant as a sparrow—and yet her responses are not uncriti-cal, undercut by a certain sly wit.

Baochai finds herself even telling about Zhang Hua's murder. As she reaches the end of her recital her momentary relief shades into the familiar sense of dread. She falls silent, half brac-ing herself for Daiyu's recoil of shock and horror, perhaps for herself as well as for Pan.

For a moment Daiyu says nothing. Her hand gropes for Baochai's under the covers, her fingers warm and sweaty. "No wonder you and your mother always seem so anxious," Daiyu says, as if finally receiving the answer to a question she has long pondered.

At the unexpectedness of Daiyu's reaction, Baochai gives a little laugh despite herself.

"I never suspected. He seemed perfectly pleasant the few times I saw him."

"That's the hard part. In many ways, he is a kind person. Only he seems to have no control over himself when he loses his temper ... "

"It's frightening to think that he beat someone up so badly, even if he didn't mean to kill him."

"But he was horrified by what he'd done." Baochai is surprised by her instinct to defend him.

"If he was horrified by it, then perhaps he will change."

Baochai sighs, shaking her head. "We have pleaded with and scolded him for years."

"But other people telling you is different from feeling something yourself. My mother ..." Daiyu pauses, as Baochai has observed that she always does before speaking of her mother, as if she must gather her composure to mention the topic. "Before my mother was sick, she used to have the neighbors' children over to teach them a few characters, and I would help her. Sometimes I'd get frustrated that they learned slowly, or forgot what we taught them the day before. My mother always said that people learn at different rates, but that everyone learns in the end. She said that someone who can learn nothing is just as rare as someone who can learn everything. So perhaps Pan has just been slow to learn ..."

Feeling herself relaxing against the warmth of Daiyu's body and under the gentle murmur of her voice, Baochai yawns.

"Do you think you can fall asleep again? I'm afraid you'll be tired tomorrow. But if you want to stay up, I'll light the lamp and stay up with you."

"No, we'd better go to sleep." Baochai turns onto her side away from Daiyu. With a little sigh, Daiyu curls her body against Baochai's so that her torso follows the curve of Baochai's back.

"Are you warm enough?" Baochai asks.

"Yes, I'm fine."

For a long time they lie silent. It has been several years since Baochai has slept with anyone. She used to sleep with her mother, but then when she moved into the Garden she became accustomed to sleeping by herself. She notices that Daiyu's breathing has slowed and deepened. She turns her head to look at her cousin. The faintest gray light is coming through the window; it must be getting close to sunrise. She sees Daiyu's parted pink lips, the purplish smudges under her eyes beneath her straight lashes. The little pucker between her brows has relaxed into smoothness. Baochai smiles as she hears the gurgle of a snore in Daiyu's nose. Then she lets herself slip into sleep.

14

Xifeng wakes in the chilly autumn dawn and shuffles out from her bedroom to the front room. The room is cold and dark, the blinds still down. The fire in the *kang* has all but gone out. This is the fourth time in six weeks that Autumn has failed to arrive on time. As she stoops down to poke at the dying embers, she thinks about how she will have the maid beaten, and deduct a month's salary as well. Despite all her threats and scoldings, Autumn has not become more dependable. In her heart, she admits to herself that she had promoted Autumn to senior maid simply because Ping'er disliked her.

Xifeng pours water into a kettle, letting the metal bang against the stove. She goes to the wardrobe and begins to dress. She glances at the clock on the wall, knowing she should hurry to get to Lady Jia's on time. Still, she feels a heavy sluggishness weighing on her limbs, as if she has not slept enough. She puts on a fur-lined vest over her robe, then goes to her dressing table and sits before the mirror.

Since Lian started neglecting her for Ping'er, she has felt old; but after all, she is only nine months older than Ping'er, and even the most unforgiving scrutiny does not reveal any wrinkles or lack of freshness in her complexion. She only looks tired and spiritless, with tiny creases in her forehead and at the corners of her mouth. She dislikes doing her own hair, since Ping'er always did it for her, and starts instead on her makeup. She forces herself to smile and open her eyes wide as she applies the powder and rouge and kohl, taking a little heart from the lively, pretty countenance that appears in her mirror.

She has just finished combing her hair when she hears a sound in the hallway from the room where Lian sleeps with Ping'er every night. Ping'er comes in, yawning and buttoning up her tunic, which is the only thing she wears besides a pair of loose undertrousers. Xifeng tries to keep her eyes fixed on her reflection in the mirror. All the same, through the corner of her eye, she cannot help noticing how flushed and rosy Ping'er is, suffused, she thinks sourly, with a glow of contentment and sexual satisfaction.

Without even saying good morning, Ping'er goes to the cupboard by the stove and starts to rummage inside it. "Have you seen the Pu'er?"

Pu'er is Lian's favorite kind of tea.

"I think we're out." Xifeng does not take her eyes off her reflection. It is Ping'er's responsibility to keep the cupboard stocked.

"Oh, well, I'll make another kind. What's this?" She emerges from the cupboard holding the metal canister of herbs that Dr. Wang had prescribed to help Xifeng conceive.

Xifeng does not answer.

Ping'er realizes what it is. She shuts her mouth and stands there looking a little foolish. She shakes the canister, feeling how full it is. There is a silence. Then she says, "Why haven't you been taking your medicine?"

Xifeng takes her eyes off her reflection to look at Ping'er, as she begins to pin her hair into a knot. "I don't have time to make it for myself in the mornings. I barely have enough time to wash and dress as it is, before I have to go to Lady Jia's."

"Why don't you have one of the other maids, like Autumn, make it for you?"

Xifeng is silent for a moment before replying. "What is the point?" She looks back at her reflection. Lian has not spent a single night with her since he took Ping'er as a concubine.

Ping'er does not speak. Without bothering to pin her ornaments in her hair, Xifeng rises to go to Granny's.

"Wait a moment," Ping'er says.

Xifeng continues towards the door.

"What is the date?" Ping'er asks, just as Xifeng puts out her hand to swing it open.

Xifeng pauses, faintly surprised at the irrelevance of the question. "It is the thirteenth of the Tenth Month."

Ping'er rushes over to Xifeng. She grabs her arm and whispers in her ear. "That means you are fertile now. Doesn't your period always come around the first of the month?"

Xifeng tries to draw her arm away, sickened by this attempt to act as if they are still intimate. Ping'er holds on, looking at the calendar on the wall. "It was the first of the month, wasn't it?"

"Yes, but what of it?"

Ping'er glances down the hallway. "Find some excuse to send me away tonight," she whispers. "And get him to sleep with you."

"He's not interested in me."

"You know what he is like." Ping'er nudges Xifeng confidentially. "All you have to do is order some wine and wear a low-cut gown."

Xifeng does not move, mortified that the intimate knowledge of Lian's sexual proclivities is now something she shares with Ping'er.

"Come on. Why not?" Ping'er urges. "Otherwise you'll have to wait another whole month for a chance." Now she is at the stove shaking the medicine into a cup, pouring the water from the kettle. "Come on," she repeats. "You can't afford to give up."

She brings the steaming cup to Xifeng.

Xifeng does not take it for a moment, filled with distrust, as if the cup holds something poisonous. Why is Ping'er being nice to her all of a sudden after ignoring her for weeks?

Regardless of Ping'er's motives, Xifeng cannot afford to let the opportunity slip. She takes the cup.

"Why don't you let me fix your hair while you drink it? The back is uneven." Ping'er shepherds Xifeng back to the dressing table and starts to pluck out the pins.

"Ouch, you're hurting me," Xifeng complains, when a pin snags in her hair. Inside, she feels abjectly grateful for Ping'er's help.

Baoyu walks quickly through the Inner Gate, rejoicing that in honor of the Spirit Festival the day after tomorrow, the school-master has let the class out early. He will tell Granny that he is home, then he will go to Baochai's, in the hope of spending his afternoon with Daiyu. When he enters Granny's apartment, he is surprised to find the front room empty, although it is nearly four o'clock. He goes down the corridor to her bedroom. Even before he pushes through the door curtain, his nostrils are assailed by the strong medicinal smell of the *baiyao* liniment that Granny has Snowgoose rub on her legs. When he slips into the room, the blinds are still down, the wardrobes and chests that line the walls shadowy hulks. He advances towards the *kang*, his eyes adjusting to the dimness, and sees that Lady Jia is still sleeping on the *kang* while a maid massages her legs. As he creeps nearer, he sees that instead of Snowgoose, it is the pretty, flirtatious Silver, one of Granny's senior maids. She seems half asleep herself, her eyelids half shut and her head nodding, as her hands mechanically knead Lady Jia's legs. He knows that he should leave again, but something about her unconsciousness, her fluttering eyelids and red lips falling apart to reveal small white teeth, makes him want to linger. She does not seem to notice as he climbs onto the *kang*. He leans over and tweaks her earring. Her eyelids fly open in surprise, but her lips curve into a smile when she sees who it is.

He leans close to her and whispers in her ear, "Isn't Granny feeling well?"

She turns her head so that her lips brush his hair, and whispers back, "No, she has a headache."

"Where's Snowgoose?"

"Lady Jia sent her to the doctor to get some medicine."

Baoyu is glad that Snowgoose is not there. It always seems strange to him that so pretty a girl should have so forbidding a personality. She keeps him at a distance, and he has the vague feeling that she disapproves of him. It is different with Silver and the other maids. He has known them for years, watching them transform from gangly, giggling girls to lovely young women. He remembers when Granny bought Silver, a skinny monkey of a girl with some of her teeth still missing. His mother was still alive then, so she must be seventeen or eighteen by now. He wonders what will become of her. Usually the Jias marry the maids off, to stewards or grooms, when they reach their early twenties and are too old to be maids. Sometimes they are freed and allowed to return to their families, if they have any. For some reason, the thought of Silver getting married and leaving the mansion makes him feel like crying.

"Can you get me something to eat, there's a dear," he whispers in her ear.

"How can I? I'm afraid she'll wake up if I stop," Silver whispers back. "Besides, I'm the one who needs a drink. I've been massaging her legs for the last hour and a half."

"I'll get you some tea from the other room."

"How can I drink it?" she pouts. "I can't use my hands."

"I'll hold the cup for you."

"No, that's all right. Now if I could only have something to suck on, to wet my mouth ..."

He remembers the Fragrant Snow lozenges that he carries in a little embroidered purse attached to his sash. He takes one out. She sees it, and opens her mouth, shutting her eyes. The sight of her red lips parting to reveal her little pink tongue arouses him, and on an impulse he leans forward and gives her lips a quick kiss before popping the lozenge between them.

She opens her eyes at him. "Why did you do that?" She speaks coyly, with pretended innocence. She shuts her eyes and begins to suck on the lozenge, a little smile puckering the corners of her mouth.

He can tell that she is pleased by his kiss. It takes away his embarrassment, and goads him to go further. He leans close to her again. "Shall I ask Granny if I can have you, so we can be together?" he whispers jokingly.

Silver does not say anything, her eyes still closed.

"I'll ask her about it when she wakes up," he adds.

She opens her eyes and looks directly into his. She gives a little shrug, and says, "*Yours is yours, wherever it be,*' as they said to the lady who dropped her gold pin in the well." The expression in her eyes, a frank mixture of appraisal and desire, almost frightens him, and he draws back a little.

Lady Jia sits up and deals Silver a ringing slap across her face. "You little whore! So this is how you talk to Baoyu when you think no one is around! How can a young boy keep himself decent with someone like you giving him ideas?"

Baoyu is so startled by Granny's fury that for a moment he cannot think of what to say. Silver bursts into tears, nursing her red cheek with one hand. He starts to explain, "We were just joking."

"Oh, no." Lady Jia does not even look at him. "What this young lady said was no joke. Aren't you ashamed of yourself? After working here so long, after all that I've done for you, this is how you treat me—"

What she says strikes Baoyu as all wrong. Silver has slaved faithfully for Granny for almost ten years. How can Granny treat her like this? Silver does not protest. She weeps and apologizes as Granny upbraids her.

He tries again. "You shouldn't blame her. It was my fault for flirting with her."

Granny looks at him this time, and for a brief instant he thinks he sees dislike in her eyes. "I'm sending for your mother to take you away," she tells Silver.

Silver falls down on her knees with a little cry. "Beat me or call me names, I don't mind. But please don't dismiss me! I have served you for ten years. How will I have the face to see people if you dismiss me now?" She had looked so charming only a short time before, but now she is red-eyed and distraught, her face distorted by weeping. She seems to have forgotten his presence.

"What is the matter?" Snowgoose comes in carrying a small packet of medicine.

"Send for Mrs. Bai, Silver's mother," Granny tells her.

"Why on earth?"

Silver falls on her knees before Snowgoose, begging her to intercede with Granny on her behalf.

As Silver tells what passed between her and Baoyu, what seemed innocent and playful now seems dirty, and he is overcome by shame. He tries to defend Silver one last time. "Please, Granny. We didn't mean any harm. Please don't dismiss Silver."

"You stay out of it," Granny says. There is no mistaking her hostility.

Now Granny is calling Silver names again, while Snowgoose tries to reason with her. He slips out of the room, unable to bear the shrill voices and tears. He blames himself, but does not know how to fix the situation.

Lian had told Ping'er that he would be having dinner with friends, but would return afterwards. As soon as dinner at Lady Jia's is cleared, Xifeng hurries to her own apartments to prepare for his return. She rubs coarse salt on her teeth, and chews a clove to sweeten her breath. She scrubs her face and redoes her makeup with a lighter hand, rubbing her lips with almond oil to make them look soft and full. Finally, she goes to her bedroom and strips off her clothes. She stands in front of the wardrobe, puzzling over what to wear. In the end she chooses a tight peach-pink sleeveless tunic with a low-cut neckline in the shape of a *pipa* guitar, and a pair of loose trousers in ivy-green brocade.

She trips out to the front room, her feet thrust into a pair of high-heeled slippers. The food she has ordered from the kitchens has arrived. She opens the food boxes. All Lian's favorites are there—pine-nut rolls, goose-fat dumplings, tiny sesame-seed cakes fried in the shapes of flowers—as well as ordinary drinking snacks: roasted melon seeds, dried plums, anise-scented beans. Two kinds of wine are warming on the brazier. She is just blowing out a lamp when she hears Lian's footsteps outside. She pours out a full cup of *samshoo* and greets him.

"Where's Ping'er?" he asks.

"Have some *samshoo*." She ignores his question. "This is the 'Red Dew' *samshoo* that the Countess of Xining sent us from Shaoxing last year. I decided to open the cask."

She holds the cup to his lips. He swallows a mouthful.

"Good, isn't it?"

"Mmm." He nods. "Where's Ping'er?" he asks again.

"Out," she says over her shoulder as she climbs onto the *kang*. She nips a pine-nut roll onto a plate and offers it to him.

Instead of using the chopsticks, he takes it between his thumb and index finger and bites into it. He has always had a weakness for deep-fried foods.

"It's late for her to be out," he says with his mouth full.

"She's a big girl. She's allowed to be out late if she wants to." She points to his oil-slicked fingers laughingly. "At least sit down and use chopsticks!"

He perches on the edge of the *kang* instead of climbing up and settling himself on the cushions. She kneels beside the food boxes and puts a selection of the snacks on a plate.

"Just one more." He grabs a goose-fat dumpling with his fingers and washes it down with the rest of the *samshoo*. He gets up and walks towards Ping'er's bedroom.

"Aren't you going to have any more?"

"I don't want to eat too much," he says over his shoulder. "It's 'Fatty' Jin's birthday, and I told him I'd stop by."

She climbs off the *kang* and hurries after him. He is already unwinding his sash before the open door of the wardrobe. It surprises her to see how full the wardrobe is, how many of his clothes have imperceptibly migrated from her own bedroom to this one, where Ping'er keeps them immaculately laundered and pressed. He selects a peacock-blue sash and puts it around his waist.

"Here, let me do that for you." Standing behind him, she wraps her arms about his waist, smoothing the heavy silk against his torso. She presses her body against his back and lets one hand travel from his belly to his chest, while the other slides downward towards his groin.

"I can do it myself." He takes the two ends of the sash, but she holds on to him, her hand slipping under his gown and sliding over his thigh, in its thin trouser. She rubs his thigh and his buttock, her fingers splayed over his bulging muscles. Then she trails her fingers down the inside of his leg towards his crotch.

"I'd better go." This time he steps firmly out of her grasp.

"It's still early. They won't expect you for another hour or two at Jin's house," she says, a little breathlessly, steadying herself on the door of the wardrobe.

"You know the saying: 'Go out early and come home early.'"
He ties the sash without looking at her.

"This wine is a lot better than anything you'll get there. Why don't you have another cup?"

"No, thank you." His politeness chills her. He straightens his gown beneath the sash and moves towards the bedroom door.

She cannot help herself. "Can't even spend an evening at home with your wife—" she begins, her voice shriller than she intended, following him out to the front room. She stops herself. It will not help for her to seem like a nag. He strides out without a backward glance.

She is alone. Suddenly she feels how cold she is in her thin clothes, with her arms and neck uncovered. She wraps her arms around herself. She wants Ping'er to come back, so she has someone to complain to about Lian. It is not even ten o'clock, and Ping'er had said that she would try to stay out as late as possible. She wraps a robe about her shoulders, looking around the empty room: the decanters and cups arranged on a tray, the kettles of wine still steaming on the brazier. Most of the food boxes have not been touched.

It comforts her to pretend to herself that she has ordered all these things for her own enjoyment, that she is pleased that she will get them all to herself. "Mmm," she murmurs in the silent room, opening the boxes. She is fond of wine, but never gets to drink much, for fear of what people would say. Now is her chance to drink all she wants. She kicks off her uncomfortable shoes, climbing onto the *kang*. She rearranges the cushions, and settles herself beside the table of food.

She pours a full cup of *samshoo* for herself. She sips it. It is hot and sweet and burns her throat. She takes a bigger mouthful, and grabs a handful of sesame cakes, letting the crumbs shower onto the red Kashmiri rug covering the *kang*. She takes a flat black melon seed and cracks it open between her front teeth. When she was a little girl, she had developed a slight gap between her front teeth from eating so many of them. She still finds it deeply relaxing: positioning the shell perfectly, biting down with just enough force to split the two halves apart, and then nibbling the tiny flat kernel; but now she never has time to sit still for so long. She eyes a goose-fat dumpling. She never eats foods like that for fear of pimples, but decides that one can't hurt. The dumpling's meaty juices ooze in her mouth. She finishes her wine, and pours herself another cup. Even though her head now feels unpleasantly warm, at the same time she feels strangely comfortable, as if her body is melting into the cushions beneath her. It really is good wine, she thinks, letting it play over her tongue. Rich and complex, not like that yellow rotgut that Lian drinks.

She picks up the kettle to pour herself more *samshoo*. To her surprise, it is almost empty. She pours herself a cup from the other kettle. When she tastes this, she is a little surprised by how strong it is. It is different from the *samshoo*. Not as rich, as soft in her mouth, but somehow cleaner and sharper. She drinks a little, then eats a few melon seeds. She drinks a little more. Because this wine is so much stronger, she must eat more to get it down. She reaches for another goose-fat dumpling. Lian won't look at her anyway. After the second bite, she becomes aware of a slight queasiness. She puts the cup down, thinking that she must take a rest. Her head spinning, she has to reach a hand out to stop herself from toppling forward onto her face. She eases herself down among the cushions.

She opens her eyes, startled out of a heavy sleep. Something is pressing against her face. She raises her head, and sees that she is lying facedown on the *kang*, with a porcelain spoon against her cheek. Her head is pounding, her mouth dry. With a groan she pushes herself to a sitting position amid the jumble of pillows and dirty dishes. She turns her stiff neck painfully and rubs her eyes. Though the lamp is still burning, she can see the faint dawn light through the paper windows.

She looks around vaguely, wondering what woke her, and then hears a cough, followed by retching and a muffled gurgle. Someone is vomiting. Despite how awful she feels, she almost laughs out loud. So Lian has drunk himself sick somewhere and has come crawling home at sunrise. So much for "Go out early and come home early!" She listens to him gasp for breath, and then begin to retch again. She raises herself off the *kang* to make some jibe. He is squatting in the corner of the room, doubled over the chamber pot.

Suddenly she realizes that it is Ping'er, not Lian. Ping'er retches again, and then turns her face halfway towards Xifeng. She looks like a wild animal crouching there, her hair hanging about her white face in damp strands. Ping'er grips the chamber pot and vomits again, and Xifeng understands.

15

By the time Jia Zheng arrives home from the Ministry, it is almost nine o'clock. After his long day, he does not feel equal to seeing his mother, and goes straight to his own apartments, hoping that his concubine Auntie Zhao has had the sense to set aside something for him to eat. He finds her on the *kang* talking to Huan.

"She wouldn't stop crying and defending herself, and she hasn't had a bite to eat or drink since she came home ... " she says. Huan is seated at a small *kang* table, bending over to slurp from a big bowl of noodles. The spicy smell of the noodles reaches Jia Zheng's nose, making his mouth water.

"It's about time," Auntie Zhao says. "Can't they even let you go home at a decent hour the night before a holiday?"

He does not bother to explain that no one had made him stay at the Ministry; in fact, he had been the only one there. "Is there anything to eat?"

"No. What they sent me was hardly fit to eat in the first place." Auntie Zhao is always complaining about the rudeness of the servants, how she gets the worst of everything. "Why don't you order something from the kitchens?"

"I'm sure they've already closed up for the night."

"What does that matter? It's not like they have anything better to do," she says. This is the attitude that makes her so unpopular in the household.

"No. I don't need to force them to make up their fires again at this time of night. Why don't you just make me some of the noodles that Huan is having?"

At the mention of his name, Huan, who has continued to eat steadily, looks up from his food.

"And what are you doing here anyway?" Jia Zheng says, annoyed that the boy continues gorging himself when his father stands by hungry.

Auntie Zhao answers for her son, banging the pots and pans pettishly as she prepares to boil more noodles. "It's a holiday, isn't it? Can't he take a break to see his mother?"

"See that you're back to work the day after tomorrow." As he unbuttons his gown, he thinks of the question he meant to ask before he was distracted by his hunger. "What was that you were saying when I came in? Who has been crying all day, and won't eat or drink?"

Mother and son exchange a quick glance.

"Oh, that was nothing," Auntie Zhao says, shrugging; but he has the distinct impression that she wants him to pursue the matter.

He repeats his question.

"It's just Silver," she answers at last.

It takes him a moment to remember who Silver is. "Oh! Mother's maid," he says, relieved that it is something so trivial. He takes off his gown. "What happened to her?"

He senses another exchange of glances.

This time Huan answers, "My brother Baoyu tried to force his attentions on her. She resisted him, and he took it out on her by complaining to Lady Jia. Then Lady Jia dismissed her ... "

"How do you know this?" he says quickly.

"My mother went to pay a visit to Silver's mother today, to say how sorry she was that Silver was dismissed. Silver's mother told her."

Jia Zheng turns to Auntie Zhao. "Is this true?"

"Yes, it is," Auntie Zhao says. "It's what Mrs. Bai told me. She told me that now Silver is at home crying her eyes out about how unfairly she's been treated. Lady Jia wouldn't listen to a word she said. This shows you what Baoyu really is, even though everyone treats him like a living Buddha—"

Jia Zheng throws his robe back on, fumbling with the fastenings. He rushes out of his apartment, shouting, "Send Baoyu to me in my study!" He realizes, even in his fury, that if he beats Baoyu in the Inner Quarters, someone will report to his mother, who will try to stop him. Arriving breathless in his study, he finds the bamboo switch in the corner, half hidden by the bookshelf. He paces the room, rehearsing what he will say. He is formulating a line about how the Jias have always been renowned for their kindness to their servants, and how base it is to take advantage of those under one's protection, when he turns and sees that Baoyu has entered the room silently.

At the sight of his son standing there warily, he forgets his prepared speech, overcome by disgust at Baoyu's falseness, the disparity between his noble appearance and his vile behavior. He grabs the bamboo. "You act like an animal, so I see that I will have to treat you like one."

Baoyu is quiet for a moment before he says, as if reasoning with a madman, "Will you kindly tell me what you're talking about?"

"I am talking about what you did to Silver." Jia Zheng cannot bring himself to use a more specific word. He pictures Baoyu pressing Silver down on the *kang* beneath him, and her fluttering helplessly against him in her panic. He tries to block out the image, frightened by its bestiality. His own father had been a high-tempered man, brutal to his sons while doting on his daughter. As a boy, Jia Zheng never had a thought beyond studying hard and passing the Exams. Yet his father had beaten him on a regular basis. He never understood what he had done to incur his father's rage. At the time, he could only assume it was his own stupidity: he was not a bad student, but even the schoolmaster, who was kind to him, called him "slow."

When his own sons were born, he had resolved not to be the fearsome tyrant his father had been. With Zhu, this had been easy. Though Zhu was one of the brightest students in the clan school, he never lost his diligence and humility, his fear of making a mistake, which he expressed in the quick inquiring glances he directed at Jia Zheng for reassurance or guidance, even after he had passed the Exams. With Baoyu it had been otherwise. From almost the moment of Baoyu's birth, because of the jade, both Jia Zheng's mother and wife had united in spoiling him, and interpreting his every utterance and act as a sign of latent brilliance. Jia Zheng by nature regarded all that was uncanny or unusual with deep suspicion; and the jade filled him with distrust. He could see with his own eyes how the jade warped everyone's treatment of the boy. Was it any wonder that Baoyu was lazy and filled with a ridiculously inflated vision of his own importance and ability? Thus it had fallen upon Jia Zheng alone to instill in him some sense of discipline and duty.

At the mention of Silver, Baoyu looks down. "You're right. What I did to Silver was unforgivable."

At Baoyu's admission of wrongdoing, Jia Zheng's anger fades a little despite himself. "Huan told me what happened."

"What did he say?" Baoyu asks quickly.

"I don't want to go through it again."

"But obviously you know everything because Huan told you."

At Baoyu's sarcasm, Jia Zheng's anger starts to rise again. "What does it matter what he said? You're not denying it."

Again, Baoyu pauses and looks down before answering. "No."

"Is that all you have to say for yourself?" Jia Zheng's hand grasps the switch convulsively. "Aren't you ashamed of yourself?

I could hardly believe that a son of mine could be guilty of such a thing, taking advantage of an innocent girl—"

Baoyu looks up. "No, of course Zhu would never have done such a thing."

Jia Zheng is taken aback. Baoyu almost never mentions Zhu. "What does he have to do with this?"

"I'm sorry I disappoint you. I'm sorry I'm not as perfect as Zhu."

"What are you saying? Are you saying anything against your older brother?"

"How could anyone say anything against Zhu?" Baoyu's eyes are lowered again, but he speaks with a sort of suppressed intensity. "Besides, you wouldn't listen to me. Yet you listen to what Huan says about me."

"What are you bringing up Huan and Zhu for? This has nothing to do with them. We are talking about the shameful thing that you did!"

Baoyu looks up again. "Yes, I deserve to be punished."

This time, Baoyu's seeming submission galls him. It is as if he is determined to take the authority of punishment away from Jia Zheng.

"Take off your robe!" Jia Zheng rolls up his right sleeve.

Baoyu takes off his robe, folds it neatly, and places it on a chair. Jia Zheng had hoped he would make excuses or plead. He should have known that Baoyu was too proud, too convinced of his own superiority, to ever give his father that satisfaction.

"Turn around!"

Baoyu stands with his back to Jia Zheng, his arms hanging by his sides, in only a light tunic and trousers.

Jia Zheng beats him. He puts his whole arm into the strokes, careless about whether he strikes Baoyu's back or buttocks. Again and again the switch snaps smartly against Baoyu's body, the only sound in the room. He had thought that beating Baoyu would relieve his anger, but the more he hits Baoyu the angrier he gets. He is angry that Baoyu forces him to become the sort of brutal, vindictive father he himself fears and despises. He is angry because he is certain the beating will have no effect. He is tempted to yell at Baoyu some more, but he knows that Baoyu does not respect or listen to him, and that he will just make himself more ridiculous in his son's eyes. All he can do is continue to swing the switch, even though his arm is beginning to ache.

Now he is running out of breath, and can hear the rasp of his own lungs between the blows of the switch. Why doesn't Baoyu moan or cry out? If he did, Jia Zheng could end the beating. Even by his silence he defies Jia Zheng, refusing to acknowledge the effect of the blows, and so Jia Zheng must go on beating him. Only by the unevenness of his breathing, and the awkward stance of his body, does he reveal that he is in pain. It is Baoyu's fatal weakness that his stubbornness is spent on being recalcitrant, never for any worthwhile purpose.

With a sort of clinical distance, Jia Zheng sees blood soaking through the seat of Baoyu's pants, the thin material clinging where the skin has broken underneath. His right arm aches. He switches the bamboo to his left hand. It feels awkward, but he keeps on hitting, though he feels his strength is reaching its limit. He swings more and more wildly, pausing only to wipe the sweat from his eyes.

By now, he wishes desperately that the boy will cry out. Even though the fabric of his clothes is worn through in places, and the switch strikes raw, bloody skin, he still will not make a sound. Jia Zheng's heart feels overwhelmed by despair that Baoyu will never change, and it is this despair that drives his blows. His heart is pounding. His arm is on fire. The sweat pours off him.

A tiny whimper escapes Baoyu. Jia Zheng lets the switch fall from his hand as Baoyu crumples to the ground.

16

Daiyu walks down the shore of the lake towards Baoyu's apartments. That morning when she and Baochai arrived at Lady Jia's for breakfast, they found the household in disarray over Baoyu's beating. Neither Granny nor Uncle Zheng had appeared. Xifeng had supervised the serving of breakfast as usual, but seemed distracted, in momentary expectation of the doctor's arrival. Mrs. Xue had sat silently, barely eating or raising her eyes from her bowl, as if to make her presence as unobtrusive as possible. Only by overhearing the Two Springs whispering did Daiyu understand the vague outlines of what had happened: Uncle Zheng had given Baoyu a terrible beating, so bad that he had passed out.

She hesitates at the bamboo trellis before Baoyu's front gate, wondering whether it is too forward to go to Baoyu's apartments uninvited. Still, she crosses the forecourt planted with plantains and crab apples, her breath, quick from shyness, forming a plume in the cold air.

The front room is empty except for Baoyu, who is lying awkwardly on his stomach under a quilt on the *kang*, and his body servant Pearl. His head is turned to the side so that it faces the door. His eyes are shut, but they open at her entrance. He is almost unrecognizable, his once radiant face deathly pale, with dark circles under his eyes. She is surprised by the sting of tears in her own eyes. She blinks them away. "Are you all right?"

"I'm not too bad." His voice sounds weak.

"Does it hurt very badly?"

"A little."

She thinks he is lying. "I don't want to disturb you. I just wanted to see how you were, and to tell you how—how sorry I am. What does the doctor say?"

"He says there isn't any lasting damage. Only"—he musters a smile—"it will be impossible for me to go back to school until my backside heals enough for me to sit down."

"Did he give you any medicine?"

"He gave me a decongestant to disperse the bad blood, and something for pain so I can sleep better."

"I thought you said it didn't hurt much."

"Just a little, when I'm trying to fall asleep."

"I'm sure you must be tired, so I won't disturb you any longer."

His mouth curves again in a ghost of his old smile. "Do you suppose I'm going to let you go now that I've finally gotten you to visit again? Stay and talk to me."

"You can't possibly want to make the effort to talk at a time like this."

"You're wrong. It takes me away from my aches and pains to have you to talk to." He shifts his head slightly so that he can direct his words to his maid sewing on the *kang*. "Pearl, why don't you go to the bedroom and rest? You barely slept last night. My cousin is here to keep me company."

Daiyu suspects he is sending the maid away so the two of them can talk in private. Her suspicion is confirmed by the slightly offended air with which Pearl puts away her sewing and crawls off the *kang*. "Be sure not to talk too long. Master Baoyu needs his rest," she says, sniffing a little.

"Come and sit beside me," Baoyu says.

Realizing that it will strain his neck and voice more if she sits farther away, she climbs onto the *kang* beside him. "Can I get you anything? Is there anything I can do to make you more comfortable?"

"No, just talk to me."

"Why did your father beat you like that?"

His face darkens. "It was something to do with Granny's maid Silver. Huan told him something that wasn't true, and my father chose to believe it."

"Didn't you tell him the truth, then?"

His eyes meet hers challengingly. "I refused to tell him what really happened. He should trust me. If he chooses to think the worst of me ... "

"But how can he know if you don't explain?"

"What good would that do? Do you think he would believe me?" His eyes blaze with anger and despair, before shifting away from her gaze. "Besides, I had done something wrong. I deserved to be punished." He falls silent, his face somber and remote.

She looks at him doubtfully, wondering what exactly he had done. She is indignant on his behalf, and at the same time pained by the hostility and distrust between Baoyu and his father. Uncle Zheng has always struck her as kindly beneath his reserve. It is hard for her to imagine him losing all control over his temper. She remembers, however, the sardonic edge in his voice when he talks to Baoyu. She is beginning to understand why he is so frustrated with his son. Baoyu cares nothing for state affairs, the isms and ideologies that govern other men, including her father. Instead he follows his own chivalric code, as intricate and fine as old brocade.

"Tell me about your mother," she says. "I've never heard anything about her."

"She died more than seven years ago. Sometimes, I'm afraid I am starting to forget what she looked like. I remember how soft and dry her hands were, without the tiniest trace of oil or sweat on them. They smelled of jasmine. When I was upset, all I wanted to do was hold her hands, and then I would feel better."

She laughs to hide the tears that come to her eyes. "Yes, that was how it was with my mother. When I was little and couldn't fall asleep, she would make up stories, about my favorite toys, or people we knew, like the tofu seller, or a spirit who lived in the well . . . "

"Just like you made up a story about the jade."

"Her stories were far better. She was usually so gentle and patient, but she had a hot temper, too. There was a bully on our street who terrorized all the smaller children. Once, she caught him dangling me by the ankles over the canal. She was so livid that she dragged him by the ear all the way back to his house. She told his parents that if they didn't beat him, she would."

She laughs, but the memory makes it even harder for her to keep back her tears. He pulls his arm out from under the quilt, grimacing a little at the movement, and takes her hand.

"You miss her terribly," he says.

She nods, stifling a sob. "You must miss your mother, too."

"Mine died much longer ago. Besides, she was different after my brother died."

"How do you mean?"

"It's hard to explain. She seemed to stop caring about anything. She stopped running the household, or paying much attention to Tanchun or Huan or me. It was as if she had no interest in living anymore."

"My parents had a son, four years younger than me, but he died when he was three years old. After he died, it was the same way with my mother, but she came to herself after a year or two."

"It was different with Zhu. Both my parents thought he was absolutely perfect. They worshipped him. He was hardworking, and respectful, and well-mannered, and he passed the Exams." She thinks she can hear the faintest note of derision in his voice. Then he falls silent, his eyes slipping away from hers.

"Didn't you love him, then?" Having lost her younger

brother, she was always jealous of people with brothers and sisters, and assumed that siblings loved and cherished each other. At Rongguo she has seen that it is far otherwise.

"Of course I loved him." He raises his eyes to hers again. "But when he died, I was just reaching the age when I was starting to go out in society more, and I saw that he wasn't exactly how he presented himself to our parents. He was intelligent, and it was true that he studied hard. Because he had passed the Exams, my parents never paid any attention to what he did outside the house. Actually, he gambled and drank, and kept a mistress. Not that those things are so terrible, but it was important to him to maintain his perfect image before our parents.

"Lian knew. His friend Feng Ziying's older brother was one of Zhu's cronies. He never told, either. After Zhu died, Lian scraped together some money to pay off his gambling debts and give his mistress something."

She is shocked, recalling the reverent tone in which Zhu's name is always mentioned. "This household is filled with secrets."

"I hate it," he says, turning his face away from her towards the wall. She has never heard him speak so bitterly. "You know, that's why I don't mind Huan. He hates me, but at least he makes no pretense about it. Everyone else . . . "

He is silent for a long time. Daiyu says, "Do you remember my mother at all from when you were a little boy?"

He turns back to look at her. "How could I? I'm only a few years older than you. I was probably barely two when she went south with Uncle Lin. I remember our great-aunt the Imperial Concubine, though. The last time she came to visit before she died I must have been around ten."

"What was she like?"

"I remember we were up at dawn waiting for her, and then it turned out that she wasn't supposed to come till evening, only no one had bothered to tell us. Then, just as the sun was setting, she arrived with an army of eunuchs. We weren't allowed to be alone with her for a minute. Even when she was supposed to be allowed an 'informal chat' with Granny, there were three or four eunuchs in the room, and she didn't dare speak freely in front of them.

"I had the impression that she was trying not to cry. She was only allowed to stay a few hours. And then when she was being carried off in her golden palanquin, I was standing on my tip-toes to get a last glimpse of her. There were two tracks of tears, one beneath each eye, through the powder on her face. She didn't seem to dare to wipe them for fear of drawing attention to them . . . "

"Why was she so unhappy at the Palace?"

"I can only guess—but imagine how restricted and confined her life must have been, a hundred times worse than it is for you girls here. And then to be kept away from everyone she trusted and cared about—"

Pearl comes in. "Master Baoyu, it's time for your medicine." She does not attempt to disguise her displeasure at how long Daiyu has stayed. "You really must rest now. Remember the doctor told you not to overtire yourself."

Daiyu scrambles off the *kang*. "I'm sorry. I wasn't paying attention to the time."

"Nonsense. It did me good to have you talk to me," Baoyu says.

Daiyu slips out of the room, chilled by Baoyu's account of the Imperial Concubine. Entering the Palace and being elevated was the highest honor a woman could aspire to. She had never dreamed that it might offer so little happiness. As she turns onto the path along the lake, she sees Jia Huan skipping stones from the bank.

He turns at the sound of her steps.

"What are you doing here?" she says. "I thought you weren't allowed in here anymore."

"I snuck in," he says, with his queer mixture of sulkiness and vulnerability. He shies a stone at the water. Instead of skipping, it sinks into the dark water with a plop. "What are you doing on this side of the lake? Visiting Baoyu, I suppose."

She catches the note of malice in his voice. "You should be happy. Your father nearly beat Baoyu to a pulp."

"What makes you think it had anything to do with me?"

"What did you tell him about Silver?"

Huan's eyes shift away from hers.

"And what you told your father wasn't even true," she adds.

"Who knows what really happened? Silver wouldn't say anything. So I guessed," he admits sullenly.

"Why do you want to get him in trouble anyway? He hasn't done you any wrong—"

"What do you mean?" Huan bursts out. "You see the way that everyone treats me, and the way they treat him—"

"That isn't his fault."

"Isn't it? When he's always showing off, and trying to make me look bad—"

"That isn't true at all," she cries. "He protects you and stands up for you even when you injure him! He knew that you dropped that candle on his face on purpose. And still he defended you and insisted it was an accident."

Huan's face looks startled. "What do you mean?" He catches himself. "It was an accident."

"I saw the look on your face. I knew that you did it on purpose."

He stares at her. "Why didn't you say anything?" he asks after a moment.

"I don't know." She tries to think back to the incident, just a few weeks after her arrival at Rongguo. "I was too flustered. And then I was going to say something, but Baoyu insisted it was an accident. Later, when I said you'd done it on purpose, all he said was not to tell anyone, so you wouldn't get in trouble."

Again, he stares at her wordlessly. She can tell how struck he is; maybe he even regrets the way he had slandered Baoyu. She turns away.

"Wait a minute."

"Yes?"

"Thank you—for not tattling on me." His face is flushed, and he is biting his lower lip.

"It's nothing. Baoyu is the one you should thank."

He looks as if he would like to say more, but she continues down the path towards Lady Jia's. Her mind is filled with her encounters with the two half brothers, and she wants to talk to Snowgoose. She could tell Baochai, of course, but it would not be as satisfying. Baochai is too diplomatic to ever speak ill of anyone in the household. Baochai has been so kind to her that Daiyu feels guilty that the two of them have not become better friends. That night she had comforted Baochai from her nightmare, she was sure they would become close; but with daylight, Baochai's old reserve had returned.

No one is in the front room when she arrives at Lady Jia's apartments. She tiptoes down the hall to Lady Jia's bedroom and pokes her head through the door curtain.

"Who's there?" She hears Lady Jia's voice, sharp and suspicious, from the dimness of the *kang*.

Wishing she could run away, she says, "It's me, Daiyu."

"What do you want?"

"I was looking for Snowgoose." All of a sudden, she feels shy and awkward. She realizes that since coming to Rongguo this is the first time she has been alone with Granny, without any of the maids around.

"What do you need from her?"

"I—I just wanted to talk to her."

There is a silence. "Peculiar taste for a young girl, wanting to spend time with a maid, when she has her cousins to play with," Lady Jia mutters at last.

"I like to spend time with my cousins, too," Daiyu stammers.

"Well, don't just stand there. Come massage my legs. I'm aching all over. I was up half the night worrying about Baoyu. I sent Snowgoose to get a tisane, but she must be dawdling somewhere."

Daiyu advances reluctantly. The few times she has entered the room, she has always hated how dark and stuffy it is. No matter how often the maids scrub and sweep, they can never get rid of the smell of dust and decay that seems to emanate from the old trunks and wardrobes. She kneels on the *kang* beside Granny and tentatively rubs her legs.

"Harder!"

She applies more pressure to the loose flesh of Granny's calves.

"Now pound them."

Daiyu chops the edges of her hands against Lady Jia's shins.

"The thighs, too. Harder!"

She moves up and down Lady Jia's legs, pounding as hard as she can, certain that she will hurt the old lady. However, the blows seem to please Lady Jia. She shuts her eyes with a sigh. The exertion soon tires Daiyu, and she starts to lose her breath. She forces herself to continue, but her breath catches raggedly in her throat and she coughs so hard that she doubles over, covering her mouth with her hands.

"I didn't know you were sick," Lady Jia says disapprovingly.

"I'm not," Daiyu says, panting. "I usually get a cough in the fall. It will go away in a few weeks. It's worse this year because I'm not used to the climate here. Should I keep rubbing your legs?"

"No. You can't do it properly anyway. And I should think that anything would be better than the climate down there, like a swampy jungle—"

"It's beautiful—lush and green . . . "

Granny makes a skeptical sound. After a brief silence, she asks, almost grudgingly, "How did Min like it down there?"

"She loved it." Daiyu peers at Lady Jia's face, unable to see her expression in the gloom. "You never talk about my mother. What was she like when she was a little girl?"

There is a long pause. At last Lady Jia says, "She was the merriest child, always chattering and laughing. She was head-strong, like Baoyu, but so sweet and pretty that no one could resist her."

Daiyu listens eagerly, but then the incongruity strikes her: If Granny had been so fond of her mother, why hadn't her mother remained close to her family?

"She was so stubborn," Lady Jia continues. "Once she threw a tantrum because she wanted to wear the same red shoes every day. How she kicked and screamed!" There is another pause. "You remind me of her."

"I'm glad. How do you mean?"

Instead of answering, Lady Jia says, "What did Min like about the south?"

"She loved the weather, the scenery. She liked being able to see the places she'd read about in ancient poems. She loved it when my father would take us boating on Tai Lake, because it reminded her of that poem by—"

"How like her!" Granny Jia bursts out. "Always caring more about some old poem, instead of what was right before her eyes. That was the only reason she wanted to marry your father in the first place. Do you think he was the only one who wanted to marry her? She could have married General Xue Ke, the Area Commandant for Chang'an!"

She hears the sarcasm in Granny's voice, but does not understand it. "Xue? Is he related to Baochai?"

"All the powerful families are related to each other. I was so pleased when he sent a matchmaker. She would have married him, but then your father had the nerve to send a matchmaker. He placed third in the whole country in the Triennial Exams; but he had no money, and the Lins were all but dying out. On top of that, he was posted to go south."

"Then what happened?"

"She wouldn't have Xue Ke. She wanted to marry Lin Ruhai! Why?" Lady Jia answers her own question. "His poems! It was Zheng's fault. Some of Lin's poems were enjoying a little vogue. Zheng had copied them onto a fan, and Min had read them."

"His poems," Daiyu echoes, glad that the darkness hides her smile. So her parents, without meeting, had recognized each other through the medium of poetry. She had always known that what was between her father and mother was something sweeter and more intimate than the sense of duty and shared interests that seemed to unite other married couples.

"I swore that if she disobeyed me and married Lin, I would never speak to her again." Granny's words strike Daiyu like stones. "I kept my word. I didn't go to the wedding feast. And I never wrote a word to her in twenty years.

"Oh, I knew that she wrote to her father when he was alive. That was how I knew she had you, and a little boy, who died. But until she wrote Zheng, to tell him that she was dying, I never wrote a word to her. Then I wrote to tell her to send you up here, so I could see you."

Daiyu suddenly feels that she is in the presence of an enemy, this woman who forced her mother to choose between marrying the man she loved and her own family. She remembers what her mother had said before she died. Had she come to regret her choice, the long estrangement? She pictures her mother as a young woman, in silks like the ones Daiyu now wears, with her phoenix tiara on her sleek hair. That young woman had never swept a floor, never washed a dish. How could being with Daiyu's father have made up for the life of ease she had lost? Then, with a desperate effort, her mind leaps back beyond her mother's illness to recall the unshadowed period before: Her mother holding on to the side of a punt as the wind whipped her hair out of its knot, laughing as Daiyu's father boosted her to reach a high-hanging peach. Even if she had felt a twinge of regret at the end, Daiyu cannot believe that she wasn't happy for all those years.

Granny Jia breaks the long silence. "The climate down there killed her."

Her mother is dead. Why does Granny still need to prove herself right? "That's not true."

The old woman struggles to a seated position. A dim shaft of light falls onto her face. Her black eyes shine like prunes from their sunken recesses. "Everyone knows the climate down there brings on all sorts of fevers—"

"It isn't true!" Daiyu has an urge to shake her grandmother. She clutches her hands together in her lap. After all, she has been sent here by her mother in an attempt to patch over the long estrangement. But how can she patch it over when her grandmother's anger is still blazing?

PART TWO

Eleventh Month, 1721

Everyone said that the South would be fine,
But the years slipped away till I was old in the
    South:
Springtime waters bluer than sky,
I drift to sleep in the rain.
A woman like the moon beside the stove,
Her wrists gleam like snow.
Never go home till you're old,
For your heart will surely break.

        Wei Zhuang, song lyric to the tune
        "Boddhisatva Barbarian"

1

At the beginning of the Eleventh Month, word finally comes from Daiyu's father. The letter is addressed not to her, but to Uncle Zheng. All it says is that he, Daiyu's father, is ill, and will they send Daiyu home to him as soon as possible. She stares at the letter, trying to extract more meaning from its brief lines. Is his illness serious? Or does he merely want Daiyu with him when he is not feeling well? She runs her fingers over the handwriting. There is no evidence of shaking, or weakness. She imagines her father writing it, bent over his desk in the corner of the front room, the desk so worn that the varnish has come off in spots and she could feel the smooth grain of the walnut with her fingers.

It is settled that she will set out the following morning accompanied by Jia Lian. Originally, Lady Jia proposed sending her in the care of some senior stewardesses. Jia Zheng objected that it was neither proper nor safe to send her with servants alone. Moreover, he wished Lian to visit the family's farms in the south. For the first time in as long as anyone can remember, the harvest was so meager that Xifeng will have to buy rice to keep the household fed. Daiyu feels shy of taking a long journey with Lian, whom she has hardly spoken to. She fears he will resent having to leave Rongguo with Ping'er pregnant. However, Uncle Zheng, ignoring Daiyu's protests, had dispatched Lian, complaining bitterly, to the docks that very morning to hire a barge for their journey south.

In her bedroom before her empty trunk, she stares at the tangle of gowns and jackets as if they belong to someone else.

Snowgoose comes in and begins to sort through the clothes. "When are you leaving?"

"Tomorrow at dawn."

"What did your father's letter say?"

"Barely anything. That's what makes me scared. Just that he was sick, and that I should come back."

Snowgoose takes Daiyu's cold hand in her warm one. "Well, you said you wanted to go home."

Mrs. Xue and Baochai come. Mrs. Xue puts her arms around Daiyu. "We just heard about your father. You poor dear."

Daiyu has an urge to let herself be held in that soft embrace, to burst into tears in the shelter of Mrs. Xue's arms—but another voice warns her not to let herself go, to steel herself for what is ahead. She stands stiff and dry-eyed.

"We brought you something." Baochai opens a small paper parcel. It is filled with the largest ginseng roots that Daiyu has ever seen, as thick as her thumb. "These days, unless you have special connections, all you can get are those skinny little rootlets, 'whiskers,' they call them. We were only able to get these because my father was friends with the Imperial Physician years ago."

Daiyu shakes her head. "They're too valuable. Besides, I don't even know what kind of sickness my father has."

"Ginseng is good for almost all sicknesses, because it strengthens the *qi*."

"No, keep them for yourselves. What if one of you should become ill?"

Baochai gently forces Daiyu's fingers around the parcel. "You take them. They'll lose their strength if we keep them too long. Granny had some, even thicker than these, from when she was a girl, but they crumbled into dust the instant she touched them.

"Also," she speaks over Daiyu's attempt to thank her, "your lungs aren't as strong as they should be. I hear you coughing at night a lot. If you don't strengthen them now, when you are young, they will get worse as you grow older. These are bird's nests. You should stew one of these every morning."

Smiling at Baochai's tone of authority, Daiyu accepts the second package. In the three months she has lived side by side with Baochai, she has come to understand how the older girl conceals her emotions beneath her bossy manner. It is too hard for her to reveal her vulnerability through a tender gesture or word. Weeks ago, when Daiyu poured out the story of Granny's anger towards her mother, Baochai had looked shocked but didn't say a word of commiseration. Daiyu had been hurt and angry, resolving never to confide in her. Then, remembering Baochai's thoughtfulness and generosity, she tried once more to draw closer to her. Now she wonders if they will ever see each other again. She takes Baochai's hand. "Don't you think that you and Aunt Xue will come south to visit your relatives sometime? You must be sure to come and see me."

Baochai's fingers return the pressure of her own. "Of course."

Xifeng enters with her arms full of clothes. Daiyu has never overcome her initial dislike of Xifeng, with her patronizing air, her brittle gaiety. Now, as Xifeng spreads the fur-lined jacket and red camlet cape on the *kang*, Daiyu sees that they show signs of wear.

"These are your things, aren't they?" she asks in surprise. Xifeng's offer of her own clothing seems an act of generosity and not condescension. "Are you sure you can spare them?"

"Good Heavens, do you think I'll ever get a chance to travel?" Xifeng laughs. "Now, tell me, do you need any medicines, or anything else for your journey? Come now, I hope you don't feel shy anymore, after being with us so long."

"No, thank you. Auntie Xue and Baochai have given me all I need."

"Then let me give you a piece of advice, even though you haven't asked for it." Xifeng's voice is missing the tone of faintly superior mockery she often adopts when speaking to the unmarried girls. "When you get back to Suzhou to nurse your father, everything will be clamoring for your attention. You'll be tempted to sacrifice yourself to get all of it done. But remember: Get enough sleep. Eat properly. Everyone forgets the nurse, but you are the one on whom everyone depends." Her face, with its brilliant, dramatically lined eyes, holds a mixture of shrewdness and kindness.

Daiyu understands. When she returns to Suzhou she will be carrying the weight of the household on her own. For the first time she takes Xifeng's hand of her own accord. "Thank you," she says. "I will remember."

After naptime, Xifeng rapidly sorts through Lian's tunics and undertrousers for his trip. The suddenness of the departure has thrown the whole household, already strained by preparations for New Year's, into disorder. She will probably have to stay up all night to get Lian's luggage ready. Ping'er might lend a hand, of course, but she spends her days in bed, claiming morning sickness. When Lian told them about the trip, Ping'er had actually burst into tears. Somehow to Xifeng this seemed the measure of her alienation from her maid. Even at the best of times, she could never have imagined being so upset by Lian's absence. Now she considers it a rare stroke of luck that Uncle Zheng is sending him away, so that she will be spared having to see the way he and Ping'er cling to each other.

Autumn comes in. "The Abbess from the Water Moon Priory is here to see you."

"What does she want?" Xifeng asks, annoyed at being interrupted.

"I don't know."

Xifeng hesitates. The Water Moon Priory, one of the largest temples in the Capital area, is frequented by noblewomen and officials' wives. The Abbess is an important personage, and an excellent source of gossip and political news.

"Very well. I'll see her."

She suppresses a shudder of distaste when she sees the coarse black stubble dotting the Abbess's shaved head, and her fleshy, asexual body in her shapeless gray robes. "Ah, my dear Abbess. How kind of you to come."

"Of course." The Abbess's broad face crinkles into a smile. "I only regret that I am not able to come oftener. How are you keeping?"

"I am well, thank you." She leads the Abbess to the *kang*, looking around for Autumn to serve tea. To her annoyance, Autumn is nowhere to be seen. She is about to call for the maid when the Abbess waves her hands.

"I just had tea at Lady Jia's." She pats the *kang* beside her. "We'll sit and have a cozy chat, just you and me." Her eyes twinkle at Xifeng between folds of fat. "Lady Jia told me the wonderful news." She is referring to Ping'er's baby, of course. "When is the happy event?"

"At the beginning of the Fourth Month."

"The baby will be born in the Year of the Tiger! What a piece of good fortune for the whole family." The Abbess nods and smiles, but her eyes tell Xifeng that she understands very well that it is far from good luck for Xifeng.

"Well," the Abbess continues, "I know you are always so busy, so I'll get straight to the point. You can probably guess what I've come for." She folds her plump white hands in her lap. "Every year before New Year's I ask all the important ladies in the Capital to contribute a little for oil, to keep the lamps in front of our Blessed Lady Guanyin burning all the year round—"

"Oh, yes!" Xifeng jumps up. "I'd completely forgotten." She

hurries to her bedroom, opens the box where she keeps her small cash, and quickly wraps up fifty *taels* of silver, almost everything in the box. She returns to the Abbess with the money. "Here you are. Thank you for reminding me. It completely slipped my mind this year." She knows it is a strange incongruity in her, which others, including Lian, have remarked on: even though she is hardheaded to the point of stinginess when it comes to buying and selling, when it comes to religion, she is so generous that she has never let a single monk, no matter how disreputable, leave the mansion empty-handed. And Lady Guanyin, the goddess of mercy, with her remote yet gentle face and snow-white robes, has always been her favorite.

The Abbess climbs off the *kang*, nodding and chuckling. "That's just like you, Mrs. Lian. Always so generous. May you receive blessings in your next life for your kindness."

The Abbess is just offering Xifeng a farewell benediction when she adds, as if an afterthought, "Oh, yes, there was one more thing I wanted to talk to you about."

Her casualness strikes Xifeng as calculated. "What is it?"

"The Countess of Xiping came out to the temple the other day to burn some incense for her little son, who is sick." The Abbess leans closer to Xifeng. "She happened to mention that she was a little short of cash, and was looking for a loan ... "

Xifeng lowers her eyes to hide her excitement. Ever since coming to Rongguo, she has been looking to make a little money of her own. She knows, even if everyone else chooses to ignore the fact, that every year the household's expenditures outstrip its income. The Jias' wealth, as enormous as it is, is slowly being whittled away by their extravagance, the dishonesty of their servants, and the mismanagement of their estates. She had long suspected the stewards overseeing the farms in the south of siphoning off profits for themselves. She knew also that the Jias had been putting off maintenance and repairs of the irrigation system and farm buildings for years. She alone had not been surprised at the meagerness of this year's harvest. Having no faith in Uncle Zheng's and Lian's ability to set matters right, she has squirreled away four or five hundred *taels*, so she can feel secure if anything happens; but she knows that she will never make real money by saving alone. She needs to find a way to invest her capital.

"Really?" she says, hoping that her eagerness does not betray itself in her voice.

"Yes. She wants to buy a promotion for her oldest son."

Xifeng knows the Countess of Xiping slightly. She had been a contemporary of Xifeng's mother-in-law, and when Lady Xing was alive, the Countess had come to Rongguo several times for holidays or birthday parties. Xifeng remembers her as a woman in her late thirties or forties, who insisted on wearing the rouged lips and butterfly silks of a young girl. She had given birth to a son the first year or two after her marriage, but then had not been able to conceive again until quite suddenly, nearly twenty years after her first child, she gave birth to a second son. "I see. How much does she want?"

"Two thousand *taels*."

"For how long?"

"A month or two."

Xifeng calculates rapidly. In a few days the rents from the Jias' properties in the Capital will come in. Usually she uses these to pay the allowances on the first of the month, and spends the rest on food for the kitchens and other operating expenses. She can lend the rent money to the Countess, and then pay the allowances and kitchen expenses out of her own money. If she falls short, she will divert some money from one of the other accounts—for instance, the money she has been putting aside for the Two Springs' dowries—for the time being. It will be difficult, because of all the expenses for the New Year's celebrations coming up, but she will put off nonessential purchases.

"There is one more thing," the Abbess continues, when Xifeng says nothing. "It has to be kept very quiet. If her husband ever got to know of it ... "

Xifeng wonders why the loan must be kept secret. In her own case, she does not want Lian to know of it, because he would try to claim a share of her profit. But why wouldn't the Countess's husband wish to pay for their son's promotion as well? The Countess must have spent the money meant for the promotion elsewhere, and is trying to conceal this fact from her husband. "Naturally."

She says nothing more. She wants the Abbess to make the request for a loan directly, in order to make it perfectly clear who is asking the favor, and who is granting it.

"Well, Mrs. Lian," the Abbess says at last. "Do you think you can help her?"

"That all depends. What about interest?"

"She is willing to pay interest, of course."

Xifeng gives a sigh of barely suppressed impatience. "Did she suppose that she could get a loan of that size *without* interest? It's all a matter of how much."

"Why, how much do you want, Mrs. Lian?"

If she is going to put herself through so much risk and trouble, she had better make it worth her while. "Ten percent a month," she says recklessly.

"Ten percent a month!" The Abbess opens her eyes wide. "That's well above the legal rate. You could be charged for usury!"

"I thought this was a private loan, between two people," Xifeng says coldly. "What does the law have to do with it?"

"Yes, you're right, of course," the Abbess says hastily. "It's just a little high."

Xifeng shrugs. "If the Countess thinks it's too high, she can borrow the money from someone else." She speaks confidently, knowing that it will be difficult for the Countess to borrow that kind of money elsewhere. How many other women in the Capital can get their hands on that kind of cash on such short notice? The Countess can try to pawn some jewels, but then would risk her husband's or servants' discovering they were gone.

The Abbess hesitates for a few moments. Then she nods. "All right. I'll go see the Countess and see what she says." She looks Xifeng over, her eyes no longer twinkling. "I've always heard people say you were stingy, but you were so generous to the Priory I never believed it."

Xifeng smiles, untroubled by the Abbess's words. "I don't see what generosity has to do with it. This is business, not charity."

After Xifeng sees the Abbess out, she returns to her bedroom. She opens her wardrobe and shifts the piles of clothes onto the *kang*. She kneels on the ground and wedges the sharp end of a poker into the seam where the back wall meets the wardrobe floor. She jimmies up the bottom panel of the wardrobe. Beneath is a gaping black hole. She leans forward, reaching her hands into the darkness. Her fingers touch the old rice bag, the type they use to send up the harvest from the south, in which she keeps her money. She feels the hard shapes of the silver inside through the fabric, and checks her calculations: if the Countess borrows the money for just two months, Xifeng will be able to more than double her savings.

She hears Lian coming into the front room. He is yelling something about his woolen leggings: Did she remember to pack them? He calls her only when he needs something, never speaks to her for any other reason. She replaces the false panel, shoving the clothes back into the wardrobe. The last thing she wants is for him to realize that she has any money. She slams the wardrobe door, and hurries out to meet him.

Daiyu looks around her emptied room to make sure she has not left anything. As she pads in her bare feet towards the lamp, shivering in her thin underclothes, she checks her trunk, neatly packed by Snowgoose. On the edge of the *kang* lie the clothes that Xifeng has given her for the journey tomorrow. She is bending over to blow out the lamp when someone hisses her name outside the door curtain.

"Who's there?" she calls.

"It's Baoyu."

So he has come to say goodbye after all. He had not come home for dinner after school, so she had resigned herself to leaving without seeing him. "What is it?"

"I came to say goodbye. Can I come in?"

"Yes." She snatches up a gown and throws it over her shoulders.

He enters, dressed as if he has just come back from a party, wearing the "peacock gold" cape he was trying on when she first saw him. Granny must have convinced him to wear it after all. It must be snowing outside, for a few unmelted flakes glitter on the glossy black feathers.

He stands there on the threshold of the room staring at her, his breath coming quickly, as if he has hurried to get there. "I didn't know you were going. I was at the Prince of Beijing's party, and Tealeaf came to fetch me. He said you were leaving first thing in the morning. Why didn't I hear anything about this?" To her amazement, he speaks in a tone of accusation. "What were you going to do? Disappear without even saying goodbye?"

Confused by his anger, she feels her color rising. "I only got the letter from my father today."

"What did it say?" He notices the traveling cloak on the *kang*. He picks it up, looks at it, and then flings it away. She has never seen him in this kind of mood before.

"Only that he's sick, and that I must come home at once." At her own words, fear for her father floods over her. She huddles her arms around her chest and shivers.

"You're cold. Get under the covers."

She shakes her head. She cannot get into bed with him in the room.

"Holy name, forget propriety!" he says impatiently. "It's not going to help matters if you catch cold."

After hesitating a moment, she eases off her robe and slides her legs under the covers. She sits on her pillow with her knees up to her chin, and her quilt tucked up to her neck.

Baoyu unfastens his cloak and lays it on a chair. Underneath, he is even more gorgeous, in a narrow-sleeved robe of crimson damask with a sash of elaborately braided and knotted colored silks. He sits down on the *kang* beside her bed. She lets herself stay close to him, not forcing herself to draw away. She feels herself glowing with the happiness of his presence, of being alone with him one last time—only she is put off by his abruptness, so unlike his usual suavity. She catches the scent of wine on his breath.

"I was looking forward to spending my New Year's vacation with you," he says, in the same tone as before. "Granny hires an opera troupe, and they set up a stage. There's a banquet in the pavilion, and we guess lantern riddles in the moonlight ... "

She has the impression that this is not really what he means to say to her. "Well, perhaps you can use your vacation to study, so you can be sure to pass the Exams in the spring—"

He interrupts her. "Don't go spoiling our last minutes together with that kind of drivel."

She shuts her mouth, offended.

He bursts out, "I'm not going to let you go!"

He speaks so passionately that she wonders whether he has drunk too much.

He can read her expression. "I'm not drunk. I'm afraid I'll never see you again."

Her heart gives a quick, happy flutter, and yet, deeper down, in her belly, there is a movement of fear. Does he speak thoughtlessly, or does he understand the import of his words? She says, as coolly as she can, "Who knows what will happen? I may come to visit again in a few years. Or perhaps you will travel down to your family's estates in the south."

He shakes his head vehemently. "In a year or two, you'll be married. Who knows where you'll be, or whether your husband will let you come see us."

"How do you know I'll be married?" she objects. "My parents always said they weren't in any hurry to let me go. I don't think I'll be betrothed until I'm at least twenty. You will probably be married before I am."

"I'll ask Granny to betroth me to you," he says.

She feels a rush of anger. He is just being flippant after all. "You shouldn't joke about something like that."

"I'm not joking."

Is he just pretending not to understand the gap between them? Is he just teasing her to see how she will react? "Don't be ridiculous. You know you're going to marry someone rich and well-connected—"

"I don't care about any of that."

"Granny and Uncle Zheng will care for you."

Suddenly he puts his arms around her and pulls her against him. His hands are warm on her bare arms, and she feels his breath ruffling her hair. "Kiss me."

She shakes her head, trying to pull away, but he only draws her closer. "Kiss me," he says. "We may never see each other again." She is frightened and embarrassed, yet she feels a queer excitement at his touch. He puts his hand on her chin and pushes it up gently to make her look at him, but she resists. He leans down to her, and she feels his lips on her hairline, on her eyelids. Beneath the soap and shampoo, she catches the odor of his body, with its undertones of animal sweat. It draws her to him, making her want to bury her face in his shoulder. She feels the quickness of his breath, his hands slick with sweat, and understands that he is nervous, too. She stops resisting. His lips move across her cheeks, closer and closer to her lips. She is excited by the roughness of his stubble. On his breath there is the slight scent of wine, but stronger than that is the familiar, comforting scent of rice. Stroking her hair, he kisses her mouth now, his lips firm and warm.

"Daiyu!" Baochai's voice comes from outside the door curtain.

She and Baoyu jerk apart. He scrambles off the *kang*.

"I thought I heard voices, and came to see why you hadn't gone to bed yet," Baochai says. "Can I come in?"

"Of course." Daiyu drags on her robe, uncomfortably aware of her disheveled hair and flushed face.

Baochai comes in fully dressed. She must have heard Baoyu's voice from out in the hallway, yet she stands there looking at him as though surprised by his presence.

Daiyu rushes into an explanation. "Baoyu just came to say goodbye—"

Baochai cuts her off. "It's so late, and you have a long journey ahead of you. Don't you think you'd better get to bed? I came over to see if anything was wrong, whether you'd forgotten something."

"No, everything is fine."

"Then, come on. Let me braid your hair so it won't be tangled in the morning." She climbs on the *kang* and kneels behind Daiyu. Before she touches Daiyu's hair, she looks at Baoyu and waits.

Daiyu looks at him, too, her body still throbbing from the

way he had touched her. Barely daring to glance at her, he says, "Goodbye. Have a safe trip."

"Goodbye," she says, and then he is gone.

She feels Baochai's fingers gently separating and plaiting her hair. "This way," Baochai says, "you won't even have to comb it in the morning. You won't have much time to get ready. You're supposed to be at the dock by dawn. I was afraid that you were too worried to sleep. Aren't you tired?"

"Yes," she says, although she feels wide awake.

"I'll blow out the light." Baochai rises and goes towards the lamp. Halfway there, she turns back. "Are you sure you don't want me to sleep with you? That way, if you get scared in the night ... "

Daiyu is surprised by the offer. With her natural reserve, it is unlike Baochai to foist her company on someone. Daiyu wants nothing more than to run after Baoyu, but she feels that she can't refuse. "Yes, thank you. That's very nice of you."

Baochai smiles, and then blows out the lamp. In the darkness, Daiyu hears her removing her robe. Daiyu moves over to make room for her. Baochai slips under the covers without touching Daiyu. She reaches over, gives Daiyu's hand a quick squeeze, then withdraws her hand, and turns on her side.

"Sleep well," she says.

2

Ten days before the Twelfth Month, Baochai sits in her mother's room preparing New Year's gifts for the servants. Her own rooms seem empty without Daiyu, and she has taken to spending more time with her mother. For weeks she has regretted the way she parted from Daiyu. Startled by the rush of jealousy she had felt on overhearing Baoyu's voice from Daiyu's room, she had deliberately interrupted their tête-à-tête. She had hidden her jealousy under a calm exterior, but had been unable to infuse any warmth into her last moments with Daiyu. Now she misses Daiyu, and wonders what Daiyu had made of her coldness. And her jealousy is pointless, she knows: Baoyu has never paid the least attention to her since that day he almost kissed her last summer.

She looks up from stuffing the embroidered purses with little medallions of gold and silver. Her mother, instead of helping, is staring off into space with a frown. "What's the matter, Mother?"

Mrs. Xue doesn't respond. Baochai sighs, knowing that she is worrying about Pan. There has been only one letter from him, from almost two months ago, saying that he had arrived in Nanjing. To distract her mother, she says, "Granny is hiring the best troupe of child actors to perform on New Year's Eve. Their soprano is supposed to be excellent in ingénue roles. What scenes do you want to hear them perform?"

"What?" Mrs. Xue jumps.

Baochai repeats her question. Her mother does not answer, her eyes fixed on the window. "Someone's coming."

Baochai looks towards the door. Pan walks in, dressed in traveling clothes.

"Surprise!" he says, as Baochai and her mother jump up from the *kang*.

"What's wrong? Are you sick?" Mrs. Xue exclaims. She grips him by the upper arms and looks searchingly into his face.

"Old Feng told me to write you," Pan says, laughing. "But I thought it'd be more fun if I just walked in and surprised you ... "

"Yes, but why are you back so early?" Baochai says. "I thought you weren't supposed to come back until spring."

"I wasn't, but something came up."

Baochai braces herself. It is impossible to believe that Pan's sudden return does not foretell disaster.

"Wonderful news!"

"What is it?"

"I've met a girl. I want to be married!"

She looks at her mother and sees that Mrs. Xue is looking alarmed as well.

"Do you mean a concubine?" Mrs. Xue asks.

"No, I mean a wife. I want to marry the Xias' daughter. I came back so you could arrange the match."

"The Xias?" Mrs. Xue's eyes widen with surprise. "You mean Xia Jingui?"

He nods, beaming.

Mrs. Xue looks at Baochai. "They're old family friends!"

Baochai frowns. "I've never heard that name."

"They were Imperial Purveyors, too. Immensely wealthy: they made their fortune selling cassia. Your father used to do business with Mr. Xia, but he died not long after your father, and we fell out of contact." Mrs. Xue begins to laugh, apparently delighted. "How did you meet them, Pan?"

"Old Feng reminded me that they used to be friends with Father, so I went to visit them in Nanjing. Mrs. Xia was so pleased that I had visited after all those years, and insisted that I meet her daughter. She said we had played together as children. The moment I saw Jingui, I knew—"

"What's she like?"

"She's nineteen, and the most beautiful woman I've ever seen. She's educated and accomplished, too. Mother, you'll send a matchmaker, won't you?"

Mrs. Xue laughs again. "I don't see why not, when you've chosen such a perfect match!"

After Pan leaves to wash up and rest, Mrs. Xue says, "I can't believe it. What luck!"

Baochai has not seen her mother so happy in a long time. Her cheeks glow with excitement. "It seems fortunate that his fancy alighted on a girl from a decent family," Baochai says. "But tell me more about the Xias."

"Let me see. I remember your father and Mr. Xia used to have a joke, about how Mr. Xia would trade your father cassia for a son like Pan. They were desperate for a son, you understand. They couldn't seem to have more children even though Mr. Xia had two or three concubines."

Baochai wonders at the idea of Mr. Xia wanting a son like Pan, but says nothing.

Mrs. Xue continues, "Mr. Xia was a nice man, always laughing and joking, but your father said that he was very shrewd as far as business was concerned. Mrs. Xia was stiffer, as I recall. I remember she was very proud of Jingui's accomplishments even when she was just a little girl."

"You don't remember anything about Jingui herself?"

Mrs. Xue frowns in concentration. "I remember she had very long fingernails, because of playing the *qin*. She had long slender fingers to begin with, so it gave her a very odd look: a grown woman's hands on a little girl." She laughs, as if the recollection is endearing. "I must ask Pan if her hands are still like that."

Baochai sees that her mother is too happy to be cautious. To her, this match seems to mean an end to the life they have been living: Pan settling down properly to his duties, a good daughter-in-law to serve her, a stable home life, and grandchildren. "You have no objections to the match, then?"

"I don't see why I should. The girl couldn't have been more suitable if I had chosen her myself."

While Baochai sees no real objection to the match, her native caution makes her consider the worst-case scenario. "Has it occurred to you that they may say 'no' to Pan? Family background aside, it is not as if he himself is a desirable catch, since he has not passed the Exams. With Jingui's qualifications, they may be hoping for a Palace Graduate."

"They may say 'no,' of course. But it doesn't hurt to ask, since Pan has his heart set on it."

"If they say 'no,' they say 'no,'" Baochai says. "And maybe it will do Pan good, not to get something that he has set his heart on."

There is a scuffle of feet outside the door and Pan bursts back into the room. "I was already on my horse before I remembered!" He goes to where Baochai sits on the *kang* and unstraps his saddlebag. "I brought these for you all the way from Nanjing."

"What is it?" she asks curiously, as he takes out a rolled-up vest. He unfurls it to reveal a jumble of brightly colored figurines.

"Look at this." He places one on a *kang* table. The little figure of a man begins to move by itself and actually turns a somersault. Baochai begins to laugh. She has never seen anything like this.

"And look at this!" He takes another figure, holds it upside down for a moment, and then places it upright next to the first one. This one slowly wiggles its arms and legs.

"How do they work?" Mrs. Xue says, marveling and laughing.

"This first one has mercury in it. When the mercury runs to its head, it turns a somersault. The other one has sand in it. I got them at a place called Huqiushan, where they specialize in making these things. And look at these!" He takes out another rolled-up article of clothing, this time a jacket. Only Pan would present his gifts wrapped in his dirty clothing.

These are figurines of characters from plays and operas, molded out of colored clay. Baochai picks one up and is wondering at how finely it is made when Pan holds another figure before her eyes. It is a replica of Pan himself, perfect in every detail, from the large, flat feet and slight paunch, to the slouched posture. She collapses in laughter, showing her mother.

Pan laughs delightedly also. "I knew that you would like it," he says, putting his arm around her. "I wanted to make you laugh, after all that you've been through." He stops short of saying "after all that I've put you through," but she knows that that is what he means, nevertheless.

She sees his simple pride and joy at amazing her and her mother, and realizes that this is why it is so difficult to harden her heart against him. She puts her arms around him, torn between laughter and tears. "Welcome home, Pan. I'm glad you're back."

3

"You wanted to see me, ma'am?" Cook Liu stands in the doorway of Xifeng's front room, nervously drying her red hands on her apron.

Xifeng does not look up from the ledger on her desk. Very deliberately, she makes an infinitesimal check in the margin beside one of the numbers, before raising her eyes from the ledger. She puts down her ink brush.

"I have been going over household accounts," she says. Still not looking at the cook, she pulls another ledger, this one for kitchen expenditures, from the corner of the desk. She opens it to a page marked with a bamboo slip.

Finally, she looks up. "It seems to me that you have been spending quite a bit more than you used to."

"Oh, my lady." Cook Liu's hands twitch under her apron, as she rushes to explain. "It's getting close to New Year's, you know, and with all the parties, and visitors, and preparing for the sacrifices, we've been spending three or four times as much as we do in a usual month—"

"If you think I don't know that, you're more of a fool than I supposed," Xifeng interrupts. "No, I don't mean just the last month or two. I mean that for the last six months or more, the kitchens have consistently exceeded their budget. And with things as tight as they are, we simply can't afford to be so extravagant. Take this, for example." She runs her finger down the page in the ledger and finds a line near the bottom. She lays the bamboo slip below it, to mark the place, and turns the heavy ledger so it faces the cook.

Cook Liu steps forward and squints at the tiny characters. "'Two dozen black-boned chickens,'" she reads.

"And how much did they cost?" Xifeng prompts.

"Twenty-four *taels*."

"One *tael* apiece, for chickens! And we already have a standing order for twenty-five chickens a month to begin with. To order more chickens, and by far the most expensive kind at that—"

"But, my lady," Cook Liu says, opening her eyes wide. "Surely you know that we stew one every couple of mornings with some jujubes and ginkgo nuts for Miss Ping'er. You know that chickens, especially the black-boned kind, are good for pregnant women, with how much blood and *qi* they lose at delivery, and nursing the baby—"

Xifeng cuts her off. "Well, with things as tight as they are, we really can't afford it. Please don't order them anymore." She shuts the ledger and pushes it back to the corner of the desk. She picks up her writing brush again.

The cook, however, remains standing there, still twisting her hands in her apron. Xifeng turns to a new page in the ledger and begins to tally up the columns.

"The moment he heard she was pregnant," the cook says, "Master Lian came to the kitchens himself. He told us to see that she got a stewed black-boned chicken every few days."

"Did he give you the money to pay for them?" Xifeng does not look up.

The cook shakes her head.

"If he wanted her to have them, he should have paid for them," Xifeng tells her.

"But he's away down south!"

"That's not my problem, is it?" Xifeng reaches for her abacus and begins to click the beads.

A few days later, when Ping'er is opening the lacquered box that the kitchen has delivered for her breakfast, she says, "That's strange."

"What is?" asks Xifeng, glancing over from the dressing table, even though she knows perfectly well. Now that Lian has been gone for more than a week, Xifeng and Ping'er have fallen back, on the surface at least, into something of their old companionship.

"Well, I used to get some stewed black-boned chicken every morning, but for the last few days I haven't been getting it."

"Really?" Xifeng gets up and walks over to where Ping'er sits on the *kang*, with the just-opened box steaming before her. There is an egg custard, its creamy yellow surface dotted with dried scallops, some tiny silver fish crusted with salt, pickled radishes, a few *mantou*, and tofu, as well as shreds of crisp-fried pork and a bowl of rice porridge.

"You're right," she says. "Well, Cook Liu was saying just the other day that the prices of things, eggs and so on, have gone up so much these days that they've really had to tighten their belts."

"Is that so?" Ping'er picks up her chopsticks, shrugging. "Oh, well. There is plenty without it."

Xifeng goes back to her dressing table. As she picks up her comb again, some impulse makes her say, "But a pregnant woman can't be too careful about getting proper nutrition, you know." She smiles at Ping'er. "I'll talk to Cook Liu, and tell her to set aside all the chicken necks and wings to make a nice stew for you every morning."

Ping'er looks up from her breakfast, her eyes shining with pleasure. "That's very kind of you."

"It's no problem." She begins to comb her hair again. "Your morning sickness is better, isn't it?"

"That's right. I've felt a lot better since the beginning of the

Twelfth Month. I have even been meaning to go out to the Water Moon Priory to burn incense to Guanyin for a safe delivery."

"That's a good idea." Guanyin is the goddess of childbirth, as well as of mercy. Xifeng had miscarried so many months before her baby was due that she had not gotten a chance to go to the temple to pray to her. She makes an effort to speak lightly. "When you go out there, let me know, will you? I have something to deliver to the Abbess."

"Of course."

Autumn comes in. "There's a servant here from Feng Ziying. He says that Master Lian owes him a debt from dice. He says he wouldn't ordinarily bother you while Master Lian is gone, only he needs the money right away to pay a debt to someone else."

"Is that so?" Xifeng rises from the dressing table, irritated. "Well, you can tell him that he'll just have to wait until Lian comes back to get paid, because I am certainly not going to throw away money on his gaming debts—"

"How much is the debt for?" Ping'er interrupts.

"One hundred *taels*," Autumn says.

"I can pay it," Ping'er says, struggling to rise from the *kang*. "Lian left me some money."

Torn between indignation that Lian has kept money without her knowledge, and triumph that she is about to discover where he hides it, Xifeng rushes to help Ping'er off the *kang*. Ping'er does not really need help, but she wants an excuse to follow Ping'er into her bedroom. In the bedroom, Ping'er points to the far corner of the *kang*. "It's under a loose brick."

Xifeng kneels on the *kang*, turning back the rug. She dislodges the brick and finds a small bag. She empties it out, noticing with a feeling of contempt that it is not quite enough, only about eighty *taels*. She also finds a tiny drawstring bag. She feels it with her fingers and realizes it contains the small stone block carved with Lian's name, which he uses to imprint official documents.

Concealing her excitement, she says, "There isn't enough. I'll have to give you twenty *taels* or so."

"Thank you. I'm sure Lian will repay you when he gets back."

She grunts skeptically, wondering at Ping'er's naïveté.

In the afternoon, she sends Ping'er on an errand elsewhere in the mansion, and goes into Ping'er's bedroom with an unsigned loan agreement. The Countess of Xiping has repaid her, and now the Abbess has helped her set up an even larger loan. She takes out the chop from its hiding place and prints Lian's name in the corner of the loan agreement with red ink. Because women cannot make contracts, the agreement will be more binding if Lian's name is on it. She hears a sound in the front room and hurries out, carefully folding the document.

Chess, Xichun's maid, is waiting for her. "Mrs. Lian, I wish you'd come over to Miss Xichun's apartment. Her pearl and gold phoenix necklace is missing!"

"Missing!" Lady Jia had given the Two Springs the matching necklaces last year, the most costly pieces of jewelry that each of them owns. "Did you ask Miss Xichun and the other maids about it?"

"Yes, but they all say they haven't seen it."

"Is anything else missing?"

"Not that I know of."

"Very well. I'll go over with you." While Xifeng has resigned herself to a certain amount of petty theft in a household of this size, this is the first time something so valuable has disappeared.

When they arrive at Xichun's apartments, Xichun has her nose buried in a book on the *kang*.

"What's this about your pearl and gold necklace disappearing?" Xifeng demands.

"Oh." Xichun looks annoyed. "It's nothing. Why did Chess have to go bothering you about that?"

"What do you mean it's nothing? Do you know where the necklace is or not?"

Xichun shrugs. "I'm sure it will turn up sometime." She looks back down at her book.

Xifeng snatches the book out of her hands, noticing that it is a sutra, as usual. "What do you mean it will turn up sometime? How long has it been missing?"

"I don't really know." Xichun blinks up at her, as if surprised by her anger.

"Where did you keep it?"

Chess answers, pointing. "We kept it in a box in Miss Xichun's dressing table drawer."

Xifeng pulls open the drawer. All the smaller pieces, the bracelets and rings and hairpins, seem to be in their places. Only the largest box is empty. "You should really keep better track of your things."

"Why should I? The sutras say we shouldn't have attachments to the material world—"

"Is that so?" Xifeng cries, losing her patience. "Why don't you explain that to Granny when she asks you where your necklace is at New Year's?"

Xichun looks scared. Xifeng begins to suspect that Xichun knows who took the necklace but is afraid to say.

She sits down on the *kang* beside her sister-in-law, trying to speak calmly. "Don't you understand that if there's a thief here, it's a serious matter? Who knows what she will take next, and not just from you?"

She pauses, waiting for Xichun to speak. Xichun looks down at her hands.

"Well." Xifeng rises. "If you really have no idea, I'll have to question the maids one by one. If no one speaks up, I'll have to beat it out of them."

"No!" Xichun cries.

"Why not?"

"It isn't one of the maids."

Xifeng pounces on this. "If you know it isn't one of the maids, then you obviously know who did it."

Xichun starts to cry.

"It's no use crying. Until I find out who it is, I will beat every person who has reason to come to these apartments."

Chess bursts out as if she can no longer restrain herself, "Nanny Li took the necklace!"

Xichun starts to cry harder.

Xifeng whirls to stare at Chess. "Nanny Li?" She cannot, for the moment, place the name.

"Miss Xichun's wet nurse."

"Ah!" No wonder Xichun is protecting her. "How do you know?"

Chess is almost crying now too. "It's not the first time she has taken something to pawn. I've begged Miss Xichun, but she refuses to do anything about it. I've told her again and again that she had to stop it, or else we'd all end up getting in trouble."

"What on earth does Nanny Li need all that money for?"

"At night, some of the old women in the Garden have a gambling ring," Chess says.

"What!" In her surprise and alarm, Xifeng takes a quick step backwards and almost falls against the *kang*. She steadies herself quickly. "A gambling ring? Where?"

"They stay up late in the gatehouse after everyone goes to bed. Lots of the stewardesses and gardeners and old nannies play. Nanny Li is one of the bankers."

"You knew about this? And didn't tell me until now?"

Suddenly, her palm itches to slap Chess. She controls herself, knowing that if she beats the bearers of bad news, no one will ever tell her anything. She turns to Xichun. "You knew, too, and didn't tell me?"

Xichun and Chess both stare at her as if bewildered by her anger.

"Don't you understand? With gambling comes drinking, and with drinking comes carelessness, and letting in strangers who have no business in the Inner Quarters! We should count ourselves lucky that all that happened was that a necklace was stolen. What if a man had snuck in?"

She sees Xichun's eyes widen with fear. She continues, wanting to impress her with the seriousness of the situation, "At night, there'd be no one to protect you but some maids."

She feels a chill of fear at her own words. Xichun and Chess both begin to sob again. The way they cling to each other, their ineffectual tears, make her feel alone. They can sob all they want, but she will be blamed if any of the terrible things she imagines come to pass. She decides to resolve the matter quickly, before Granny Jia can hear anything about it. She has Nanny Li dragged in and beaten. After a few strokes of the bamboo, Nanny Li breaks down and confesses. It is worse than Xifeng imagined: more than two dozen women gather in the gatehouse nearly every night. She cannot believe that it has come to this without her being aware of it. Two hours later, she has dismissed Nanny Li and the other two ringleaders, and identified the regular and occasional participants. She tells Mrs. Lai to have them all beaten twenty strokes and to dock them two months' salary.

When Xifeng rises from her chair in Xichun's room to return to her own apartment, she is hoarse from yelling. Xichun, who has not offered her so much as a cup of tea, is still weeping on the *kang*. "Why are you crying?"

"Because my wet nurse was dismissed," Xichun sobs. "I've been disgraced in front of the whole household, because she was my servant. None of the other girls' servants were dismissed."

Xifeng realizes that this is true. Most of the gamblers were gardeners and porters and gatewomen, rather than personal servants. "Then let this be a lesson to you. You have no one to blame but yourself. It's your duty to keep your servants in line. If you had done something about it earlier, it wouldn't have come to this." Unbidden, an old saying comes to her: *The beast of a thousand legs is more than a day in dying.*

Xichun weeps, "If only I could be a nun, I wouldn't have to deal with any of this shouting and beating."

"What kind of nonsense is this?" She knows that Xichun constantly pores over Buddhist texts, but she has never heard her mention becoming a nun before. Praying and making offerings at the temple is one thing; it is another matter entirely to shave one's head and cut oneself off from one's family.

"If I could join a nunnery, I wouldn't have to live here, and deal with all the servants—"

"You'd *be* a servant, in all but name! Who do you think does the Abbess's laundry, and washes her dishes? Don't you know enough to be grateful for what you have—"

Xichun ignores her. "I want to withdraw from the 'red dust' of the world and read sutras."

"Girls from families like ours don't leave home to become nuns. Only girls from poor families, who can't arrange decent matches for them, are sent off like that. It would be considered a real disgrace if someone like you entered a nunnery!"

"I don't care."

She shakes Xichun by the shoulders, unable to contain her exasperation. "You'd better not let Granny hear you speaking like that."

She leaves Xichun crying helplessly, and starts to cross the

Garden, fuming at her sister-in-law's foolishness. Dusk is falling, and it is almost time for her to go to Granny's to prepare for dinner. It is not enough that Xichun lives pampered and protected from every worry and household care. It is not enough that she never has to lift a finger. She still wants to "escape" to what she imagines to be the peace and seclusion of a nunnery. Xifeng must speak to Lian when he comes back. He does not usually concern himself with his sister, but he might bestir himself for something like this, affecting the reputation of the entire family.

She is so absorbed in her thoughts as she skirts the frozen lake that she almost screams when a man in dark robes comes out of the leafless rosebushes onto the path in front of her. Her first panic-stricken thought is that her words have come true: the gatewomen have already grown so slack that a strange man has managed to slip into the Garden. Her whole body throbs with a visceral panic, and her instinct is to run away. Then she remembers she is not some innocent girl, to be stricken by terror at the sight of a strange man. "Who are you? What are you doing here?" she shouts. She is pleased by how loudly and fiercely her voice echoes in the silence of the Garden.

The man is only a few feet from her. She sees from his face in the gathering dusk that, far from lying in wait for her, he looks as startled as she is. "I'm sorry I scared you. I'm here with permission."

"Whose permission?"

"Lord Jia's. I'm a friend of his." He lowers his head and shoulders in a little kowtow. "My name is Jia Yucun."

"Jia Yucun?" she repeats. After a moment, it comes to her: he is the distant cousin that Uncle Zheng had befriended in the fall. "If you are here to visit Uncle Zheng, you should wait for him out in his study, not in the Women's Quarters."

"I often visit him here in his private apartments."

"Really?" She is disturbed. The only men allowed into the Inner Quarters are close relatives. It is unlike Uncle Zheng of all people to break the rules like this.

She peers at the young man curiously. Now she sees through the dimness that he is wearing official robes. He looks young, at most Lian's age. He is good-looking, with pale, clear-cut features. She notices he is looking back at her, and feels flustered.

"See that you stay in Uncle Zheng's apartments next time. It won't do for you to go wandering around with so many unmarried girls living here." Resolving to speak to the gatewomen, she dismisses him with a nod, then continues down the path.

"Just a minute." He hurries after her. "You call Lord Jia your uncle. Are you Jia Lian's younger sister?"

She curls her lip scornfully. Anyone but a rube would realize from her clothing that she is a matron, and not an unmarried girl. "If you must know, I'm Lian's wife." She imagines how her husband must seem to a young man like this, an official at the start of a promising career, and feels a pang of mortification at being associated with Lian.

"Good Heavens!" He sounds shocked.

"Why do you say that?"

"It's just that—it's just that I would never have imagined that Jia Lian could be married to someone like you."

She looks away, flattered despite herself.

"What I mean is," he continues, "you don't look old enough to be married to anyone."

She cannot help laughing at his blatant flattery, but then she thinks of the sadness of her situation. "But I have been married four years," she says soberly. She begins to walk down the path again, and he falls into step beside her.

"What is your name?"

"Why should I tell you?" she says. After a moment, though, she blurts it out.

"Wang Xifeng." He repeats the syllables slowly. "What characters are they?"

"'Xi' is 'brilliant,' and 'feng' is 'phoenix.'"

She is used to having people laugh at her name, for it sounds like it belongs to a boy. Her parents had expected her to be a boy, and her father insisted on giving her the name he intended for a son. Jia Yucun does not even smile.

"How old are you?"

"Twenty," she lies for some reason. She is actually twenty-three.

"Where did you live before coming here?"

"In Chang'an."

"Do you have any brothers or sisters?"

"I have two younger brothers."

"Your parents?"

"They are both dead."

It has been such a long time since anyone asked her even these simple facts about herself. Even though she has lived at Rongguo for over four years, she does not feel that anyone here knows anything of her history, or who she is. No one imagines that before she was married, she had been as treasured and pampered as Baoyu himself. Although her father had wanted a son, he was soon delighting in her quickness and spirit. Even after her younger brothers were born, she did not lose her place of eminence in the household. A favorite family story concerned a fierce, half-wild dog that somehow found its way into the compound. The seven-year-old Xifeng managed to heave her brothers into the crook of a tree, and was found holding off the cur by throwing stones.

Her father, a retired general, did not believe that girls should learn more than a handful of characters and basic arithmetic, but Xifeng far outshone her brothers in her facility with numbers. While she knew nothing of such "cultured" accomplishments as calligraphy and landscape painting, her sharp eye and nimble fingers enabled her to excel at the feminine arts: weaving, sewing, embroidery, paper cutting, and knotting. She cannot help sighing when she thinks of how different things are now from her childhood days. Her mother first and then her father had died in the last four years. Now no one bothers to send messages all the way from Chang'an. Despite her seemingly high status as manager of the household, her position feels precarious. She is too busy to spend much time cultivating her relationships with the other women, and the servants hate her for her harshness and attempts to save money.

Jia Yucun beside her looks at her more boldly, his eyes traveling up and down her body. His gaze frightens and excites her. It has been so long since someone looked at her like that, not since she was young, and careless about letting men see her. She remembers her wedding night. When Lian took off her veil and undressed her for the first time, his eyes traveled over her face and body, and she had had the distinct impression that he was disappointed. She was not his type, she supposed.

Yucun's gaze reminds her of the danger of talking to a strange man in the middle of the Garden. Failing to hide behind a screen when a man other than a close relative entered the room would subject her to severe rebuke; how much more so conversing openly with a stranger? Anyone might see her, a maid or a gardener. If they tattle to Granny, no explanations will shield her from blame.

She begins to run.

"Wait." He grabs her by the arm, but she jerks it away, terrified that he actually has the effrontery to touch her. She runs faster, not stopping until she reaches Lady Jia's. Her heart is pounding the way it did when he first appeared out of the rosebushes.

4

It is the Lantern Festival, the fifteenth day of the New Year, the last big party of the New Year's celebrations. All the members of the Jia clan in the Capital have been invited. The large reception hall in the Garden is ablaze with lights: great palace lanterns on carved wooden frames with crimson tassels; lanterns made of horn and glass and gauze; embroidered ones and painted ones, ones patterned with cutouts of paper or silk. All the female guests are sitting inside the reception hall, while the male guests are sitting on the verandah, separated from the inside by carved wooden partitions. At one end of the hall, a covered stage has been erected, and a famous troupe of child actors is performing scenes from popular plays to the accompaniment of strings and flutes.

On the verandah, Jia Zheng makes his way from table to table, making sure that he greets each of his twenty-five or thirty male guests. "Welcome! Welcome! So glad you could come!" As he goes around the tables, refilling his guests' cups, it strikes him that he barely knows most of them, and has nothing to say but a few polite commonplaces. It used to be that, thanks to the clan school, men from less prosperous branches of the family would pass the Exams as well. Lacking the Rongguo Jias' close connections to the throne, they would not advance as quickly, often stagnating in the lower middle ranks. Nevertheless, Jia Zheng would see them at Court functions, or run into them in the streets around the Ministries. Now, for some reason, the few men who have made it into the Civil Service are ·all well into middle age. In the last seven or eight years, none of the young men have managed to pass. He knows that Cousin

Rong, who is being raised by his widowed mother, Loushi, is said to be a bright boy; perhaps he will pass in a year or two.

As he struggles to make conversation, he wishes that Baoyu or Lian were with him. But Lian is in the south with Daiyu, and Baoyu has seemed so wan and subdued lately that Lady Jia insisted on having him sit with her on the women's side. Jia Huan is there, of course, but his manners are so gauche that Jia Zheng avoids drawing attention to him in company.

He pauses near the wooden partition, craning his neck to peep through. All he sees through the cracks in the screen are flashes of brilliant color from the women's robes. On an impulse he ducks around the partition into the women's side. He sees Wang Xifeng going from table to table, just as he has been doing, greeting all the female guests. She shows none of the awkwardness that he felt, joking and chatting, leaving every table in uproarious laughter. In the blaze of light from the innumerable lanterns, she is dressed even more gorgeously than usual, wearing a coquettish little headband of red sable fastened with a large pearl brooch. Beneath the headband her face is so beautiful and animated it almost hurts his eyes. He finds her vivacity a little unseemly, and wonders whether to offer a reproof.

Then he reminds himself that it is New Year's, after all, and that she is the only woman in the family fulfilling her social duties. Granny is half reclining on a carved wooden settle with her legs covered by a fur rug. Beside her, Baoyu is murmuring into her ear, as she caresses his hair with gnarled fingers. Sitting at the same table are Tanchun, Xichun, and Baochai. None of them leaves the table to speak to other guests. Instead they are chattering among themselves, and Jia Zheng sees from the slips of paper and ink brushes scattered across the table that they are writing lantern riddles.

Before going to greet his mother, he stops to say a few words to Mrs. Xue, who is conversing quietly with Cousin Rong's mother, Loushi, at another table, their sober widow's gowns standing out against the blur of brightness.

"I hope you are enjoying yourselves," he says.

"Ah, brother Zheng, everything is just perfect," Mrs. Xue says, her face breaking into a wide smile.

"And now we have something else to celebrate."

"Yes, indeed! The Xias' betrothal gifts arrived the day before yesterday."

"Have you chosen a date for the wedding yet?"

"We'll send a bridal party down to fetch Miss Xia as soon as the New Year's celebrations are over."

"Wonderful. Is Pan going to buy a house in the Capital?"

"Oh, no. The Xias have a very good house here. They will live there."

It galls Jia Zheng that after escaping scot-free from the troubles of his lawsuit, Pan is now making a match with a family that seems, from all accounts, both exceptionally wealthy and cultured. Taking leave of Mrs. Xue, he approaches his mother's table. She looks up from what Baoyu is saying to her. "What are you doing here? Shouldn't you be on the other side entertaining the guests?"

It is clear that she finds his presence unwelcome. He forces a smile. "I came over to see whether you were enjoying yourselves."

"We're writing lantern riddles to try to cheer Baoyu up." Xichun points at the square white lantern in the middle of the table stuck with handwritten strips of paper.

Jia Zheng looks sternly at his son. "What do you have to be unhappy about, at New Year's of all times, Baoyu? I thought you loved parties. Are you ill?"

Baoyu does not answer, looking down. Jia Zheng notices again that he looks pale and dispirited, with dark circles under his eyes.

It is Xichun who answers. "It's because Cousin Lin went away. He's been moping ever since."

"Nonsense," Baochai interjects quickly. "He just hasn't been feeling well."

Although Xichun's version of events has never occurred to Jia Zheng, it does not surprise him. It accords with his estimation of his son's self-involved and self-dramatizing character that Baoyu should have brief, violent crushes, imagining himself deeply in love with one girl until his fancy shifted to someone else. Because he does not want to spoil the party, and also because it is inauspicious to scold children at the New Year, he changes the subject. "Well, don't I get to guess some lantern riddles?" he says, with an attempt at joviality.

There is dead silence. He sees his nieces and daughter looking at one another. Tanchun shyly passes him a slip of paper. "Here's mine, Father."

He reads it out loud:

At Grave Sweeping, the little boys look up and stare,
To see me ride so proudly in the air.
My strength all goes when once the thread is parted
And on the wind I drift broken-hearted.

He laughs heartily and pretends to have to think hard, scratching his head and furrowing his brow. At last, he ventures, "A kite?"

The girls all smile. Tanchun claps her hands.

"Who else?" He looks around. No one else volunteers, even though Baoyu seems to have a completed riddle in front of him. To break the awkward pause, Jia Zheng plucks one of the riddles already attached to the lantern. "Let me try this one." He sees that it is written meticulously in tiny "fly's-head" characters.

"That one is Baochai's," Tanchun tells him. He reads out loud:

My "eyes" cannot see and I'm hollow inside.
When the lotuses surface, I shall be by your side.
When the autumn leaves fall I shall bid you adieu,
For our marriage must end when the summer is through.

He realizes the answer must be a "bamboo wife," those wicker
cylinders that are placed between the bedclothes in summertime
to make them cooler. He is struck by the sadness of both the
girls' poems. Both are about loss and parting. Don't they realize how inauspicious it is to speak about such things at the New
Year? And they are both just young girls. What can they know
of such things? He looks at their faces. Tanchun is gazing at him
with bright eager eyes, wondering if he will guess the riddle cor-
rectly. Baochai's eyes are cast down demurely into her lap, as if
she is afraid that by meeting his eyes, she will inadvertently give
him a clue.

He shakes his head. "I can't guess."

Everyone is delighted by his defeat.

"You've got him stumped, Baochai," Tanchun crows.

Baochai smiles as she tells him the answer, "It's a bamboo
wife." He is surprised by her air of triumph. She is always so
sedate that he did not expect her to become excited about guessing lantern riddles.

Walking back towards the men's side, he feels even stranger
and more out of sorts. He almost bumps into Xifeng, who is
whirling from one table to another, a decanter in one hand and
a wine cup in the other. "Oh, excuse me!" she exclaims, with a
dazzling smile, but she seems scarcely to recognize him. She has
clearly had too much to drink. He makes his way back to his seat
on the men's side, feeling too dispirited to greet any more
guests.

As he passes Jia Yucun's table, the young man leaps up. "Lord
Jia! Good to see you."

He forces a smile. "Ah, Yucun. How are you? I heard when the promotions were announced for the year you received quite an elevation."

"Yes, Under-Secretary to the President of the Board of War."

"Splendid!" It is quite exceptional for a young official to be promoted so fast. "You must have really impressed someone."

Now the young man is babbling on about what a wonderful occasion it is. "There is just one thing," he adds. "I wouldn't bring it up, except that you've been so kind to me."

"What is it?"

"When you were kind enough to invite me to your ancestral offerings on New Year's Day, I couldn't help noticing a pair of gilt lions in the Ancestors Hall."

"What lions?" Jia Zheng says blankly. He casts his mind over the statues and tripods and scrolls that decorate the Ancestors Hall, many inscribed with the names of their givers. "Oh, yes, the ones from Prince Yinti."

"Yes. You must get rid of them." Yucun lowers his voice.

"Why on earth?"

Yucun speaks with the air of someone explaining something obvious to a dimwit. "If another prince becomes Emperor, you don't want evidence of your ties to Prince Yinti."

"Good Heavens!" Jia Zheng exclaims, not bothering to lower his voice. "I know you think Prince Yinti may not succeed to the throne, but even if he doesn't, it's hardly a crime to receive gifts from him. Get rid of them?" He shakes his head in irritated disbelief.

He sees that Yucun wants to say more, but the evening has already tried his patience. He returns to his own seat, pours himself a cup of wine, and drinks half of it in one gulp. He turns his eyes to the actors, trying to lose himself in the drama onstage.

5

When Daiyu glimpses the stone bridges and canals, fringed with leafless willows, from the window of the sedan carrying her and Lian from the barge, she is filled with a sense of peace and well-being she had almost forgotten. When she left, the city had been abloom with wisteria and crape myrtles. Now, she catches the aroma of wintersweet and jasmine. After the dust and grit of the Capital, the soft air envelops her like a cloud. She breathes it deep into her lungs, reveling in its humidity and scent of greenery.

The instant the sedan is set down in Bottle-Gourd Street, she rushes inside. Her father is sitting in the front room with a book on his lap.

"Daiyu!"

"Father!" She rushes to him and throws her arms around his neck before he can struggle to his feet.

"How are you, Father? How do you feel?" She releases him so she can look at him more closely. He is pale and thin, even thinner than when she left, but his color is good.

He smiles at her. "I'm a bit better. I've been seeing a doctor, and he says I've been working too hard. So I asked for a leave of absence, and am taking it easy for a while."

She clasps his hand in both of hers, understanding that his illness is not after all so serious. "Why didn't you write me?" she says, half laughing, half tearful in her relief. "Didn't you know how worried I would be? I thought that you couldn't write more because you were too sick!"

He looks surprised. "I was extremely busy with work this fall, and sending a messenger is so expensive. Besides, I knew that you would be home soon. How did you enjoy your visit?"

She hesitates. "At first I hated it. I hated being away from you, and I hated how cold and formal everything seemed." She thinks of her conversation with Granny Jia, and decides not to mention it, though he must know the whole bitter history. "But in the end, I grew fond of some of my cousins."

"Which ones?"

"Xue Baochai, and Baoyu." She feels herself blushing when she says Baoyu's name.

"Ah, Baoyu," her father says with a teasing smile. "Tell me what you thought of him."

Lian comes in and Daiyu introduces him.

"Jia Lian!" her father says. "The last time I saw you was at Rongguo twenty years ago. You must have been about five years old! I must thank you for coming all this way for Daiyu."

"It's no trouble. The truth is, Uncle Zheng wanted me to come south to look at the family estates anyway."

She goes into the kitchen to make tea. When she enters the familiar room, she is struck by the lowness of the ceiling, the simple rough shapes of the table and cupboards, the dinginess of the paper windows. This must have been how her mother felt when she first arrived from Rongguo. She opens the cupboard and runs her finger along the rim of a familiar blue-and-white bowl, picturing her mother picking it out twenty years ago when she was a new bride. Her mother is gone. From now on she must preside over this kitchen alone.

That afternoon, before setting off for the Jia estates, Lian arranges for her father's examination by a well-known doctor. Dr. Hu confirms the diagnosis of the previous physician: Mr. Lin's *qi* has been damaged by worry and poor sleep and diet. He is suffering from excessive fire in the stomach, and his spleen has been harmed, resulting in acute fatigue and digestive problems.

Although her father's condition is serious, with proper care and medication, it may not be irreversible.

Daiyu settles in to caring for her father. She goes to market to load her basket with winter bamboo shoots and fresh carp from the lake. She makes soups and rice porridge, and spends hours hovering over the stove brewing her father's medicines. For the first time, she forces herself to kill and pluck a chicken. When she feels the frantic leaping of the pullet's heart beneath her fingertips, she almost gives up and calls Granny Liu. Then, thinking of Baochai's calmness, she firms her trembling hands and twists the poor creature's neck. As she plucks the now limp body, she wonders what Baoyu would think if he were to see her. Although she missed him passionately all through her barge trip south, he has receded from her thoughts now that she is home. Still, sometimes she wonders if he misses her, and whether she will ever see him again.

Fortunately, her anxiety about her father is fading. His color is better. He has gained weight. Although he says little, he is tender and gentle to her. In the evenings, she asks him to read aloud from the histories and poets that he likes, while she does the mending. If she does not ask him, she will often catch his gaze drifting from the book before him, a sad and distant expression in his eyes.

And then the New Year is upon them. For the first time she must clean and decorate the house, prepare the offerings, and make new clothes all by herself. Her father's health excuses them from entertaining guests or making New Year's visits among his colleagues. Lian, however, has written that he will return to Suzhou for the holiday, and then, if Mr. Lin's health appears stable, he will make the return trip to the Capital.

On New Year's eve, she and her father and Lian burn incense and make offerings before the small altar in the corner of the front room. As the evening darkness gathers, her father says for the first time that he feels strong enough to take a short walk in the streets. She bundles him up, and they walk out onto Bottle-Gourd Street, Daiyu holding one arm, Lian the other. The streets are full of neighborhood children, racing around shouting and setting off firecrackers. The light of the firecrackers falls on her father's face, and she sees him smiling at their antics.

Two days after New Year's, a messenger comes from the Jia estates to say that one of the barns had caught fire during the celebrations. The fire spread to the adjoining barn, and both buildings had sustained significant damage before the blaze could be extinguished. Lian, cursing that the mishap must delay his trip back to the Capital, sets off to the estates. Daiyu and her father are left alone, and pass the first two weeks of the New Year quietly. On the Lantern Festival, Daiyu decides to hang up a few paper lanterns. It had been one of the family's favorite holidays. Her mother and father had always delighted in stumping each other with difficult riddles. When Daiyu grew old enough, she had participated as well.

"I'll bet you can't guess my riddles, Father," she says after dinner, putting one of the lanterns in the middle of the table to hold the riddles, and setting out paper and brushes.

Her father looks up from his book with a smile, and comes to the table. "Don't be too cocksure. I have lots of experience guessing riddles." He sits down to grind some ink. "In fact, I'm pretty sure that you'll have trouble with *mine*."

On her mettle, she does not answer, and sits there trying to devise a riddle while she grinds her own ink. She decides that her riddle will be about an incense clock, and takes up a brush and begins to scribble on her paper. When she reads the four lines she has written, she thinks that her clues are too vague. She decides to make it an eight-line poem. She writes two more lines, but then cannot think of any more rhymes. After about half a minute, a way of ending the poem occurs to her and she quickly jots down the last couplet.

"I've got it!" she says triumphantly, and holds up the paper to read it aloud:

At court levee my smoke is in your sleeve:
Music and beds to other sorts I leave.
With me, at dawn you need no watchman's cry,
At night no maid to bring a fresh supply.
My head burns through the night and through the day,
And year by year my heart consumes away.
The precious moments I would have you spare:
But come fair, foul, or fine, I do not care.

"Can you guess it, Father?" she cries, looking at him.

He is sitting with a sheet of paper before him and a brush in his hand, but the paper is blank and his face is wet with tears.

6

"How are you feeling today?" Xifeng asks Ping'er, returning to her own apartments after serving breakfast at Lady Jia's.

"Pretty well, thank you." Ping'er sits on the *kang*, embroidering golden plum blossoms on a tiny red vest.

Because she wants Ping'er to do her a favor, she refrains from commenting on how Ping'er is squandering her time on embroidery while she wears herself out running the household. The dishes from Ping'er's breakfast have not been cleared. She sees the spiny, finely reticulated neckbones of chicken that Ping'er has left behind after gnawing off the meat, and feels a touch of satisfaction that they are the pale color of ordinary chickens, not the black-boned kind. "Then would you mind running an errand for me?"

"Of course not. What do you want me to do?"

"I need something delivered to the Abbess at the Water Moon Priory. Would you mind going? I've already ordered a carriage. I'd take it myself, only I still have to go through all those presents we received for New Year's."

"That's fine," Ping'er says.

"And then you can pray to Guanyin for a safe childbirth, like you wanted to."

As Xifeng watches Ping'er struggle clumsily off the *kang*, she is struck by the size of her belly, pressing tautly against the waist of her gown. Even her legs look swollen, her feet bulging plumply over the tops of her shoes like rising dough. She turns away in disgust and goes to her bedroom to check the money she is delivering to the Abbess. It is her largest loan yet, three thousand *taels*, neatly wrapped in six bundles on the *kang*. In one of the bundles is the loan agreement Xifeng had stamped with Lian's chop when Ping'er was out of the room. It is so much money that she prefers to send it with Ping'er in charge, rather than an ordinary servant. Her only fear was that Ping'er would ask what it was, but Ping'er no longer takes any interest in household matters.

As soon as Ping'er has been sent off in the carriage with the money, Xifeng goes to Ping'er's bedroom. She flings open the wardrobe door. She does not know what exactly she expects to find, but she flinches at the sight that meets her eyes. What remain of Lian's clothes have been pushed to one side. In their place are meticulously folded piles of tiny robes and jackets, a mountain of snow-white diapers, and, on top of that, a pair of minuscule slippers. They are barely longer than her pinkie, and yet every inch is covered with painstaking embroidery. She turns them over and looks at the soles. Even though shoes for so young an infant will never touch the floor, Ping'er has quilted together four layers of cloth with countless tiny stitches, to make a thick, sturdy sole. She has an urge to cut them to pieces.

She hears a sound from the front room. Ping'er must have forgotten something and come back. Quickly she replaces the slippers, arranging them at the precise angle at which she had found them. She gently shuts the wardrobe door. At random she grabs a pair of shears off the side table.

She hurries to the front room, saying, "I couldn't find my scissors, so I went into your room to look for yours—"

It is not Ping'er, but Jia Yucun. He stands a few feet inside the front door, slouched and uneasy. Her throat is suddenly so dry that she hears the rasp of her breath. She had caught glimpses of him at the New Year's celebrations almost a month ago. In the Hall of the Ancestors, when Uncle Zheng burned the silk offering and made the libation, she felt Yucun staring at her from the male side of the courtyard. When she helped Granny make the

food offerings to the ancestors' portraits, she picked him out
from among the watching masses of servants and relatives. He
was gazing at her with an almost painful intensity. It made her so
nervous that her hand slipped and nearly dropped the dish of
cakes that she was passing to Lady Jia. Two weeks ago, at the
Lantern Festival, knowing he would be there, she had dressed
and made herself up with more care than usual. Under the pretense of seeing that the servants were doing their job properly,
she slipped around the partition onto the verandah where the
male guests were seated. As she stood there in the light of one of
the great tasseled palace lanterns, she saw him staring at her from
a corner table. She knew she could get him in trouble, even for
just looking at her. Instead she had kept silent. She had never
imagined he would dare come to her room like this.

"I came to see you." He tries to speak jauntily, but in the late
morning light filtering through the paper window, she sees how
scared he is. The part of her mind that can still think rationally,
that coolly observes the scene like an uninvolved witness, tells
her that she has nothing to fear from a junior official from the
country. The rest of her body, her heart, her breath, is throbbing to a panicky rhythm. She does not move from where she
stands a few steps from the hallway. The quality of the light this
morning is merciless, she thinks, revealing the stubble on his
cheeks, the pale purple under his eyes.

"You shouldn't be here," she says.

"You think I don't know that?"

He does not move. There is a brief silence. He rubs his hands
together, and she notices that his knuckles are raw and chapped.
"Could I have some tea?" he says. "The wind is blowing fit to
freeze a man."

She hesitates, then slowly crosses the room to the stove, placing Ping'er's scissors on the desk. "You must go as soon as
you've had it."

"All right." He remains standing close to the door.

Her fingers shake a little as she gets out the tea and spoons some into a pot.

"Where is your maid?" he asks.

"I sent her to the temple."

As she pours the steaming water, the spout of the kettle knocks uncontrollably against the teapot.

"I want to tell you something," he says, still standing awkwardly on the other side of the room. "That time I ran into you in the Garden wasn't the first time I had seen you." He speaks with an intensity that makes her stare at him, wondering what he is trying to say.

He looks down. "I was only pretending I didn't know who you were. Lian talked to me about you before." He smiles wryly and she sees the intelligence and quiet humor in his face. "He used to complain about you. He told me he was tired of you, and that he'd taken your maid as a concubine. Even then, I thought it was strange—marrying his wife's own maid.

"One night, he invited me to go to a party. He was supposed to meet me in the outer part of the mansion, but he didn't show up. I asked the women at the Inner Gate to let me go in to his apartments. I didn't want to disturb anyone if he wasn't there. It was a warm night and the window was open. I peeked in and saw you weaving at your loom."

On his face is a strange and dreamy expression, as if he has just read a poem, or is gazing at a beautiful painting. A part of her wants to laugh, but another part of her is moved.

"I couldn't believe you were the person he had been talking about. You were bent over your weaving, concentrating so hard that you never even heard me. You looked so beautiful, so untouchable." He laughs, a little bitterly. "In my world, the women are very different. There was my mother. She took in sewing to keep the two of us alive. She was always bad-tempered

and tired, and never took care of herself. It was all she could do
to comb and put up her hair."

This remark about his mother surprises her. While she knew
he was from a less wealthy branch of the Jias, she had not
guessed the extent of his poverty.

"When I came to the Capital, I met other sorts of women.
Not women like you, of course—upper-class men lock up their
wives and daughters—but singing girls. Now, *they're* quite orna-
mental, but . . . " He pauses as if groping to find the right words.
"You can never really know them, because they have to sing and
be merry no matter how they feel."

She wants to tell him that she is no different from the singing
girls; all women have to smile and chatter and charm.

"And yet," he continues, "when I saw you there weaving,
looking so beautiful, I felt sorry for you, too."

"You felt sorry for me?" she repeats, taken aback, and wondering whether to be offended.

"Yes." Again he struggles to find the words. "You looked so
frail and alone—" He breaks off, with a deprecatory laugh.
"This must sound ridiculous to you."

Despite herself, tears come to her eyes. She shakes her head.

"That was when I realized what Lian was like, what the Jias
are like. They're selfish. They think they're entitled to anything
they want, and will trample everyone else to get it. To have a
wife like you—a woman whom most men would die to possess—and to treat you like that. Making you compete with your
own maid." He looks away from her, as if ashamed by his own
words. "And then, after that time I spoke to you in the Garden,
I couldn't think about anything else but seeing you again."

"You don't even know me," she says, her voice quivering.

He comes a step closer. All this time he has been standing
across the room from her. Now he takes another step. Her heart
starts to hammer again.

"You'd better go," she says.

He continues to walk towards her.

"Someone could come in."

He goes to the door, bolts it, and then walks towards her again.

"My maid may come back."

He is only a few steps away from her. She tries to dart past him into the hallway. He catches her before she has gone more than a few steps. She struggles to break free of his hold, but half-heartedly. Now that he is so close, she can smell him. He smells faintly of stale sweat. She notices this objectively, without disgust or judgment. In fact, she finds his scent pleasant, reassuring, like her own smell, after a long day. He is touching her hair, she notices vaguely, as if it is happening to someone else. His touch is gentle and slow, not like Lian's, as if there is all the time in the world. He says her name.

She tells herself to resist him, to push him away, but somehow she cannot move. She is aware of a grave danger. He is kissing her hairline now, but his caresses, his endearments, fill her with a sense of ominousness. Still, rather than resisting, she throws her arms around his neck. She stares blindly over his shoulder, as he buries his lips in her throat, holding her body against his.

She is falling, and has nothing to hold on to. There is no one to stop her, no one who cares. Not her family in the west, whom she has not laid eyes on since the day she was married. Not the Jias, who make her slave for them, but have no mercy when she falls short. For so long, she relied on Ping'er. But Ping'er is lost to her. She can tell that Ping'er loves Lian, in a way that she never did. And besides, Ping'er's heart is filled by her coming baby.

Now Yucun is kissing her on the lips. It gives her no pleasure. Since leaving her family and marrying Lian, she has long been turned to stone. Yet she holds Yucun tighter, burying her face in his neck. She is falling, and there is no one to stop her. She lets him lead her into the bedroom.

7

Ordinarily, Baochai and her mother would have spent the month and a half before the arrival of Pan's bride furnishing and preparing an apartment for the new couple. Because the Xias already own a mansion in the Capital, however, Pan has agreed to live there with Jingui, at least for the time being. The Xues should have hosted the wedding at their house, thus receiving the bride into her new home and family. Given that the couple will marry in the Capital, however, the Jias have offered to host the wedding, which will be small, since nearly all of the Xue and Xia relatives live in the south.

This strikes Baochai as awkward, because the relationship between the Jias and the Xias is tenuous at best; but she cannot come up with a better solution. Finally, Baochai and Mrs. Xue have decided to move in with Pan now that he is setting up a household in the Capital. Pan agrees, but no plans can be made until Jingui arrives, he says, because he is as yet unfamiliar with the layout and arrangements of the new house. In the meantime, none of them, even Pan, has set foot in the house, although they have sent over bridal gifts and furniture.

While each of these deviations from normal procedure can be explained by the circumstances, together they fill Baochai with a deep unease. It is almost as if the social roles have been reversed. Rather than Mrs. Xue receiving Jingui as a daughter-in-law into her own household, it is as if Xue Pan is being given to the Xias. She wonders whether it is generosity or some more selfish motive that leads the Xias to offer their house to the new couple. After all, with no son of their own, they may be eager to annex Pan into their family rather than giving up Jingui to the Xues. Such an arrangement will not be advantageous either to Pan or to Baochai and her mother.

Both Mrs. Xue and Pan are too elated by the approaching wedding to understand her reservations and warnings. Pan is infatuated with his bride. Mrs. Xue, enjoying the long-anticipated role of mother-in-law, is preoccupied with furnishing the bridal suite. "Do you think Jingui would like satin brocade, or gauze, for the bed hangings?" she says.

"I really don't know, Mother. Do whatever you think is best."

"Maybe if there's time, we can do one of each kind. I do want her to be happy with her new apartments. Tell us, again, Pan, what she is like."

"Don't ask me," Pan demurs. "You know I'm no good at describing things."

"Is there anyone we know that she reminds you of?"

"She's a little like Xifeng."

Baochai does not find this comparison reassuring. While she admires Xifeng for her abilities as a manager, her desire for control does not make her easy to get along with, either as a wife or as a daughter-in-law. "In what way is she like Xifeng?"

"I don't know."

"Is she lively, and fond of joking, like Cousin Xifeng is?" Baochai prompts.

Pan's brow creases from the effort of reflection. "Not exactly. She is more serious, and—and dignified than Xifeng is."

"In what way is she like Xifeng, then?" Baochai persists.

"Oh, I don't know. I suppose she's not quiet, like you. She's more sure of herself, like Cousin Xifeng. That's what I meant. But she is a hundred times prettier than Cousin Xifeng!"

Baochai hesitates before asking, "Is she fond of having her own way, like Xifeng is?"

Pan bursts out laughing. "Of course not! You must think me

a fool, if that's the sort of girl you think I would want to marry! She's not like that at all. Quite the contrary! She's very gentle, always eager to do what would please me the most. You know, since her mother and she have been without a man in the family for so long, they were especially interested in my advice and opinions."

This speech does not set Baochai's mind at rest as much as Pan seems to think it should. She says nothing more, and settles back to her sewing, waiting for the bride's arrival in the Second Month.

Many years ago, when the Xues still lived in Nanjing, an older girl had come to visit and had taken away Baochai's favorite doll. Her father was alive then; Baochai must have been only four or five. The girl—Baochai could remember nothing about her or her family—had noticed Baochai cuddling the doll and pretending to put it to bed. When she snatched it out of Baochai's hands, Baochai was more startled than anything else. She at first assumed that the girl meant to play with it for a while and then give it back. But the girl did not play with it, just put it in her sleeve so that Baochai could not have it. Eventually Baochai got up the nerve to ask for the doll back, but the girl simply turned away and started to play with another of Baochai's toys. Baochai thought about tattling—her mother and father were sitting in the next room chatting with the little girl's parents—but she was too polite and too shy, too deeply imbued with her duties as hostess, and said nothing. Eventually, the girl left, with the doll still hidden in her sleeve. It was only that night that Baochai had wept silently in bed, trying to fall asleep without her doll to cuddle. She had never had a favorite toy again.

At the sight of Jingui's face, when Pan pulls off her red veil, the incident comes back to her after all these years. She recognizes the high cheekbones, the smallish, bright eyes under thin brows, and, especially, the short nose with its pinched nostrils and unusually pointed tip. Of course, Jingui has changed a great deal. She is now a tall young lady, undeniably handsome in her bridal finery, with the sort of willowy figure that Baochai envies. Her eyes are darkened with kohl, and her thin lips are heavily rouged. Yet there is still something about her, some harshness to her expression, some hard, fixed quality to her gaze that reminds Baochai of that girl from so many years ago.

Now as Pan, beaming with pride, leads Jingui to greet Mrs. Xue, she notices that Jingui carries herself confidently, as Pan had said. Jingui flashes a bold smile at her mother-in-law, hardly a blushing bride. Mrs. Xue, so happy that she is nearly crying, embraces her. Jingui receives her caresses with composure, but does not return them. Then Pan leads her to greet Lady Jia and Uncle Zheng. Xia Jingui handles these introductions with the same smiling aplomb. Baochai hears Lady Jia commenting to Mrs. Xue that the new bride is not shy and tongue-tied like so many young ladies these days. Baochai is surprised by Granny Jia's favorable impression of Jingui. For years it has been drummed into her that young girls should be demure and submissive, barely daring to meet the eyes of their elders. However, she has long ago discovered that behavior that would be considered a grave shortcoming in ordinary people is easily forgiven in those of unusual physical beauty.

Now it is time for Baochai to meet Jingui. She moves forward, smiling, knowing that she must on no account stint on the courtesies. For a moment she wonders whether Jingui will recognize her, but Jingui seems hardly to look at her. She bows as low as possible, saying, "Older sister." When she rises from her bow, she smiles and takes Jingui's hand, saying, "I am so glad that you have come. I hope we will soon be as close as real sisters!"

At her words, Jingui's attention finally seems to focus on her. Jingui gives no sign of recognition. Instead, her eyes sweep Baochai from head to toe with an appraising look that makes her feel dowdy and clumsy. She wishes she had dressed up more, like the other girls.

"Little sister," Jingui says, dismissing her with a flick of the eye, before moving on to greet Baoyu.

When Xifeng steps out of Xue Pan's wedding feast to ask a maid to bring more *samshoo*, someone grabs her and pulls her into the shadow of a pine tree. She knows as soon as he touches her that it is Jia Yucun. All evening at the wedding feast, she has sensed him looking at her. She has had to force herself to keep her eyes severely away.

"Will you stop looking at me? Someone is going to notice—"

Her words are drowned when he kisses her on the mouth.

"Stop it. Someone may see." She puts her hand up and pushes his lips away, yet she leaves her fingers on his lips, and he kisses them.

"Slip away with me."

"It's too dangerous."

"Just for a few minutes. Aren't there any empty rooms any-where?"

She thinks for a moment. Without a word, she leads him to the other side of the reception hall where there are some unused rooms. This side of the hall is deserted. She fumbles at the heavy ring of keys at her waist, and opens a door.

"Clever girl, to have the key," he murmurs, kissing her neck.

They step into the room. She shuts the door behind them. They are in pitch blackness. They find each other by feel and sink to the ground. He is on top of her, kissing her, his hands scrabbling against her as if frantic to touch her bare skin. To her surprise, she is just as frantic to touch him. Unlike last time, when she was so numb, she feels every touch of his lips and body, her pleasure so sharp that it is almost pain. He is pulling down her trousers beneath her gown. She feels his hand warm and firm against her bare buttocks. She presses her buttocks against his hand. He slips his finger inside her and she feels how wet she is inside. With a groan, she presses against his shoulders and pushes with her legs so that she is on top of him. She tugs at his trousers, feeling his hardness through the silk.

"What do you want?" he whispers teasingly.

"I want you inside me," she says, pressing her body against his. She has never spoken to Lian like this.

With a laugh, he pulls down his trousers. She feels his penis rearing up between her legs and lowers herself down on him so quickly that they both gasp. What has gotten into her? she thinks, as she shuts her eyes, feeling heat suffuse her. She feels like she is waking up, coming to life, after the numbness of long misery.

8

"Mother, can I speak to you alone?" Instead of going to the Ministry after breakfast, Jia Zheng pokes his head into Lady Jia's room.

His mother looks up from the bowl of red date soup she is spooning into her mouth. "Well, what is it?"

He does not speak, looking at Snowgoose, who is rearranging the cushions on the *kang*.

"Well, what?" his mother repeats impatiently.

"I said 'alone,'" he mutters, embarrassed.

"Snowgoose, you will have to go someplace else. Lord Jia doesn't want you to hear what he has to say," Lady Jia says.

He burns with stifled resentment at the way she seems to trivialize what he will say, even before she knows what it is. He does not speak until Snowgoose has left the room. "Baoyu's schoolmaster came to see me at the Ministry yesterday afternoon."

Interested, she puts her soup down. "What did he say?"

He hesitates, knowing his words will wound her. Deep inside he feels a secret pleasure at giving her evidence that Baoyu is not as wonderful as she has always believed. "He discouraged me from registering Baoyu for the Exams this year. He said that Baoyu will most probably fail, and maybe even make a fool of himself—"

"What nonsense! He's just prejudiced against Baoyu."

"Why would he be?"

"Oh, I don't know! Jealous, perhaps."

"I'm afraid not. I asked Jia Yucun to come over last night to read Baoyu's essays and give me a second opinion. He also said the essays showed a very poor grasp of the Eight-Legged form. Also that Baoyu's attempts to interpret the Classics are so strained as to be almost laughable."

"Why would you listen to some nobody from the country?" his mother says indignantly.

"He's now Under-Secretary to the President of the Board of War—"

His mother shakes her head, bewildered. "But I don't understand. Just a few months ago, we were getting reports about what wonderful progress he was making . . . "

"The schoolmaster said that he *was* doing well, until about a month before New Year's, when he suddenly started to not pay attention in class, and not hand in homework. What do you think could have happened?"

Lady Jia is silent for a moment. Finally, she says unpleasantly, "Well, that was around the time you beat him half to death, wasn't it?"

He has to control his anger at this attempt to blame him for Baoyu's shortcomings. "No. That occurred to me as well. I asked the schoolmaster specifically whether Baoyu's performance started to suffer after the beating. He was out of school more than two weeks then. The teacher said that he remembered that Baoyu's work when he came back was still good. The change came later, closer to the Twelfth Month."

"Then what could it have been?"

"Nothing happened then? Nothing with Huan?"

"Not that I know of."

"Then I can't think of anything either." He pauses before saying hesitantly, "Only, there was that remark that Xichun made at New Year's."

"What do you mean?"

"She said Baoyu was moping because Daiyu had gone back to the south."

Lady Jia is silent for a moment. Finally, she gives a little laugh and says, "He'll forget her in a month. He never could have thought seriously about her."

From her reaction, Jia Zheng realizes that what Xichun said was true: Baoyu was attached to Daiyu, and his mother knows it. "You think he did care for her?"

His mother shrugs. "You know what he's like. He is always infatuated with someone or other."

"It was my impression that it was usually a maid. This is the first time he's been infatuated, as you call it, with someone he could actually be betrothed to."

His mother stares at him incredulously. "You would actually consider betrothing him to her?"

"Why not, if he is so distressed by her departure that he can no longer study?" He pauses, trying to remember the reports from the schoolmaster over the last six months. "In fact, now that I think of it, he never made such good progress as this fall when she was here. That was why I thought that this year he would finally be ready to take the Exams."

"It's nonsense to think that how he does in school has anything to do with her. Such a match is entirely out of the question."

He senses, as he has a few times before, that his mother for some reason holds Daiyu in dislike. "Why not?" He tries to reason with her. "It is not an ideal match, but it's not a bad match by any means. Daiyu is a sensible, intelligent girl, and the Lins are a good family. In general, I don't believe in first cousins marrying, but if his heart is really set on her—if he still cares for her in a year or two, after he has passed the Exams, I see no real objection to the match."

"No objection to the match!" his mother cries. "She doesn't have a penny, and the Lins have all but died out! What's worse is her upbringing. Her manners are disgraceful."

As he watches his mother's brows draw together over her nose, it strikes him that her old anger at Min, far from dissipating at her death, has transferred itself to Min's daughter. While it pains him that his mother's resentment against Min is so implacable, he knows it is useless to argue, so he falls silent, willing to let the subject drop.

His mother takes up her soup again and begins to drink it noisily. "And besides, I believe that you are wrong about Baoyu."

"What do you mean?" The anger on her face has been replaced by a look of shrewd calculation.

"I don't think he cared particularly for Daiyu. Don't you see his infatuation with her is a symptom of a larger problem?"

"What problem?"

"You treat him like a child, but he has been shaving for more than four years. You can't expect him not to have natural appetites." She casts him a significant look. "He is nineteen and has always been physically mature for his age. He is more than old enough to be betrothed."

"I've told you my position on that before," he retorts. "He can be betrothed after he passes the Exams, like Zhu was."

"But he is already several years older than Zhu was. How long are you going to make him wait? You will just be bringing trouble on us if you do."

"What exactly do you mean by that?" He is disquieted by her insinuating expression.

"He isn't a little boy anymore. You will have to deal with other incidents like that affair with Silver, and maybe even worse, if you keep denying him."

"Denying him! How is it denying him to require him to concentrate on his studies until he passes the Exams?" he says, but his mother's words have set spark to the fear that he has harbored since the Silver incident. "I've always told you that it isn't

right for him to live in the Women's Quarters. It gives people
something to gossip about. And besides, how can we be sure
that some silly maid won't sleep with him and get pregnant?
Then we'll have a scandal on our hands."

His mother gives a knowing laugh. "If he has a good-looking
wife, why would he sneak around with maids?"

He winces a little at his mother's crudity. "But if I let him
marry, how will he be able to concentrate on his studies?"

"Why not betroth him, to give him something to look forward to? And then he can be married after he takes the Exams."
She laughs again. "I assure you, you'll be surprised at what a
powerful incentive it is!"

He hesitates. Every time his mother has brought up making
a match for Baoyu, he has strenuously resisted. In the first place,
he feared Baoyu was so easily distracted that the novelty of
being married would make it impossible for him to concentrate.
He worried also that Baoyu, moody and unpredictable, was
incapable of treating a young wife with the forbearance and
steadiness she might expect. He begins to feel that he is trying
to put off the inevitable. He reminds himself that even Pan, who
is less reliable than Baoyu, is now married. Pan's example
reminds him of the importance of finding a suitable match,
which may take months or even years. "I suppose we can start
to make some preliminary inquiries ..." he begins slowly.

Lady Jia begins to laugh, as if he is being very foolish. "Why
make inquiries when the answer is right in front of our noses?"

"What do you mean?"

She laughs merrily. "Didn't your wife always joke with Mrs.
Xue about Baoyu and Baochai marrying, when they were little?"

"Yes, but I hoped that nonsense would be forgotten."

She opens her eyes at him. "Why is it nonsense?"

"In the first place, I disapprove of first cousins marrying."

"You were willing to make an exception for Daiyu. Why not

for Baochai when the match is so much better? Then there's that saying about gold and jade being a perfect match."

"What has that to do with anything?"

"You know, Baoyu has his jade, and Baochai has her gold locket."

"I don't have any patience for those sorts of superstitions," he tells her. "I've always thought you made far too much of that jade."

"It isn't a superstition. It's predestination. All I know is that I couldn't think of a better match for him," his mother says. "Tell me, what fault can you find with Baochai? The Xues are extremely rich and influential. Baochai has been well brought up, and knows perfectly how to get along in a big household like ours. Of all the girls in the family, she has always been the most considerate and capable. I don't know what you could possibly have against her."

"I didn't say I had anything against her." The truth is he has no particular objection to her, only he has never grown the least fond of her over the years she has lived at Rongguo. She is too cold, too composed, for him to find her endearing, as he does his other nieces, Daiyu and Xichun. "But there are many other excellent families in the Capital. I don't understand why you are so set on this match."

"The one thing you might say against Baochai," she continues, ignoring him, "is that her looks are only passable. Her hands and figure are all very well, but her face . . . On the other hand, it's possible to be *too* attractive . . . "

"I don't consider having a brother like Pan to be an advantage."

"Well, I don't think there's any real harm in Pan. There's always a scapegrace in every family."

"Are you sure their temperaments are suitable?" Baochai and Baoyu strike him as polar opposites: Baoyu suffers from a surfeit of emotion, while she seems to have too little. "She seems so old for her age. Won't she find Baoyu rather childish?"

"That's all the more reason it is a good match. She is so level-headed and mature that she is sure to exercise a steadying influence on him."

Nettled by the way that his mother keeps dismissing his objections, he falls back on his old habit of denigrating Baoyu. "Granted that all you say is true, I wonder why the Xues would want to throw away a fine girl like Baochai on a good-for-nothing like Baoyu."

In an instant, his mother is up in arms. "That's just like you. Always running down your own son! I don't say that it isn't a good match for Baoyu, but Baochai is a lucky girl, too, to get someone so handsome and talented. And in a year or two, he'll have passed the Exams, maybe at the top of the lists."

"Haven't you forgotten the point? He hasn't passed the Exams yet, and won't even be taking them this year."

"I haven't forgotten. My point is that if we settle his future for him now, he will buckle down and pass the Exams next year. I'll talk to Mrs. Xue about it, shall I?"

"What's the rush?" he exclaims, still reluctant to commit to the match.

"What's the rush?" his mother repeats indignantly. "You expect a girl like Baochai to be available forever? Now that Pan's married, Mrs. Xue is sure to start to think about making a match for Baochai."

He shakes his head distractedly. He is irritated at his mother's obstinacy, yet he feels helpless to resist her. In the end, he does not much care whom Baoyu marries as long as the girl is well brought up and from a good family. If Baoyu was attached to Daiyu, he saw no reason not to let the two of them marry; but it is now clear to him that his mother would prevent this. He knows and trusts Baochai. Perhaps it is better to acquiesce to the match than to brave the unknown. "All right." He sighs. "But promise me one thing in return."

"What is it?"

"Don't say a word about this to Baoyu yet."

"Why not?"

He looks at his mother, struck by how little regard she has for Baoyu's feelings. They have just been talking about how Baoyu is moping about Daiyu. Surely the news that he has been betrothed to someone else will pain the boy. By the time Baoyu actually marries Baochai, many months will have passed, and Jia Zheng hopes that he will have forgotten Daiyu by then. He knows that mentioning Daiyu again will only anger his mother, so he says, "I'm afraid he'll find it harder to concentrate."

She gives a scornful snort, but agrees.

9

The morning of the third day after Pan's wedding, Mrs. Xue insists on paying a visit to the bridal couple.

"Are you sure we should go so soon?" Baochai says, climbing into the carriage after her mother. "Perhaps we should give them a little more time to themselves." At the wedding feast, beneath Jingui's surface politeness, Baochai had sensed a hostility towards herself and her mother.

"Time to themselves?" Mrs. Xue looks at her in surprise. Of course a bride ordinarily had no respite from her in-laws from the moment of her wedding. "I don't want Jingui to feel slighted because we haven't been welcoming enough to her. Besides, we need to take these cushion covers over."

When the carriage pulls up to the address that Pan has given them, Baochai sees that the place looks to be a good-sized mansion, though by no means as big as Rongguo. She looks out the window, observing the carvings on the pillars, the freshly painted gates.

"It looks like it's well kept up," her mother says. "It's in a good location, too, although it's a bit noisier here than at Rongguo."

Baochai hears the coachman's voice raised in argument from outside. "What do you mean you need to check with your mistress before you let us in? Don't you realize that it's your master's mother here coming to visit?"

"Our orders are not to admit anyone without Miss Xia's permission," she hears the gateman reply. It is strange that he still calls his mistress "Miss Xia" rather than "Mrs. Xue."

"What badly trained servants," Mrs. Xue says. "We'll have to talk to Pan about them."

"But they are the Xias' servants. It will be awkward for us to criticize them."

"You're right, of course."

To Baochai's amazement, the carriage is forced to wait outside the gate for ten minutes. Despite their fur-lined jackets and muffs, they rapidly grow cold. Baochai can see that her mother is trying to control her annoyance.

When they are eventually admitted, they are led to the Inner Gate by a maid. Baochai sees that the courtyards and buildings are large and well laid out. Finally, they arrive at what seem to be the principal apartments of the Inner Quarters. The maid precedes them across the courtyard and announces them from outside the door curtain, but leaves them to enter by themselves.

They pass into a large room that despite the opulence of its furnishings gives the impression of messiness: there are tea things and articles of clothing scattered across the *kang*. Both Pan and Jingui are still undressed: Pan in a tunic and loose trousers, Jingui in a tight, low-necked jacket that reveals the white expanse of her breast. Below her flowing, pomegranate-red trousers, her feet are bare. She leans against a backrest eating with her fingers. There is a kettle of wine heating on a brazier.

Pan scrambles off the *kang* to greet them. "Mother! Baochai! We were planning on going to visit you ourselves this morning, only Jingui is a little tired." Baochai catches the scent of wine on his breath.

Jingui does not rise from her place, continuing to chew on the morsel she has just popped in her mouth. Her long, slender fingers are greasy, and she wipes them on a napkin before taking a sip of wine. She is eating what appear to be crisp-fried chicken bones.

Baochai sees that her mother is taken aback by Jingui's failure to greet her properly, but all Mrs. Xue says is, "It's no wonder you are tired after your long journey. We came to see if there was anything you needed. Also, we just finished making these cushion covers this morning."

"Actually," Jingui speaks up, "the quilt you gave us wasn't very comfortable."

Baochai senses Jingui looking covertly at her. Jingui must know that Baochai had made the quilt. She began it almost as soon as the betrothal had been arranged, staying up late to complete the elaborate embroidery. She forces herself to smile. "I'm sorry you don't like it."

"The embroidery was scratchy, and the lining was sewn on crooked," Jingui says.

Although Baochai tries to keep her face expressionless, she feels herself flushing. She has always been praised as an exceptional needlewoman. She waits for her mother, or even Pan, to come to her defense, but they remain silent. Pan looks uncomfortable, while Mrs. Xue wears a forced smile. "I'm sorry," Baochai repeats. "Perhaps I can make you another one."

Jingui shrugs. "Don't bother. I'll have one sent up from home."

"Well," Mrs. Xue attempts to change the subject. "We were also wondering when it would be convenient for us to move in. Have you decided which rooms to put us in yet?"

"Moving in?" Jingui stops eating. "What do you mean?"

Baochai tenses, sensing the impending danger. Flustered, her mother says, "We were just waiting until you'd settled in to pick a date."

Jingui scrambles off the *kang*, planting herself a few feet before her mother-in-law. She fixes her eyes on a spot above Mrs. Xue's head. "Strange," she says, as if addressing an unseen person standing there. "Making arrangements about my house without consulting me! I suppose they'll want to pawn my jewelry next."

Mrs. Xue stares at her, two red spots burning on her cheeks. "There is no need to speak like that."

"It's my fault," Pan intervenes. His face is flushed, either from wine or embarrassment. He addresses his wife, without looking at his mother. "I shouldn't have said anything to my mother before you came," he says apologetically, his head lowered submissively. He turns to Mrs. Xue. "Don't you think it's better for you to stay with the Jias for the time being? You can keep Lady Jia company, and Baochai has the Two Springs to spend time with."

"What kind of nonsense is this?" Mrs. Xue cries, unable to control herself. "Even if you said nothing, it's still our right to live with you." She turns to Jingui. "*You* are marrying into *our* family. And if you think that you are entitled to trample everyone underfoot, just because the house belongs to you, let me assure you that we are perfectly able to buy a house in the Capital for you to live in as well."

"If you can, then why don't you?" Jingui sneers. "Instead of relying on my family to foot the bills. I asked Pan whether he had money to buy a new house, and he said that he had always turned over most of the profits from the family business to you."

Baochai is horrified that the new couple are arguing about money within a few days of the wedding. She knows that these are arguments to which there is no end.

"It's true that Pan has always been generous to us," Mrs. Xue says. Her voice is shaking with anger. She turns to Pan. "Yes," she says. "I used a great deal of that money to pay Zhang Hua's medical bills, so his family wouldn't press charges for murder." Baochai is amazed that her mother is mentioning Zhang's case in the presence of Jingui, but she seems beside herself. "I also had to bribe the doctor who examined him, and one of the clerks in the court as well. Before that, I had to pay more than twenty thousand *taels* to cover your gambling debts, not once but twice! And before that, in Nanjing, I had to bribe the husband of that woman you harassed at the temple, as well as paying off the district magistrate. And then of what remained, I paid about half for Jingui's bridal price. The other half is for Baochai's dowry. Perhaps she'd like that as well?"

Pan looks so wretched that Baochai pities him. "Oh, no. She wouldn't want to touch that."

But Mrs. Xue is growing hysterical. "Baochai, why don't we go home and get our jewelry boxes for Jingui—"

"Mother, don't be like this," Pan pleads.

She turns on him, her face white with rage. "I think we'd better go, Pan. I'm not sure there's much to be gained by this conversation."

In all these years of trouble with Pan, it is almost the first time that Baochai has seen her mother really lose her temper with him. Mrs. Xue starts to sob. "I gave birth to you and raised you for twenty years, and now that you are finally settled and I am getting older, I am not allowed to live with you?"

"Mama, it isn't good for you to upset yourself like this," Baochai says, trying to stroke her mother's hand.

"Don't cry, Mother," Pan mutters. "Why don't we talk about it later?"

"There's nothing to talk about," Jingui says. "The day they move in is the day that I move out."

Baochai leads her mother from the room. "It's no use, Mama," she says. "Let's go home." As they cross the courtyard, she whispers, "Control yourself, Mother. We don't want the servants to talk."

Mrs. Xue starts to weep again as soon as they are alone in the carriage. "Don't cry, Mother. He doesn't know what to do. It's all so new to him. And he's in a terrible position."

"I know. It just hurts me that now he is so loyal to a woman he has barely known for a few months. He never listened to a word I said." She starts to sob even harder. "After all those years of worry, and scolding him, and pleading with him—it never occurred to me that one day he would someday belong to someone else."

Her mother's words strike an unexpected chill in Baochai's heart. Will she, too, "belong to someone else" when she is married? She shakes off the unwelcome thought. "They've only been married such a short while. Perhaps things will change in a month or two. Maybe he will learn to stand up to her."

Her mother shakes her head. "I don't think so. What happens in the first months of marriage usually sets the pattern for the future." She shakes her head again, wiping her eyes. "What a terrible mistake. I thought this marriage would be the making of him."

"How could we have known?"

"I should have known. It always seemed too good to be true." Mrs. Xue leans back against her seat for a moment, shutting her eyes. When she opens them, some of her shrewdness, which seemed to have been in abeyance for the last few months, has returned. "If Jingui was such a good match, why didn't one of the families in Nanjing snap her up? She is already more than twenty-two. And the Xias were so quick to accept our offer.

"Maybe everyone in Nanjing knew what Jingui was like. Why didn't I make inquiries about her? Why didn't I write our relatives down south? I think we could have discovered the truth. But I was so eager for things to work out that I turned a blind eye to all the signs."

Baochai knows this is true, but says, "Don't be so hard on yourself. Everything looks clear in hindsight."

"And now what? Are we going to lose Pan?"

For so many years, Baochai has regarded Pan as an impossible burden. Why, then, does she feel such sadness?

"Father! What's the matter? Are you all right?" Daiyu hears the note of panic in her own voice.

The two of them have just gone for a walk. Her father has been steadily improving since New Year's, and they had even talked of his going back to work at the beginning of the Second Month. Now, crossing the threshold of their apartment, he suddenly clutches his right side and sinks to the floor. She throws her arms around him, using all her strength to prevent him from falling too heavily.

"What's the matter?"

He does not answer, but she can see from the fixed look in his eyes that he is in pain.

"Can you get to the bed?"

He nods, and using his left arm helps push himself off the ground. With their combined strength they manage to stagger to the bed, where he collapses again. When she pulls a quilt over him, he says, "My right side hurts."

"Let me get a doctor."

"There's no need. It will pass."

She hesitates, looking at his face. It is paler than she has ever seen it, slightly twisted with pain, with an unhealthy sheen on it. Afraid to leave him alone, she rushes to the door and shouts to a neighbor's child to fetch the doctor.

"Do you want something to drink?"

"No, just sit by me."

She sits down and takes his hand, which is cold and clammy.

"Is the pain very bad?"

He does not answer. She continues to hold his hand gently, hoping that he will fall asleep.

When the doctor finally arrives, Daiyu watches him take her father's pulse, first on the right hand and then on the left. His face wears an expression of great concentration. He asks her to leave the room while he does a physical examination. At the doctor's call, she returns to the front room. Her father is still lying with his eyes open on the bed.

"I can't understand what has happened. Last time I examined your father, he seemed to have excessive fire in his stomach, and his spleen was acting up. However, both his spleen and his stomach appear to be functioning well now."

"Yes, we thought he was getting better—"

"But now, his lower left distal pulse is rapid and the lower left median pulse is strong and full." The doctor speaks quickly, as if thinking aloud. "On the right side, the distal pulse is thin and lacks strength, and the median pulse is faint and lacks vitality."

"What does that mean?"

"It means that the liver's humor is blocked, giving rise to a deficiency in the blood. On top of that, I believe that the controlling humor of the heart is causing it to generate too much fire."

"But last time you said there was too much fire in the stomach."

"Yes, but now I see a gross deficiency of humor in the lungs. You see, I thought that the fire of the stomach was creating the problem with the spleen. Now it seems that the earth of the spleen was being subdued by the woody element of the liver."

She shakes her head in frustration and confusion. "You mean, you were wrong the last time?"

The doctor is silent for a moment. "I am not entirely certain. The last time I came everything seemed to indicate a problem with the stomach, but this time I feel that the evidence points to a problem with the liver."

"The liver! But that's more serious, isn't it?"

He does not reply.

"But what about the medicine?" she says. "I've been giving him the medicines you prescribed last time. Should he be taking something else?"

"I think I must give you a new prescription." He hesitates. "It must be something to fortify the spleen and calm the liver, perhaps hemlock parsley and white peony root. I'm not entirely sure. Why don't I think more about it, and I'll send someone to you with the prescription this afternoon."

"Yes, that's fine," she replies, but it troubles her that he is uncertain enough to need more time to devise a prescription.

The doctor hesitates again. "And he seems to be in some pain. Let me give you something for that. You can have this made up right away." He writes a prescription. "This should make him more comfortable."

"I'll go to the druggist right away."

After the doctor leaves, she goes to her father. To her relief, he is asleep. She looks at his face, which seems to have changed even over the last hour. There are lines etched around the eyes and mouth, and his skin has taken on a waxy pallor. She looks down at the prescription in her hands. She believes that the doctor is a good one. He had taken care of her mother, and she has always trusted him. Still, she wants another doctor to examine her father, perhaps the famous Dr. Hu, whom Lian had found for them when they first arrived in Suzhou. She has the impression that Dr. Hu is expensive; Lian had insisted on paying his fees. She rummages in the trunk of winter clothes and finds the tiara from her mother's dowry. She calls Granny Liu to sit with her father, before hurrying to the druggist and the pawn-shop.

Three weeks after his wedding, Pan comes to Rongguo. Baochai, seeing the weariness on his face, is filled with foreboding. Her mother is so happy and relieved to see him that she shows no resentment at their last encounter.

"How are you?" Mrs. Xue says. She settles him on the *kang* and bustles about to get him a snack.

"All right."

"Look." Mrs. Xue uncovers pickled turnips fried in gluten batter. "Your favorite."

"Thank you." Pan picks up the chopsticks, then sets them down.

"What's the matter? Aren't you hungry?"

Pan does not speak.

"What's the matter?" Mrs. Xue repeats.

"Jingui wants me to go south again," he says.

"But you just came back! Why?"

"There are some repairs that have to be made on one of the Xias' estates outside Hangzhou. Also, she says that there's a shortage of stationery and perfumed goods in the Capital. She wants me to go down south and buy up as much as I can, and bring them up here. She says we should be able to make several hundred percent profit."

"If she wants it done, surely she can send some of their clerks. And it's so much closer for them to send someone from Nanjing," Mrs. Xue cries indignantly. "Surely there is no reason for you to go, when you have just made the trip."

"She says she doesn't trust servants with such important work."

"That's a fine way to treat a husband. You've barely been married a month, and now she is sending you away. Why don't you tell her 'no'?"

Pan looks down, saying nothing. Baochai stares at him, reading the shame and defeat on his face. Who knows what battles are waged between the married couple? She thinks of how Pan had beaten a man to death, and how frightened she had been at the thought of his brutality. But in that case Pan had been emboldened to attack a single opponent by the presence of three or four servants. Perhaps the truth is that Pan is neither a strong nor a brave man.

"When does she want you to go?" Mrs. Xue says.

He pauses again, knowing that the answer will infuriate his mother even more. "In two or three weeks," he says in a low voice.

"Two or three weeks! Tell her you won't go then."

"How can I tell her that?" he says helplessly.

"Make some excuse! Tell her we have to consult an almanac for a lucky date."

"She won't listen."

"I won't stand for this. I'll go and speak to her myself."

"No, no. She'll be so angry ... It's better if you—I mean, we—don't say anything ... " Pan loses himself in a tangle of words.

Baochai cannot tell whether he is afraid that Jingui will be angry at him for involving his family, or whether he is afraid of how Jingui will treat Mrs. Xue. She has wanted to stay silent, but now she feels inevitably drawn into the crisis.

"It's no use, Mama." She puts her hand on her mother's arm.

"What do you mean?" Her mother turns to her, her eyes uncomprehending in her anger and grief.

"It's best if we don't interfere. It will only make things worse for Pan."

"For Pan? What about us?"

But Baochai sees from her mother's eyes that she understands that if Pan is caught between them and Jingui, he will be the one to suffer. Her mother starts to cry, and Baochai puts her arms around her. She understands the peculiarly bitter twist to her mother's pain. After all these years of sacrificing herself for Pan's sake, she had expected one day to be rewarded by having a good son to care for her in her old age. Instead, she is being asked to sacrifice herself once again, this time to facilitate his relationship with Jingui.

Over her mother's shoulders she meets Pan's eyes. His face wears the doltish, stubborn expression in which he takes refuge when he is pained or uncomfortable. With a quick jerk of the chin, she tells him to leave, and he slips out of the room. She feels that she is caught in an elaborate web. She is trapped between her mother and Pan, who is caught between them and Jingui, who is perhaps in turn caught between the rest of the Xias and the Xues. So many people, many of whom have never seen one another, bound together by the invisible, sticky filaments that form the social fabric of the Empire's elite. She cannot move a muscle without feeling the pull of the tiny clinging threads.

10

Xifeng waits for Yucun in the loft of the big storeroom on the edge of the Women's Quarters. She sits in the usual place, among the hulking shapes of the unused furniture, hidden behind the back of a large armoire and an old dusty screen. She has brought a fur-lined cloak to spread over the rough boards of the floor. It is a cold day, so she wraps herself in it, absently rubbing her cheek against the softness of the fox collar. There is only a small round window at the near end of the loft. She clasps her knees before her and dreamily watches the dust motes float in the dim sunlight. These times are the happiest moments of her week, when she waits for him, poised between the past and the future: allowing her mind to skip and drift over the time she has spent with him, at the same time her whole body glowing in anticipation of being with him again.

She hears the scrape of the door opening downstairs.

"Hello?" he calls.

"I'm up here."

She hears his quick, light steps crossing the floor below. Then he is at the ladder. She rushes out to meet him. As soon as he has climbed up, he gathers her in his arms and kisses her. He stops to pull up the ladder and shut the trapdoor. He spreads out the fur cloak and he lies down on it, putting his arms out to her. She lowers herself onto his chest, sighing.

"How was your week?" he says.

"All right," she tells him. "They are talking of betrothing Baoyu to Baochai."

"How will that affect you?" he says, lifting his head a few inches to look into her face.

She shrugs. "I don't think they will actually be married for a while. It won't make much difference to me."

"Maybe she will be able to help out with some of the work."

"Maybe," she agrees, nestling the top of her head into the space below his chin. Even a few months ago, she would have been worried by the betrothal: afraid that Baochai would quickly bear Baoyu a son, further undercutting her own status in the household, afraid that Baochai would vie with her for control of the household. Now she no longer cares.

"And you?" she says, turning her face so she whispers into Yucun's neck.

"I heard a rumor the Emperor's health is getting worse. I don't know how much longer he can last."

"Do you think His Highness will finally appoint Prince Yinti as the Heir Apparent?"

"I don't know. He hasn't made any mention of it so far."

She nods, knowing that he is deeply concerned about the succession, hoping he can use the ascension of a less favored prince to advance his career. Locked up in the Inner Quarters, she has little sense of the political situation beyond what he tells her. Uncle Zheng almost never mentions official matters. Lian, with his fraternity of bon vivants, neither cares for nor knows much of politics. She herself feels an instinctive interest in the rivalries and intrigues among the various Princes and eunuchs and officials. Yucun, unlike other officials, has befriended the eunuchs as a means of keeping abreast of Palace affairs. Far from despising him for this, she respects him for his ambition and pragmatism.

"I missed you," he says, pulling her to him. They would talk for hours if they could, but always there is the awareness of time slipping away, the sense that she must return before someone misses her. They begin to kiss, more passionately this time. They kiss for a long time with her lying on top of him. Then slowly, when they have grown warmer, they begin to undress each other.

She watches their bodies in the soft, dim light, entwining their limbs, pushing and pulling. She lifts her head to kiss him, and then lets it loll back, looking at her leg, wrapped around his trunk, and at her arm, draped over his shoulder, as if they belong to another person. He runs his hand up her thigh, passing it over her buttock. Sometimes his touch is gentle, sometimes rough; but always he watches her, noticing her pleasure or her discomfort, quick to adjust to her moods. It is totally unlike being with Lian. She is relaxed, her mind filled with the strangest fancies. As she looks at their bodies, soft and gray in the dim light, she thinks of underwater creatures, giant blunt-nosed catfish wrestling and surging in the muddy depths of a river.

After they are done, they lie and talk, piecing together each other's lives. By now, she has described to him in detail the twin mansions where she grew up in Chang'an. One mansion belonged to her father, the other to his younger brother, and all the children of the family grew up running back and forth between the two houses. Of the twenty cousins of her genera-tion, she was the leader, a regular tomboy. Ping'er had been her sidekick and constant companion. Together the two of them could take on any of their cousins, older or younger, boy or girl, in any sport, any game. Sometimes it gives her pleasure to speak about Ping'er when they were children. More often, the pain at their present estrangement makes her break off. "Everything changed after I got married," she tells him, sighing and shaking her head.

In turn, he tells her of his bitter childhood: how his mother scraped together a living by doing other people's sewing and sent him to the village school. He talks of being filled with envy because the other boys devoured meat and vegetables at lunch, whereas he had plain rice without even a sprinkling of salt to make it more palatable. He tells her how, after attending the school for three years, he had advanced beyond the teacher, and was ready to study himself. He stayed up late at night with a single candle at his desk, both in order to save money and so as not to wake his mother, snoring a few feet away. He learned to immerse himself in the Classics so thoroughly that a whole day would go by, and then he would realize that he had forgotten to eat or drink or even go to the bathroom. This ability to disappear into texts helped him through the death of his mother when he was twelve. But his hard work and suffering had paid off, and here he was, Under-Secretary to President of the Board of War.

Whenever he describes his childhood to her, she cannot help thinking how he must resent the Jias in their arrogant, spoiled luxury. She fears he must resent her as well, but he always says that he considers her as much a victim of their wealth and power as any servant. Despite the luxury of her own life, she agrees with him. Even he does not understand the way that the favoritism and gossip, the petty rivalries, of the household have warped her.

As always, a glance at the West Ocean watch that Granny had given her tells her that she has stayed too long. She sits up and starts to pull on her underclothes. "I have to go now."

He reaches out to stroke her bare arm. "Just a little bit longer."

"No, I really have to go. Lady Jia is going to the Marquise of Nan'an's birthday party tonight, and needs me to find something for her to bring as a present."

With a groan, he sits up, too, and starts to dress. In the light from the window, she notices how his robes are fraying at the elbows and cuffs. His underwear is so worn from repeated washings that the fabric is as delicate as old gauze. She is filled with a sudden tenderness, and has to stop herself from putting her arms around him and kissing him again.

"Your robes are getting old. Let me get you a new set."

"These? They're not too bad," he says, tightening his sash.

She has an urge to see him smart and handsome, like Baoyu or Lian. She smiles to herself, deciding she will surprise him with some new clothes.

"What are you smiling at?" he says.

"Oh, nothing."

"Yes, something. What is it?"

"I'm thinking about when I will see you again."

"When?"

"Not for a few days. It's too dangerous. I don't want anyone to miss me."

"The day after tomorrow, then," he says, putting his arms around her.

She laughs, and kisses him. She knows that they are taking crazy risks, but the joy that fills her leaves no room for caution.

Baochai slips out of her mother's bedroom, careful not to make a sound. Worried about Pan's departure for the south in only ten days, Mrs. Xue had not been able to fall asleep last night until the third watch. After lunch, Baochai coaxed her to lie down for a nap. She was so tense and restless that Baochai had had to rub her legs for nearly an hour before her eyelids finally began to flutter shut. Now Baochai is stiff and tired. She recalls that she has been neglecting her social obligations lately because she has been busy attending to her mother. Shaking off her sleepiness, she decides to skip her own nap and sit with Lady Jia, who has probably awoken from her sleep by now.

She finds Granny sitting against her backrest in the front room while Snowgoose pounds her legs. She seems to be in a fretful mood, and barely acknowledges Baochai's greeting.

"How was your nap, Granny?" she says.

Instead of answering, Granny waves Snowgoose off, and says, "Now, where's Xifeng got to?"

"She is probably still napping," Snowgoose says.

"I *told* her to find me that alabaster Buddha's hand that the Shis gave me last year. I'm going to the Marquise of Nan'an's birthday party tonight, and I was going to bring it as a present."

"You don't have to leave until after dinner. There is still plenty of time to get it," Snowgoose says soothingly.

"Xifeng shouldn't have forgotten," Lady Jia complains. "Go tell her to get it now."

"She is probably still resting."

"Then wake her."

"Mrs. Lian needs her rest, too," Snowgoose tries to reason with her. "She has been complaining of a headache for the last few weeks."

Baochai also has noticed that Xifeng has not seemed herself lately. She seems absentminded and distracted and, more than once, Baochai has heard Granny scold her for some trivial mistake in the household routine.

"She is just pretending, to get out of work," Lady Jia says. "Where does she keep disappearing to, anyway? Any time I want her, I can't find her."

"It's these headaches. We really should send for a doctor," says Snowgoose.

"She is just faking it, I tell you!"

While Baochai is mindful of the respect she owes Lady Jia, sometimes she is surprised by the old woman's capriciousness and eagerness to find fault even in those whom she claims to favor. "Why don't I go look for the Buddha's hand?" she offers, trying to spare Granny from working herself into a rage.

Lady Jia looks at her. "You don't know where it is."

"It's in the storerooms, isn't it? Why wouldn't I be able to find it?"

"The storerooms are enormous. You'll never be able to find it without knowing where it is beforehand."

"Well, if I can't find it, then we can ask Xifeng," Baochai says, smiling.

"We don't have the keys. We'll have to wake Xifeng anyway," Granny says, apparently determined to disturb her.

"No," Snowgoose says, unhooking a key from the large bunch that she carries around her waist. "I have an extra set. You had better take a lantern," Snowgoose adds, lighting one for Baochai. "It's pretty dark in there."

When Baochai arrives at the storerooms, she is startled to find the door unlocked. She stands there for a moment, staring at the opened lock. As she swings the door gently open, she hears a tiny scuffling somewhere in the building. She wonders if someone is there already, or whether there are mice or rats. It is not like Xifeng to leave it unlocked by mistake—perhaps she really is becoming absentminded. Leaving the door wide open, she advances a few steps, wondering whether to call out. Squinting into the dimness, she can see no trace of a light and concludes that the place must be empty.

Something about the quiet, shadowy space frightens her, and she must force herself to go in. She thinks the Buddha's hand must be in the back of the storeroom, where she has seen many shelves of objets d'art. Wishing she had never offered to come, she weaves between the hulking wardrobes and bedsteads, darker and darker now that she has left the stream of light from the door. At every step, she is convinced that cobwebs are cling-ing to her face, and waves her hand to brush them away.

Looking around, holding the lantern high, she feels like the darkness is filled with whispering voices. She has never been superstitious before, but it is almost as if the place is haunted.

She gets to the shelves at the back and runs the lantern hurriedly over the rows of vases and tea trays and table screens. She spies the Buddha's hand on the second shelf. As she reaches for it, she hears a woman's voice moaning, and realizes that it is not her imagination after all. There is someone here, in the loft of the storeroom. She sees that the ladder leading to the second floor is gone. Then she hears a man's voice, and understands that some couple is using the place to meet secretly.

She grabs the Buddha's hand, careful not to bump against anything, and begins to walk quickly back to the entrance. Her first thought is that some maid has smuggled her lover in and is meeting him here. But that cannot be right. A maid would not dare to sneak a man in. The thought flashes into her mind that it is Xifeng.

She catches her breath at the risk, the danger. She is too frightened to even think about who Xifeng could be meeting. She stumbles the final few steps and bursts out into the sunlight.

11

"Baochai, dear. Can I talk to you about something?"

Baochai jumps. She has been sitting with her embroidery on her lap in her mother's front room. As she looks down, she realizes that she has not sewn a stitch for the past half hour. She has been too preoccupied by what she had heard in the storerooms two days before. Her thoughts have gone around and around the event until it feels like they have worn a groove in her mind. Could Xifeng really be so reckless? She wants to go to Xifeng, to test her somehow in order to confirm her suspicions. But what would be the point, except to put Xifeng on guard and make her treat Baochai as an enemy? Baochai cannot imagine what man could be sneaking into the Inner Quarters, nor what would happen if Xifeng were discovered. A divorce? A court case? Xifeng would be sent back to her family and neither the Jias nor the Wangs would be able to hold their heads up for shame. She knows that Xifeng is in her power; yet she does not wish for such power, and fears Xifeng all the more now knowing what she is capable of.

"Yes, Mother. What is it?" She tries to shake off her pre-occupation.

"There is something I want to talk to you about."

Baochai sees from her mother's face that it is something important. "What is it? Something about Pan?"

"Not about Pan. About you."

"About me?" Baochai raises her brows, smiling.

Her mother hesitates before speaking, her expression half

eager, half worried. "Lady Jia spoke to me yesterday about a match between Baoyu and you."

Baochai sits perfectly still for a moment, looking unseeingly down at the embroidery in her lap. She does not know whether she should be flattered or surprised. She is not really surprised, after all—she knows how her mother and aunt used to joke about the match. Her heart gives a queer bound of pleasure— but it is nothing compared to the elation she would once have felt. She remembers that day last summer when he put his arms around her and almost kissed her. What has changed since then? Was it the night of Daiyu's departure, when she had discovered him in Daiyu's bedroom? But now Daiyu is gone, she reminds herself, and most likely he will never see her again.

"What is it, Baochai? Don't you like the match?" her mother says, mistaking her long silence for reluctance.

Baochai looks at her mother, taken aback by her mother's question. "I don't have any opinion, Mother. It is for you to make my match."

Her mother smiles. "You don't have to prove to me that you are a dutiful daughter, Baochai. I am sure that no one ever had a more filial child. I'm asking you your opinion, because I want you to be happy."

"I really don't know, Mother." A part of Baochai wishes that her mother would simply tell her what to do. She finds it too difficult to express her feelings on such a matter, even to her mother. The truth is, she does not know what she wants. Her attraction to Baoyu is still there, buried but still alive. Yet he no longer seems to her the shining and glamorous hero he once did. He still has not passed the Exams, for one thing.

"To tell you the truth," her mother says slowly, "I am not sure myself. On the one hand, Baoyu is gentle, even tenderhearted. He would never trample on your feelings, or be cruel to you, like Lian is to Xifeng."

Baochai finds her mother's sympathy for Xifeng misplaced, wondering what she would think if she knew the truth about Xifeng.

"I remember finding Baoyu in tears once when he was a little boy," Mrs. Xue says. "I asked him what the matter was. He said he was crying because one of the maids had told him how she had been orphaned when she was four years old. He was always more sensitive than most boys.

"On the other hand," Mrs. Xue goes on with a wry smile, "he is so soft that he has no self-discipline. That's the only reason he hasn't passed the Exams yet. He is certainly bright enough. And he has such an odd perverse streak." Mrs. Xue shakes her head. "If you want him to do one thing, he is sure to do the very opposite."

"He's just a little spoiled and rebellious, because Uncle Zheng is so strict with him."

Mrs. Xue shakes her head. "It's more than that. In any case, if everyone knew each other's faults, no one would ever get married." She pats Baochai's hand. "Now, I want you to know you should feel free to say 'no' to this match. After all, I'm sure this is not the only proposal we will get for your hand—"

Embarrassed, Baochai tries to draw her hand away, but Mrs. Xue holds it. "Baochai, you are a sensible girl. There are some other things you might want to consider, before you make your decision."

Baochai is surprised by her mother's serious tone, and looks nervously into her face.

"First of all, you know as well as I do that Jingui is going to be difficult about money. That being the case, it as an advantage for you to be betrothed as soon as possible, so that your dowry will already be paid, and she won't be able to get her hands on it. If we make this match with the Jias, we can arrange it right away, and Pan can even pay your dowry before he goes. That would give me some peace of mind.

"Secondly," Mrs. Xue continues, "at least the Jias are known to us. After this experience with Jingui, I have come to think that marrying you into a family that we do not know well is too great a risk." At the mention of Jingui, her mother's attempt to speak in a cool, rational tone starts to come apart.

"Thirdly"—Baochai sees the tears glistening in her mother's eyes, but Mrs. Xue rubs them away—"now that I cannot live with Pan, if you marry Baoyu, I can continue living here with you. If you married someone else, they might not be willing to let me continue to live with you."

It is the first time that it has occurred to Baochai that she need not leave her mother when she marries. She has always assumed that according to custom her mother would live with Pan, while she herself would be forced to live with her new in-laws. She has always dreaded the prospect of parting from her mother. But given that Jingui is so intolerable, wouldn't it be best if she and her mother could remain together at the Jias'?

Her mother picks up her embroidery, and resumes sewing, not looking at Baochai. Baochai knows her mother does not mean to manipulate her with tears. She begins sewing, too, taking comfort in the soothing rhythm of drawing her needle through the silk. As always, when she thinks of Baoyu, she compares him to Pan and what she has seen of other young men, like her Xue cousins in Nanjing. Her mother is right. No matter how Auntie Zhao and Huan try to backstab Baoyu, he never attempts to protect himself, much less take revenge. She cannot imagine him being brutal or harsh to anyone.

"I agree with you, Mother." She does not take her eyes off her sewing. "I think it is a good match."

She feels her mother's eyes on her, but does not meet them. "Are you sure, Baochai? I don't want to put pressure on you."

Baochai nods, feeling a strange desire to cry. Instead, she says, "There is just one other problem."

"What is it?"

"If I am to be betrothed to Baoyu, how can I go on living in the Garden with him, seeing him every day?"

Her mother nods. "It will be highly improper for you to see him once you are betrothed." She thinks for a moment. "I know. Why don't you move in here with me? It is somewhat separate from the rest of the Inner Quarters, and we can arrange to have our meals here, so that you will hardly see him. Granny and Xifeng will understand our reasons without our having to say anything directly."

"All right," Baochai says. She does not mind moving in with her mother, for her own place seems so lonely now that Daiyu is gone. She hesitates for a moment before adding, "And what about Baoyu?"

"What do you mean?"

Baochai looks back down at her sewing before saying, with a little difficulty, "Does he know about the betrothal? What does he say?"

"Actually, I don't believe they intend to tell him as yet," her mother says. "I think they're afraid that if they tell him, it will distract him from his studies." She tries to speak as if this secrecy is perfectly natural, but does not quite succeed.

Baochai also feels the strangeness of the whole transaction, but she does not know what to do. She pushes her uneasiness aside, and tells herself that she prefers that Baoyu not know.

PART THREE

Fourth Month, 1722

When you grieve, I also am sad.
When you laugh, then I too feel joy.
Don't you see the trees with boughs joined?
From different roots, the branches intertwine.

Song of Ziye

1

For the second time, Daiyu is carried in a sedan past the stone lions through the massive triple gate of Rongguo Mansion. This time, she leans quietly in the corner of the sedan with her eyes shut, exhausted by her father's funeral and the barge trip back north. The journey, long to begin with, was rendered more grueling by their pace. Eager to be in the Capital before Ping'er gave birth, Lian had insisted on starting every day at sunrise and traveling until it was dark, with the result that a journey that ordinarily took over a month had been accomplished in a little over three weeks.

The sedan is set down before the Inner Gate. As they walk towards Lady Jia's, she gazes at the manmade mountain towering over the Garden. Its humped jade-green form seems at once alien and familiar, as if she had been another person when she last saw it five months ago. As they walk into Granny Jia's courtyard, through the cages of twittering birds, she can see how happy Lian is to be home. His eagerness reminds her that her own home is gone. She tries not to dwell on her loss, thinking instead of Baoyu and Baochai and Snowgoose. The thought of seeing them has sustained her through the journey.

When they walk into the front room, only Lady Jia and Uncle Zheng are there on the *kang*. She hurries forward to give Lady Jia her kowtow, but instead of greeting her, Lady Jia stares at her. "What are you doing here?"

Taken aback, Daiyu stops short.

Lian steps forward. "Didn't you get my letter?"

"No," Uncle Zheng says, climbing off the *kang* to greet them. "What has happened? How is Lin Ruhai?"

"He passed away in the middle of the Second Month."

"Passed away!" Uncle Zheng exclaims, shocked. "But your letter after New Year's said he was getting better."

"He was, but then he got worse suddenly at the beginning of the Second Month. There was nothing the doctors could do. I wrote, and said I was coming back with Cousin Daiyu."

"We didn't get any other letter. What was it that killed him?"

Lady Jia cuts in, "Wouldn't it have been wiser to leave her with some of her Lin relatives?"

A sort of bewildered anger and shame pierces the dullness of Daiyu's grief. Even though she knows that she and Granny are not especially fond of each other, now that she is orphaned she never supposed that Granny would not welcome her into the household. She wishes she could turn on her heel and leave, but she has no choice but to throw herself on the mercy of the Jias.

"I wrote to ask you what I should do," Lian says. "There were some distant cousins in Yangzhou. I went to see them, but they wouldn't take her." He casts an embarrassed glance at Daiyu for fear that the bluntness of his words may hurt her. "They said they could barely make ends meet as it was. Besides, they were fourth cousins. They said we were a lot more closely related to her than they were. Besides, Cousin Lin had never seen them in her life."

"That may be," Lady Jia says. "But she's a Lin, not a Jia."

"What did you expect me to do?" Lian says. "Leave her there alone?"

"You should have written and asked for permission."

"What is this nonsense?" Uncle Zheng, who has been silent, apparently brooding about the death of Daiyu's father, cuts in irritably. "Where should she go but here?"

Lady Jia turns on him. "So you want to play the great benefactor! That's your affair. Don't come to me when you want money for her dowry."

"It's not a question of her dowry," Uncle Zheng says. "She is Min's daughter. Where else should she go?"

"Min turned her back on her family. I don't know why—"

"Can't you understand that it is not the time for this?" It is the most harshly Daiyu has ever seen him speak to his mother. He turns to Daiyu and forces a smile. "You must be tired. You've had a long journey. Why don't you go rest?"

"Where shall I have her luggage put?" Lian says.

"Oh," Jia Zheng says, looking around for Xifeng, who usually manages such matters. Frowning when he realizes she is not there, he looks at Daiyu. "You slept in Baochai's apartments last time, didn't you? Why don't we put you there again?"

She nods, and tries to thank him, but he says, with brusque kindness, "There is no need for that. There's no question of your not staying with us."

Baochai comes in. Daiyu cries, "Baochai!" Just as she is reaching out to embrace her cousin, she notices a strange expression on Baochai's face. She is not smiling. Her face looks grave, and in her eyes is—can it be?—a look of hostility. Confused, Daiyu stops, and lets her arms drop. "Baochai, you've heard ... my father ... "

"I just heard. I'm so sorry." But Baochai makes no move to embrace Daiyu.

"And you, how are you?" Daiyu stammers. Is Baochai acting so serious as a way of expressing sympathy? Had she simply forgotten how cold and reserved Baochai was?

"You know that Pan got married after New Year's."

"That's wonderful news."

"Yes, but he has gone south again."

From these few words, Daiyu understands that there is some

sort of trouble with Pan again. Perhaps that is the reason that Baochai is so subdued and distant.

"I was just going to your apartments in the Garden. Come with me. We can talk there."

If possible, Baochai's face grows even more forbidding. "I'm not living there anymore."

Daiyu is surprised. "Why not? Where are you living, then?"

"I've moved in with my mother."

"But why?"

"She has been feeling lonely, and needs my company."

"I see," Daiyu says, but she does not understand why Mrs. Xue would feel more lonely now than she had earlier. "Well," she says, "if you will not be living with me, then I will have to go to see you at Mrs. Xue's."

"Yes, of course."

Daiyu notices that Baochai says nothing about being happy to see her again. Baochai climbs onto the *kang* and seats herself beside Lady Jia.

Daiyu walks slowly from the room. Through the door curtain, she hears Lady Jia and Uncle Zheng starting to argue again. As she crosses the courtyard, the birds, disturbed by her presence, burst into indignant scoldings and twitterings. It needed only this, she thinks, shrinking from the furious barrage of sound, to give her return to Rongguo the quality of a nightmare.

Xifeng pulls her wrist out from under Yucun's body and squints at her watch in the dim light. It is only seventeen minutes from seven o'clock.

She gasps, pushing Yucun off her. "I have to go!" She rolls herself out from underneath him and begins to pull on her underclothes.

"Don't go yet," he says, putting his arms around her and kissing her bare neck.

She thrusts him away. "Stop it!" she says angrily. "This time I really will be late!"

She pulls on her robe and ties her sash, her fingers twitching in her haste. She drags on her stockings and shoes. He silently hands her her fur-lined jacket, which she shrugs on. Then, without even looking at him or saying goodbye, she is rushing down the ladder and out of the storeroom. After weeks of close calls, this time she has really done it: made herself late for dinner, where the whole family will be expecting her. She feels a twinge of annoyance at Yucun, for making her forget the time and urging her to linger, without realizing the terrible risk that she will run if she is detected. She hastens down the passage behind the kitchens, all the way to Lady Jia's place, patting her hair and straightening her clothes as she runs.

When she reaches Lady Jia's courtyard, she forces herself to slow to a walk, so she can catch her breath before going in. She passes through the door curtain, hoping that her makeup hasn't been too smudged by Yucun's kisses. She sees to her dismay that Lady Jia, Uncle Zheng, and the Two Springs are all gathered for dinner, and that Snowgoose is already helping Lady Jia into her seat at the head of the table. Acting as if nothing is the matter, she hurries towards the *tansu* to get out the serving utensils as usual.

"What are you doing here, Xifeng?" Lady Jia says.

Xifeng jumps. "What do you mean?"

"Didn't you get my message?"

"No," Xifeng says, terrified that someone has been looking for her while she was with Yucun. "What is it?"

"I told Lian to tell you that you didn't need to help with dinner tonight, seeing that it is his first night back."

She is bewildered. "Lian! He's back?"

It takes her one instant to comprehend Lady Jia's words, and to stop herself from saying more. It is too late. All around her she sees the servants exchanging smirks and glances. Lian has returned from a five-month journey without even coming to greet her.

"I—I was in the storerooms," she stammers, desperately trying to save some face. "I think no one knew where I was, so that's why . . . " She trails off. "Well, then, if you don't need me tonight, I will go back and make sure he is comfortable."

She whirls on her heel, feeling all the curious and malicious gazes on her. All across the courtyard, she concentrates on keeping her back straight, her head up, her pace slow and deliberate. As soon as she passes through the front gates, however, she begins to run, panic flooding her. She wonders why Lian has come back without warning, and without informing her of his arrival. In the back of her mind, she is afraid that he has heard some rumor of her affair with Yucun. This fear makes her compose her features into a smile, rather than scolding him for humiliating her, when she pushes through the door curtain into her own apartments.

"How was your trip? Why didn't you write that you were coming home?"

Lian is leaning against a backrest on the *kang* wearing a tunic and loose trousers, freshly bathed, his hair wet. Ping'er is serving him dinner from a *kang* table beside him. He does not answer, instead draining a cup of wine that Ping'er has just poured him.

"How was your trip?" she repeats, taking a step closer to the *kang*, wondering if he had not heard her. "Is everything all right?"

He puts the empty cup on the table. Ping'er hands him a napkin. He wipes his mouth.

Xifeng stares at him, half bewildered, half frightened. "What is it?"

He looks back at her, his face expressionless. Finally, he says, "Why did you cancel the order for the black-boned chickens for Ping'er?"

"What?" she says blankly.

"I said," he repeats, louder and with an edge to his voice, "why did you cancel the order for black-boned chickens for Ping'er?"

It comes back to her. It seems a lifetime ago, and so trivial compared to what she had feared, that she almost laughs. "Oh, that," she says, recovering herself. "The kitchens were exceeding their budget, and I spoke to the cook about cutting down their expenses." She speaks quickly. "I left it entirely up to her. I really can't remember what she ended up cutting out, but maybe—"

"I called Cook Liu to ask her," Lian interrupts. "She said you specifically told her to stop buying the black-boned chickens."

She begins to feel flustered by his tone of accusation. "I really can't remember every little thing I told her to cut out. It was months ago—"

"Name one other thing that you told her to stop buying."

"Good Heavens, how do you expect me to remember—" She is humiliated at being caught in such an imposture, but her pride refuses to let her admit the fault.

"You've never forgotten one thing having to do with money in your whole life," Lian says.

"What a to-do about nothing! If you don't like the way I manage things, then why don't you do it?"

"You lied to me." Ping'er speaks for the first time from beside Lian on the *kang*. "You made it seem as if you were helping me, when it was you who told Cook Liu to stop ordering the chickens in the first place."

Xifeng has almost forgotten how she had deceived Ping'er. Ping'er gives a sob, and suddenly she feels ashamed. As she tries to think of some way to make light of the deception, she sees Lian slide an arm protectively around Ping'er's shoulders.

Something breaks loose inside of her. She, Xifeng, raised Ping'er from among dozens of maids at the Wang mansion to be her personal servant. Ping'er had been only a junior maid, who swept the yard and fetched water. Xifeng had brought her inside and given her the chance to learn more sophisticated skills, without which a female servant could never advance: the ability to speak formally and precisely in a way that would impress the masters and mistresses, the knowledge of how to dress hair and apply makeup, the authority to organize and direct other servants. She instructed her in manners, and how to hold her head and walk with small steps. She taught Ping'er how to count and figure, even to recognize a few basic characters. Since the two of them were twelve or thirteen, she has treated Ping'er like a sister, sharing her clothes and jewels and cosmetics. She had turned Ping'er into someone capable of attracting Lian. Now the two of them act like Xifeng is a monster, someone from whom Ping'er must be protected.

Suddenly, she is screaming, calling Ping'er a whore, and Lian obscenities that have never crossed her lips before. She is almost frightened by the sound of her own voice in the silence of the room. She starts to tell Lian what she has always thought of his stupidity and laziness, and then, just as abruptly, she stops herself. She narrows her eyes and the words form themselves without her thinking. "Get out."

"What do you mean?" Lian looks at her as if she is crazy.

"You heard me. I said, 'Get out.' The two of you. This is my apartment." Now her voice is calm. She stabs her fingers at the furniture, the scrolls on the wall. "All this is mine." Nearly every piece was part of her dowry, a dowry fit for a princess.

Lian stares at her. She is gratified by how helpless and scared he looks. "Where—where should we go?"

"I don't care. Find someplace else to live. There are plenty of other places in the house."

Ping'er and Lian look at each other, like a couple of bereft children. She almost laughs at their scared expressions. It is so easy, she thinks. If she had known how easy it was, she would have done it long ago.

Alone in the apartments she used to share with Baochai, Daiyu pours cold water into a basin. In the silence of the night she hears the emptiness of the rooms around her, the empty space between this apartment and those of the other girls. She wishes she had asked Baochai and her mother to let her sleep at their place for the night, but given Baochai's strange coldness, she would not have dared, even if it had occurred to her. A feeling of desolation overcame her when she walked into these rooms, so different now that they are uninhabited. The air smells of damp and disuse. Someone has hastily made up a bed on the *kang*. When she was last here, one of Baochai's maids had always helped her, but now there is no one. She wonders whether she has not been assigned a maid because Lady Jia has made it clear how unwelcome she is.

She props a window open. She feels the coolness of the night air on her arms and shivers. She feels her breath slowing after the last weeks of hurry and stress. During her mourning and the journey, she has never been by herself for even a moment. She slumps on her knees on the floor and presses her face into the mustiness of the *kang* rug. She does not cry at first. Then the sobs seem to rise out of her stomach, slowly at first, with long intervals in between, then more quickly, making her gasp for breath. She slides onto the floor against the *kang*, letting the tears roll down her cheeks. She cries, her big gulping sobs echoing in the room, for she does not know how long. Eventually, she gets cold sitting on the floor. She blows out the lantern and gets into bed without taking off her clothes. She sits there under the covers, holding her knees before her chest, still weeping. Strangely, the crying gives her no relief. It feels like merely a physical reaction, like yawning or hiccupping, and does not loosen her knot of grief.

When the sobs finally start to recede, she holds a handkerchief to her mouth, wiping the tears that still occasionally well from her eyes. She hears a sound outside the open window. "Snowgoose?" she calls.

"It's me. Baoyu."

"What are you doing here?" she says, drying her eyes. She had been hoping to see him at dinner, but he had not come home.

"I'm going to climb in through the window," he says.

"I don't see why you can't come through the door."

She hears the window hinge creak, and sees his silhouette against the moonlit darkness outside. Then she hears the scuffle of his feet on the floor, and another creak as he shuts the window.

"You've heard about my father ..."

"Yes." He comes towards her. "But tell me what happened. Lian wrote that he was getting better."

"He was, at New Year's. But then, all of a sudden, he collapsed one day." She feels her tears rising again. "The doctor said it was his liver, when all along he had been saying it was his stomach and his spleen. He got worse so quickly. We tried all sorts of medicines, all different doctors, but nothing seemed to help." She puts her face in her hands and sobs.

His arms are around her protectively. "One morning, I woke up and went to his room. He was already dead, his body all cold, and shrunken." Baoyu holds her tighter, his hand gently stroking the back of her head.

He lets her cry for a while. When she grows calmer, he says, "How were you able to manage everything?"

"I knew what to do, because when my mother died—but my father had taken care of almost everything then. I didn't know how many little things there were to do. I almost didn't have time to feel sad . . . "

"I understand."

She feels insensibly soothed by being able to spill out all the hardships of the past months to him. "Lian helped—but he was in such a rush to come back here, he wanted me to cut short the Forty-Nine Days. He had done so much for us already that I didn't feel I could refuse. But there was so much to do before we left. We had to sell or give away everything, and settle all the bills, and say goodbye."

"It must have been hard for you to leave Suzhou."

"How could I stay? There was no place for me. But when I got back here, Granny made it perfectly clear that I wasn't welcome." With a sob, she tells him what Lady Jia had said.

She has the impression, although she cannot see his expression, that he is not surprised. "You mustn't let it bother you. You know what her moods are like."

"It's more than her moods. Why does she hate me so?"

"I'm not sure."

"Thank you for not pretending. I told Baochai that Granny disliked me, and she said it was my imagination."

"Never mind Baochai. I used to think Granny hated you because of your mother."

"I thought so, too."

"I am not sure that explains it all. But you mustn't let it worry you." He holds her to him. "This is where you belong. My father knows that. He'll see you are treated properly."

The thought crosses her mind that Uncle Zheng pays so little attention to the mundane affairs of the Inner Quarters that he will have no idea how she is treated. But all she says is, "Yes, your father was very kind."

"Well, he knows that—" He breaks off abruptly. "I'd forgotten how late it is. I shouldn't keep you up. You must be terribly worn out by taking care of your father and the journey. It's very important that you take care of your health now." He slips off the *kang* towards the window.

She remembers how quiet and desolate the room felt before he came. "Stay a little longer."

"You need to rest," he says, but he comes back to the *kang*, and she senses him peering at her in the darkness. "Lie down. I'll stay with you until you fall asleep."

She eases herself into a lying position under the quilts, still in her clothes. She wonders whether he will lie beside her, but he sits beside her pillow clasping his knees. She is glad that he does not speak or try to touch her now. She does not want anything more than his silent presence. Her exhaustion begins to overtake her. She feels her breath lengthening and her eyes growing heavy, and lets herself slip into sleep.

2

"Baochai, would you mind bringing this note to Lady Jia?" Mrs. Xue says after breakfast. "Baoyu should be at school already, so you won't be in any danger of seeing him."

"Of course, Mother." She is about to ask what the note is about, when she realizes that it probably concerns her betrothal gifts and dowry. The arrangements for her betrothal had been completed last week, before Pan left for the south.

As she passes through the front gate of Granny's apartment, however, out of the corner of her eye she sees Baoyu and Daiyu speaking in the shelter of the verandah along the side of the courtyard, half hidden by the cages of birds. He must be going to school late for some reason. She cannot hear their words from this distance, but something about the way they speak to each other pierces her heart like a small poisonous dart. Daiyu is pale and drooping, as she has been since she came back from the south. She is looking down, and Baochai thinks she can see tears on her cheeks. Baoyu is standing close to her, his body bent protectively towards hers, his head lowered in order to catch her words. There is an intimacy, a tacit understanding, between the two of them. Baoyu loves Daiyu; she has been foolish to ever think otherwise. Daiyu's feelings towards Baoyu are less clear. She is nodding and listening to what he says, but from the way that her body slumps away from him, Baochai thinks she is too caught up in her grief to be open to Baoyu's advances.

The two of them are so intent on their conversation that they do not notice her. She turns on her heel without delivering the note. Hoping the scenery will soothe her, she goes to the Garden and walks along the lake. Lotuses bloom on the green water, but she hardly sees them, instead picturing Baoyu and Daiyu, barely half a pace apart, talking to each other with their voices lowered so no one else can hear. Daiyu exaggerates her sorrow and helplessness to make herself appealing to Baoyu, Baochai thinks. Daiyu knows how tenderhearted Baoyu is, and uses this tenderness to manipulate him and bind him to herself.

Then she remembers that Daiyu does not know of her own betrothal to Baoyu. It remains a secret, and Baochai has never mentioned the match, even to Baoyu's half sister Tanchun, as it is considered proper for young girls to behave as if they are oblivious of their impending marriages. She must overcome her reserve to tell Daiyu of the betrothal. For the sake of her friendship with Daiyu—more importantly, for the sake of her marriage—she must quash this dangerous intimacy between Baoyu and Daiyu.

Having come to this decision, she feels calmer. She turns around and begins, more slowly, to retrace her steps back to Lady Jia's. By the time she reenters Lady Jia's courtyard, there is no trace of either Daiyu or Baoyu. She delivers the note, then walks towards her old apartments in the Garden. At first she steps quickly, in her eagerness to resolve the misunderstanding. However, the nearer she comes to the apartment, the more she realizes how difficult it will be to bring up the betrothal. She resents Daiyu for forcing her to speak about so embarrassing and painful a topic.

She finds her old front room empty. Even though all the old furniture and decorations are still there, the place has the air of being uninhabited, even a little dusty. She remembers that Daiyu has no maid. This time, she feels little inclination to let Daiyu borrow one of hers. She is surprised by the sound of girls' voices from Daiyu's bedroom. She had not expected the Two Springs to take the initiative to visit. When she pushes through the door curtain she finds Snowgoose, so close to Daiyu that their knees touch. They break off their conversation when they see her.

Snowgoose climbs off the *kang* and stands respectfully. "Lady Jia gave me the day off to visit my family, and I came here to see how Miss Lin was doing before setting off," she explains.

"I see," Baochai says. It is not wrong for Snowgoose to spend her time off gossiping with Daiyu, but such intimacy strikes Baochai as improper.

"Snowgoose was telling me that now that I am staying here, and not just a visitor, I must be more careful to stay on Lady Jia's good side," Daiyu says.

Snowgoose breaks in. "Won't you tell her, Miss Xue, that she can't go on like this, showing up late for breakfast, and then only eating a bite or two? Sometimes she even misses breakfast. It offends Lady Jia, and is hurting her health." She speaks as if she and Baochai are united by concern for Daiyu. "I'm afraid that if the other servants see that Lady Jia does not favor her, they will start to mistreat her, just as they do Auntie Zhao and Master Huan."

Baochai feels a prick of guilt that Snowgoose should be the one warning Daiyu how to get on in the household; she realizes how much she has been neglecting Daiyu herself, caught up in preparations for her betrothal. "Naturally you owe the Jias as many gestures of respect and consideration as possible," she says stiffly.

When Snowgoose takes her leave to visit her family, Baochai is again disturbed by how affectionate Daiyu's farewell is. When she and Daiyu are alone, she sits down beside Daiyu on the *kang*. "I hadn't realized that you weren't going to breakfast on time. You must take better care of yourself."

"How would you?" Daiyu says, raising her brows. "You never eat with us anymore."

Although Baochai has come to explain why, she finds herself saying evasively, "My mother hasn't been well, and prefers to eat in our own rooms."

"*Your* own rooms?" Daiyu echoes. "*These* used to be your rooms, but this is the first time that you have come here since I arrived."

She catches the sharpness in Daiyu's tone. "I'm sorry. I've been busy with my mother. But Snowgoose is right. You should make every effort to show Lady Jia how grateful you are."

Daiyu's face takes on an obstinate expression. "Why should I be grateful to her? She has made it perfectly clear that she doesn't want me here."

"But she's your grandmother."

"So what? I'd never seen her until this year. No, the ones I love here are Snowgoose and you, and your mother. I don't owe anything to anyone else."

Baochai is shocked. "How can you say that? Granny is your mother's mother."

"But Granny abandoned my mother. No, I can't love people just because they are related to me by blood."

Baochai has never seen Daiyu in this perverse mood, in which she seems to repudiate everything that Baochai holds dear. "Since she has taken you in, even though you aren't fond of her, that's all the more reason you should be grateful to her." She tries to change the subject. "There is something else I wanted to tell you."

"What is it?"

"I was surprised at the way you were discussing your behavior with Snowgoose, even allowing her to give you advice on how to conduct yourself."

Daiyu smiles. "I don't see why I wouldn't take her advice. She knows this household better than anyone else."

Baochai suspects Daiyu of deliberately trying to misunderstand her. "Don't you see that if you want the servants' respect, you must keep a proper distance?"

Daiyu laughs. "Why shouldn't I talk to Snowgoose? Everyone here spends lots of time gossiping with the servants."

Irritated by Daiyu's naïveté, Baochai says, "Gossiping is one thing, but you let her get above herself by allowing her to comment on your relationship with other mistresses. Even I wouldn't presume to give you such advice!"

The smile fades from Daiyu's face. "Good Heavens, Baochai! I never thought you were such a snob."

Baochai has to bite her lip to keep from retorting, feeling the distance yawning between them. If only there were some neutral topic on which they could converse amicably; it seems that everything she has said today, no matter how innocuous, has rubbed Daiyu the wrong way. Bringing up her betrothal seems impossible. Forcing a smile, she makes an excuse to leave. Daiyu makes no attempt to keep her. Walking across the forecourt, she realizes that she has not told Daiyu about her and her mother's troubles with Jingui; nor has she learned the details of Daiyu's father's illness and death. Their old camaraderie is gone.

Xifeng moves around the newly emptied space of her apartments, deciding what to do with the now unoccupied rooms. She opens the wardrobe in Ping'er and Lian's old bedroom; it is empty. If there were anything left, she would throw it out into the middle of the courtyard, where the two of them could see it from their new rooms on the other side. She decides to use this room for the baby and wet nurse. She goes back to the wardrobe in her own bedroom. Inside it, besides her own clothes, are the baby clothes and diapers she has had made, not as elaborate as the ones Ping'er has sewn, but solidly stitched from the best materials nevertheless.

When she had realized that she, as the principal wife, was entitled to take charge of Ping'er's baby, she nearly laughed out loud. Here was the way to punish Lian and Ping'er for the way they have treated her: when the baby is born, she will take it from Ping'er's arms and bring it back here. Humming a little, she carries the piles of baby clothes to the wardrobe in the other bedroom. Then she goes to the linen chest and selects the softest bedding she can find.

Hearing a sound in the front room, she hurries out and finds a roughly dressed young woman with rosy cheeks.

"Mrs. Lian?" the young woman says in a sing-songy Shandongese accent. "They told me you were looking for a wet nurse."

"What's your name?"

The girl gives a jerky bow. "They call me Zhang's wife. I'm married to Zhang He, over in the stables."

"Don't you have a name of your own?"

"When I was a child, my family called me 'Number Five.'"

"I can't call you 'Number Five.'" In some lower-class families, girls are held so cheap that the parents do not even bother to name them, simply addressing them by their birth order. "We'll have to think of something else."

"Just as you please."

"How many children do you have?"

"A little boy, six months old."

"How will you nurse another child?"

Zhang's wife smiles and jerks a thumb at her plump bosom, straining against the coarse blue cotton of her shirt. "I've got plenty for two."

"Are you in good health?"

"Strong as an ox. I was scrubbing the floors three days after I gave birth."

"Do you ever drink?"

"So help me, never."

"Gamble?"

Zhang's wife laughs as if Xifeng has cracked a very funny joke, revealing a mouthful of uneven teeth. "What do I have to gamble with?"

"That's your own concern, as long as you don't get into bad company. You'll live here, with me and the baby. I'll pay you three *taels* a month. You'll get your meals here, too. You'll be responsible for the child: feeding it, changing it, bathing it, sleeping with it at night."

Zhang's wife nods. Xifeng can tell that she is pleased by the amount of the salary.

"You can bring your own son here with you, as long as he behaves himself."

Zhang's wife smiles broadly now, bowing again. "There's just one thing."

"What is it?"

"Er—when exactly is the baby due?"

"In about two weeks."

Xifeng notices the woman eyeing her own flat stomach, but all she says is, "Yes, ma'am."

After the wet nurse is gone, Xifeng sits down in her bedroom with a brush and paper to calculate the interest on her latest loans. Someone is always wanting to borrow money, and when she has finished she realizes that when she is repaid she will have nearly seven thousand *taels* at her disposal. It is not much compared to what Lady Jia probably has, yet it is a significant sum, enough to make her feel a little safe.

Hearing another sound from the front room, she hurriedly

folds the paper up and goes out to see who it is. Yucun is standing there inside the door curtain. In the last week of daily battles
with Lian, she had almost forgotten about him.

"What are you doing here?"

He looks surprised. "You were supposed to meet me in the
storerooms four days ago, but you didn't show up. I came to see
what was wrong."

"Something is wrong," she tells him. "Lian is back."

"Yes, I know. I saw him yesterday, but—"

"You knew he was back and you still have the nerve to come
here looking for me? Are you crazy? He could walk in here any
minute!"

"Then meet me at the storerooms."

"It's too dangerous."

He steps closer to her. "Or we can find someplace to meet
outside the mansion. Say you want to burn incense at the
temple."

She shakes her head. With Lian's return, her sense of the
impossibility and danger of being with Yucun has come rushing back to her. How could she have allowed herself to be
caught up in such a foolish dream for the past months? When
she realized how easily she might have been caught if Lian had
come looking for her, she had come to her senses. As much as
she may dream about escaping from it, her life, her future, is
contained within the confines of this mansion. Unhappy as she
may be, what would be left for her if she were discovered? She
would be sent back to her family in Chang'an, dishonored and
despised, to be a hanger-on, like Daiyu, with no standing or
security in the household. No, she cannot throw away the
position she has consolidated over the years by some foolish
misstep.

She pushes him towards the door. "You have to leave."

"No, we have to talk."

"Don't you understand? Lian is back. I can't see you any-more."

"So you were just looking for some amusement while he was away—" he says bitterly.

His expression pains her, and she allows herself to be drawn into a discussion instead of sending him away immediately as she had intended. "What more do you want from me? You've slept with me. Isn't that enough? Why don't you go away and leave me alone?"

He takes her roughly by the hands. "Is that what you think I wanted from you? If that's all I wanted, do you think I would have come sneaking in here at all hours, risking my career—"

She jerks her hands away. "And what do you think I'm risking? Don't you know what will happen to me if anyone finds out?"

He is silent for a moment. Then he says, "Lian will divorce you, and I will marry you."

She stares at him. The way he says it, quite calmly, not as a rhetorical flourish, but as a simple fact, strikes her silent. "You couldn't marry me. I would be disgraced, a fallen woman."

"Why not? I don't have a family to care what I do."

"But what about your career? You need to make a good mar-riage so that you will have influential in-laws, a patron—"

"I don't care about that. I've made it this far without a patron—"

"Yes, but you'll be able to go still farther if you have one. One day it will make all the difference in your career—"

He grips her by the shoulders. "You keep on talking about me, but what about you? Would you be willing to marry me?"

She wrenches herself away, angry that they have spent so much time discussing something so ridiculous. "Why are we talking about this? It's impossible! How can you ask me to—"

She catches a faint sound outside the door and instinctively springs away from him.

Baochai enters, saying, "I'm sorry to bother you, but Granny wants to know what you did with the tribute satin that Her Highness gave us—" She breaks off, her eyes widening in shock at the sight of Yucun, even though he and Xifeng are by now several feet apart. She quickly backs out of the apartment.

Seized by panic, Xifeng runs after her, calling, "No, Baochai, wait!" She rushes out the door, but Baochai is already hurrying out of the courtyard. She goes back inside and vents her anger on Yucun. "Now see what you've done! What if she tells someone?"

"What does it matter? We have to talk, decide what to do. Don't you see we may not have many chances to see each other again?"

At his words it sinks in for the first time that this may be the last time she sees him. For an instant she remembers the wild sweetness she had felt in his arms, but she thrusts the memory away. "Go away and don't come back," she cries, fear giving violence to her words.

3

Daiyu suddenly feels that her robes are wet. She raises herself up on her elbows to look around, and discovers that she is lying on a raft in an endless, surging ocean. The raft is of thin boards, stitched together with string and vines. The waves are lapping over it and seeping through the cracks. She wants to tighten the string and vines, yet she fears that undoing any of them would simply cause the raft to disintegrate. She scans the four directions for help. There is nothing, just miles of empty, restless sea. She kneels and looks over the edge, glimpsing the limitless depths beneath her. She is overtaken by a strange dizziness, almost vertigo, as if she is perched not on a raft but on the top story of a pagoda. She squats down and clings to the edge of the raft with her eyes shut, feeling the uneasy heaving as she tries to stop herself from being sick.

She wakes up, blinking, from the nightmare. She had slept badly the night before, and slipped into a heavy slumber when she lay down after lunch. The familiar dream had come to her again, leaving her dull and dispirited. She gazes around the empty room, tempted to spend the afternoon in bed. Then she recalls Snowgoose's injunctions that she take better care of herself: faithful Snowgoose, who comes over before Granny wakes to make sure that Daiyu gets out of bed. Sighing, she puts on her shoes.

She decides to visit Baochai, and begins to walk along the shore of the lake towards Mrs. Xue's apartments. Baochai has visited her only once since her return to Rongguo, and she continues to be baffled by Baochai's coldness. Doesn't Baochai understand how lonely Daiyu is at Rongguo? Why doesn't she show any sympathy for Daiyu's loss? Could she have inadvertently offended Baochai?

She hears someone calling, and looks up to see a punt in the middle of the lake, Baoyu poling it from the stern, Huan seated in the bow. Her spirits rise at the sight of the half brothers together. She hardly sees Baoyu these days. He is busy until ten o'clock every night working with a "crammer" to prepare for the Exams. Sometimes he slips into her bedroom to see her afterwards, as he had on her first night back, but he stays for only a few minutes. She clambers down the bank to the water's edge. "What are you doing here? Aren't you supposed to be in school?"

"The schoolmaster wasn't feeling well. He let us out early, so we thought we'd take out one of the boats," Huan says, as Baoyu pilots the boat in her direction. "We wanted to ask you to come, but were afraid that you were still napping."

"I was. I just woke up," she calls back, smiling. She has come to like Huan since her return to Rongguo. He has been kind to her, asking about her father's illness and death, saying how sorry he was. He has grown taller, almost as tall as Baoyu, and no longer teases his cousins. She has heard Tanchun say that he was making good progress in his studies.

"My turn," Huan says.

"All right." Baoyu passes him the pole, and squats down to change positions. The boat rocks wildly and nearly tips as Huan scrambles to the back of the boat.

"Do you think you should come so near the shore?" Daiyu calls. "You might scrape the bottom."

"We're coming to get you," Baoyu says, as Huan thrusts the boat nearer.

"Me? Do you think it can hold three people?"

"It's supposed to hold four."

"I'm not sure I trust you not to tip me over."

"Don't worry. Huan here is a good boatman. Besides, the lake isn't supposed to be very deep."

"That's comforting."

The punt is only a few feet away now. Baoyu holds out his arm to help her aboard. She hesitates, then puts her hand out to take his. His strong grip pulls her towards him and in an instant she is standing in his arms on the bobbing boat.

"Sit down before we tip over!" Baoyu says.

Laughing, she crouches down in the bow as Baoyu sits down beside her.

"Where do you want to go?" Huan asks from behind them.

She gazes around, at the pavilion perched over the rippling waters, the lotuses in bloom, and the snowy froth of the waterfall as it bursts out of the mountain. For the first time since returning to Rongguo, she is overcome not by the bitterness of missing home, but by a sense of wonder and beauty.

4

"Who wants to sit rattling around in a carriage the whole day?" Xifeng cries gaily. "We'll have a better time here at home! Why don't we have a picnic of our own, in the pavilion in the Garden?" As Xifeng orders the servants to prepare a picnic lunch, Baochai looks at her, wondering what other secrets she hides beneath her gleaming eyes and smiling lips.

It is the Grave Sweeping Festival, when families must visit the graves of their ancestors and offer sacrifices. Granny Jia, Mrs. Xue, and all the men in the family, from Uncle Zheng down to Jia Huan, have driven out to the Jia family burial grounds in the suburbs of the Capital. Baochai, Daiyu, and the Two Springs are staying behind, because Lady Jia disapproves of unmarried girls going on excursions outside the mansion. Ping'er, too, is staying at Rongguo, as her pregnancy is too far advanced for her to sit jolting in a wagon for two and a half hours. Xifeng was to have gone with the rest, only, at the last minute, as the carriages were setting out, she changed her mind, telling Granny, with a roguish wink, that she would stay home and look after the girls.

Now the six of them are in the pavilion having lunch. The table is spread with food and wine: jellyfish salad, slivered pig's ears, dainty platters of sausages and hams. Because in honor of the holiday no fires can be lit, all the food is cold. Everyone is drinking wine, because, as Xifeng laughingly points out, the only thing worse than cold wine is cold tea. The Two Springs are joking with each other, as if the absence of the adults frees them from constraint. Baochai notices the other three seem in little mood for celebrating. Ping'er sits quietly, with her hands clasped over her enormous belly, her forehead sweaty even though it is not particularly warm. She does not touch the wine, and takes only a bite or two of food; even that seems to make her queasy. After a few joking remarks, Xifeng also has fallen silent, fidgeting nervously, a preoccupied frown on her face. She also does not eat much, drinking wine and cracking melon seeds instead.

Daiyu sits quietly on the other side of the table next to Xichun, her brows puckered in a pensive little frown. Probably the holiday makes her think of her parents, and her inability to visit and care for their distant graves. She does not eat either, looking out over the railing towards the water lilies in the middle of the lake. Baochai feels a pang of guilt for how she has been treating Daiyu. She still has not found the courage to tell Daiyu of her betrothal. She knows her jealousy is distorting her behavior, and that Daiyu is hurt and baffled by this. She resolves to try to put aside her resentment. She will find some way to make a gesture to Daiyu to show that she harbors no ill feeling towards her.

Xifeng rouses herself to ask Xichun to pass the wine. As she takes the kettle, she licks a finger and holds it up in the air. "I thought we would fly kites, but I'm afraid there isn't any wind."

"Kites?" Baochai says. "Oh, yes!" She had almost forgotten the custom of flying kites on Grave Sweeping Day.

"Maybe the wind will pick up in the afternoon," Xichun says.

Tanchun says, "I hope so. I can't remember the last time we flew kites."

"Me neither," says Xichun. "It rained last year, so we didn't do it then."

Baochai notices Snowgoose coming down the nine-angled bridge. When the maid enters the pavilion, one look at her face tells Baochai that something is wrong.

"What is it?" The sharpness in Xifeng's voice makes the others fall silent.

Snowgoose says, "Silver's mother has come to see Lady Jia. Since Lady Jia is not here, I thought I would carry her message to you."

"What is the message?"

"She says that Silver has killed herself, and she has come to ask Lady Jia for some money for the funeral expenses and some clothing for the burial." Snowgoose's eyes are lowered, but Baochai hears a quiver in her voice. She remembers that Snowgoose and Silver had served Lady Jia together for many years.

"Killed herself!" Xifeng exclaims. "What on earth for?"

"Her mother says that she had just been moping around ever since Lady Jia dismissed her back in the autumn, and then this morning they couldn't find her. When someone went to draw water from the well, something caught on the rope. They drew it up, and it was Silver's body."

"Good God!" Xifeng is shocked into silence.

A chill of foreboding sweeps over Baochai, but she says, with an air of certainty she does not feel, "Surely there's no reason to suppose that she killed herself. Probably she was fooling around near the well, and accidentally slipped and fell in."

"Yes, I suppose that makes more sense," Xifeng says slowly.

Snowgoose looks at Baochai, and she sees that Snowgoose's eyes are red. "I am only telling you what Silver's mother told me. She says that all Silver did since her dismissal was sit around and cry."

"Then it was foolish of her to take it so much to heart," Baochai says. Inside, she tries to push away the thought that Baoyu is in some way responsible. She does not know what happened between him and Silver; she assumes it was something more than the casual kiss he had once almost given her, and that

Silver was willing. Yet such a careless act had produced so terrible a result. It occurs to her that he brings only misfortune to the girls who fall in love with him. The thought frightens her, but she reminds herself that Silver was punished for illicit behavior, while she herself will be Baoyu's wife.

"What shall I do about Silver's mother?" Snowgoose asks Xifeng.

"Give her fifty *taels*."

"What about the clothes for the burial?"

Xifeng hesitates. "I would like to give her a new outfit, but we don't have anything made up. The only one of you who has gotten new clothes lately is Daiyu ... "

She looks questioningly at Daiyu. Baochai sees the horror on Daiyu's face that her clothes are to be used for so inauspicious a purpose, so she says quickly, "I have some new outfits I have never worn. Why don't you use those?"

"Aren't you superstitious?" Xifeng asks.

"You know I have never believed in that sort of thing." It occurs to her how upset Granny Jia and Baoyu will be at the news. "The more important question, I suppose, is whether or not to tell Lady Jia about any of this when she comes home." As usual, she does not allow Baoyu's name to pass her lips.

Xifeng looks at her, surprised. "Don't you think we should tell her?"

In turn, Baochai is surprised that it has not occurred to Xifeng to keep the news a secret. "Why should we? It would only upset her, and she might blame herself for dismissing Silver."

"Do you really think we can keep it from her?"

"Why not? If none of us mentions it, no one else will ever know."

Xifeng thinks a moment, frowning. "I suppose you're right." She looks at the other girls. "Did you hear that, all of you? No one is to say a word of this to Granny. Snowgoose, you won't say a word either."

"No, Mrs. Lian," Snowgoose agrees, but Baochai thinks that the carefully expressionless look on her face hides disapproval.

After Snowgoose goes, there is a long silence.

"Poor Silver," Tanchun says at last.

Xifeng gives a harsh laugh. "Do you think so? I think she was saved a lot of trouble by dying young!"

Baochai looks at her. "What on earth do you mean?"

"Do you think her fate was really worse than most women's?" Xifeng's voice and look are challenging.

This time it is Tanchun who asks, frowning, "Why, what do you mean?"

"Just what I said," Xifeng answers. "Do you think her fate is any worse than most women's?" The wine or the shock of Silver's death seems to have loosened Xifeng's tongue. Her gay smile is gone. Without it, there are hard lines at the corners of her mouth. "A woman doesn't have any choices in life. Even from a good family like ours, she has to marry whomever her parents choose for her. If, by a stroke of luck, he is a decent fellow, then she might be fortunate. But if he is a bad man, as is far more likely, she will suffer." Xifeng tosses off another cupful of wine. "How much more so in a poor family like Silver's, where girls are usually sold off as maids and concubines to the highest bidders?"

Xichun looks shocked and a little scared. "But don't Granny and Uncle have our best interests at heart? Can't we trust them to make us good matches?"

"They might wish to, but what can they really know of a man's character?"

"They can choose someone from a good family," Tanchun says. "That way, they'll know he's been properly raised."

Xifeng gives another harsh laugh. "There's no way of really

knowing. Think of Lian and Zhu. They were from the same family, first cousins who grew up together, but they couldn't have been more different. Look at Jingui. The Xias are a perfectly respectable family—" Xifeng sees Baochai's face, and then shuts her mouth. She resumes after a moment. "But my point is, a woman has no choice. What is she going to do? Go out and find someone to marry herself? What can she do but accept what her parents choose for her, good or bad?"

"Yes, I think Xifeng is right," Daiyu speaks up. "A girl has no choice, over anything in her life. If her parents choose to let her learn a few characters, she may be lucky enough to be able to read and educate herself. But she can't do anything with that education."

Xifeng nods. "We've all been lucky that our parents decided not to leave us in total ignorance—but how often have we all heard that old saying: *'A virtuous woman is an uneducated woman'*?"

The pessimism of Xifeng and Daiyu's vision disturbs Baochai. Although she dislikes debates or arguments of any kind, and had not meant to join in the conversation, she says reprovingly, "You are wrong to say that a woman cannot do anything with her education. She can use it to teach her children and run her household. Surely that's the best use of a woman's education."

"But a woman can't take the Exams," Daiyu says. "Or even make a living as a teacher."

"She doesn't need to," Baochai says.

"But then," Daiyu points out, "because she cannot support herself, she has no choice but to marry when someone else chooses for her, good or bad. Xifeng is right. Women have no choices at all."

For some reason, Baochai feels a need to refute this argument. Daiyu and Xifeng's insistence that women have no choices makes her feel that by doing her duty, she is somehow trapped and helpless; whereas she has always thought that in doing her duty, she would find contentment and freedom. "Perhaps you think you are being very insightful and profound," she says, forcing a laugh. "But actually, your vision is rather narrow. What about a man? If he is born in a poor family, he has to do hard labor for a living. In a good family, then he studies for the Exams. What choice does he have, either?

"Perhaps it doesn't make sense to talk about choices," she continues. "Perhaps it'd be wiser to say that men and women have different responsibilities and duties."

Xifeng gives a scornful snort, pouring herself another cup of wine. "Let's see how you feel about it after you are married."

Baochai feels her face growing hot, believing that Xifeng is not making a general statement, but is referring to her betrothal.

Xichun pipes up, "There is one choice that everyone can make. Each person can choose to become a nun or a monk, and to renounce the 'red dust.'"

Xifeng looks irritated. "I don't understand you—always dreaming about becoming a nun, as if that would solve any problems."

"Don't you know that all the problems that human beings suffer are caused by attachment to the material world? If only we could give up our attachments—"

"Spare us the sermon," Xifeng interrupts.

Xichun, abashed, falls silent.

After a little while, Tanchun says, gazing around the pavilion, "When we're older and married and have children of our own, how do you think we'll look back on the time we've spent here?" She looks at the others. "Do you suppose we'll think this was the happiest time of our lives?"

"There's not a doubt of it." Xifeng laughs unpleasantly. Daiyu turns away, but not before Baochai sees tears glistening on her cheeks.

Baochai looks around at the Garden where she has spent so much of her girlhood: at the moss-green mountain, the tangle of roses over the pergola, the willow and *wutong* trees fringing the far shore. If she carries any nostalgia, it is for her childhood in Nanjing, when her father was still alive. But, yes, with the exception of her worries over Pan, her time at Rongguo has been happy, and she believes that she will look back on it with fondness.

Out of the corner of her eye, she notices a napkin hung over the railing begin to flutter. "Look, the wind is picking up. Shall we send for our kites?"

Everyone springs up, calling to the maids to fetch their kites, eager, it seems, to put an end to the painful conversation. Only Daiyu does not move, still sitting on her stool looking out at the water. She does not have a kite, Baochai knows, so she sends a maid to fetch two of hers.

The maid reappears with the two kites, a many-jointed centipede and a butterfly with long streamers. Baochai takes the kites to Daiyu. Everyone else has already gone to the bank to launch their kites. "Which one do you want?" she asks.

Daiyu shakes her head, forcing a smile, but does not rise from her seat. "No, thank you, Baochai. That's kind of you, but I don't feel like it."

There is a squeal from Tanchun as the wind snatches the kite from her hands and flings it high into the air.

"No, I insist," Baochai says. "It's good luck to fly kites, today of all days." She pulls Daiyu to her feet. "You fly the butterfly," she says. "And when it's high in the air, we'll cut the string, and send away your bad luck and sadness."

Now there are several kites high in the air above the lake, a scarlet bat, and a "beautiful lady." Even Ping'er, sitting on a stool that someone has brought for her, is holding the string of a crab-shaped kite.

Daiyu nods. Together, they walk down the bridge to the bank. Baochai throws the butterfly into the air, while Daiyu holds the spool of string. Instead of rising in the breeze, however, the butterfly loops crazily a few times before crashing to the ground.

They retrieve it, and Daiyu rewinds the string.

"Perhaps it's a little top-heavy," Daiyu says. "I'll try running with it."

This time, as Baochai tosses it up as hard as she can, Daiyu sets off running down the path beside the lake. It stays aloft as long as she is running full speed, but plummets from the air the moment that she slows. Again and again, the two of them try to launch the kite, even retying the strings to correct the balance. Daiyu runs and runs, until her usually pale cheeks are suffused with color. Still, the kite refuses to fly.

5

After the kite flying, Xifeng walks back from the lake to her own apartments. She feels obliged to make a pretense of walking with Ping'er, but the sight of Ping'er waddling along so irritates her that she cannot watch, and walks ahead. Then, after she has gone fifteen paces or so, she feels guilty and stops to let Ping'er catch up, listening to Ping'er's noisy puffing behind her. After Ping'er catches up, Xifeng walks ahead again. So it continues until they are about halfway to the apartments, when Xifeng notices that Ping'er has fallen silent. She turns to see Ping'er sink to her knees.

"What is it?" She hurries back and stoops beside Ping'er.

Ping'er's hand presses her side. She gives hoarse, gasping breaths. "I think—the baby's coming."

Even though Xifeng has been anticipating this moment for months, and had stayed home for fear that Ping'er would give birth while she was gone, she feels a rush of excitement. "Can you walk?"

Ping'er does not answer. She grasps Xifeng's hands, so hard that Xifeng almost cries out. For about the time it takes to count to thirty, Ping'er holds on, her lips pulled back from her teeth, her face contorted unrecognizably into an animal expression of pain. Then she relaxes, beginning to breathe again. Xifeng pulls her hand away and massages it.

"It's better now," Ping'er gasps.

"We'd better get back to the apartment."

Xifeng wedges her shoulder under Ping'er's armpit, and somehow gets Ping'er to her feet. Supporting what feels like

most of Ping'er's weight, she staggers forward. Once, when
they were children, the two of them had run away to the
servants' quarters behind the Wang mansion. She still remembers the rabbit warren of alleys, the people bathing their
babies and brushing their teeth on their doorsteps, dumping
the water into a ditch of greenish-brown sludge that snaked
along the main avenue. The two of them had run along hand
in hand, laughing and shouting from sheer excitement. But
then Ping'er had twisted her ankle on a loose stone, and Xifeng
had had to half carry, half support her home, just as she is doing
now.

They have almost made it to the apartment by the next contraction. Xifeng tries to detach Ping'er's hands. "Stay here. I'll
get help."

"Don't leave me."

Xifeng tries to tug away. "I have to send for the midwife." She
is terrified by the thought that Ping'er might give birth before
the midwife comes, with only her, Xifeng, in attendance.

"Help me." Ping'er turns pleading eyes to Xifeng.

"What can I do?"

Ping'er does not answer, crushing Xifeng's fingers again, lost
in the throes of another contraction.

When this one ends, Xifeng half drags her across the courtyard, shouting frantically for Autumn. She has pulled Ping'er
onto the *kang* in her own bedroom when Autumn shows up.

"Send for Old Woman Ma," she barks, scrambling to get pillows and blankets to prop Ping'er up. For once Autumn does
not dawdle and rushes out of the room.

By the time the midwife arrives, Xifeng has, between contractions, helped Ping'er undress, stoked up the fire, and set a
pot of water to boil. She is leaning over Ping'er on the *kang*,
wiping her brow with a wet towel. Already, she can hardly move
her hand after the way that Ping'er had gripped it during the

contractions. When Old Woman Ma walks in, Xifeng yells at her to hurry and wash her hands, believing that, with contractions so intense, the birth is minutes away.

After the midwife examines Ping'er, she laughs and says that the baby is still a long way from coming. "It is her first time, don't forget," she says, rolling her sleeves back down. "You'd be surprised at how long these first births can take."

"How long do you think it will be?"

Old Woman Ma tilts her head consideringly. "I would be surprised if the baby came before midnight."

"That's more than eight hours!"

"It might not even be here by then."

Given that it will be so long and that she will have to stay up late, Xifeng decides to lie down in the front room to rest. As she moves towards the doorway, Ping'er says, "Don't leave me."

"You don't have to worry now. The midwife is here."

Yet, as another contraction begins, Ping'er reaches out her hands piteously to Xifeng. Xifeng climbs back on the *kang* to let Ping'er hold on to her. Again, Ping'er crushes her hands mercilessly, seemingly aware of nothing but her own pain.

"That won't do," the midwife says, noticing Xifeng wincing. "If you go on like that you won't even be able to hold a pair of chopsticks." She knots and twists an old sheet, loops the middle around the leg of a table, ties the ends, and gives the big knot to Ping'er to hold. The next contraction, Ping'er pounces on and kneads and tears at the knotted sheet like a jungle cat.

At the end of the contraction, Ping'er turns bloodshot eyes to Xifeng. "Can't you stay with me?"

"I was just going to rest a little. I'll come back later. I can call Autumn to stay with you now."

Ping'er shakes her head against the pillow, already darkened with sweat. "I don't want Autumn. Can't you stay?"

Sighing audibly, Xifeng climbs back onto the *kang*. Though she acts as if she is being put upon, she feels a strange satisfaction that in Ping'er's hour of need, she, Xifeng, is still indispensable. She tells herself that it would serve Ping'er right if she were to leave, yet she feels little inclination to go.

Her satisfaction only increases when Lian and the others arrive back from the burial grounds near dinnertime. Lian seems put off by the sight of Ping'er's swollen body half-naked under the soaking sheet. He pats her hand awkwardly, and makes an excuse to leave the room before Ping'er has had even one contraction. Now Ping'er can see for herself how much Lian is to be depended on, Xifeng thinks, but Ping'er, asking Xifeng for a drink of water, hardly seems to notice his departure.

The hours drag by, broken only by Autumn and Snowgoose coming in to ask about the progress of the labor. Xifeng has left the room only once, at about ten o'clock, to go to the bathroom and to send a message to the wet nurse to wait in the other bedroom. Mercifully, Ping'er falls into an uneasy doze about an hour after midnight. Xifeng lies down beside her on the *kang* and falls asleep immediately. She awakens to the sound of Ping'er moaning. Ping'er's eyes are shut, but she is clearly awake. She looks terrible, with huge bluish hollows under her eyes, her bottom lip bloody and torn.

Watching Ping'er, she senses a change in the rhythm of the contractions. They come more frequently, longer and more intense than before. Ping'er begins to whimper and groan out loud. Xifeng sees beads of sweat pop out on her upper lip. When Ping'er sees Xifeng is awake, she gasps, "I can't bear it any longer."

She takes Ping'er's hand. Ping'er's fingers, cold and clammy, cling to hers.

"I think it's almost over," she says. She scrambles off the *kang* to where the midwife is dozing near the stove, and shakes the old woman by the shoulder. "Don't you think it's almost time now?"

Old Woman Ma shakes herself awake, startled. Rubbing her eyes, she goes to Ping'er and stoops to examine her beneath the sheet. "You're all the way open. Push!"

Time seems to take on a different rhythm. Ping'er strains as if trying to shift some crushing weight. Her face is tomato red, the veins in her temples bulging darkly. Old Woman Ma kneels on the *kang* pressing Ping'er's knees wide apart. She alternately shouts at Ping'er to push and allows her to catch her breath for a few seconds, before beginning to shout again. Xifeng leans over, expecting to see the baby's head emerging, but does not see anything different from before. Ping'er strains and strains, almost crying, but it doesn't seem to do any good.

Suddenly Old Woman Ma shouts. Xifeng sees a round blackish circle about the size of a mushroom cap between the reddish folds.

"Push! Push! Push!" Old Woman Ma shouts.

The circle gets larger, about the size of a goose egg. Then, quite suddenly, the whole head is through, and Old Woman Ma kneels there guiding the tiny slime-covered shoulders and elbows out of Ping'er's body, until the whole baby lies there in her hands, as Ping'er moans and shudders with pain.

Xifeng leans over and sees there is no penis between the skinny, feebly twitching legs. She can hardly believe it is a girl after all these months of suspense. Exhausted, she stumbles to a chair. She had been possessed by a bitter certainty that the baby would be a boy, who would permanently cement Ping'er's place in Lian's affections and in the household.

"It's all right," the midwife says, pressing Ping'er back down onto the *kang*. "You can rest now."

Ping'er lifts her head. "Is it a boy?"

"No. It's a nice little *guixiu*." Old Woman Ma uses the

euphemistic term "beauty of the Inner Chambers," instead of the word "girl."

"Oh. Lian was so hoping for a boy," Ping'er says weakly, letting herself fall back with a little sigh. She opens her eyes and reaches out her arms. "Can I hold her?"

"Just a minute." Old Woman Ma has cut the cord and is carrying the baby to a basin near the stove. It is an ugly thing, its skin blotchy, its head tapered to a blunt point. Xifeng feels a twinge of pity for the helpless creature, born into the world only to suffer.

"Why isn't she crying?" Ping'er asks from the *kang*.

"Sometimes they swallow a lot of water during labor, especially during a long labor like yours. Let me dry her off, and I'll slap her back—we'll see if she doesn't cry then!"

She takes the baby over her knees and slaps her on the back, so sharply that Xifeng winces. The baby whimpers and squirms a little. After a few more blows the baby begins to cry weakly.

"Is there something wrong with her lungs?" Xifeng says, at the same moment the midwife asks, "What are you going to call her?"

Ping'er says, "Lian will have to go to an astrologer to choose something lucky."

"Of course I meant a 'milk' name," Old Woman Ma says, putting the baby in a diaper. "Surely you can choose that yourself."

"I suppose you're right. I think I'll call her 'Qiaojie.'" Ping'er reaches out her arms. "Let me hold her now."

Old Woman Ma hands Ping'er the baby. Ping'er lies awkwardly with the infant across her breast. She notices Xifeng standing there. "Help me up, will you?"

Xifeng climbs onto the *kang* and helps prop Ping'er into a sitting position.

"Thanks." Ping'er gazes down at the baby. "Isn't she beautiful?"

Xifeng kneels next to Ping'er. Although she would hardly call her beautiful, the baby looks more presentable now that she is cleaned up and her skinny monkey limbs are covered. She bends over and looks at the puffy face with its scattering of pimples. Gingerly, she touches one tiny hand. To her surprise, the baby opens her hand and holds on to her finger. Her skin is warm and moist, her grip surprisingly strong.

Ping'er laughs. "Oho! Qiaojie! Do you know your Auntie Xifeng?'"

Xifeng tugs her finger gently, as Qiaojie still maintains her grip. She is bewildered by Ping'er's behavior, as if now, after the course of the labor, they have suddenly become as close as before. Ping'er rocks Qiaojie gently back and forth, burying her lips in the soft, sparse hair. "Oh, she smells good." She draws Qiaojie's feet from the blanket, fingering the toes. She looks up. "Do you want to hold her?"

Xifeng hesitates, then puts her arms out to take Qiaojie. The infant is unexpectedly light. She hardly knows what to do with it. She moves her arms back and forth as Ping'er had done, calling, "Qiaojie! Qiaojie!"

The baby's eyes pop open, first one, and then the other. They are coal black, and full of light, like Baoyu's.

Ping'er laughs delightedly. "Look! You already know your auntie!"

Xifeng cannot help laughing. Her eyes fill with tears. Before she can wipe them, one of them falls on the baby's nose, and she starts to whimper again.

"You crying? I don't believe it," Ping'er says, with her old playfulness.

The wet nurse enters the room, rubbing the sleep from her eyes. Probably she has heard the baby cry. She approaches the *kang*. "Should I take the baby now?"

"Who's that?" Ping'er says in surprise, as Xifeng clambers off the *kang* with the baby.

Suddenly Ping'er understands. She cries out hoarsely and claws herself to a sitting position. "No! Jiejie, no!"

At the name "Jiejie," Xifeng stops. "Older Sister" is the name Ping'er had always called her when they were children. Once they grew up and came to Rongguo, Ping'er had taken to calling her "Mistress," as the other servants did. Half suspecting Ping'er of trying to manipulate her, Xifeng turns and looks at her. On Ping'er's drawn face, dawning realization struggles with disbelief. There is shock, uncertainty, but not yet anger or accusation. Like a person who has just been bitten by a favorite dog, Ping'er's first impulse, before the realization has sunk in, is to soothe and pet the creature with her torn hand. Xifeng had thought that the bond between her and Ping'er was long broken; she had nothing to lose. Looking at Ping'er now, she understands that all the bad blood of the past months counts for nothing. The old love is still there. She has only to step back into her old place.

The wet nurse is barely a pace away. If Xifeng hands her the baby, she can give back every ounce of humiliation and pain that Lian and Ping'er have inflicted on her. Instead she turns and thrusts the baby back into Ping'er's arms. Ping'er bursts into tears, but Xifeng turns away dry-eyed. How will she survive in this world if she can't harden her heart?

6

Daiyu sits up waiting for Baoyu. He has not come for three or four days, so she hopes he will visit tonight. When he still has not come by eleven, she puts aside the book of poems she is reading and, disappointed, blows out the lamp and climbs into bed. She falls asleep almost immediately, but at some point she half wakes and finds him sitting beside her in the darkness.

"You came," she murmurs. "Why are you so late?"

"I was at a party at the Prince of Beijing's and they started to talk about the political situation." He shifts so that he is sitting only a few inches from her head with his knees clasped to his chest.

"What did they say?"

"His Highness's health is getting worse quickly, but he still hasn't called Prince Yinti back from the Tibetan front."

"What does that mean?" Hearing the excitement in his voice, she pushes herself up onto her elbow.

"Well, if Prince Yinti isn't back by the time His Highness departs from this world, more than one Prince may try to seize the throne."

She sits up, rubbing her eyes. "Why doesn't His Highness just appoint Prince Yinti as Heir Apparent?"

"No one knows why. I can't understand why he didn't do it seven or eight years ago, when he demoted Prince Yinreng. Surely he knows that if the Princes end up fighting over the throne, there may be bloodshed, or, Heaven forbid, civil war . . ."

"Really?" She peers at him in the darkness, suddenly a little scared.

"It's possible. I really don't know."

"Do you think it will affect us?" Here, in the Inner Quarters, she feels so insulated from the outside world that it is hard for her to imagine the political situation making any difference in their day-to-day life.

He is silent for much longer than she expects. At last, after more than a minute, he shakes his head. "I don't think so. My father doesn't involve himself in this sort of thing. He doesn't belong to any faction, and doesn't have close ties to any of the Imperial Princes."

She senses that he is still uneasy. "Then what is it?"

"I just don't know what will happen."

He falls silent. She can make out his profile in the faint moonlight coming through the window and sees that he is gazing somberly before him. Wanting to comfort him, she reaches out and takes his hand. He interlaces his fingers with hers and gives them a gentle squeeze. "Never mind. I didn't mean to scare you." He does not release her hand right away, but draws it up to his lips, warm and slightly bristly against her skin. It is the first time that he has touched her like this since she had left for Suzhou months ago, and she feels a strange crawling sensation on the back of her neck, at once pleasurable and disquieting. He lets go of her hand. "I shouldn't have woken you. You'll be tired tomorrow." He moves towards the window.

Suddenly she feels bereft. "Aren't you going to kiss me?" she blurts out. At her own words she feels her face go hot with embarrassment. She hears him laughing softly.

Suddenly he is on the *kang* beside her again. His arms go around her, catching her to him. He kisses her once, lingeringly, on the lips, and then he is gone.

At first Xifeng tries to sleep through the whimpers from beside her on the *kang*. She turns away, pulling a pillow over her head to muffle the noise, and manages to fall asleep again. Eventually, the sound of Qiaojie's full-blown wailing penetrates her ears. She turns back over and sees Qiaojie writhing and red-faced, her hands balled into tiny fists. It is six o'clock, an hour before breakfast. Ping'er, on the other side of Qiaojie, is sprawled fast asleep, her tunic still open from the last time she nursed the baby.

Xifeng drags on a robe and stumbles out into the courtyard with Qiaojie so Ping'er can sleep. As soon as she is picked up, Qiaojie's piercing wail quiets to a soft whimper. Xifeng walks back and forth, jiggling her knees to produce the little bounce that Qiaojie seems to find soporific. She glances across the courtyard at the rooms where Lian has slept alone since the baby's birth. At least she assumes that he sleeps alone, although she has recently begun to suspect that Autumn shares his bed. She looks back down at Qiaojie's half-open mouth and fluttering eyelids. Ping'er insists that Qiaojie will be pretty when she grows up, but Xifeng does not see any evidence of this. However, she is forced to admit that Qiaojie is cute, with her crescent-moon-shaped eyebrows, and snub nose with its tiny nostrils. Now her eyes are shut and her breathing is peaceful and even. With a sigh of relief, Xifeng eases herself into a sitting position on the front steps. She rests there enjoying the rare moment of peace, feeling an unexpected happiness. Even though the baby is not her own, Qiaojie, with her diapers and burps, her need to be cuddled and bathed, has pulled Xifeng away from the dry world of ledgers and tallies. She feels the light, warm bundle on her lap, alive with breath. Without opening her eyes, she draws one of Qioajie's hands from the swaddling clothes. As always she is surprised by the velvety tenderness of Qiaojie's skin. Her fingers touch the tiny dimples at every knuckle, the larger crease around the wrist.

She sits there resting with her eyes closed until Qiaojie begins to whimper again. She can tell by the sun that it is almost time for her to prepare to go to Lady Jia's. She goes back into the apartment and lays Qiaojie beside Ping'er. "I'm sorry to wake you. I think she's hungry again."

"Thank you for taking her," Ping'er murmurs. Half asleep, she pulls Qiaojie towards her breast, curving her arm around the baby.

"How did she sleep last night?"

"Much better. She nursed only three times. I think she's getting more milk."

Xifeng looks down at Qiaojie, the corners of her mouth puckering in a rhythmic sucking. The only thing that has worried her is that Qiaojie is not growing as robust and vigorous as she should be. Sometimes it even strikes her that there is a languor about Qiaojie, strange in an infant. As she prepares to serve breakfast at Lady Jia's apartments, she tells herself that as Qiaojie eats more, she will sleep better, and grow more lively.

Her happy mood lasts until the end of breakfast. As Uncle Zheng rises from the table, he says, "I meant to ask you, Lian, have you seen Jia Yucun lately?"

She stops in the middle of stacking teacups to listen.

Lian shrugs. "No. Why?"

"He used to come over all the time, but he hasn't come for quite a while. I was wondering whether he was ill or something."

"Not that I know of. Maybe now that he's Under-Secretary to the President of the Board of War, he's too busy to associate with us."

She stoops down before the *tansu* so no one will see her expression. Sometimes in a spare moment, she has found herself wondering what Yucun is doing. She has even wondered whether it would be possible to meet him somewhere outside of the mansion, as he had suggested, but fears that he would only importune her to see him again. Now that she is so happily absorbed in caring for Qiaojie with Ping'er, she is no longer willing to take such risks. Her feeling for him is like a nicked finger, she tells herself. It hurts only when it's bumped.

Daiyu walks along the shore of the lake, trying to shake off the restlessness that has filled her since Baoyu's visit the night before. She passes beneath the pergola, with its twining clumps of crimson and white roses, towards the farther end of the lake. For three months, caught up in grief for her father, she has been content not to question the nature of Baoyu's visits, but simply to accept the comfort of his presence. Last night's kiss, however, makes her think of how he had talked of marrying her the night before she left for Suzhou. She had taken it as a joke, and had not allowed herself to dwell on it. But since last night, she has been filled with joyous expectation—yet she cannot dispel a competing sense of foreboding. She has no dowry, no family, and Lady Jia dislikes her so much. She remembers how angry Lady Jia had been at her mother, for marrying her father instead of General Xue. Why would she be any more lenient with Baoyu?

Following the path beneath the grove of spotted bamboo, she almost stumbles upon Jia Huan, stooping by the water's edge. "What are you doing?"

He shows her how he is balancing pebbles on bamboo leaves and pushing them out onto the lake to see if they will float. "I finished my homework early today."

"How are your studies going?" She stoops down beside him to pick up a bamboo leaf too.

"Better. Once, after I'd made a fool of myself in class, Baoyu offered to help me with anything I didn't understand. Since then, I go to him when I have trouble. I have to admit, sometimes he makes things clearer than the schoolmaster."

Her heart swells with pride. "I'm so glad. You see, he wants to help you." In her excitement, she fumbles a little with the flat black pebble that she is trying to balance on her leaf.

"I suppose so," Jia Huan concedes. "He's still a show-off."

"He is not."

"Yes, he is. He's always trying to charm everyone into liking him."

"That's not true."

He looks intently at her. Nervous that her face somehow betrays her, she looks away and stoops to pick up another rock.

"You're in love with him, aren't you?"

"Don't be ridiculous." She feels herself blushing, but manages to force a laugh.

"Yes, you are. I can see it in your face."

"You're dreaming!"

"Now that I think of it, I can see it in the way that you look at him. All the girls fall in love with him." He speaks jeeringly, as if his old jealousy of Baoyu has flared up. "What has he been saying to you, to make you blush like that? But don't take anything he says seriously, you know. He flirts with all the girls."

"That isn't true!"

Again he stares at her, and then gives a short laugh. "Well, whatever he's been promising you, it won't happen. They would never let him marry you. Besides"—his face is alive with malice—"he's already betrothed."

"What do you mean?" She is too shocked to feign indifference.

"He's going to marry Baochai."

"Baochai!" She takes refuge in incredulity. "Why have I never heard anything about it—"

"Granny arranged it all after you went back south. They're keeping it secret."

"Then how do you know?"

"My father told my mother, and she told me."

She cannot speak. It all makes sense now: why Baochai moved in with her mother and no longer has meals with the rest of the household. But why hasn't Baochai simply told her? She can no longer convince herself that Jia Huan is lying or mistaken. "Does Baoyu know?"

"I would think so."

She turns and runs down the path towards her own apartments, so Huan will not see her tears. It makes perfect sense: gold and jade, the perfect pair. She could never hope to penetrate their charmed circle of wealth and power. Why has Baoyu deceived her? Why has he taken advantage of her vulnerability after her father's death to make her love him? How could she have imagined that she could be with him? She is a nobody, a poor relation living on charity, and Granny Jia will never let her forget it.

The throne room is so tightly packed with officials that it takes Jia Zheng fifteen minutes to make it to the door. Everyone is buzzing with His Highness's latest edict, recalling Prince Yinti from the front. Jia Zheng squeezes through the crowded doorway and makes his way down the steps, eager to get back to his Ministry to talk over the announcement with his colleagues. At the bottom of the stairs, he catches sight of Jia Yucun and hurries over to say hello. Only then does he see that Yucun is deep in conversation with "Daddy Xia," the head eunuch in the

Forbidden City. The Eunuch Chamberlain is leaning so close to Yucun that his pendulous lips almost touch the young man's ear.

"Ah, Lord Jia," Daddy Xia says, breaking off. "I never run into you these days." In the old days, when the Imperial Concubine was still alive, Jia Zheng had often had dealings with the eunuch. "How is your esteemed mother?"

Barely waiting for Jia Zheng's reply, however, the Eunuch Chamberlain moves away, nodding at Yucun over his shoulder. "We will talk another time."

Left alone with his young relative, Jia Zheng cannot help gloating over the fact that his own predictions about the succession are about to come true. "So," he says, tucking his hand into Yucun's elbow as the two of them are pushed towards the main gate. "Prince Yinti will probably be back in the Capital in six or seven weeks."

"Yes."

"And then His Majesty will name him Heir Apparent."

Jia Yucun says nothing.

Jia Zheng notices that the young man does not look well. His color is bad, and he has lost weight. "Have you been sick? I haven't seen you in so long."

"No, no."

Then, as Jia Zheng continues to stare at him with a concerned face, he adds, "I'm just getting over a bout of stomach flu, that's all."

"You should eat rice porridge for a day or two until your system is cleaned out." Jia Zheng squeezes the young man's arm. "Are you free now? Why don't you come back to Rongguo with me and have dinner?"

"I'm sorry." Yucun shakes his head, and tries to smile. "I can't come now. I just saw Minister Nian in the crowd, and I want to ask him about a petition I am drafting."

"Are you sure you are all right?"

"Yes, I'm fine."

"Then you'll come another time?" Jia Zheng wonders whether Yucun, having found other senior officials to mentor him, no longer needs his help.

"Yes, another time," Yucun agrees, already backing away.

7

When Daiyu hears the tapping on her bolted window, she lies still, resolutely not moving or making a sound. Baoyu taps again. Then comes his voice, "Daiyu! Daiyu!"

She does not answer. He calls louder, starting to rattle the window in its frame.

Finally, he starts to shout, "What's wrong? Are you sick?"

After a minute of this she jumps out of bed and rushes to the window, unable to keep her resolve. "For goodness' sake, will you be quiet? Someone will hear you."

"Why won't you open the window?"

"Go away. I don't want to speak to you."

"Why not?"

"I said, 'Go away'!"

"Not until you tell me what's wrong."

She walks back to her bed and climbs under the covers.

"Daiyu! Daiyu! Will you please open the window so we can at least talk?"

She pulls the covers over her head.

"If you don't open the window, I'll just break it."

She still does not move.

"All right. Have it your way."

She hears a crashing sound as he tries to knock the window out of its frame. She rushes to the window and opens it. "Stop it!"

The moment she opens the window, he sticks his head through so she can no longer close it. "What's the matter?"

She does not answer.

He climbs quickly inside and shuts the window. "Tell me."

Now that he is actually standing in front of her, the picture of bewildered innocence, instead of being coolly sarcastic, as she had intended, she blurts out, her voice shaking with anger, "Why didn't you tell me you were betrothed to Baochai?"

He stands silent and motionless before her. She tries to see his face, but all she can make out is the pale gleam of his forehead and nose in the moonlight.

"So you've heard about that," he says at last.

"Yes. Huan told me." She crosses her arms over her chest and climbs back into bed, turning her back towards him.

There is a long silence. She can sense him standing there awkwardly near the window. She hears him approaching the bed. She pulls the covers protectively about herself as he sits down on the *kang* next to her. She thinks about telling him to get off, but decides that it is more dignified to preserve her silence.

"I should have told you."

She does not answer.

After another pause, he says, "At first I wasn't sure, you know. No one actually said anything to me. But I sensed it, from the way Baochai was acting."

When he says the name Baochai, she is possessed by an unreasoning flame of jealousy, and huddles more tightly into herself.

"I don't want to marry her. I've been thinking of a way to get out of the betrothal."

She lies there without moving. Then she says over her shoulder, as nastily as she can, "I don't know why you wouldn't want to marry her. She's rich, and well connected, and well behaved. You'll make a lovely couple, the perfect *caizijiaren*, 'beauty and scholar,' like in all the romances—"

He bends over her and takes her ungently by the shoulders, turning her to face him. "Why are you doing this, Dai? Don't you know how I feel about you?"

"No, I don't," she says, turning her face away. "How would I know anything? You've been betrothed for all these months and I haven't known it!"

"I don't want to marry her. I was just figuring out how to get out of the match—"

"Well, and what did you figure out?" She is pleased at how sardonic her voice sounds.

"It's not so simple. I was trying to figure out whether you cared for me—"

"But why didn't you tell me? Why did you leave me in the dark?" She wrenches herself so violently out of his grip that her shoulders hurt.

"How could I tell you? You would have been angry and wanted nothing to do with me—"

He tries to hold on to her again, but she shoves his hands away. "Don't try to defend yourself. I should have listened to all those rumors about you."

"What rumors?"

"About Silver." She hurls the name at him.

He stares at her. "What about Silver? I told you what happened."

"No, you didn't. You never told me anything! You were vague and mysterious, just like you are about everything! She killed herself, did you know that? She killed herself and it was your fault!"

She hears his sharp intake of breath. "What do you mean?"

"Her mother came and said she had thrown herself in the well."

"When?"

"More than two months ago, at the Grave Sweeping Festival. Your precious Baochai told everyone not to tell. She didn't want you to be upset by what you'd done."

He is silent. Instead of defending himself, he buries his face in his hands. "How could it have gone so far?" he says. She can tell from his voice that he is crying. "It was nothing, but Granny got so angry. How could it have gone so far?"

She is slightly mollified by his tears but still she challenges him. "What do you mean, it was nothing?"

He lifts up his face from his hands, and she can see the gleam of tears on his cheeks. "My father assumed that I raped her. All I did was kiss her, and she was perfectly willing! Then Granny got angry and dismissed her. That's all that happened, though Heaven knows I blamed myself afterwards for getting her in such terrible trouble."

She had never really believed that he was capable of forcing himself on anyone, but the phrase that he uses cuts her to the quick. "Is that what you're going to say about me, that all you did was kiss me?"

"You think this is the same as Silver?"

"What am I supposed to think, when you didn't even tell me about your betrothal—"

"I was just flirting with Silver—"

"Just like you flirted with me!"

"I haven't been flirting with you. I love you, and I want to marry you!"

She feels a rush of joy, but then she remembers how meaningless such words are when he is already betrothed to Baochai. "Why should I believe you? You—you insult me by coming here and sneaking into my bedroom and"—she cannot bring herself to say the word "kiss" after what he said about Silver—"and all along you knew that you were going to marry someone else!"

He looks at her with narrowed eyes for a moment, apparently unable to speak for his fury. Then he turns away, and before she can understand what he is doing, he has looped the cord of his jade from around his head and is pressing the cool, hard stone into her palm.

Instinctively she recoils. "What are you doing?"

"What do you think I'm doing? I'm giving you my jade."

"Are you crazy?" She thrusts it back at him.

"No, I'm saner than I've ever been in my life. I want you to have it." He takes her hand and forces her fingers around the stone.

"Why?" She tries to pull her hand away.

"As a promise. I want you to wear it until I manage to break my betrothal."

She starts to tremble. "But that's impossible. How on earth will you do that? Granny will never consent—"

"I'll speak to my father first. And then if that doesn't work, I'll ask Xifeng to speak to Granny for me. And if that doesn't work, I will beg Granny myself."

"But I don't know if they'll agree. Granny doesn't like me, nor Xifeng either—"

"Never mind. I won't rest until they agree. Until they do, I want you to wear this."

"You can't give this away." She tries to give it back again. "It's your good luck charm. It's almost a part of yourself."

He does not answer. Instead he loops the cord over her own neck, careful not to let it catch in her hair. "Wear it inside your collar. You don't want anyone else to see it."

"You don't even like it," she says, half crying, half laughing.

"I do like it now." He pulls her to him and buries his face in her hair. "I like it because it is the only thing that I can give you that is truly mine."

8

Even though the unlit *kang* has been covered with cool bamboo mats, Baochai wakes up sticky and uncomfortable from her nap. Summer's heat has begun to gather, and her mouth and lips feel dry from the close, still air. She glances towards her mother, asleep beside her. Mrs. Xue had had a bad headache last night, and Baochai sat up with her until one in the morning. She herself feels heavy and drowsy, but she rises from the *kang* and dresses and does her hair. She goes out to the front room, and sits on the *kang* with her embroidery. She sews for several minutes, but feels so hot and dull that she is tempted to go back to sleep. Trying to shake off her lethargy, she decides to walk to Tanchun's to see what the other girls are doing.

She finds the Two Springs and Daiyu in Tanchun's front room listening to one of the old nannies telling stories. They have all taken off their robes and sit on the *kang* in light tunics and undertrousers. She is surprised that Daiyu has made the effort to visit the other girls; she has seemed in better spirits lately. When Baochai climbs onto the *kang*, Daiyu smiles at her, and makes room for Baochai to sit between her and Xichun. Baochai settles herself and begins to listen to the old woman with her heavy Hubei accent. She looks to be one of the oldest servants in the household, perhaps more than sixty, and she is talking about the Great Fire that destroyed large portions of the Capital more than fifty years ago. The nanny had only been a little girl then, she says, but she remembers everything vividly: the wall of flame, as high as the tallest tree, that came sweeping and crackling through the city, as it leapt from building to building, from lane to lane; the constant roar, so loud that you could not hear a shout from only a few feet away. With lively gestures and dramatic expressions, she tells of the beams cracking above her head, the paper windows suddenly combusting from the intense heat. She tells of people running and screaming to plunge themselves into ponds and rivers, whatever water they could find. Baochai does not enjoy this sort of thing, just as she refuses to listen to ghost stories: she suspects the old woman of taking advantage of her listeners' gullibility to exaggerate. She listens politely, but allows a slight smile to play on her lips to express her incredulity.

Beside her, Daiyu is silent, utterly absorbed in the story. As she stares at Nanny Chen, her eyes wide with terror, she fingers something small and round beneath her tunic at the base of her throat. It comes to Baochai in a flash: it is the jade. Daiyu has no jewelry of her own. Baoyu must have given it to her as a pledge. She tells herself that she is being fanciful, but she cannot rid herself of the idea.

She cannot sit there any longer, and climbs off the *kang*. Daiyu tears herself away from Nanny Chen's story. "Where are you going? Don't you want to listen to more stories?"

"I must go see if my mother is awake."

"I wish you would stay. I feel as if I rarely see you anymore."

Baochai musters a smile. "Then why don't you come over to see me tomorrow afternoon?"

When Daiyu walks into Granny Jia's for breakfast, she finds Snowgoose alone in the front room.

Snowgoose smiles. "There you are. Why haven't you been coming over early to see me like before?"

Daiyu is embarrassed to tell her friend that because Baoyu

has been staying so late when he comes to visit her at night, she has not been able to wake up early. Seeing the expression of concern on Snowgoose's face, she has an urge to share her happiness. "Come into the courtyard with me. I want to tell you a secret," she whispers.

They go out onto the verandah, and under the cover of the twittering birds, Daiyu tells about Baoyu's secret visits, about how she had found out about his engagement to Baochai, and how he had reassured her by giving her the jade and promising he would marry her. She is so giddy with excitement that she is almost at the end of her recital before she notices Snowgoose's grave expression.

"Haven't I told you to be careful with Baoyu?" Snowgoose says.

"No, I don't think you have." Daiyu laughs. "But it's not like that. He's given me his jade." Daiyu looks to make sure no one is around, then steps close to Snowgoose and pulls the jade out of her collar.

Instead of being reassured, Snowgoose stares at the jade as if it is a poisonous snake. "Put that away," she hisses.

Daiyu tucks it back inside her collar.

"Now listen to me." Snowgoose takes Daiyu's hand and looks intently into her eyes. "You must give the jade back, and break things off with Baoyu. He must never, never visit you at night again. I should have realized there would be trouble when they had you live all alone in those apartments with no one to watch over you!"

She has never heard Snowgoose speak with such urgency before. "Don't you see, Snowgoose? He isn't just flirting with me. Giving me the jade means that I'm the person he wants to spend his life with—"

"You must give it back to him," Snowgoose repeats, unheeding. "Don't you understand how much trouble there will be if anyone finds out—"

"But I want them to find out. Baoyu is going to talk to Uncle Zheng and Granny."

"Talk to them! Do you really think that will do any good? Of course they want him to marry someone rich and powerful, like Baochai."

"Why does it matter? They are rich and powerful enough themselves."

"That's the very reason that they want him to marry someone else rich and powerful."

"But don't you think that Lady Jia cares about Baoyu's happiness? She loves him so. If he can convince her that the only way he will be happy is with me ... "

"The only one Lady Jia loves is herself."

"But what if he passes the Exams? Won't they be satisfied then, and let him marry whom he chooses?"

"If he passes the Exams, he'll need a rich and powerful wife to advance—" Snowgoose breaks off suddenly as if a new thought has occurred to her. "And what about Baochai?"

"Oh, she won't care," Daiyu says confidently. "She would just as soon be betrothed to someone else, as long as he was from a good family, too."

Snowgoose shakes her head. "No one wants to suffer the loss of face and embarrassing questions of a broken betrothal."

"But she won't really suffer very badly, because the betrothal was kept secret in the first place. Besides, it's not as if she loves him."

"What makes you so sure she doesn't love him?"

Daiyu only smiles. Snowgoose does not know Baochai as she does. Of course she is only marrying Baoyu because her mother arranged the match. It is inconceivable to Daiyu that Baochai has any feelings for him.

Before Daiyu's visit, Baochai asks Oriole to heat some water. She has Oriole set out soap, a hair string, fresh towels, and a bottle of Oil of Flowers. Her mother, who has had another migraine, is still sleeping in the back bedroom.

When Daiyu comes in, Baochai greets her warmly, and then says, smiling, "It's such a nice sunny day. I was about to wash my hair. Do you want to wash yours, too, as long as I have everything ready?"

Daiyu smiles back, apparently pleased by Baochai's friendliness. "That's a good idea."

Baochai tells Oriole to set the basin on a small table in a sunny patch near the open door. She goes to her dressing table to take off her bracelets and roll up her sleeves. "Why don't you go first?"

"Of course not. You should go first."

"There's no need to be so polite." Baochai laughs. "You go first."

Baochai insists, and eventually Daiyu gives in. She drapes a towel over Daiyu's shoulders, and begins to pluck out her hairpins.

"I can do that myself."

"Good Heavens, why are you being so polite today? It's easier when someone else does it for you. Besides, I'm very good at giving head massages, don't you remember? I'll wash your hair, then you wash mine."

Daiyu sits on a stool next to the basin, and Baochai uses her own comb to smooth out the tangles in Daiyu's hair. She notices how different it is from her own. Thin and fine and inky black, the clinging strands are so delicate that Baochai has to be careful not to tear them. Baochai's hair is coarse and heavy, with reddish brown tints. When she can finally draw the comb smoothly through the long, silky strands, she asks Daiyu to stand up and lean over the basin. "I am afraid of splashing on your robe. Why don't you unbutton it a little so it won't get wet?" she says.

"All right." Daiyu opens the tight collar of her gown, undoing the top three fastenings, so that she can roll the fabric away from her neck. She bends over the basin, flipping her hair up over the crown of her head so that it hangs into the water. Almost without surprise, Baochai sees the jade, dangling on the familiar black and gold knotted cord around Daiyu's neck. She is glad Daiyu cannot see her face. How strange, she thinks, that Daiyu is having an affair with Baoyu—for his giving her the jade can mean only that—but is able to face Baochai and receive favors from her, without apparent guilt or shame.

She cups her fingers and splashes water onto Daiyu's hair, then rubs soap into Daiyu's scalp, using her fingernails to loosen the oil at the roots. Sometimes she digs her fingernails into Daiyu's scalp more roughly than she has to. More than once she feels Daiyu wincing a little beneath her hands. When she has subjected Daiyu's scalp to a merciless scrubbing, she pushes Daiyu's head into the basin to rinse it. She feels Daiyu relaxing as she scoops the warm water over her head. Below Daiyu's notched hairline, her skin is snow-white and flawlessly smooth. Her neck is long and slender, curving away from the graceful sweep of her shoulders. Baochai's own shoulders are fleshy, with a sprinkling of pimples. Her neck is short. Perhaps if she had been as beautiful as Daiyu she would have been able to keep Baoyu's notice.

Looking down at Daiyu's neck, she pictures Baoyu touching it and kissing it, and is filled, not with jealousy, but with disgust. She has no doubt that such scenes really do occur, and suspects Baoyu of sneaking to Daiyu's bedroom under the cover of night. Now Daiyu's freedom from constraint, which she had previously liked, strikes her as dangerous. She has broken the trust of the family that had taken her in, wantonly crushing the dignity and propriety of the household, and Baochai's own feelings. Didn't she understand that belonging to a large household was like being suspended in a web? You could not move a muscle without feeling the cling of gossamer threads, without knowing that your movements sent reverberations up and down the entire structure. Didn't she know how she would fall without those invisible threads to hold her safely aloft?

She wrings Daiyu's hair dry with the hair string, then gathers it into a lazy knot. "That's better, isn't it? Now it's my turn."

9

After slipping back to his own room from Daiyu's the night before, Baoyu had hardly slept. He had resolved to approach his father after dinner before his crammer came. He is afraid of his father's anger; but despite their constant conflicts, he trusts his father more than anyone else in the family. His father doesn't play favorites. He is principled, despite his blustery temper and old-fashioned ideas. His decision made, Baoyu lay awake till dawn rehearsing various speeches, trying to figure out how to convince his father that marrying Baochai will result in a lifetime of misery for the two of them, and Daiyu as well.

At dinnertime, his father does not appear. His father's absence is not unusual. What is strange is that he has not sent a message excusing himself and telling them to eat without him. Granny delays dinner forty-five minutes, grumbling the whole time, before growing impatient and ordering the meal to be served. By then, the whole evening's schedule is off. A page comes in to announce the crammer, and Baoyu has to rush off to his study in the outer part of the mansion without exchanging a word with Daiyu.

He muddles through the lesson, so distracted that the tutor threatens to tell his father. At the end of the lesson, he rushes out to look for his father at his apartments. Jia Zheng is still not home. Only Auntie Zhao is there, playing dice in her nightclothes with one of her maids.

"Hasn't my father sent a message?" he asks.

"No." Apparently unconcerned by Jia Zheng's lateness, she

climbs off the *kang*. "Why don't you stay here and wait for him? Fivey here can prepare some snacks and wine."

He knows that Auntie Zhao hates him and slanders him behind his back, but to his face, she is sugar sweet. In order not to offend her, he stays and has a little wine and a few cakes. Under the best of circumstances he finds it hard to make conversation with such a harsh-tempered and narrow-minded woman. He does his best to nod and smile at whatever she says, while surreptitiously watching the progress of the hands on the West Ocean clock.

When the clock strikes ten thirty, he takes his leave, telling Auntie Zhao he is going to bed. Instead, he goes to the Inner Gates. They are shut at this hour, and he has to call the gate-women to open them. They look at him in surprise when he tells them he is going out to his father's study. He lights the lamp in the silent, empty room, examining his father's things to distract himself from his worry. On the corner of the desk he notices a well-worn book. Careful not to let the bookmark slip out of its pages, he finds that it is a copy of Mencius. He smiles despite himself. Most officials, after passing the Exams, never open the Classics again; but here is his father, reading Mencius in his spare time.

At last he hears footsteps outside and glances at the clock. It is almost midnight.

"Father, I need to speak to you—" he begins, but breaks off at the sight of his father's face. "What's the matter? Why are you home so late?"

His father does not answer. Baoyu pushes a chair towards him. "Here, sit down."

Jia Zheng slumps in the seat, staring blankly before him. Baoyu forces himself to go on, afraid his courage will fail him. "I must talk to you about something important. I want to break my betrothal to Baochai and marry Daiyu. I don't care for

Baochai. If I don't marry Daiyu, it will break my heart and I will—"

His father shakes his head, raising both hands as if trying to thrust Baoyu's words away.

"What's the matter?" Baoyu cries. "Why won't you say anything? Aren't you feeling well?"

Jia Zheng's face twitches. Baoyu realizes that his father is trying to keep from bursting into tears.

"Father." Baoyu sinks to his knees, taking his father's hands. "Tell me what the matter is."

"His Highness is dying."

"What! But I heard today at school he was getting better."

"He had some kind of seizure this evening at dinner."

"Isn't there anything the Imperial Physician can do?"

Jia Zheng buries his face in his hands, shaking his head. "They say he is in a coma and may never wake up."

Baoyu stands there, strangely unmoved by the Emperor's plight, his mind racing. Prince Yinti is not yet back in the Capital; perhaps there will be a struggle for the succession. The prospect of unrest in the Capital makes him more determined to resolve the issue of his betrothal, so that if anything happens, he will be able to take care of Daiyu.

"Father."

Jia Zheng ignores him, still sobbing.

"Father, I know that you are worried about His Highness. I am, too. But this can't wait. I need to speak to you about my betrothal."

After a moment, Jia Zheng lifts his face up from his hands. "What do you want?"

"I want you to help me break my betrothal to Baochai. I want to marry Daiyu."

Jia Zheng's face is red and puffy, but his tear-swollen eyes seem to focus on Baoyu. He pauses, then repeats, "You want to break your betrothal?"

"Yes."

"And marry Daiyu?"

"Yes."

His father slumps back in the chair and shuts his eyes. He seems to be absorbing what the words mean with an effort. Finally, he opens his eyes. "I understand, but this is not the time to talk about it. You can bring it up with me later. I will see what I can do."

Baoyu slips into Daiyu's room and wakes her with kisses.

"What is it?" she says sleepily.

"I spoke to my father tonight."

"Yes?" She rubs her eyes.

"His Highness had some sort of attack and has fallen into a coma."

"That's terrible."

"Yes." He climbs under the covers. The night air has turned cool, and her body is warm against his. "My father was crying. I've never seen him so upset before."

"What will happen?"

"I don't know." He puts his arms around her. He does not want to worry her. "Maybe His Highness will linger on until Prince Yinti comes back to the Capital."

"But he might not." She lifts her head and looks into his face. "What do you think will happen?"

"No one can know. But I spoke to my father about breaking my betrothal."

"What did he say?"

"He was very upset about His Highness, but when I pressed him about it, he said that he would see what he could do."

"You mean he doesn't object?" He hears the joy in her voice.

"No, he didn't seem to."

"Then, that means ... I'd hardly dared hope ... " She flings her arms around him and buries her face in his neck. "I'm so happy!" One of the things he loves about her is her spontaneity. Other girls are too self-conscious ever to be unguarded.

He puts his arms around her and squeezes her tightly. "But we shouldn't let our hopes get too high. He still has to convince Granny," he reminds her, though he, too, feels giddy with hope. As they lie in each other's arms, she lifts her face to his and kisses him, a little timidly. At the butterfly-like touch of her lips, he kisses her back gently at first, and then more urgently. He tangles his fingers in her hair. She returns his kisses, her mouth clinging to his. Her mouth is soft, with the faint, sweet-sour taste of the rice that she has eaten for dinner. Their kisses are bolder now, their mouths half open. He had taught himself to resist the urge to touch her, but tonight, he no longer holds back. He buries his face in the softness of her hair, scented with Oil of Flowers, and lets his hands move over her body, following the indentation of her narrow waist, feeling the curve of her buttocks. He touches her tentatively at first, but she puts her arms around him and draws him to her. He grows bolder, and slides his hand beneath her tunic. He hears the catch of her breath.

Still kissing her, he feels the smoothness of her belly, the delicate tracery of her ribs and backbone. She reaches up and begins to tug at his gown. He shrugs it off so that he too is only in tunic and undertrousers. He presses his body against hers, and touches her small pointed breasts with his hands. She moans and her whole body stiffens and jerks against his. He loosens the waistband of her pants and lets his fingers travel down her slim hips. His hand moves slowly towards the damp, slick place between her legs. She wraps her legs around him and buries her face in his throat. He strokes her gently and she whimpers against him. Loosening the drawstring of his pants, her fingers close around his penis. At the feeling of her warm hand gripping him, he gasps and almost doubles over. She tugs on him gently, looking at his face. In the darkness, he can see the gleam of her eyes, although he cannot see her expression. He is amazed at her unself-consciousness. He feels like crying. He has never felt so close to another person in his whole life.

He feels an irresistible urge to make love to her. He has made love to a woman only once before. On his sixteenth birthday Lian had taken him to a *qinglou* and arranged for him to sleep with one of the singing girls. The girl had been pretty enough, and had known how to make Baoyu comfortable, but somehow the act, though pleasurable in itself, had felt empty and sordid. Now he wants to become one with Daiyu, to erase any sliver of separation between them. He pulls his pants down all the way, and then tugs at hers. She lets him draw them down. He guides his penis so that its tip touches the wet spot between her legs. Both of them gasp and leap apart at the intensity of the sensation.

"Daiyu."

"Yes?" she breathes.

"Is it all right if I—if we . . . " He trails off in embarrassment, not knowing what words to use.

"I don't know." Her voice is barely audible.

"Do you—do you know what I mean?"

"Yes." As if embarrassed, she buries her face in his chest. The movement brings his penis in contact with her again. This time they do not jerk apart. Between his own gasps, he hears her quick, shallow breaths. "Do you want to?" she says.

"Yes. Do you?"

She is silent for a moment. "Yes."

He puts up his hand and strokes her hair. "Are you sure?"

"Yes," and as if to affirm her statement, she moves against him so that the length of his penis slides between her legs.

With a groan he rolls her onto her back so that he is on top of her. For a few minutes, he rubs against her and the sensation is both exquisite and excruciating. Then he uses his hand to guide himself. His tip slides in and meets resistance. As gently as he can, he pushes past it. He hears her give a tiny whimper.

"Did I hurt you?" he says, drawing back.

"Just for a moment." She pulls him back towards her, and he is deep inside her. She seems beside herself, shuddering almost as if in pain. He feels so overwhelmed by sensation that he is afraid he will not be able to control himself if he moves a single muscle. Slowly, their breathing calms, they look at each other, and he begins to move deliberately and rhythmically inside her. She puts her arms around his neck and starts to rock her hips, awkwardly at first, and then more smoothly, to match his movements. As he thrusts, smelling the sweat on her body, hearing her gasps, he feels as if a giant bubble of something, joy perhaps, is swelling up inside his chest so that he can hardly breathe. The room and everything else around them recedes until he feels like the two of them are the only two people in the universe. She clings to him, pressing his face to her breasts.

Later, he looks down at her lying against his arm, and sees that she is falling asleep.

"You can't stay," she murmurs.

"No, I know. I'll go back to my apartment after you fall asleep."

A few minutes later she is snoring gently. He strokes her face, touched by a sense of wonder and joy, before slipping away.

10

Daiyu wakes to bright sunshine. Instinctively she looks around for Baoyu, then remembers that he promised to go back to his own rooms. Slightly disappointed, she shuts her eyes again, imagining him touching her. She is startled by the sound of voices from the front of the apartments. Realizing that her trousers are not on, she jumps out of bed and pulls them on. She has just slipped back under the covers when Granny Jia, leaning on Xifeng's arm, enters the room.

"What is it?" she says, sitting up, surprised to see Granny, who rarely leaves her own apartments.

Granny approaches the bed. "Give me the jade."

Her first instinct is to deny that she has it. Then she shakes her head. "No."

"Do you have the jade or not?"

"I have it, but I won't give it to you. Baoyu wants me to have it."

Daiyu expects Lady Jia to be angry, but her impassive expression does not change. She looks over her shoulder towards Xifeng. "So Baochai was right. Take it from her."

With a flash of anger, she realizes that Baochai must have seen the jade while washing her hair—had perhaps even manufactured the pretext as a means of discovering whether Daiyu had the jade. She puts her hands protectively over the stone as Xifeng advances towards her.

Xifeng smiles a trifle apologetically. "Why don't you just give it to me, Cousin Lin?"

"No." She grips the jade tightly.

Xifeng tries to pull the cord over Daiyu's head. It catches in Daiyu's hair, and Xifeng's tugs bring tears to her eyes. Xifeng's roughness makes her afraid, but still she will not loosen her grip. "Baoyu gave it to me. You have no right to take it away."

Xifeng lets go, and looks questioningly at Lady Jia.

"What are you waiting for?" Lady Jia snaps.

This time, when Daiyu resists her, Xifeng uses both her hands to force Daiyu's left wrist back. Daiyu cries out in pain, and lets go.

"Give it to me," Lady Jia says.

Xifeng hands Lady Jia the jade.

"Now pack up your things," Lady Jia says.

"Why? What are you going to do with me?" Daiyu jumps out of bed, her fear sharpening.

Lady Jia looks at her coldly, and then turns back to Xifeng. "Have her things moved to that storeroom in the back of my apartments."

"You can't lock me up," Daiyu cries, but Lady Jia ignores her.

Xifeng raises her brows. "A storeroom? Surely you can't be considering putting her in a storeroom! If you don't want Baoyu sneaking in to see her, why not have a maid guard her, or send her to Cousin Rong's?"

"You think a maid can stop him? And they don't have room at Cousin Rong's."

Xifeng sighs, avoiding Daiyu's eyes. "If you insist on locking her up, there's a storeroom in the back of my apartments with a high window she can't possibly climb out of. If you don't want Baoyu talking to her, you can post two maids to watch her."

Granny Jia nods. "I suppose that will do." She turns towards Daiyu. "Now pack your things."

They speak of her as if she isn't there. Struggling against a feeling of helplessness, she cries, "You can't do this! Baoyu won't let you."

Lady Jia does not deign to respond.

"He wants to marry me."

Instead of being angry or surprised as Daiyu expects, Lady Jia gives a little laugh. "No doubt that's what he told you. What else would he have said if he wanted to sleep with you?" She turns to Xifeng. "I suppose the best way to avert a scandal is to arrange a match for her at once."

Xifeng frowns. "What sort of match did you have in mind? You'll have to provide a dowry and—"

Daiyu breaks in. "Baoyu won't let you. He's not afraid of you—"

A deep bonging echoes through the Garden, drowning out her words.

"What's that infernal noise?" Lady Jia says.

Xifeng holds up one finger for silence, an arrested look on her face. "It is the big iron chime bar by the Inner Gate. One. Two. Three. Four." She counts the ominous strokes. "Four strokes for death," she says, her face suddenly scared.

The street to the Imperial Palace is clogged with vehicles. Jia Zheng, sweating in his mourning robes in the summer heat, fidgets at the slow progress of the carriage through the crowds. Wiping his eyes, he looks around at his weeping family. Across from him, Mrs. Xue and Xifeng are trying to comfort Granny Jia. Jia Lian looks stunned and a little scared, while Baoyu, his eyes bloodshot and his face pale, is looking out the window. Pushing aside the blind, Jia Zheng looks out to see a river of white mourning snaking up the street towards the Palace. White banners flutter sluggishly in the faint wind. Every vehicle, every person, every horse, has been swathed in the color of death. The tears prickle in his eyes, and he pictures His

Highness's face, with its fine wrinkles and expression of benev-
olence. He cannot stand to sit any longer in the carriage inching
at a snail's pace.

"I'm getting out and walking," he says.

"Oh, Zheng, are you sure?" his mother quavers. He had not
realized how shaken she would be by His Highness's death.
"The crowds out there are terrible."

"That's all right. I'll probably get there faster than you. I'll
meet you by the front entrance. Baoyu, Lian, you take care of
Granny."

In a moment, he is out in the blazing sun. There is little
pedestrian traffic, and he walks briskly, quickly losing sight of his
own carriage in the crush of other vehicles. He notices that all
the stores are closed, their doors shut and awnings down. Other
than those hurrying to the Palace to mourn, there is no one on
the streets. It is eerily silent.

Within a few hundred yards of the Palace, the pedestrians
grow denser. When he approaches the enormous flight of stairs
up to the throne room, he is caught in the crowd of mourners
disembarking from their carriages. He tries to find a spot to wait
for his mother and the others, but is driven towards the stairway
by the press of people. He is forced through the entranceway,
and then up the stairs. On the fourth or fifth step, he turns and
sees Jia Yucun a few steps back. It is too solemn an occasion to
call out, so he raises his eyebrows and nods his head, trying to
get Yucun's attention. It seems impossible that Yucun does not
see him—he is looking right in Jia Zheng's direction—but
Yucun turns away without acknowledging the greeting.

He catches sight of numerous other colleagues and acquain-
tances on either side of him, escorting the female members of
their families, wives or elderly mothers, some of whom have not
appeared in public for years. He notices that same eerie silence.
It strikes him that few people are actually crying, but instead

wear tense, watchful expressions. What do they fear? Near the top of the stairs, he sees the Prime Minister, Nian Gengyao, looking haggard with grief.

With a surge like the breaking of a wave, Jia Zheng is thrust through the great doors into the throne room. Raising his eyes over the heads in front of him, he sees the massive black coffin on a dais flanked by rows of kneeling monks. Half blinded by tears, his eyes go automatically to the throne to the right of the coffin where he has so often seen the Emperor. To his amazement, it is not empty. Prince Yongzheng is in his father's place. He stares at the ugly, clever face blazing with triumph, at the golden robes embroidered with dragons that only the Emperor himself can wear. He had thought his grief was so great that it left no room for any other emotion, but he was wrong, for now his heart pounds with fear.

11

By the fourth day of mourning, Baoyu is exhausted. He has spent the last three days, from daylight until ten o'clock, at the Palace kneeling and kowtowing amid the crowds of mourners. The first night back from the Palace, he had gone straight to Daiyu's rooms in his mourning robes. Discovering them empty, and all her possessions gone, he rushed to Tanchun's room in a panic. The gates of Tanchun's apartment were locked, and he had had to sneak back to her bedroom window to wake her. All she could tell him was that Lady Jia was angry at Daiyu and had moved her into a storeroom in Xifeng's apartments. He had rushed to Xifeng's apartments, leaving Tanchun in midsentence. To his relief, the gates of Xifeng's apartments were still open— he could see lit lanterns in Xifeng's rooms, and could hear Qiaojie crying. When he got to the storeroom, he found two maids standing watch outside. He begged and pleaded with them to let him speak to Daiyu, even offering them bribes, but they refused, saying that Baoyu was expressly forbidden to see her. At a loss, he had gone back to his own apartments to lie down, and then returned two hours later. This time, Xifeng's front gates were locked. He climbed into the compound by scaling a crab apple tree outside the wall. There were two different maids standing guard, and they had been so scared by his sudden appearance in the middle of the night that they threatened to start screaming if he did not go away.

Now, after the third night of failing to see Daiyu, he puts on his mourning robes and walks straight to Lady Jia's. In the front room he finds Xifeng helping Granny dress. His father, already in mourning clothes, slumps in a chair. He looks terrible, his face a ghastly yellow, and Baoyu wonders whether he, too, has passed a sleepless night. He feels guilty for bringing up something to worry and upset his father even more, but forces himself to begin. "I need to speak to you."

Xifeng shoots him a look. She seems to know what he wants to talk about. "This isn't a good time, Baoyu. We have to set out for the Palace in an hour, and no one has even had breakfast."

Baoyu stands before his father. "Father, Daiyu is locked up in a storeroom."

"What?" His father lifts his bowed head. "Locked up?"

"Yes," Baoyu says, before Granny can strike in with an explanation. "Shouldn't she be released at once?"

Jia Zheng looks bewildered. "Yes, of course." He gives his head a shake as if to clear it. "Why has she been locked up?"

"You don't know what the two of them have been getting up to at night," Granny Jia puts in. "I had to stop it, and didn't know what else to do!"

"Is this true?" Jia Zheng looks at Baoyu. Baoyu is struck again by how wretched his father seems, almost physically ill. He asks the question not as if he is interested in the answer, but as if respect for his mother obliges him to ask.

"I did visit her in the night sometimes. It was very wrong, and I won't do it again." He looks around at them, first his father, who hardly seems to be taking his words in, then Xifeng, and then Granny. He wanted to find them all together: If he could get even one of them to support his marriage to Daiyu, surely he would be able to convince the other two. "I want to break my betrothal to Baochai. I love Daiyu, and I won't be able to live"— he had meant to say "to be happy," but somehow these words had come to his lips instead—"without her."

"Break the betrothal? We'll do no such thing," Lady Jia says. He wonders how he could ever have thought that she loved him. Confusedly, he recalls all those years when she had doted on him and indulged him in every way. Now, everything has shifted, and looking into her eyes, he feels that they have become enemies. "It's an excellent match. Baochai is a well-brought-up young woman, not like Daiyu, who is arrogant and—"

"Why are you worrying about it now, Baoyu?" Xifeng says. "We are in national mourning. No one will be able to get married for six months." Her voice is not ungentle. He sees from her face that she is exhausted as well. He remembers how he hears Qiaojie crying when he goes to Xifeng's apartments late at night. He realizes that she wants to avoid an argument when they are about to set off for another long day at the Palace.

"I understand that getting married now is impossible, but I need this to be settled. What if Granny arranges Daiyu's betrothal to someone else, or has her sent away? What if Daiyu is mistreated? She has already been locked up like a criminal, when she has done nothing wrong!" He is beyond caring whether he offends his grandmother. He cannot afford to hold anything back. He goes to Xifeng and takes her hand. "Xifeng, you of all people understand how hard it is—to be married to someone, when the couple isn't well suited ... " He stumbles awkwardly.

She jerks her hand away. "I don't know what you're talking about. What do you expect me to understand?"

He realizes he has made a misstep. Xifeng's pride will not allow her to admit her miserable situation with Lian. How often has he heard her repeat the saying: *"You must hide a broken arm in your sleeve"*?

She seems to recover, for she says after a moment, "If you insist on talking about your betrothal at a time like this, let's try to talk about it in a sensible manner. In the first place, in theory, breaking off the betrothal is not in itself impossible, if handled with proper tact. After all, it is not as if the betrothal was ever made public." Here, she pauses and darts a quick look at Jia Zheng. Baoyu receives the impression that she does not care for Baochai, and would not be displeased if the betrothal were broken. She wishes to show his father that, if he himself does not approve of the betrothal, she will be his ally against Lady Jia. But his father remains slumped in his chair, not even looking at her.

"I tell you," Lady Jia cries, incensed by Xifeng's defection. "It's not to be considered. What will people think if we break off the betrothal, especially after Mrs. Xue and Baochai have lived with us so long? People would assume we had backed out because there was some problem with Baochai's reputation, and then Mrs. Xue would have trouble making a new match for her. She would never agree!"

"I was just saying," Xifeng says, "that it was possible in theory, but difficult in practice." She looks at Baoyu. He cannot tell whether she is changing her position, because she has received no support from his father and is now trying to please Granny Jia, as usual. "For one thing, the dowry has been paid, and in fact has already been spent on some major repairs on the farms down south."

This objection strikes him as laughable. "Why can't we just pay them back?"

She looks at him as if his question is singularly foolish. "Because we can't afford to."

Baoyu is dumbfounded. "What do you mean?" he says, with a little laugh. "I thought we had plenty of money."

"The men in this family are all the same. They never pay the least attention to money until they want to spend it! The household has been running on a deficit for two years. Last year we had to borrow money. We've been spending all the money from the farms for years, but not putting anything back into maintaining the properties. Why do you think we waited until we got Baochai's dowry to do the repairs?"

He is stunned, then furious. Never in his life has it occurred to him that money might present an obstacle to anything he wished to do. "Why was I never told before?"

"You never asked, did you?"

He has to admit that he has never shown the least interest in the practical affairs of the household. He would have made more of an effort to pass the Exams if it had ever occurred to him that the family might actually need his official salary. "Father, Granny, did you know this? Is this true?"

Granny appears not to be listening. Perhaps she has so much money hidden in her apartments that she is unconcerned about the finances of the rest of the household. His father shakes his head despairingly, and buries his face in his hands. "What does it matter? We're ruined anyway. That's what I came here to tell you this morning, but I didn't dare." He is speaking to his mother, but does not turn his face in her direction.

"What do you mean?" Baoyu says.

"Haven't you been paying attention to the political situation?"

"No, I—" He had been so absorbed by his worry for Daiyu that he had hardly thought about it. "I know Prince Yongzheng must have staged some sort of a coup ... "

Jia Zheng lifts his face from his hands. "One of Prime Minister Nian's clerks came to see me this morning before sunrise because he didn't want to be seen." His voice drops to a hoarse croak. Baoyu kneels on the floor before him to catch the words. "They say Prince Yongzheng paid the eunuchs to poison His Highness, and then wouldn't let the Imperial Physician treat him. He brought his soldiers into the Palace when His Highness was dying. That was how he seized the throne. When I think about His Highness, spending his last moments helpless and betrayed by the people who were supposed to serve him ... " His father buries his face in his hands again.

Baoyu puts his hand on his father's shoulder. "But the other Princes? Surely they'll contest the legitimacy of such a succession."

"As soon as Yongzheng's soldiers were in the Palace, they arrested Prince Yinsi and Prince Yintang." Prince Yinsi and Yintang are the eighth and ninths sons of the late Emperor, also his favorites. "Even before he seized the throne, he had sent out soldiers to intercept Prince Yinti. He was arrested yesterday, halfway between Shouzhou and the Capital, while everyone was at the Palace mourning." Prince Yinti had made it to less than one hundred *li* from the Capital, barely a few days' march. His imminent arrival must have been the reason that Prince Yongzheng had taken the drastic step of having the Emperor poisoned.

Baoyu sees that his father is horrified by these arrests, but to him they mean something different. Perhaps there will not be fighting after all, because the rival Princes have all been imprisoned. "But what does this have to do with us? I know Prince Yongzheng dislikes the Imperial Bondsmen, but do you really think that will affect us?"

His father gives a little laugh that strikes Baoyu as almost hysterical. "What does it have to do with us? Nian Gengyao was arrested last night when he got home from the Palace. They didn't even wait until the first few days of mourning were over! And not just Nian himself—all his sons and brothers were arrested, too, and his household confiscated. And then early this morning, Cao Fu and Li Xu were arrested ... "

For the first time, fear grips Baoyu's heart. If the new Emperor is so insecure about his own power, he will purge everyone known to be a supporter of one of the old Emperor's favorites. "But, Father," he stammers, "those men, Prime

Minister Nian, and Cao and Li, were known to be proponents
of Prince Yinti—"

"Not necessarily. Li Xu was arrested for having once given
Prince Yinsi a couple of singing girls."

"But Father"—Baoyu looks searchingly into his father's
face—"you have never gotten involved in this sort of thing. *I*
knew you wanted Prince Yinti to succeed, but you haven't been
indiscreet enough to say so in front of other people."

"I can't remember what I said!" Jia Zheng thrusts himself violently up from his seat and begins to pace the room. "I made no
secret that I thought Prince Yinti the rightful heir. Why would
I? It's what His Highness intended. No, wait—" He stops short.
"At New Year's, Jia Yucun told me to get rid of those gilt lions
that Prince Yinti gave us, and I refused and said . . . "

"Jia Yucun?" Baoyu's hope ebbs. "Haven't *you* heard?"

His father stares at him. "What?"

"I always wondered why he spent so much time with the
eunuchs. Not long ago the Prince of Beijing told me that he had
become very close to Prince Yongzheng, a member of his inner
circle, in fact."

"No wonder he has been acting so strangely lately!" Jia
Zheng exclaims at the same moment that Lady Jia cries, "It's all
your fault for bringing that upstart here in the first place!"

Baoyu looks from his father towards Lady Jia. Her face is
ashen and her hands are shaking. "You never know when you
should keep quiet! You went around blathering about the
Princes just to make yourself seem important. If you are
arrested, what's to become of us?"

"I didn't mean any harm—"

"You should have thought about your seventy-four-year-old
mother before you tried to show off—"

Pained by the sight of his father being scolded like a child,
Baoyu rouses himself. "That doesn't matter." He takes his

father's hand. "Isn't there anything we can do to help our-selves?"

"Can't we get rid of the gilt lions?" Xifeng interrupts. She is pale but perfectly composed.

"It's too late for that. If we tried to do anything now, we could be charged with destroying state's evidence." Jia Zheng sits down again, staring at the floor. He says, as if thinking aloud, "Our only hope is to get someone to pull strings for us. Most people will want nothing to do with us, but our relatives by marriage have no choice but to stand by us." He looks at Xifeng. "If we only have time to send messengers to your family before anything happens. I'll ask Mrs. Xue to send to her brother-in-law in Nanjing ... "

The mention of Mrs. Xue stabs Baoyu. "Do you have to ask the Xues?"

His father looks at him. "Why wouldn't I ask the Xues? They're extremely well connected."

He manages to stammer, "How can we break the betrothal if we ask them to help us?"

Jia Zheng's startled expression makes it clear that he had entirely forgotten Baoyu's desire to break the betrothal. "Good Heavens, how can you be thinking about that at a time like this? We need to stay on good terms with the Xues."

"Can't we just ask the Wangs?"

"Don't you understand? We have to do everything we can, and even that might not be enough. Do you realize what's at stake? If—Heaven forbid—I end up in prison, what do you think will happen to Granny and your sister and cousins?"

"But—" he begins, and stops. For the first time he under-stands the chains that bind him to his family, each link forged from obligation and sacrifice, from which he can never escape. No wonder Granny had looked at him with such hatred. She is bound to him as much as he is bound to her. He thinks about how he has misled Daiyu into thinking he could marry her. Locked up without any word from him, she must believe that he has betrayed her.

Xifeng says, "Look at the time. We have to leave for the Palace in ten minutes."

Baoyu does not move. His father, also, remains silent and motionless. At last, Jia Zheng heaves himself to his feet. "I suppose we must go."

"Where is the jade?" Granny says.

Baoyu is startled, wondering why Granny is thinking about the jade at such a time. "I gave it to Daiyu."

"I know, but I took it from her."

For an instant his anger jerks him out of his despair. "You had no right to! I want her to have it."

Ignoring him, Lady Jia says, "Where did you put it, Xifeng?"

"I gave it to you."

"Are you sure?" Lady Jia says, frowning. "I don't know where it is."

"Maybe you gave it to Snowgoose for safekeeping. Why don't you ask her?"

"Snowgoose!" Lady Jia calls. The maid does not appear. "Oh, yes. I sent her out to the stables. I don't know why she isn't back yet."

Baoyu feels a perverse triumph. If Daiyu cannot have the jade, he does not want anyone else, including himself, to have it.

There is the sound of running feet outside the front room. A gatewoman rushes in, wild-eyed. "Some men—they look like soldiers—have broken into the mansion. They're coming into the Inner Quarters—"

"What sort of men?" Jia Zheng turns pale.

"They are wearing yellow robes and pointed helmets—"

Jia Zheng sinks down on the *kang*. "It's the Embroidered Jackets."

"The Embroidered Jackets!" The Emperor's Secret Police. Baoyu feels his heart knocking against his ribs. "It must be a confiscation!"

"How many of them are there?" his father asks.

"Dozens!"

His father lurches to his feet. "I must go see them. I must try to reason with them."

Baoyu is dimly aware of being surprised by his father's courage, but his mind is picturing what will happen. If the Embroidered Jackets find Daiyu locked up, they will not realize that she is a member of the family. At best, they will assume that she is a concubine, or a maid. Who knows what will happen to her? She might be sent to serve in another household. He must release her before the Embroidered Jackets arrive, even if he has to break down the door.

"Baoyu, come with me and help me speak to them," his father says, starting towards the door.

"I can't." He pushes past his father and begins to run as he has never run before.

12

A key scrapes in the lock. In an instant Daiyu is out of her makeshift bed. Finally, after four days of waiting, Baoyu is here to rescue her. When the door swings open, however, it is Snowgoose, not Baoyu.

"Snowgoose! What's happening—"

Snowgoose takes her hand and tugs her out the door.

"What is it?" Daiyu says, stumbling.

"You have to get out of here." Snowgoose pulls Daiyu towards the front gates of Xifeng's apartments.

"But why?" Infected by Snowgoose's urgency, Daiyu begins to run as well.

"The Embroidered Jackets are here. They're confiscating the Jias." Snowgoose gets the words out between gasps of breath. "I saw them out near the stables. I ran in here to let you out. You can get out the side gate before they come."

"Confiscated? But why?" Now they are circling around the back of Xifeng's apartments.

"I don't know."

"Will anything happen to Uncle Zheng and Baoyu?"

"I'm not sure. It doesn't have anything to do with you, does it?"

Daiyu slows her steps. "I can't just run away and leave them—"

Snowgoose's grip on her hand tightens. "What could you do? You don't owe them anything after the way they've treated you." They have arrived at a small gate in the back wall of the Inner Quarters, which Snowgoose opens with a key from her waist.

"Now when you get out into the streets, you must go straight to Flowers Street near the Chongwen gate in the southern part of the city. You must ask for the blacksmith Zhen Shiyin. Anyone on Flowers Street will be able to tell you where he lives. Can you remember?"

"Of course, but how can I stay with your family?" She knows the Zhens are too poor to be able to feed an extra mouth.

"We'll manage. When you get there, tell them who you are and what happened. I've told them all about you." Now they are running down a back passage in the outer mansion.

At last they come to the outer wall. From the other side Daiyu hears the hubbub of the streets: the clopping of hooves, the scrape of wheels, the babble and screech of a hundred voices. Snowgoose unlocks the gate. "You remember where to go?"

"Yes, but what about you?" She takes Snowgoose's hand. "Aren't you coming with me? Is it safe for you to go back?"

"I'm only a servant. I'll probably just be sent to another household. I'll come see you as soon as I can."

Snowgoose pushes her out the gate. She hesitates, the thought of Baoyu holding her back. Then she remembers how she has not heard from him for the last four days. "If Baoyu wants to know where I am, you'll let him know, won't you?"

"Of course. Now go!"

The gate clangs shut behind her. She is alone outside the mansion. The bracing air of the streets hits her, so different from the air inside: smokier, grittier, yet somehow clearer and more invigorating. Breathing in deeply, she looks around the back alley, then walks towards the main thoroughfare, orienting herself by the increase in noise. When she reaches it, she stands for a moment amid the stream of people and animals and vehicles passing in both directions, conscious that she has nothing but the clothes that she wears. Her hand goes up to her throat to finger the jade, a habit she developed in the few weeks she had worn it, before she remembers it is gone.

As he runs towards Xifeng's apartments, Baoyu hears all around him evidence that the Embroidered Jackets have already broken into the Inner Quarters: loud male voices, the tramping of heavy feet, the splintering of wood. He takes the alley behind the apartments to avoid the police. He hears Auntie Zhao and the maids screaming from his father's rooms. The Embroidered Jackets must have ignored his father's pleas and must already be searching the mansion. He runs faster.

At the back wall of Xifeng's compound, he swings onto a low branch of a nearby tree. The back gate bursts open and a half-dozen Embroidered Jackets emerge. He turns to run but they are on him in an instant.

"Let me go!" He wrenches himself out of their hands and runs a few steps, but they catch hold of him again.

"Let me go!" He struggles wildly. One of them twists his forearm behind his back. Half bent over from the pain in his arm, he glares up at the Embroidered Jackets. With their flapping sleeves and peaked helmets, they look like ill-omened birds of prey.

"You have no right to detain me." He tries to pull his arm away, but the Embroidered Jacket wrenches it so hard he cries out.

"Who are you?" the soldier shouts.

"I'm Jia Baoyu."

"Jia Baoyu, I hereby arrest you."

Strangely, he is not frightened. His mind latches on to the hope that if he stops resisting and speaks reasonably to them, they will let him explain about Daiyu, and will see that she is released and placed with the other women in the family.

He stops struggling and says as calmly as he can, "On what charges?"

"Didn't you hear the Edict read?"

"No."

"I'll take you to the lieutenant. He can explain it to you."

Still twisting Baoyu's arm, the soldier leads Baoyu to the courtyard of Xifeng's apartments. The place is swarming with Embroidered Jackets, but there is no sign of Daiyu.

"Do you know if they found a girl locked in one of these rooms?" he asks.

"If you have questions, you'd better ask the lieutenant."

However, the lieutenant is nowhere to be seen. At last the soldier releases Baoyu's arm and allows him to wait, flanked by two soldiers, in the corner of the courtyard. Baoyu watches the stream of police going in and out of the apartments. Occasionally there is the sound of crockery breaking, or of some heavy piece of furniture being shifted.

Finally, a policeman in a more elaborate uniform enters the courtyard. The soldier who had twisted Baoyu's arm accosts him. "This is Jia Baoyu. He wants to know on what charges he is being held."

The lieutenant looks Baoyu up and down expressionlessly. "We were sent to arrest Jia Zheng, Duke of Rongguo, as well as Jia Lian, Jia Huan, and yourself on the charge of treason and collaborating with enemies of the State. Also on the charge of receiving gifts from enemies of the State."

Baoyu is stunned. Treason and collaborating with the enemy are serious crimes, carrying significant prison sentences. While it is not unheard-of for all the adult male members of a family to be included in a charge for a political crime, it strikes him as unusually harsh that all four Jia men are to be arrested. How will the women manage on their own?

The lieutenant continues, "Jia Zheng is also charged with

obstruction of justice in the case of *Surviving Relatives of Zhang Hua vs. Xue Pan.*"

"Obstruction of justice?" Baoyu repeats dumbly. Had Xue Pan killed someone, and had his father intervened on Pan's behalf? With a flash of insight, he at last understands why his father had befriended Jia Yucun, and what secret, tortuous ties bind the Xues and the Jias.

"Jia Zheng is hereby stripped of his rank as Duke of Rongguo," the lieutenant goes on, speaking with the clipped precision of a military man. "We have also found evidence of additional crimes."

Baoyu knows that this is how it happens in confiscations: Even if the evidence against a family is weak to begin with, a top-to-bottom search of their property usually turns up sufficient evidence to arrest them.

"We found Prohibited Articles on the premises: more than two dozen bolts of Imperial Use silk, which are restricted for Palace use. Therefore, you will also be charged with illegal possession of contraband goods."

"But Her Late Highness the Imperial Concubine sent those to us!"

"The law clearly specifies that it is a crime for a private household to be in possession of articles reserved for use in the Palace."

Baoyu wants to protest that it is a universal practice for Palace women to smuggle out items as gifts for their families, but he suddenly feels ashamed, and stops himself.

"The last charge is for usury." The lieutenant speaks contemptuously.

"Usury! We haven't loaned any money—"

"Promissory notes, imprinted with Jia Lian's chop, were found in these very apartments."

"Lian couldn't have made those loans." Generous to a fault,

Lian is incapable of calculating the price of a few casks of wine. The thought occurs to him: Could Xifeng have made them? She had told him that very morning how precarious the family finances were. He wonders if he should tell the lieutenant the truth—but the idea that Xifeng too would be arrested is unthinkable.

"Do you have any other questions, before we take you to the *yamen*?" the lieutenant asks.

"Yes. Have you finished searching these apartments?"

"Yes."

"Did you find a girl locked up in one of the storerooms?"

The lieutenant looks surprised, but answers, "No, we didn't. We did find a storeroom with a bed and a trunk, but no one was there."

He is flooded with relief. Someone must have remembered Daiyu and released her. He lets himself be led out of Xifeng's apartments towards Granny's place, wondering if he will find her there. Granny's courtyard is crowded with people. After the first moment of confusion he sees that, besides the Embroidered Jackets, there are three groups. One group, in the far corner, consists of Granny and Xifeng, Ping'er and Qiaojie, and Tanchun and Xichun, as well as Baochai and Mrs. Xue. Daiyu is not among them. Granny is hunched on the verandah steps, while Xifeng supports her. All the women but Xifeng are crying. Baochai, her face swollen with tears, has her arms around her mother. He feels a twinge of dislike.

The far larger group in the middle of the courtyard consists of maids and stewardesses and other senior women servants. He scans it quickly for Daiyu, but she is not there. His eyes go to the final group, in another corner, surrounded by Embroidered Jackets, to which he himself is being led. As he approaches it, he sees that it consists of his father, Lian, and Huan. At the sight of his father, something—shame or pity—twists in his stomach.

Jia Zheng is boxed in by four Embroidered Jackets, as if they suspect him of trying to escape. One even holds his upper arm. Although Baoyu was not angry when the police seized his own arm, he feels a mad urge to thrust this policeman away. His father's head and shoulders are bowed, his eyes fixed on the ground.

The full disgrace of their situation hits him. He is sufficiently well versed in court life to understand that his father had done nothing to warrant the treason charge, but is a victim of factional strife. The other charges, though probably carrying lighter sentences, trouble him more: the usury, his father's intervention in Pan's murder case, the smuggling of items out of the Imperial Palace. As insignificant as each may seem, exposed to the harsh glare of public scrutiny, they stink of corruption and abuse of power. For the first time it occurs to him that the grandeur and pomp of their whole life have been built on these small acts of wrongdoing. While Xifeng had been earning interest on illegal loans, he had worn the best clothing, had ridden the finest horses, without ever understanding their price. He had been self-righteous, posing as a freethinker above ambition and duty. In the meantime, his father and Xifeng had done the dirty work. He feels a wave of self-disgust.

Gently, he pushes past Huan and Lian, and stands next to his father.

Xifeng walks away from the huddle of sobbing women near the Inner Gate. Ping'er is trying to soothe Qiaojie, soiled and wet from not having had her diaper changed all day. Lady Jia, her face rigid with shock, is sitting on the steps beside Baochai. When Baoyu had been taken away with the other men, Xifeng saw Baochai's composure break for the first time. She cried out

his name, and even ran a few steps after him. Perhaps she cared
for him more than Xifeng supposed. Now Baochai's iron composure is back as she divides her attention between Granny and
her mother. The Two Springs are crying in each other's arms.

The men have been taken to prison; she does not know when
she will hear from them again. Rongguo no longer belongs to
the family, and the women must leave the mansion by nightfall.
She can think of nowhere to go to sleep tonight but Cousin
Rong's two-room apartment. Before they leave she must go
back to her own apartment. They need diapers and clothes for
Qiaojie, and she must check whether her secret cache of money
has somehow escaped discovery. They need cash urgently: to
bribe the prison guards, to send messengers to friends and relatives begging for their intervention. If only she can get her
hands on some silver, she will not feel so helpless.

She has heard of people hanging themselves during confiscations. Now she understands why. At first, she had thrown herself
onto the *kang*, terrified that the police would grab her. They did
not do so, but had simply ordered her out into the courtyard.
However, the few moments before she helped Granny out of the
room were enough for her to see what they were doing: the lock
on the *tansu* had been smashed, wardrobes jerked open, drawers
upended. Watching the police paw over the objects of her daily
life, she felt a burning sense of violation, as if they had dared to
touch her own body. As she had tended to Granny, making a
pillow out of her vest and settling her in the shade of the verandah, she noticed a stream of Embroidered Jackets coming out of
the apartment, carrying trunks opened to reveal jumbles of
scrolls and antiques and jewelry. She caught sight of a pair of
solid gold Buddhas—so heavy that two policemen were needed
to lift the trunk—strings of pearls, "mutton-fat" white jade gir-
dles, West Ocean clocks and watches, tiger skins and fox furs and
Tibetan yak's serge, all the treasures that Granny Jia had hoarded

over her lifetime. As the Embroidered Police continued to
stream out, some of them carrying trunks of silver and copper,
she calculated that sixty or seventy thousand *taels'* worth of property was being taken in one fell swoop. She held on to a wild
hope that her own stash, better hidden, would somehow escape
the search.

Now she hurries towards her own apartments, struck by the
eerie silence. That morning, there had been more than one
hundred and fifty servants in the Inner Quarters. The
Embroidered Jackets had rounded up the forty or so most
senior maids and stewards and stewardesses for "questioning."
The rest of the servants, she suspects, have run away in the
panic. As she walks, she calls out to see if anyone is there. Her
voice sounds weak and small in the empty spaces. All her life,
she has had to take great pains to avoid servants whenever she
wished to be alone. Now she could scream and no one would
come.

Through the dimness she sees the front gate of her apartments padlocked and sealed over with strips of white paper
proclaiming them State Property, their loose ends fluttering in
the wind. The small door in the back wall, probably unnoticed,
has not been locked and sealed. She unlocks it with one of the
keys at her waist, and makes her way down a short alley to a
side entrance to the apartments. As she tries to swing the door
open, it catches on the piles of clothing and broken crockery on
the floor. She forces the door wider, stepping across the debris
to the front room. The cupboards have been emptied, drifts of
tea and rice spilling across the floor. Books lie facedown underfoot. Even the pillows and quilts have been slashed open, as if
the Embroidered Jackets had suspected that something was
secreted inside them. Her face powder has been dumped out on
the dressing table, all the pots of creams and lotions opened
and gouged with some sharp object to make sure nothing was

hidden at the bottom. Everything valuable is gone: the West Ocean clock, the scrolls on the wall, the mother-of-pearl screen.

She flounders over the debris to her bedroom. The wardrobe door swings open. The false bottom of the wardrobe has been removed and her hiding place lies revealed. Still she throws herself to her knees and scrabbles her fingers over every inch of the recess, breaking a fingernail on the rough brick. Nothing. The rug has been torn off the *kang*. She pries up the loose brick under which she had hidden a bag of her most precious jewelry. It is all gone. There is one last place: the bottom of a flowerpot where she kept some gold and jade rings. She finds the uprooted plant and shards of porcelain on the floor.

She cannot stop from going back to the wardrobe and searching it one last time. She plunges her torn and bleeding hands into the hiding place, digging her fingers into the crevices. Then she remembers. Besides the money, she had hidden the loan agreements there as well. With the loan agreements confiscated, she will never be repaid the thousands of *taels* she has lent. Moreover, because the agreements specify illegally high interest rates, Jia Lian, whose name is on the documents, will be charged with usury. A cold finger of fear touches her heart at the thought of Lian's fury. The fact that he is in prison and cannot vent his anger on her is a relief. But what will his anger, unable to find its object, drive him to do? Will he tell Uncle Zheng? Will he testify against her in court? She pushes such thoughts away, stooping to gather some of Qiaojie's clothing from the floor.

Mechanically, her hands sort though piles of debris, picking out diapers, trousers, a jacket, blankets, and piling them on a wrapping cloth. What a long, terrible day it has been. Was it really just this morning that she had been sitting on the *kang* with Granny and Uncle Zheng and Baoyu talking about his betrothal? What were they saying when the Embroidered Jackets arrived? They had just realized that Baoyu's jade was lost, the same moment this terrible calamity befell them. A fear sharper than any she has felt all day grips her. She has never believed in coincidence. How can anyone doubt that the family's fate is bound up with Baoyu's jade? And now that the jade is gone, the family's luck has run out, too.

PART FOUR

Eighth Month, 1722

Spring flowers, the autumn moon, when will they
    end?
How much can we know of the past?
Last night in the little tower, again an east wind,
I can't bear to look back at my old kingdom in the
    moonlight.
The carved railings, the jade steps, must still be
    there;
It's only the rosy faces that have changed.
I ask you: how much grief can there be?
As much as a spring river flowing east.

Li Yu, Last Emperor of the Southern Tang, song
    lyric to the tune "The Beautiful Lady Yu"

1

Xifeng arrives at the *yamen* nearly an hour later than she intended. The new apartment that they are renting is farther south than Rongguo, and she had underestimated how long it would take for her to walk to the center of the city. Breathless and sweaty from exertion, despite the autumn cold, she hurries to the courtroom. It is deserted but for a young clerk shuffling through a pile of papers near the judge's bench.

Attempting to quiet her noisy breathing, she advances between the empty seats. "Excuse me, has the Jia trial been held yet?"

The clerk looks up. "It was over a quarter of an hour ago."

She composes her features into a smile, and stops only a few feet from him. "Can you tell me what the sentences were?" She had prepared a bribe of a few silver *taels* in her sleeve, but money is so tight that she hopes that she will not be forced to use it. To that end, she had washed and pressed her gown the day before, and had gone to Cousin Rong's to borrow makeup from his mother. She had smeared the cheap lead powder, which she would not ordinarily touch, over her face, and brightened her cheeks with the sticky rouge. She feels the clerk's gaze on her, both curious and admiring.

He consults the papers before him. "The first charge was treason. Jia Zheng got seven years—"

She stifles a gasp. How will Uncle Zheng survive seven years in prison? He will be an old man by the time he is released.

The clerk continues, "Jia Baoyu, Jia Lian, and Jia Huan each got three years."

Three years! Everyone knew that Lian and Huan had nothing

to do with politics; even Baoyu was no more than a dabbler. The court must be making an example of them. With a growing feeling of dread, she asks, "Were there any other charges?"

"Jia Lian was also sentenced to two years for usury."

The pit of her stomach grows cold with shock. So the loan agreements had been used against him. She imagines how furious he must be at her—and Lian's anger is the type that instead of dissipating with time only grows stronger without a vent. She is abjectly grateful that she will be spared from his anger for five years. But when he returns from prison, what then? Blindly she turns away from the clerk towards the courtroom door.

"There was one more charge." The clerk's voice stops her. She is surprised. "What is it?"

"Jia Zheng and Jia Baoyu were charged with obstruction of justice, and each got sentenced to two more years."

"Obstruction of justice?" she repeats. "What for?"

The clerk consults his papers once again. "Jia Zheng's nephew Xue Pan was involved in a murder case last fall—"

"A murder case! I didn't know anything about that."

The clerk continues, "Jia Zheng was charged with illegally approaching the district magistrate and getting him to drop the charges."

A dart of suspicion enters her mind. Jia Yucun had been a district magistrate before he was promoted. Was it possible that he had been the one overseeing Xue Pan's case? She had never known how Uncle Zheng and Yucun had become acquainted in the first place. Could Yucun have given evidence against Uncle Zheng?

Another clerk enters the courtroom and begins to gossip in an undervoice with the first one. "Did you hear that he's actually going to marry the Marquis of Donghou's daughter? Pretty well for a nobody from the country!"

She has never met the Marquis of Donghou's daughter, but

has heard of her spoken of as beautiful and accomplished, someone who would have been considered a good match for Baoyu
before the confiscation, had he not been betrothed to Baochai.
She wonders who they are talking about.

"And now he's been promoted from Under-Secretary to the
President of the Board of War to Minister of Rites," the first
clerk says. "Whoever heard of such a young man being made
Minister of Rites?"

A wave of sourness comes over her as she realizes that they
are talking about Yucun. Only a few months ago he had wanted
to marry her, and had told her that he would not marry to further his career.

"Don't you know why he's been promoted so fast?" the
second clerk asks maliciously.

"I've always heard he was hand in glove with the eunuchs."

"Yes, but there's another reason." The second clerk leans
down and begins to whisper in the first one's ear. She is close
enough to catch some of the words: " . . . gave evidence against
other officials about their ties to other Princes." Her earlier suspicion hardens into bitter certainty: Yucun had betrayed them.
When she had thought of the arrests and confiscation as the
blows of impersonal fate, she had been able to endure them
philosophically. How had Yucun hated her, to turn against them
like this? Was it because she had broken off the affair? Or was
it simply his ambition?

Slowly she goes towards the door.

Again the clerk's voice stops her. "Is there anything else you
want to know?"

She sees from his face that he is hoping to be paid for his
trouble, but she turns away. "No, nothing else."

Even the long walk through the gathering dusk does not blunt the fear and ache of betrayal in her heart. She turns onto Drum Street and enters the low-ceilinged, cluttered apartment, lit by a single lamp. On the narrow *kang*, Lady Jia, Tanchun, and Xichun all turn towards her eagerly, asking for news of the sentences. Ping'er, who is giving Qiaojie loquat syrup for her cough, looks up, her face anxious. Xifeng is struck anew by Daiyu's absence. She had disappeared during the chaos of the confiscation, and none of Xifeng's inquiries has yielded a clue as to her whereabouts. Mrs. Xue and Baochai come out from the single bedroom. The apartment is so crowded that she often wonders why they continue to live with the Jias, rather than moving in with Pan's wife.

"What's the news?" From her backrest, Lady Jia's imperious voice cuts through the babble of the others.

When she tells them the treason sentences, they are all stunned into silence. Lady Jia falls back with her eyes shut, as if she cannot bear to face the news. The others begin to weep. Even Qiaojie, infected by the others' tears, whimpers in Ping'er's arms.

"Seven years," Tanchun says. "How will we ever manage without Father for so long?"

Xifeng wonders herself. She has collected all the jewelry they were wearing the day of the confiscation and sewn it into the padding of a quilt. Ordinarily all of their jewelry should have amounted to thousands of *taels*. However, because of national mourning, everyone was wearing fewer and more modest pieces. Nevertheless, there were more than a dozen pieces, including less valuable items such as hair ornaments and her West Ocean watch. She has been pawning them one by one, to pay for their rent and living expenses, but even with the strictest economy, the jewelry will not be able to keep them for more than a few years.

Trying not to look at the Xues, she forces herself to continue.

"There was another charge as well. Uncle and Baoyu were also convicted for obstruction of justice."

"Obstruction of justice?" Lady Jia exclaims, bewildered.

"It seems that Uncle Zheng intervened in a murder case against Xue Pan."

"A murder case! What are you talking about?" Lady Jia turns to Mrs. Xue, who bursts into tears.

"Yes, it's true. Pan killed someone last year in a fight, and his family charged Pan with murder. I asked Zheng to speak to the district magistrate about it, and the charges were dropped. Zheng never said anything because he knew it would embarrass us." She kneels on the ground before Granny, kowtowing. "It never crossed my mind that you would be punished for Zheng's kindness."

Baochai's expression does not change, but her face flushes an unflattering beet-red, and her small eyes look down on the ground. She kneels beside her mother. "We would never have asked Uncle's help if we had thought it would injure you, after all your kindness to us."

For several moments there is no sound but Mrs. Xue's sobs. At last Lady Jia says, "That's all right." Despite the seeming generosity of her words, her face is expressionless, her voice dry. "We're such close kinsmen. You've lived with us for more than three years."

"Yes," Mrs. Xue stammers. "We are closer than ordinary kinsmen."

"If we don't stand by each other in times of trouble, then who will?" Lady Jia says.

"We will try to be worthy of your kindness to us." There is silence as Mrs. Xue and Baochai climb up from the floor.

Xifeng forces herself to break it. "There was one more charge." All the way home she had debated whether to tell the others about the usury charge. She could have lied about Lian's sentence. She could imagine their not finding out the truth for years; but she cannot bear the idea of living with such a secret over her head, one that might be discovered and revealed at her weakest moment.

"What is it?" Lady Jia says. "I know that they found those bolts of Palace Use silks in my room. Were we charged with possession of contraband?"

"No!" Forcing herself to get the words out, she speaks jerkily, "Lian was sentenced to two years for usury."

"Usury!" Granny looks dumbfounded. "He was making loans? To whom?"

She turns on Xifeng. "How could you let him? Why didn't you—" She stops, realizing the truth. "*He* didn't make the loans, did he?" She struggles to her feet, her face distorted by rage. "How dared you? After everything we've done for you, this is how you repay our kindness."

She had decided on the way home that the best strategy would be to admit her fault, but she feels choked by injustice, and retorts, "We were spending too much. I was worried we'd have money troubles later. I didn't think it was wrong to make some money on my own."

"You dare to defend yourself after disgracing the family like this? You should be begging my forgiveness. Look at what your selfishness and greed has brought upon the family."

"I didn't bring this on the family! The loans wouldn't have been discovered if not for the confiscation, which was Uncle Zheng's fault. And if the Embroidered Jackets hadn't found it, the money I made would be supporting us right now, and you would be grateful to me!" She doesn't know what has gotten into her, why she can't be silent and meek. Somehow she is not as afraid of Granny as she used to be. Torn loose from her home, servants, and money, Lady Jia is nothing but a querulous old woman who retains power because the rest of them are weak enough to obey her. "Why was it so wrong to try to make some money of my own? The men in this family know only how to spend money, not to make it. And look at you! We all saw how much money and jewels the Embroidered Jackets found in your room during the confiscation! How did you get all of that, except by—"

Granny steps forward and strikes her on the face with the force of her whole arm. She does not move, shocked and humiliated by the blow.

"Don't say another word! You commit a crime for which poor Lian, for which the whole family, has to pay. And instead of begging forgiveness, which you don't deserve, you dare to try to justify yourself."

Xifeng puts her hand to her burning cheek. She lowers her eyes, not to hide tears, but to hide her anger. She turns and goes into the back bedroom.

2

To Baochai's relief, Jingui does not keep her waiting for more than a few minutes before having her ushered into the Inner Quarters. To her amazement, she finds her sister-in-law deep in conversation with a strange young man on the *kang*.

"Oh, this is my adopted brother, Xia San," Jingui says, in response to Baochai's shocked look. He is a flashily dressed young man, Jingui's age or a little older.

"I didn't know that you had an adopted brother," Baochai says, trying to keep a tone of reproof out of her voice. It is wrong for Jingui to be entertaining men during Pan's absence.

"My mother adopted him this spring. He's come up to the Capital on business." Jingui turns to Xia San with a tinkling little laugh. "Why don't you go amuse yourself somewhere? My sister-in-law isn't used to much company."

After Xia San leaves, Jingui waves to Baochai to take his place on the cushion next to her. Surprised at this gesture of friendliness, Baochai climbs onto the *kang*. Seating herself beside Jingui, she is more than ever aware of the disparity between their appearances. Jingui is exquisitely dressed in a sable-lined red vest and yellow brocade gown. Baochai wears the same gown that she had been wearing the day of the confiscation, a lavender-sprigged brocade whose pale color shows the smudges of dirt around the wrists. Over it, she wears a bulky padded jacket, which she had made herself when the weather began to grow cold. Even her hairpins have been given to Xifeng to pawn. The only jewelry she wears is her gold pendant. Xifeng had refused to take it, insisting that it was as much a part of

Baochai as the jade was part of Baoyu. Now she is pleasantly aware of its weight beneath her gown.

"My mother would have come," she says, "but she wasn't feeling well. She sends you her regards. Have you heard from Pan lately?"

"No, I haven't. Tell me, how are the Jias doing?" Jingui's face is alive with malicious curiosity.

Prompted by Jingui's questions, Baochai repeats the charges and sentences against Uncle Zheng. Despite Jingui's exclamations of surprise, Baochai has the strange impression that she has heard them already.

"What about Baoyu?" Jingui asks.

Managing to keep her composure, Baochai tells Jingui that Baoyu will be in prison for five years.

"Good Heavens! You can't wait that long. Why don't you break the betrothal?"

Baochai looks down, feeling her face flush. "I'm not sure we can. After all, the dowry has already been paid, and we certainly can't expect to get it back at this point."

"Yes, that's true. Besides, it's not as if you could make much of a new match at this point. Everyone knows that you've been living with the Jias for years. For you to break things off with Baoyu now would only make you look bad."

What Jingui says is true, but Baochai cannot bring herself to tell the real reason that she cannot break the betrothal: Uncle Zheng and Baoyu had been convicted of obstruction of justice for helping Pan. How can she and her mother abandon the Jias after the risks Uncle Zheng had taken, the sentences he and Baoyu must serve? She herself had urged her mother to ask the Jias' help. How could she have known how the favor would bind the families together? And buried deep in her heart is another reason for not breaking the betrothal. On the day of the confiscation, when the men were being dragged off by the Embroidered Jackets, she had at first turned away, thinking that the sight would be too painful. Then she saw Baoyu with his arm protectively around Uncle Zheng, his face full of concern for his father. He looked so noble, so handsome, that her heart started to beat wildly, and she had actually cried his name and run a few steps after him. In that moment, Daiyu, and his affair with her, faded from her mind.

"And what about the Jia women?" Jingui asks. "Where are they living now?"

"At first, they lived with Cousin Rong, but there wasn't room, and Lady Jia didn't get along with Cousin Rong's mother. So they moved into a little apartment on Drum Street, south of Rongguo. Actually," Baochai forces herself to continue, "that was one of the reasons that I came today, to ask you whether my mother and I might come here to stay with you." She does not relish the idea of living with Jingui, but the conditions in Drum Street, with eight people, including a fussy, coughing baby, sleeping in one room, are nearly intolerable.

"Here?" Jingui says. Now that she has wormed all the information she wants out of Baochai, she is markedly less cordial. "I'm afraid that really wouldn't be convenient."

"We wouldn't be any trouble. We don't need much room."

"It's out of the question."

"Surely Pan would want you to let us live here."

Jingui gives a little shrug, clearly expressing her indifference to Pan's opinion.

Baochai had expected Jingui to refuse, and hoped that she would be more likely to accede to the next request, having already refused one. "If it isn't possible for us to live here, then, would it be possible for you to give us a loan?" she says. Determined to make the jewelry last as long as possible, Xifeng is extremely stingy about buying even such necessities as food and clothing.

"Pan took almost all our cash down south to buy merchandise. I'm afraid we haven't any to spare."

"Even something like thirty or forty *taels* would be extremely useful."

Jingui shakes her head. "I'm afraid not."

Baochai has never known anyone like her sister-in-law, who seems to feel no compunction about refusing all requests, feeling no need to even offer an excuse. She makes her final request. "Well, at least can you send a messenger to Pan down south?"

"Whatever for?"

"He doesn't know anything about what has happened to the Jias. Perhaps he should come back and see if he can help pull some strings on their behalf."

Jingui frowns. "I don't want him getting involved in any of this."

"But Uncle Zheng was charged with obstruction of justice only because he helped Pan in the first place. It's not right for him to sit by doing nothing—"

"I don't know anything about that, and I don't want to," Jingui snaps.

"Even if you don't, what is there to stop Uncle Zheng from drawing Pan into this mess? He can say that Pan put pressure on him to intervene, and perhaps they'll reopen Pan's case, too."

Baochai knows Uncle Zheng well enough to believe that he will in fact do everything he can to protect Pan, but she can see that Jingui is frightened.

After thinking a moment, frowning, she says, "Very well, I'll send a messenger to Pan."

"When?"

"Xia San is going back to Nanjing next week. I'll have him carry a message."

"You're sure?"

"Yes."

With that, Baochai must be satisfied.

3

Xifeng wakes up in the cold autumn dawn, disturbed by Qiaojie's coughing. In the light from the smudged paper panes, she turns to look at the baby beside her on the *kang*. Qiaojie coughs a little more, her face reddening from the exertion, and then settles back into sleep, her tiny hands clenching into fists above her blankets. On Qiaojie's other side, Ping'er is still sleeping soundly. Xifeng hears Tanchun's high, whistling snore from farther down the *kang*, but it is Granny's deeper rumble that keeps her awake. She rolls onto her back, careful not to nudge Qiaojie, only inches away, and lies looking at the water stains on the ceiling. All eight of them sleep squeezed onto the *kang* in the back room, in order to save coal by not heating the front room at night. She thinks of the days before the confiscation when she had reckoned coal by the wagonload.

Qiaojie coughs again, harder this time. She turns and sees Ping'er patting Qiaojie's back so she will go back to sleep.

"Do you think her cough is getting any better?" Ping'er whispers.

Xifeng raises herself on her elbow and leans her head so that Qiaojie's breath ruffles the hair beside her ears. She hears it, the faint liquid rattle deep in her chest. "I don't think so."

"The loquat syrup isn't doing any good."

"Should we try bird's nests?"

"I think we need to get another doctor. I don't trust the last one."

"I didn't think much of him either." Dr. Lu was a local practitioner recommended by Cousin Rong's mother. "Who should we get?"

"Can't we get the one who used to come before the confiscation?"

"Dr. Wang from the Imperial College? He's probably one of the most expensive doctors in the city."

"But he's good. Remember how he cured Baoyu of that terrible case of bronchitis?"

"We could try another one that isn't so expensive."

"But what if he isn't any good? Then we'll just have wasted our time and money. Besides, it's getting cold. It'll be better if Qiaojie is over her cough before winter comes."

Xifeng hesitates. She knows they must be careful with money, but how can she deny Qiaojie the best doctor?

Qiaojie stirs in her sleep and starts to whimper. The room is now bright, and around them, the others are stirring and reluctantly preparing to get out of bed. Granny Jia calls for someone to help her. Instead of obeying her summons, Xifeng lets Baochai take her place. She helps Ping'er sit up, and puts the baby to her breast. "I'll go to Dr. Wang today and ask him to come," she says.

Baochai walks home quickly from Jingui's house, eager to tell her mother the news. Jingui has kept her promise. Xia San had set out for Nanjing last week with a message for Pan. As she turns onto Drum Street, lowering her head against the blustery wind, she sees a well-dressed young woman walking back and forth along the alley as if looking for an address. When the woman turns towards her, she sees that it is Snowgoose.

"Snowgoose!" She hurries towards the maid. Her first impulse is to throw her arms around her. She seems like a ghost from a remote and happier life. "How are you?"

"I'm fine, thank you. And you, Miss Baochai?"

"I'm fine. Where did the Embroidered Jackets take you? Are you serving in another household now?"

"Yes. I was sent to the Princess of Nan'an's palace after the confiscation. I'm her body servant now."

It is no wonder that Snowgoose, with her intelligence and beauty, has swiftly attained a position of status in another household. She is as dainty and self-possessed as ever, her hands thrust into a squirrel muff, her cheeks powdered and rouged. It strikes Baochai that her manner, though pleasant, is formal; and she shows no particular pleasure at seeing Baochai.

"And the other senior maids?" she asks. "Where have they been sent?"

"I think Oriole was sent to the Countess of Xiping's. Chess was sent to Academician Mei's house, and Pearl was sent to General Guo's. I haven't seen any of them since the confiscation."

"How did you find us?"

"Master Rong told me your address."

"You've heard that Lord Jia and the others are in prison?" Baochai says, surprised that Snowgoose does not seem curious as to the fate of the rest of the family.

"Yes, the Princess told me."

"I suppose you'd like to see Lady Jia. Why don't you come in?"

"Actually, I came to see you."

Baochai is taken aback. "What for?"

"I wanted to ask you a favor."

"Yes, what is it?" Baochai says, at a loss.

"Miss Lin is sick. I remember you used to have those big, thick ginseng roots, and I was wondering if I could have a few for her."

"Miss Lin!" Baochai's heart gives a funny bound. "You know where she is?"

"Yes, she came to live with my family." As Snowgoose speaks, she looks straight into Baochai's eyes. A maid's eyes ought to be lowered submissively when talking to a mistress; there is challenge and accusation in the directness of Snowgoose's gaze. The Jias had been so negligent of Daiyu's safety during the confiscation that it had been left to a servant to take her in.

"She's ill, you said?" Baochai stammers.

"She is so delicate, and she had that bad cough last winter."

Baochai bridles at the maid's presuming to explain something about Daiyu to her, before she remembers, with a pang of shame, that by her own treatment of Daiyu she has forfeited any right to claim friendship or concern for her cousin.

"It got cold so quickly this fall," Snowgoose continues. "And our place is a little drafty."

Baochai can only imagine what sort of place Snowgoose's home is. Even the Jias' present quarters are probably palatial by comparison. She might beg Granny to let Daiyu return to live with them, but she knows how implacable Granny's anger is.

"If you can spare any of that ginseng . . . " Snowgoose says.

"I'm so sorry. Everything was taken in the confiscation."

"Oh." Snowgoose's face falls.

Baochai hesitates. "Is she very sick?"

Snowgoose looks at the ground.

"What does the doctor say?"

"He says it's consumption." Snowgoose's voice is so low that Baochai must lean close to catch the last word. Her heart sinks. Consumption is nearly incurable, even by the best doctors. Daiyu's mother had died of the same disease.

"Are you sure?"

"We had a second doctor come, and he said the same thing."

It must have been a great burden for Snowgoose's family to pay for two doctors. She wishes she had a few *taels* to give Snowgoose, but Xifeng keeps all the family's cash. She sees tears in Snowgoose's eyes. The maid rubs them quickly away. "I must go. The Princess can spare me for only an hour or two."

"Don't you want to pay your respects to Lady Jia?"

"I'm afraid I can't. Perhaps I can come back another time." Snowgoose turns to go.

Again it strikes Baochai that Snowgoose speaks politely but without warmth. She thinks of all the years Snowgoose served Lady Jia, yet she has not even asked about her old mistress's health. What binds her to Daiyu, whom she seems to treat like a sister?

"Snowgoose!" she calls. The maid has already gone a few steps.

"What is it?" Snowgoose turns back.

"Can you give me your address? I'd like to see her."

Snowgoose is silent. Baochai fears Snowgoose will tell her that Daiyu does not want to see her. At last, Snowgoose says, "Do you have anything to write on?"

Baochai has a crumpled shopping list and a stump of charcoal. Snowgoose takes them from her. Pressing the paper against a wall, she writes the address slowly and painstakingly on the back.

"I didn't know you knew how to write."

"I know just a few characters. Miss Lin taught me."

Snowgoose hands Baochai the paper and disappears.

4

Xifeng stands outside the busy apothecary, fingering the small packet of medicine the druggist had compounded for her. She reads over Dr. Wang's prescription, making sure that she had seen the druggist measure out each of the ingredients: *banlangen*, coix, licorice, mulberry leaf, forsythia, wild chrysanthemum, orange peel, and ginseng. Dr. Wang had taken a serious view of Qiaojie's ailment. She suffered from excessive heat in the lungs accompanied by a serious deficiency of *yin*. In addition, it was necessary to supplement her diet in order to strengthen her *qi*. He had also recommended bird's nests as a tonic for her lungs.

This apothecary, the best in the city, is known for the purity and high quality of its ingredients. She stands outside its door wondering whether she should go to a cheaper place to get the bird's nests. After a moment, she plunges back into the apothecary and buys three drams. She walks away feeling the one silver *tael* left in her sleeve. When she looks up, she sees Jia Yucun walking towards her on the other side of the street. She has not laid eyes on him in more than half a year. He has gained weight, making him look older, more substantial, and wears robes of heavy blue brocade. She turns quickly down a side alley. How much has she changed, for the worse, with her shabby robe and her face roughened and bare of makeup?

She has gone only about ten paces when she hears the sound of hurried footfalls behind her. She quickens her pace. In that brief moment when she hears his panting breath and running steps behind her, she feels a bittersweet happiness. Whatever else has happened between them, whatever words they will exchange, it is he who is chasing her.

He calls her name, but she hurries on, ignoring him.

"Xifeng!" She feels his hand on her arm, and pulls away. He grasps her arm again, so that she swings around and faces him.

"What do you want?"

"I wanted to know—are you all right?" His voice is hoarse and his face looks pale, perhaps from the exertion of running.

"What's it to you?" She jerks herself away.

"Why are you acting like this?" He runs after her and catches her arm again.

"You think I'm a fool? You think I don't know that you gave evidence against Uncle Zheng?"

"I had no choice."

She snorts scornfully.

"It's true." He stumbles on, as if eager for a chance to explain himself. "If I hadn't mentioned Jia Zheng, they would have thought I was protecting him because he was my kinsman. And he was vulnerable already. He was too naïve, and hadn't cultivated his relationships with his superiors properly. Even if I hadn't named him, someone else would have . . . " He holds her hands, as if pleading for her understanding.

She yanks them away. "Don't try to justify yourself! Didn't you ever think what it would be like for me, for Ping'er and Qiaojie, being thrown out of our home?"

"I loved you. I wanted to take care of you." She sees beads of sweat on his brow despite the chilly autumn air. "It was you who broke things off."

She feels a rush of triumph—he loves her still and is still wounded by their parting—but also a piercing sadness. "What could I do? I'm married." In her pain, she lashes out at him. "And why should I believe you? If you loved me, you chose a strange way of showing it."

"What choice did I have? After you wouldn't see me anymore, what could I do but throw myself into my work?"

"Yes, but you've gotten married, too. You haven't wasted any time in forgetting me."

She knows him so well that she can see from the tightening of his lips that she has touched a sore spot. "The Eunuch Chamberlain arranged the match for me."

"I'm sure you wanted to refuse," she sneers. "I've heard she's perfectly beautiful."

"I did want to refuse. You know the Marquis of Donghou. Do you think I dare disobey him in any matter, no matter how trivial? If I do anything my wife dislikes, she complains to him immediately. I knew it would happen, but how could I refuse?"

Despite herself, she believes him. Without money and family of his own, how can he stand up to his powerful in-laws? Suddenly she feels very tired. She turns back towards the main road. "There's no use talking."

"Where are you going?" He trails after her.

"Home."

"Where is that?"

Without looking at him, she says, "We're renting a small apartment off Drum Street, south of Rongguo."

After a pause, he says, "Can't we see each other?" He gives an awkward laugh. "After all, Lian's in jail now."

She stares at him. Would he really risk it, now that he has so much to lose? As for herself, even if she could find a way to disappear for a few hours without anyone noticing, even if she could tear herself away from Qiaojie, would she want to? Meeting him, which had once seemed so pleasurable, now seems pure pain. What has changed? He had betrayed the Jias, but she does not after all condemn him: Wouldn't she have done the same in his circumstances? Has she simply lost hope that he could rescue her or help her in any way? She feels a welling of self-pity, but it is as much for him as for herself. He is as trapped as she is.

"Goodbye," she says, without looking at him. She slips into the surge of people on the main thoroughfare and lets herself be borne away on their stream.

5

Baochai buttons up her padded robe in the back room.

"It's windy," her mother says. "You'd better wear a scarf."

She has told no one, not even her mother, that she plans to visit Daiyu. Instead she has said she is going to see if Jingui has heard from Pan. She goes out into the front room, wrapping a scarf around her shoulders. Xifeng and Ping'er are holding a wailing Qiaojie over a pot of steaming water with a towel draped over her head. After finding the congestion in Qiaojie's lungs worse at his last examination, Dr. Wang had recommended this process as a means of clearing them. Now Xifeng is slapping Qiaojie's back, not gently, to loosen the phlegm.

Xifeng looks up. "Will you be going by an apothecary?"

"Yes, there's one on Huizhong Street."

"Would you get a dram of bird's nests? We're almost out."

"Of course."

Xifeng goes to the back room, where she keeps the cash box under a pile of Qiaojie's clothes. In a moment she returns empty-handed, her expression harried. "Never mind. We don't have enough money. I'll have to pawn a bracelet."

"I can do it if you like."

"That's all right. I'll do it. You won't be able to get as much money for it as I will," Xifeng says with a flash of her old playfulness.

As Baochai sets out, she looks down at the address Snowgoose had given her. She guesses she will have to walk across nearly the length of the city, a distance of perhaps four or five *li*, the longest she has ever walked by herself. She is nervous that strange men will harass her, but everyone scurries about with their heads bowed against the gritty wind. The wind is the worst part of her walk, making her eyes water and her head ache.

When she gets to the southern edge of the city, she is surprised to see how different it is from Drum Street. She had thought Drum Street shabby and dingy, but here, the streets are narrower, the houses denser, the corners piled with refuse. She gathers her courage to ask a woman emptying a chamber pot where Flowers Street is. The woman directs her to a street a little farther on. When she gets there, she sees a blacksmith working in front of his shop, and decides to ask him where the Zhens live. She approaches the forge, spitting red sparks, and calls to him above the roar of the fire. He steps away from the forge, and when he hears that she is looking for the Zhens, he looks at her in some surprise. "I am Zhen Shiyin. What can I do for you?"

With a start, she realizes he must be Snowgoose's brother. Beneath the soot and sweat he is quite a young man. She is appalled that Daiyu could be living here amid all this smoke and noise. "Excuse me," she stammers. "I'm Xue Baochai. I am looking for my cousin, Lin Daiyu."

She sees that his expression has become wary, even a little unfriendly, and wonders what Daiyu and Snowgoose have told him.

"Yes, she's here. Come this way." His voice is so quiet that she can hardly hear it over the fire. He turns away from the forge, wiping his hands on a cloth tucked into his leather apron. He goes behind his shop to a door on the side of the building and knocks gently. Then, sticking his head in, he calls, "There is someone here to see you," and opens the door wide to let Baochai in.

She hesitates a moment before stepping through. The door

closes behind her, shutting out much of the noise of the forge, but also much of the light. She blinks, adjusting to the darkness, and sees a small, dingy room. In the meager light of a single high window, she sees a thin figure in a welter of blankets on the *kang* struggling to pull on a jacket, one sleeve on and one sleeve off. The figure looks up, and Baochai sees that it is Daiyu, her black eyes blazing with hope and joy. She has grown so thin that Baochai hardly recognizes her. As Daiyu looks at Baochai, the glow and color drain from her face. She stops trying to dress, and lets herself flop back on the pillows with a hopeless little sigh. Baochai understands. When Daiyu heard that someone was there to see her, she had imagined that it was Baoyu. Doesn't she know that Baoyu is in prison? She has not seen Daiyu since that day more than two months ago when she had washed Daiyu's hair. Surely Daiyu's coldness means that she knows that Baochai had betrayed her.

Baochai takes a few quick steps into the room. "How are you?" she says. Impulsively, she climbs onto the *kang* to help Daiyu up. Through the jacket sleeve, her fingers feel how thin and fleshless Daiyu's arm is.

Daiyu tries to pull her arm away, but is overcome by a fit of coughing. The sound of the cough fills Baochai with foreboding. It is dry and hacking, originating deep in Daiyu's chest, racking her whole body. She coughs for a minute or so, doubled over, her face and eyes growing red. The fit gradually passes, and she leans back against her cushions. She gives a tiny shrug. "I am as you see me," she says at last.

In her horror at Daiyu's condition, Baochai speaks without thinking. "Isn't there anyone here to take care of you? Don't tell me that you lie here by yourself all day!"

She immediately regrets her words. Daiyu looks coldly at her. "Who would there be to take care of me? Mr. and Mrs. Zhen work as servants in other households in the daytime. Snowgoose stops in when she can, but it isn't very often, since the Princess's is on the other side of the Capital."

"But who cooks for you? Who makes your medicine?"

Daiyu looks at Baochai with her lips compressed, as if considering whether to answer. At last she says, "Shiyin does almost everything for me, and he comes in and sits with me when he isn't busy."

The thought that Daiyu is looked after by a man, and a rough laborer at that, sharpens Baochai's guilt to an almost unbearable point. If not for her, Daiyu would still be with the Jias, surrounded by and nursed by her cousins. Squatting on the *kang*, she looks about the small, close room, its walls darkened by leaks and smoke. The air is foul and damp because of the poor ventilation. Zhen Shiyin has begun working again, and Baochai can clearly hear the metallic striking of his hammer.

There is an awkward silence. To break it, Baochai says, "You know that Uncle and the others are in prison." She cannot bring herself to mention Baoyu's name.

"Snowgoose told me." Daiyu is silent for a while, leaning against the pillows with her face expressionless. Then, as if feeling she must make some effort to talk, she says, "How is Qiaojie?" She struggles to prop herself up higher, and after hesitating a moment Baochai helps her shift the pillows so that she is half sitting. "Let's see. She must be more than six months old by now."

"Actually, she's very sick."

"What's the matter with her?"

"She's had a terrible cough all autumn. Her lungs are congested, and she seems to be growing weaker and weaker—" Baochai, realizing that what she is describing may closely resemble Daiyu's symptoms, breaks off abruptly. Now there is an even longer silence.

"If—if there is any way I can help you—some more clothes, or some food that you would like, I could bring it for you—"

"No!" Daiyu shakes her head, and the vehemence of her refusal brings on another fit of coughing. This fit is worse, and longer, than the previous one. Daiyu lies back again, gasping against the cushion.

"Can I get you anything?"

"Yes, some tea," Daiyu pants, pointing at the stove on the other side of the room. She begins to cough again.

Baochai scrambles off the *kang*. Frantically, she lifts the covers of the pots and pans lined up on the ledge beside the stove. There is some leftover rice, some lumpy-looking stewed grain—millet, perhaps—some boiled mung beans, and a pot of murky brown liquid that she takes to be medicine. "I don't see any tea."

"It's that one," Daiyu gasps, jabbing her finger at the last pot.

Baochai pours the liquid into a cup and rushes back to the *kang*. She finds Daiyu retching into a spittoon with a cracked rim. When Daiyu is done, Baochai hands her the tea and takes the spittoon. As Daiyu gulps the tea, Baochai's eyes fall on the contents of the spittoon. The viscous liquid is filled with dark clots of blood. On top is a coiled snake of fresh scarlet. Daiyu is in the last stages of consumption.

"Yes, this is what we call tea here," Daiyu says, wiping her mouth with a crumpled handkerchief. "Although at Rongguo, it wouldn't even pass muster as mouthwash."

Baochai says nothing. She stares at the spittoon, wondering whether Daiyu has any idea of how soon she will die. She takes her cousin's hand. She is afraid that Daiyu will pull away, but the thin hand lies unresisting in her own.

"You must take better care of yourself."

Daiyu shrugs, sighing wearily.

"You must listen to me. You've always neglected your health. Remember how you didn't take care of yourself when you came back from Suzhou after your father died? I know you. You never take care of yourself when something is bothering you—" She breaks off, realizing that she cannot speak of the emotional wound from which Daiyu suffers, her separation from Baoyu and abandonment by the Jias, because that wound had been inflicted by Baochai herself.

"What's the use?" Daiyu looks up from her pillows into Baochai's eyes. "I know I have consumption. It's what my mother died of. I've heard them say the nurse often catches it as well. I seemed all right, until this winter. I suppose the seeds of the sickness were in my body all along."

Daiyu's words reproach her. She has heard that sometimes consumption lies dormant in its victim until coldness and damp and poor nourishment provide the disease the conditions in which to take root. The tears start to her eyes, but she blinks them away before Daiyu notices. She grasps for something to say to give encouragement and comfort, and a memory from what seems a long time ago comes back to her.

"Do you remember when we had a picnic, on the day of the Grave Sweeping Festival?"

Daiyu stares at her a moment, before nodding her head. "Yes. All the men were at the family burial grounds, and we girls were at the pavilion on the lake. That was when we got the news that Silver had drowned herself—"

"Yes, that's right. We were talking about girls, and whether they had any choices in life." Baochai's mind unspools the scene, remembering what everyone had said. "Xifeng said they didn't."

"Yes, and I agreed with her."

Baochai nods. "I've thought about that conversation more than once since then," she stumbles on, in a hurry to get the words out. "I didn't think so at the time, but I've come to believe that you and Xifeng were right."

For the first time, Daiyu smiles, a little mockingly. "*We* were right? Imagine that."

Baochai ignores Daiyu's interjection. "A girl's husband is

chosen for her, and whatever he does, she has to accept. If he commits a crime and ends up in jail, even if she doesn't know anything about it, she suffers for it just the same." She is speaking not just of her own experience, but of all the Jia women. It is unlike her to express her opinions and feelings like this, her shock at Daiyu's condition overcoming her reserve. "It made me unhappy. I used to think if a woman was virtuous, she could control what other people did, by teaching and example. But that's not what people are like. They're not so easy to control."

"No, they're not." Daiyu smiles again. This time her smile is a little sad.

"I suppose I should have realized that long ago from Pan," Baochai says, with a touch of bitterness. "But now I think that women do have one choice, that no one can take from them."

"What is it?"

"They can choose whether to live or die," Baochai says. She catches Daiyu's gaze with her own, holding it insistently.

Daiyu's eyes slide away from Baochai's after a moment, and she gives a nervous laugh. "Do you mean that they have a choice whether or not to commit suicide, like Silver?"

"No." Baochai suspects Daiyu of willfully misunderstanding her. "I don't mean that. I mean," she says, trying to put her thoughts into words, "that a woman can just give up, or she can struggle to survive and make the most of her life."

Daiyu is silent for a long time. She shuts her eyes, moving her head restlessly against the pillows. At last she opens them and looks directly into Baochai's eyes. "If you are saying that I have given up hope, you are right. I don't have any reason to live. My parents are both dead. I've been nothing but a burden on the Jias, and now I'm a burden on Snowgoose's family. Besides—"

She breaks off. Baochai has the distinct impression that she was going to say something about Baoyu, but stopped herself. She falls silent again.

Baochai reaches for her hand. "Things are difficult now, but who knows what they will be like, if you can only get through this?" Even as she speaks, she feels she is being falsely optimistic. Her mother has used the same words to comfort her, but her own and Daiyu's positions are very different. What does Daiyu have to look forward to? Since she has left the Jias, who is there to arrange a match for her, or provide her with a dowry? What sort of life can she possibly have now?

Daiyu receives Baochai's homily with a shrug. "No, I don't think that way. I am already resigned. In fact, I have only one remaining wish before I die."

Baochai stiffens at Daiyu's seemingly casual reference to her own death. "What is it?"

"To see my home again. But, of course, it can't possibly be fulfilled." Daiyu smiles. This time her smile is wistful. Then she closes her eyes, as if exhausted. Lacking the animation it had taken on while she was speaking, her face looks wasted, mask-like.

Baochai squeezes Daiyu's hand again, wanting to say more, when she notices Zhen Shiyin standing inside the door. He looks much more presentable, having taken off his stained leather apron, and washed his face and hands. He approaches the *kang* and whispers to her that it is time for Miss Lin to rest. She is amused by his protective air, but then she looks at Daiyu and sees that she seems to be drifting off to sleep. Looking back as long as she can at Daiyu's still figure, she follows Zhen Shiyin out into the front yard. When she passes through the door, the sunlight and wind and noise of the fire strike her like a blow. She stands there in the yard, blinking and trying to regain her composure. She sees that Zhen Shiyin is beside her.

"How long has she been like this?"

"When it started to get cold in the Eighth Month, she got a bad cough, and it's gotten worse and worse."

"What does the doctor say?"

"He says there isn't much we can do, other than make her comfortable." Looking up at him, she sees his eyebrows puckered into an expression of such patient suffering that it occurs to her that he is in love with Daiyu.

She slips her hand into her sleeve, where she has put the two silver *taels* she had gotten from her mother, under the pretense that she wished to buy a small gift for Jingui. "Is there anything that she needs? Perhaps you can use this, to make her more comfortable—"

Before she can take the money out, he stops her, with a stern look on his face.

"I insist," she says, thinking that he is merely making a show of being polite.

When she takes the silver out, however, he looks positively angry. She feels humiliated by the rebuff, and understands that he refuses out of loyalty to Daiyu, out of a sense that it would be wrong to accept money from someone who has injured her. And yet, she cannot leave without doing something for Daiyu. If only she could make her more comfortable, make her death easier—how much it would appease her own conscience. She slips her hand into her collar. Her fingers close on her gold pendant. She draws it over her head and thrusts it into Zhen Shiyin's hand.

Bewildered, he refuses to take it.

She uses her other hand to grip his wrist and forces the pendant between his fingers. "Take it. Use it for her burial expenses." She starts to cry. "I know that she would want to be buried down south, with her parents. Use this to take her body back to Suzhou."

He takes the pendant. He bows his head, seeming to acknowledge the truth of her words.

6

"Does Qiaojie feel hot to you?" Ping'er says, frowning, as she puts the baby to her breast first thing in the morning.

The morning is bitterly cold, and Xifeng is hurriedly pulling on her own robes. She stops with her robes unfastened and leans over to feel Qiaojie's forehead. It strikes her as a little warm, but not terribly hot. She pushes up Qiaojie's jacket and feels her belly. Again, the skin feels slightly warmer than usual.

"She might be a little feverish," she says, puzzled. "But I don't think the fever is very high." Qiaojie had appeared to be getting better the last few days. Though she ate no more than usual, she had actually slept through the past two nights without coughing or needing to be nursed.

"Should we send for the doctor? He said we should tell him if there was any change in her condition."

Xifeng hesitates. She has been appalled at how quickly the doctor's and druggist's bills have mounted. She has already had to pawn three more pieces of jewelry. "I don't think we need to," she says slowly. "It really doesn't seem to be anything to worry about."

After breakfast, she is restless, watching Qiaojie, wondering if she seems a little sluggish. Unable to abide by her own words, she goes to see Dr. Wang. When she tells him that Qiaojie has a slight fever, he seems unconcerned and says he will come by the following day if the fever persists. Relieved, she hurries home to Drum Street. When she feels Qiaojie's forehead, it seems no hotter than earlier. She and Ping'er begin the morning routine of giving Qiaojie her medicine and bird's nests, and of clearing her lungs. Although she braces herself for the unpleasant tasks, they go more easily than usual. Qiaojie does not cry when Xifeng gives her the medicine. She hardly struggles when they hold her over the steaming pot. When Xifeng pounds her back afterwards, Qiaojie coughs up a large blob of putrid yellow phlegm so thick that it is almost solid. Instinctively she whisks it away without saying anything, not wanting to scare Ping'er.

After the "steaming," Ping'er sits down with Qiaojie, and Xifeng tries to feed her a bit of stewed carp. To their delight, Qiaojie consumes four or five bites.

"Look at her trying to chew," Ping'er says.

Qiaojie's two bottom front teeth, just emerging from her gums, are barely visible.

Xifeng wipes Qiaojie's chin. "But most of it is ending up on her jacket." She puts a morsel of carp on the tip of the spoon, and pretends that the spoon is a bee, buzzing and circling around Qiaojie before slowly swooping down towards her mouth. Qiaojie reaches out and grabs the spoon with her still-plump little fist. Even though the fish falls onto the *kang*, Xifeng and Ping'er laugh delightedly.

"She's never done that before," Ping'er says.

Impulsively Xifeng swoops Qiaojie out of Ping'er's lap. "What a clever baby!" She buries her face in Qiaojie's stomach. Qiaojie's face breaks into her charming, toothless smile. Xifeng swings her high in the air and dances her about. "Look at that! She's laughing!" Baochai and Mrs. Xue and the Two Springs, attracted by the unusual excitement, come over and exclaim and coo over the baby, until it is time for her to nap.

The rest of the day passes quietly enough. Xifeng and Ping'er agree that Qiaojie does not seem to be getting hotter, and that it will be all right to wait until the following day for the doctor to come. Xifeng does not notice any change in her behavior except that she is more docile and less fussy than usual. She even lets Xichun hold her while Ping'er takes a nap and Xifeng goes to market.

After dinner has been cleared, when Ping'er is putting Qiaojie into her nightclothes, she says, "I think she's hotter."

Even before Xifeng touches Qiaojie, she notices her flushed cheeks and labored breathing. Her hands and stomach are scorching. "We must send for the doctor now," she says, her voice strangely harsh in the silent room.

"It's too late, surely," Lady Jia says from the *kang*. "He'll have gone to bed."

"It's barely eight thirty," Xifeng says, looking at her watch. "I don't think we can wait for tomorrow."

"I'm sure he charges an additional fee for late-night visits," Lady Jia says.

Xifeng ignores her, looking around at the others, who are pale and quiet as if sensing the impending crisis. She wonders whether she can trust any of them to fetch the doctor, or whether she must go herself.

"I'll get the doctor," Baochai says. Xifeng relaxes, knowing that she is the most resourceful of all the girls.

"I'll go, too," says Tanchun. The two of them bundle up against the frosty night and hurry out with a lantern.

"What should we do?" Ping'er says, almost crying. "She has gotten so hot."

"We can undress her at least." With shaking hands Xifeng removes Qiaojie's tunic and trousers, so that she is only in her diaper. Every time her fingers touch Qiaojie's skin, she is struck by how hot and dry it is. Even more frightening is the way she looks. She is breathing heavily, almost puffing like a toad. She does not cry, but her head moves back and forth fitfully. Her black eyes are open but she does not appear to recognize them.

"Qiaojie! Qiaojie!" Xifeng says, trying to get those wandering eyes to focus.

Qiaojie's body jerks and twitches so she almost falls out of Ping'er's arms. Her eyes roll back in her head, and it seems to Xifeng that she has stopped breathing.

"Qiaojie! Qiaojie!" Xifeng screams. She snatches Qiaojie and holds her ear to Qiaojie's chest. She is breathing, but her limbs continue to jerk spasmodically. "I think she's having convulsions from the fever!" She looks around wildly, trying to think. "Wet some washcloths! And warm some water!" She is afraid that cold water will be too much of a shock to Qiaojie's system.

Xichun and Mrs. Xue rush to get the washcloths. Now Qiaojie is lying limply in her arms. Her complexion looks slightly blue, but at least she can hear Qiaojie's stertorous breathing again. She and Ping'er hover over Qiaojie, wiping her face and neck with the cool cloths, until Xichun brings a basin of warm water. They dip the cloths into the basin and sponge Qiaojie's chest and back and legs with them. She now appears to be asleep, still breathing heavily.

"I am going to bed," Lady Jia announces, as if the others have created this disturbance for the sole purpose of preventing her from going to sleep. Xifeng does not even glance at her. After a moment, Mrs. Xue, who has been watching them sponge Qiaojie, helps Lady Jia to the back bedroom.

"Where's the doctor?" Ping'er says.

Xifeng glances at her watch. She is shocked to see that only forty minutes have passed since Baochai and Tanchun set out for the doctor.

She sees that Qiaojie's eyes are open. Ping'er calls to her, patting her hand and kissing her cheek, but Qiaojie goes into another convulsion. This time Xifeng holds her firmly, trying to stroke her hot forehead. Gradually, the spasmodic movements of her arms and legs quiet, and she falls into a heavy stupor, breathing noisily.

A little after ten thirty, the doctor arrives with Baochai and Tanchun. He feels Qiaojie's wrist, his face intent. "Her pulse is extremely rapid and powerful. Her body is suffering from an excess of heat, to the point of toxicity, and the congestion of her lungs is very severe."

"What can be done?" Ping'er cries.

"I'll make a plaster for her chest for the congestion. The toxicity can be combated with a combination of bitter-cold drugs, such as *huanglian*, *huangqin*, and *zhizi*. Usually I am cautious about using these drugs, because they can be very damaging to the stomach, but in this case, I believe the benefit outweighs the risks."

He opens his case filled with various vials and papers of herbs and begins to weigh them out and crush them together. When Xifeng tells him about the convulsions and using water to cool Qiaojie, he looks stern. "You shouldn't have done that."

"Why not?"

"The patient must sweat to dispel the toxicity."

While Dr. Wang ties a flat gauze bag of herbs and ointments across Qiaojie's chest, he orders Xifeng to mix the medicine he has just compounded with hot water. She goes to the stove, reassured by his air of calm authority. He tells the others that Ping'er's and Xifeng's help will be sufficient, and that the rest of them might as well go to sleep. He has Xifeng blow out all the lamps except the one near the stove. In the quiet dimness, Xifeng feels her panic start to recede. When she has mixed the medicine, Dr. Wang tells Ping'er to wake Qiaojie so he can give it to her. Ping'er calls Qiaojie, jiggling her hands and tugging her feet, until she finally opens her eyes. To Xifeng's relief, her eyes no longer move restlessly and unseeingly in their sockets. She lies there calmly. Her black eyes, looking now at Ping'er's face, now at her own, have never seemed so clear, so lucid. Giddy with relief, she leans over, kissing Qiaojie's cheek, patting her head and dear little hands.

She moves aside to allow Dr. Wang to administer the medicine. Skillfully he pours it down a narrow tube inserted into the corner of Qiaojie's mouth, and she swallows it unresistingly.

"Let's wait and see if this has any effect," Dr. Wang says. He makes himself comfortable against a cushion on the *kang*, and she is glad that he seems ready to stay all night if necessary. She sits down next to Ping'er so she can be as close to Qiaojie as possible. Qiaojie looks quietly at them and about the room. Xifeng takes her hand and sings a lullaby, gently swinging her hand. By the time she has sung the song twice, Qiaojie has again dropped off to sleep.

"How will we tell if the medicine is working?" Xifeng asks.

"Her fever will go down, and perhaps she'll break out in a sweat."

They watch her silently for about twenty minutes. Qiaojie's breathing seems to be growing more and more labored.

"Doctor, isn't there anything you can do about her breathing?" Xifeng says.

"Yes, I'm worried about that, too. Let me see if I can make a stronger dispersant." He opens his case and begins to weigh out some more herbs.

Now Qiaojie seems to be struggling for every breath. Sometimes she even seems to stop breathing for a moment before gasping and drawing another breath.

"Doctor, won't you look at her?" Ping'er cries. "She can hardly breathe!"

Dr. Wang puts down the half-made medicine and hurries over.

"Try to wake her," he says sharply.

Xifeng and Ping'er call to her, and tug her hands, more and

more vigorously, but she does not respond. Her breathing is getting more and more erratic. Xifeng notices, as she slaps Qiaojie's feet, no longer gently, that her face is no longer flushed but a waxen yellow. She is gasping every few breaths now. After missing a few breaths, she lifts up her chin as if to gasp for air. Her lips part, but no sound comes. She lies there, her mouth positioned for the next breath, but unable to take it. In a frenzy, Xifeng and Ping'er chafe her hands, pat her cheeks, shift her position, but there is no response.

"It's too late," the doctor says.

Ping'er bursts into tears, burying her face in her hands. For a moment, Xifeng stares at him, unable to comprehend his words. She falls on Qiaojie, unable to believe she is dead. She catches her to her breast, nestles Qiaojie's head against her cheek, holds her close, trying to engulf her with her own body, to somehow transfer her own strength and life to the baby. But even as she presses Qiaojie against herself, she can sense a change. Already, beneath her hands, she feels the unhealthy warmth of Qiaojie's body dissipating. Already she seems to feel a slight rigidity stealing over the soft limbs. The little hands are clenching into loose fists. The head bows forward stiffly. She kisses the little brow, now cooler to her touch, but senses that Qiaojie's spirit is already gone. So quickly—how quickly—has the flame of her life been extinguished, leaving her body an empty shell. She places Qiaojie's body gently on the edge of the *kang*, covering it with a blanket, and falls into Ping'er's arms.

7

Daiyu lies on the *kang* at the Zhens' house, drifting between waking and sleeping. She spends most of her time in this state these days, her dreams and her waking thoughts often flowing indistinguishably together, her mind floating free of its moorings. Her mind feels less clear than even a few weeks ago, dulled by her body's weakness and lack of nourishment—she can hardly bring herself to swallow a few bites each day—and by her long days lying in the dark apartment. It is like a slow sluggish river sweeping and tumbling the detritus of her life in its turbid flow. Between confused, fragmented dreams, she thinks of her parents' death, her time at Rongguo, and Baoyu's and Baochai's betrayals. Baochai she might have been able to forgive, but her anger against Baoyu runs far deeper. He had won her trust and her love, and then abandoned her, allowing Lady Jia to mistreat her and now leaving her to die alone. Lying there in the dark room, she feels her loneliness and resentment against him running like poison in her veins.

She hears the door open. It is Zhen Shiyin, coming in for lunch. Too tired to turn her head to watch him, she hears him moving around the stove, as quietly as he can, making lunch. Comforted by his presence, she drifts off to sleep. She wakes to find him calling to her, with the gentleness she finds so soothing. He has finished cooking lunch and, as always, has set up a little table on the *kang* next to her. No matter how little she eats, he always sets out two bowls of rice, two bowls of soup, and two saucers of pickled cabbage. "Miss Daiyu, do you think you can eat anything today?"

"Maybe just a little soup." She is surprised at how weak and hoarse her voice sounds. She can hardly recognize it as her own.

He props her up against some pillows, blows on the soup to cool it. She tries to take the bowl from him, but he will not let her, and spoons the clear broth into her mouth for her. After a few mouthfuls she shakes her head, and he puts the bowl down.

"A little rice?" he offers hopefully.

She shakes her head.

"Some tea?"

"No, thank you."

"Do you want to lie down?"

"No, not yet. Let me sit with you while you eat."

He sits cross-legged beside the little table, and, hungry after his morning's work, begins to shovel the rice into his mouth with his chopsticks. She watches him with the envious wonder that the sick feel for the healthy, but also with affection. He reminds her of Snowgoose, especially in the delicate precision of his movements, despite the roughness of his work. Like Snowgoose, he does not express himself easily in words, and yet his generosity and sensitivity are clear in the consideration with which he treats her and everyone else. She has lived with the Zhens for three months, using up his scanty earnings, and requiring his constant care and nursing, yet he has never once made her feel that her presence is anything but an honor.

He finishes his bowl of rice and the pickles. Now he is drinking the soup, sighing a little with enjoyment. She thinks of how tiring and unpleasant it must be for him to work from sunup till sundown in all that noise and soot and heat. And for what? The best he can hope for is to earn enough money to take care of his parents when they are too old to work, and perhaps to provide Snowgoose with a dowry.

"Don't you ever get tired of it?" she asks abruptly, turning her head on the pillows to look at him.

"Of what?" He looks up from his bowl.

"Of working so hard."

"Of course I get tired. You've seen how exhausted I am at the end of the day, sometimes."

"But that's all you do: work day after day. You never even take a day off. Don't you ever feel frustrated or hopeless?"

"I do sometimes, but then I think of how I can help my family by working hard. You know how my family scrimped and saved so that I could learn a trade—that was when they sold Snowgoose. It always makes me want to do as much as I can to repay them."

This is what she lacks, she tells herself, a sense of belonging, a sense of someone to work for. If her parents had lived, she also would feel a greater sense of purpose. "But is that enough? Don't you want things for yourself?"

"For myself?" he says, not knowing what she means.

"I mean, things that make *you* happy."

At first he still seems baffled by her words, but then he says, after thinking a moment, "Well, I'd like to learn how to read. You've taught me a few words, but I want to learn more, so I can read books and poems and songs for myself. And I'd like to travel. I've heard so much about how beautiful the south is that I'd like to go there someday and see it all for myself."

He pauses, and then goes on a little bashfully, not looking at her. "I'd like to get married and have children one day. You know what they say: a thousand meetings, a thousand partings, they are all predestined by the gods. For example, I would never have imagined that I would ever meet someone like you."

Something catches in her throat, and she begins to cough before she can answer him. It is a bad fit, and he has to pass her the spittoon and give her a drink of tea before it passes.

"I shouldn't have tired you out by talking so much," he says. "You'd better rest."

She gratefully lets him help her back into a lying position. A deep exhaustion wafts over her, and she feels herself drifting into sleep. The next time she wakes, she hears Snowgoose's voice. She wants to call to her, but her limbs feel so heavy that she can hardly move. She is lying there, trying to gather the strength to speak to Snowgoose, when she realizes that Snowgoose and Shiyin are talking about her.

"How much has she eaten the last few days?" Snowgoose asks.

"Almost nothing. She's had only a few sips of soup."

"Has she gone to the bathroom?"

"No, I don't think so."

"Has she gotten out of bed at all?"

"No."

"What did the doctor say?"

Shiyin's reply is almost inaudible. "He said that it would be soon."

She hears Snowgoose sobbing and wants to comfort her. But somehow, she cannot seem to even turn her head. She feels a funny tingling in her fingertips and toes. For a long time, there is no sound except for Snowgoose's sobbing.

Then she hears Snowgoose say, "I think we should order the coffin and start to make the burial clothes."

"No!" She hears the vehemence in Shiyin's voice.

"If we wait too long, we may not have anything ready ... " Snowgoose sobs again. "And besides, I've often heard that it turns the luck."

"I've heard of that saying, too, but I don't want to."

How strange, she thinks, to overhear such a conversation about oneself: to hear one's funeral arrangements discussed in one's presence as if one were already dead. She remembers how her mother had lain silently the whole afternoon before she died; maybe she had actually known everything that was going on around her, had felt Daiyu holding her hand. She wants to call out to Snowgoose and Shiyin teasingly, to tell them that she's not in such bad shape, that it's not so desperate. But a strange heaviness is overcoming her, and she feels herself sinking under its weight, as if slipping off a shallow ledge into deeper waters.

8

"If we are to have a proper funeral for Qiaojie, we must borrow some money," Xifeng breaks the dull silence of the apartment. Qiaojie had died two nights ago. Although the family—especially Ping'er—has been prostrated by grief, it is time to see to the practical arrangements.

Only Granny responds. "Borrow money? Why should we?" she says from her corner of the *kang*.

Xifeng looks at her in surprise. She had not expected any resistance on this point. "I'm not sure we have enough money for a proper funeral—"

"What happened to the rest of the jewelry that we had?"

"I had to spend quite a lot of it on rent and food and coal, and then I had to pawn my watch and those hairpins last week to pay for Qiaojie's medicine and doctor's bills—"

"What exactly did you spend?" Beneath Granny's accusatory tone, Xifeng thinks she hears a note of panic.

"I spent twenty *taels* on the rent for the fall and winter. Then we spend about two *taels* a week for food, and about one *tael* a week for coal and candles, and other little things. We had to buy some fabric and needles and thread to make winter clothes. That was about fifteen *taels*—"

"Didn't you keep proper accounts?" Granny interrupts.

"I didn't want to waste money buying paper," Xifeng says, trying to keep her patience. "Besides, I can remember everything. That comes to about seventy-five *taels* or so. We'd already spent five *taels* on that first doctor. But then I had to spend twenty-five *taels* last week for Qiaojie's medicine and Dr. Wang,

and another thirty *taels* for his coming to the house that night."
Xifeng dislikes going through these details, but she forces
herself to be as clear as possible, so that Granny will not be able
to accuse her of dishonesty or mismanagement. "There was also
the bird's nests, and the food we bought to try to get Qiaojie to
eat."

"You should have managed better," Lady Jia says. "It was
your job to make a budget. You can't just spend and spend and
spend, and expect everything to come out all right!"

"I know, but these were unforeseen circumstances. We could
hardly have just sat by doing nothing, watching her ... " She
trails off, feeling the tears rising in her throat.

"I don't say you should have done nothing," says Granny Jia,
with the air of one making a concession. "But you could have
done less. I said so at the time, but no one listened to me. Why
did you have to get the best doctor in the city? And then you
went and sent for him in the middle of the night!"

Xifeng looks down to hide her anger. One of the only things
that has given her any comfort over the last two days is that she
and Ping'er had done everything possible to save Qiaojie. "It's
difficult to know in hindsight what we should or shouldn't have
done," she says, trying to be conciliatory. "What we must think
about now is how to arrange the funeral and burial. We need at
least seventy-five *taels*."

"Seventy-five *taels*! Whatever for?"

"Even the simplest coffin is twenty-five *taels*. And we must
make her burial clothes, and arrange to take her to the Temple
of the Iron Threshold to keep vigil over her. We must hire a few
nuns to chant sutras, and then we'll need a carriage to take her
out to the family burial grounds—"

"The Temple of the Iron Threshold! What are you thinking
of? You act as if we were back at Rongguo, and had all the
money in the world! We can keep vigil for her right here. As for

nuns chanting sutras—that's hardly necessary, is it? She's a new-born infant. What sins could she possibly have to expiate?"

"Well, even if we keep vigil here, we will still need at least sixty *taels* for the burial clothes and coffin—"

"Surely we can dispense with burial clothes, for such a young child! You should be able to manage it with forty *taels*."

"Forty *taels*!" Xifeng remembers that she had given fifty *taels* to Silver's mother to bury Silver, a common servant. She had hoped to comfort Ping'er by arranging as dignified a funeral as they could manage under the circumstances. She does not care much for pomp and ritual, but recoils at the idea that Qiaojie will be dumped into a hole without the proper ceremonies to mourn her. She controls herself. "Well, even if it is forty *taels*, we'll have to pawn the coral earrings. After that, we'll have only a bracelet and a hairpin left. That won't last us more than a few months." Once she has borrowed the money, she tells herself, she will be able to divert more of it to Qiaojie's funeral.

"Are you telling me we have enough money for only a few more months?" The note of panic in Lady Jia's voice, once sub-merged, comes to the surface. "What were you thinking when you spent all that money on doctors' bills? You should have asked me first. And it was all a waste. Qiaojie would have died anyway."

The thought that it had all been futile, that they might have spared Qiaojie all the suffering and discomfort of the medical treatments, hurts her. If they had known she was destined to die, they would have spent more of her last weeks just holding her and playing with her. "Let's not talk about it. What's done is done." Her voice shakes.

"That's easy for you to say, after you've gotten us into this fix."

"I've done the calculations and thought it over again and again. I can't think of anything to do but borrow the money."

"You think it's so easy to borrow money? Who were you proposing to borrow from?"

Xifeng answers slowly, "Well, I had thought of asking Cousin Rong." In fact, she has intended to ask Mrs. Xue to borrow money from Jingui, but does not want to put Mrs. Xue on the spot by making the request before all the others.

"Cousin Rong! He barely has enough money to keep body and soul together himself."

"Well, then, I'll ask Cousin Yun."

"Didn't you ask him to petition for an appeal on our behalf, but he refused to see you?"

"Yes, but—"

"Then why would you think you could borrow from him? There isn't anyone—"

"Actually," Xifeng is forced to admit, "I was thinking of asking Mrs. Xue if she might ask her daughter-in-law for a loan for us." She looks at Mrs. Xue and catches on her face an unmistakable expression of dismay.

"Why, yes, I would be happy to ask Jingui, but . . . " Mrs. Xue trails off.

Xifeng understands that relations between Mrs. Xue and Pan's wife are so strained that even in this extremity, she does not feel confident of her ability to get a loan.

Baochai speaks up, flushing, "When Pan comes back from the south, he'll be happy to lend you anything you need. Only we're not quite sure when he'll be back . . . "

"No, that isn't right," Lady Jia intervenes suddenly. "We shouldn't ask our kinsmen to loan us money when we haven't done everything possible ourselves."

"What do you mean we haven't done everything possible?" Xifeng says. "What else can we do?"

"The solution's obvious, isn't it?" Lady Jia smiles as if pleased by her own cleverness. "We can sell Ping'er, of course."

Xifeng recoils. How cruel to think of selling Ping'er at a time like this! "Impossible! She's Lian's wife!" She wants to dissuade Lady Jia before Ping'er, who is in the bedroom with Qiaojie's body, overhears anything to frighten her.

"She's only a concubine. Concubines are often resold. Lian certainly has no use for her now."

"What will he say when he gets back?"

"He'll have no right to complain. What does he expect us to live on while he's in prison?"

Xifeng tries another tack. "It's hardly worth the trouble to sell her. A good maid goes for only forty *taels* at most."

"Why sell her as a maid, when we'd get so much more for her as a concubine or even a principal wife? She's still young and pretty. I don't see why we wouldn't get two hundred *taels* for her."

Even though she knows it is unwise to criticize Lady Jia directly, she cannot help saying, "Don't you think it's cruel to ask her to serve a new husband after she has just lost her child?" She wishes she had cut out her tongue before mentioning the idea of borrowing money. She would by far rather forgo Qiaojie's funeral than lose Ping'er.

"How is it cruel? Her job is to serve us. Now the best way for her to serve us is to go to another master. Besides, she is one extra mouth to feed, and she barely lifts a finger around here. How can we ask the Xues to borrow money when we have a lazy servant eating us out of our house and home?"

"She ate more before because she was nursing Qiaojie, and she served us by taking care of your great-granddaughter." It hurts her the way Lady Jia acts as if Qiaojie were hardly part of the family. How differently she would have behaved if Qiaojie had been a boy. "Now that Qiaojie is gone, she will help out more with the cooking and cleaning."

"We don't need her for that anymore. Besides, she is

moping around so much that I doubt we'll get much work out of her."

Xifeng is about to retort when, to her surprise, Baochai says, "You can't expect her not to grieve for a while, but she will get back to work eventually."

It is the first time that Baochai has ever come close to contradicting Lady Jia. Xifeng looks at her with real gratitude. If only Baochai and the other girls side with her, she will be able to save Ping'er.

Lady Jia pauses, gazing at Baochai, as if giving her words a weight that she no longer gives Xifeng's. "I think you are forgetting how painful it must be for Ping'er to live here, being reminded of her loss. It will be much better for her to go somewhere new. Perhaps she'll even have a new baby soon, and that will help her forget."

Xifeng cannot speak. She is too disgusted by how Lady Jia feigns concern for Ping'er to support her own selfish ends. She remembers how Lady Jia had forced her to accept Lian and Ping'er's marriage, in the hopes that Ping'er would give the family an heir. That was barely over a year ago, although it seems another lifetime. Now that Lady Jia has been disappointed in her hope, she is ready to discard Ping'er. Xifeng's old awe of Lady Jia is gone, replaced by something akin to contempt. Perhaps she would have been more tolerant of Lady Jia if she had made some adjustment to the family's fall—but she still expects to be waited on hand and foot, eating her fill of the best food without noticing whether there is enough for the others.

Yet now Xifeng humbles herself, willing to do anything to save Ping'er. She falls to her knees. "Please don't sell her. She has served me since I was a little girl."

Lady Jia looks away, her face like stone. "Don't bother pleading. My mind is made up."

9

Over four weeks have passed since Baochai's visit to Daiyu. More than once she has told herself that she must make an effort to see her cousin again, but too many events have intervened. There had been Qiaojie's death, then New Year's. They had still been keeping vigil for Qiaojie, and no one had had the heart to arrange even the simplest celebration. After that had been the funeral and burial. Then came weeks of bitterly cold weather when it was hardly possible to venture outside. The last few days there has been a slight thaw. Still Baochai has found herself making excuses not to go, afraid of what she will find.

At last she tells herself she must go. She has brought Daiyu to this. The least she can do is comfort her if she is still alive, or weep beside her coffin if it is too late. On the fifth day of mild weather, she bundles herself up for her walk to the southern part of the Capital. As she cuts south through the city she thinks about how Ping'er has been debilitated by grief since Qiaojie's death. She has stopped eating, and spends the whole day sitting listlessly on the *kang* in the bedroom. Sometimes at night, Baochai is woken by the sound of her weeping. By contrast, although Qiaojie's death had clearly been a devastating blow to Xifeng as well, Xifeng was still struggling to live. When Xifeng wasn't comforting Ping'er, she was trying to argue Lady Jia into keeping the maid. Many days she disappeared for hours, trying to borrow money from relatives or old friends, Baochai suspects. Baochai pities Ping'er, but is unwilling to ask Jingui for money to keep her. In the first place, Jingui would refuse. On top of that, practically speaking, selling Ping'er is the best solution to the Jias' financial problems. Finally, some calculating and pragmatic voice inside her, which she does not entirely like, tells her that the sale of Ping'er, while a loss to Xifeng, is a gain to herself. With the gentle and more tactful Ping'er as her delegate among the servants, Xifeng had enjoyed far greater power and popularity than she might otherwise have. If the Jias ever regain their position, Baochai will be able to establish her precedence over the household more easily with Ping'er gone.

She feels wetness on her face and looks up. A few large snowflakes drift down from the gray sky, but she thinks nothing of it, as it almost never snows heavily in the Capital. She has begun to notice this cold-hearted pragmatism in herself more often, most recently in her reaction to Qiaojie's death. She had felt sorry, of course, but a part of her had been relieved that the family would no longer be squandering resources and money on the little girl. When Xifeng and Ping'er had woken the family with their wails over Qiaojie's body, Baochai noticed that of all of them, only her own and Lady Jia's eyes were dry. She had taken out her handkerchief and lowered her face to hide this fact, but it was the first time it had occurred to her that she and Lady Jia were similar in any way.

Drifts of snow are swirling around her now, and she is having trouble seeing more than five or ten paces ahead. Her feet have grown cold, and it has become difficult to walk. She sees that already more than an inch of snow has accumulated on the ground. The snow makes everything look unfamiliar, and she gazes around, trying to orient herself. She continues walking, the snowflakes cold on her face, hoping for a passerby from whom she can ask directions. Few people are out in the storm, and she must walk half a *li* before she comes upon a knife sharpener with his heavy round whetstone slung over his bowed shoulders. He tells her that she has overshot Flowers Street and must walk one street north and one to the west. Following his directions, she backtracks, and begins to look for the Zhens', expecting to be able to see from a distance the smoke issuing from the forge. Looking back and forth up the street, however, she does not see the column of smoke. It occurs to her that Zhen Shiyin cannot work in all the snow, and that the forge is unlit. She must trudge up and down the street herself, in her now sodden slippers, to look for the place. She goes to the end of the street. Nothing looks familiar, everything blanketed by a layer of snow. Then she goes back the way she came and continues to the other end. To her confusion, she sees no sign of the forge, and wonders if the knife sharpener has misdirected her. She goes down the street again, looking for someone to ask. Eventually, she sees a middle-aged man with his legs bound up in rags sweeping the snow before his house.

"Excuse me, can you tell me whether this is Flowers Street?" she asks.

He pauses in his sweeping to stare at her, and gives a brief nod.

"Can you tell me where Zhen Shiyin, the blacksmith, lives?"

"I don't know him. I didn't know a blacksmith lived here."

The man's reply fills her with uneasiness. It seems odd that a person would not notice a blacksmith's forge on his own street. Now shivering with cold she continues down the street and starts back up again. The snow seems to obliterate everything, leaving her alone in a white, trackless wasteland. At last, she notices a house with a front yard about the size and shape of what she remembered the Zhens' to be; only there is no forge or anvil there, just a ramshackle chicken coop. She flounders through the snow to the side door and hammers on it. She waits for about a minute, then hammers again. After knocking one more time, she hesitates before pushing on the door. It opens, and she steps through. "Hello? Is anybody home?"

An old woman, considerably older than Lady Jia, squats on a three-legged stool, fanning the stove with a fan of plaited bamboo leaves. Although the woman appears to be looking directly at Baochai, she evinces no reaction to a stranger entering her house and continues to fan the fire.

"I'm sorry to intrude on you like this," Baochai begins, taking a step into the room. "I was wondering whether you could tell me where the Zhens live."

The woman makes no reply, but bobs her head vigorously, parting her lips in a gap-toothed smile.

Baochai realizes the woman is deaf. She steps closer, repeating more loudly with her hands cupped to her mouth, "Can you tell me where the Zhens live?"

The woman nods and smiles some more. To Baochai's relief, she says, "The Zhens? They don't live here anymore." She speaks in the overly loud, uninflected voice of the very deaf.

"They used to live here?" Baochai says.

There is no response. Baochai gestures at the room. "They used to live here?" she shouts. Peering around in the dimness, she thinks she recognizes it as the room where she had visited Daiyu. Because the furniture is different, she did not at first think it familiar, but now she recognizes the narrow *kang*, the small high window on the far wall, the ledge above the stove. Her heart begins to thump. Where have the Zhens gone, and why have they left? She has heard that poor families move more frequently than rich families, because they are always on the lookout for cheaper quarters, but the Zhens could hardly move with Daiyu in the state she was in. If only she could find Snowgoose and ask her what has happened—but although Snowgoose had mentioned the name of her new mistress, Baochai can no longer remember it.

"Where did the Zhens go?" She leans down to yell near the old woman's ear.

"Down south."

"And the young lady?" she persists, miming a bun at the back of the head to suggest Daiyu's hairstyle.

"Gone," the old woman says. For once she does not smile and nod. She shuts the stove with a clang and throws down the fan.

"Gone?" Baochai echoes. She pauses. "Do you mean—do you mean *dead*?"

The old woman nods.

Baochai stares at her. Surely she is mistaken. It has been barely a month since Baochai saw Daiyu. And yet, deep inside, Baochai had known the last time she saw Daiyu that the end was not far. That was why she had given Zhen Shiyin her gold locket so impulsively; she was afraid that it would soon be too late.

Though she rarely cries, the tears come to her eyes. The last time she cried was when she had seen Daiyu. Surely that brief, awkward conversation, when Daiyu was scarcely able to veil her hostility at first, could not have been the last time they would ever speak? On her last visit she had mostly been conscious of her own guilt. This time, finding Daiyu gone, she is aware of a haunting sense of loss. Even though the two of them had spoken infrequently since Daiyu returned from Suzhou after her father's death, in her mind Daiyu has always been the one person to whom she could talk the most freely. Freed from the necessity of maintaining a façade, she has spoken to Daiyu without fear of consequences and has come to know herself through her own words. This was what had happened even in her last conversation with Daiyu. She had spoken of women's choices, implicitly encouraging Daiyu to make the choice to live rather than die. But hadn't she also been speaking, without realizing it, of the choice that she herself was making? To accept the imperfections and humiliations of her own situation, to marry Baoyu when he was released from prison, to cultivate her relationship with the Jias in the meantime, to make the best of her life. Still, how much colder and emptier her life seemed without Daiyu! With her mother and Pan, she must always be strong. It was only with Daiyu that she had allowed herself to be weak. She is becoming so hard, she thinks, like a stone, locked in a prison of her own reticence and self-control.

"When did she die?" she asks, wiping away her tears.

The woman ignores her.

Baochai tries again, more loudly. "When did she die?"

The old woman stares vacantly at a spot on the floor. Baochai turns away. There is nothing more to be said, after all. She thanks the woman and walks slowly out into the snow.

10

By the time Xifeng makes it back to the city gates, the snow is well over ankle-deep, and her shoes and socks and trousers are soaked almost to her knees. The shawl that she wears over her head and shoulders has kept her upper body dry during the blizzard, the worst that she ever remembers seeing in the Capital, but her bare hands are freezing. She has trudged almost ten *li* each way through the snow to the Water Moon Priory in the suburbs. When she saw how heavy and gray the morning sky was, she had not wanted to set out on the long trip. The day before, however, Ping'er had told her that a slave trader had come while Xifeng was out. The slave trader had examined Ping'er closely, even opening her mouth to peer at her teeth. Terrified, Xifeng had forced herself to set out for the Priory to ask the Mother Abbess for a loan.

She has already gone to almost a dozen people with the same request. Before the confiscation, she had done so many little favors for people. When Jia Qiang, Lian's cousin, needed a job, she made a position for him buying new trees and shrubs for the Garden. She used Jia connections to help Cousin Yun's daughter get out of a prior betrothal when a better match offered itself. But now that she is in need, each person has an excuse why he cannot possibly spare even fifty or a hundred *taels*. People had so little *liangxin*, sense of decency, these days; they were like the wolf who had been saved from hunters by Mr. Dongguo, who then proposed to eat his benefactor the moment he was hungry. She had reasoned and pleaded until her throat went dry, and still everyone had turned her down.

Today, she had been hopeful that the Abbess, to whom she had been so generous in the past, would be able to give her something. Because the Abbess continually solicited contributions for the Priory from wealthy families, she almost certainly had a large amount of cash on hand. The Abbess had sat her down and offered her tea cordially enough. She had clucked sympathetically when Xifeng told her about the family's poverty and Qiaojie's death. But the moment Xifeng asked for a loan, she exclaimed, "Oh, I wish you had come two weeks sooner!"

"Why?" Her heart sank, understanding that she was to be put off with some excuse.

"Didn't you know? All autumn and winter I've been going around getting contributions to build a new wing with a statue of Bodhidharma in it. Just two weeks ago I gave all the money to the workmen."

"But it's the middle of the winter. Surely they can't start work on it now."

"Well, they need the money to buy materials, hire carpenters, and so forth. I am afraid that I really can't help you. I'm terribly sorry."

"We don't need very much. Even as little as a hundred *taels* would help. Perhaps you could squeeze a little out of your ordinary operating expenses—"

"I'm afraid that's impossible," the Abbess had said. Xifeng could hear the note of finality in her voice. "Now be sure to give Lady Jia my regards."

As Xifeng trudges into the city through the western gate, she seethes at how the Abbess had not even bothered to formulate an excuse. She obviously had the money and was simply unwilling to lend it. If the Jias ever get Rongguo back, Xifeng thinks, she will never contribute so much as a copper coin to the Water Moon Priory. Exhausted, she sinks down to rest on a small ledge on the inside of the city walls. Where else can she go? she

thinks. Time is running out. In less than an hour it will be getting dark. Suddenly, the answer floats up to her from her tired
brain. Jia Yucun. She has tried not to think of him since she ran
into him buying medicine for Qiaojie. But hadn't he made it
clear that he still had feelings for her? Would he really refuse to
help when he saw how desperate she was?

She remembers hearing that he had moved into a new mansion not far from Rongguo. Could she risk waiting until
tomorrow, so that she can make herself fresh and pretty for the
visit? She does not dare to wait. Who knows when the slave
trader will find a buyer for Ping'er? She must go as she is,
exhausted and cold in her sodden clothes, her face bare of
makeup. Fortunately, the snow has stopped. Smoothing her
hair, she climbs to her feet, her hope giving strength to her legs.

She sets off in the direction of Rongguo. When she is a few
streets away, she asks someone where the Minister of Rites lives,
and is directed to a street two blocks north of Rongguo. She
walks rapidly, wanting to get there before the light fades
entirely. When she turns onto the street, she can see that the
towering triple gate, only slightly smaller than Rongguo's, is
already closed. She goes to one of the side gates and hammers
on it. A gateman steps out. "What is it?"

Assuming a confidence she does not feel, she says, "I have a
message for Minister Jia from my master, Mr. Jia Lian." She
hopes that Yucun will realize that the message is from her when
he hears Lian's name.

It seems to her that the gateman is looking at her strangely.
It is unusual for a maid, rather than a page, to be carrying a message to a male recipient. He puts out his hand. "If you have a
letter, I'll take it in for Minister Jia."

She shakes her head. "There is no letter. I have a message.
My master told me to deliver it to Minister Jia personally."

The gateman looks at her even more strangely. After a

moment, he shuts the gate in her face and disappears. She is not sure whether he is shutting her out or going inside to ask whether she is to be admitted. She decides to wait a little while before knocking again. The temperature is dropping as the sun sets, and her wet stockings are starting to tingle painfully against her skin. She forces herself to jog back and forth to keep warm. After she has waited about ten minutes, the gate opens again.

"You may come in," the gateman says.

She follows him through the gate and across a large, formal courtyard. Most of the buildings are unlit; all she can see is that they are large and well-proportioned. The gateman leads her through another courtyard, and another one. She wonders whether he is taking her to Yucun's study, until she sees they are approaching what must be the Inner Gate. She is surprised. Why would Yucun wish to see her in the Inner Quarters, where his wife will certainly hear of her visit? At the Inner Gate, the gateman, forbidden from entering the women's quarters, leaves her with a waiting maid. In the light of the lanterns at the gate, the maid in her butterfly silks at first reminds her of the maids at Rongguo. However, a second look reveals that she is too plain-faced to have been chosen to serve at Rongguo. The maid leads her to what appear to be the main apartments. How strange, she thinks. Won't his wife be there? As Xifeng crosses the courtyard towards the front door, she is seized by a sudden nervousness and has an urge to turn back.

Forcing herself to follow the maid into the front room, she sees that Yucun is not there. Instead, a young woman sitting on the edge of the *kang* regards her with singular intentness. The woman wears an ermine-lined jacket and sable cap studded with a pearl pin. Her face is pretty, but is marred by the anxious frown that draws her brows together and hardens her mouth.

"Who are you?" the woman says, starting up at the sight of Xifeng. "What do you want with my husband?"

So this is Jia Yucun's wife, the Marquis of Donghou's daughter.
She is attractive enough, but her face and figure lack distinction.
She is fumbling with a small metal handwarmer shaped as a fish,
and drops it on the floor in her agitation. A maid hastens to pick
it up. Xifeng notices that this girl is as homely as the first maid. It
occurs to her that Jia Yucun's wife is a jealous and insecure woman
who deliberately surrounds herself with unattractive girls.

"My name is Ping'er," she lies, because Xifeng is too distin-
guished a name for a maid. "I'm here with a message for
Minister Jia. If you will please have a maid take me to him, I will
deliver my message."

"My husband is not here. He has gone to Tianjin on Ministry
business. Who sent you?"

Xifeng's hope slips away. Who can she go to now? All she can
think of is getting away from here. "My master, Mr. Jia Lian,
sent me. If Minister Jia is not here, I'll come back another time.
Can you tell me when you expect him back?"

"My husband won't be back for another week at least," Jia
Yucun's wife says. She refers to Yucun as "my husband," instead
of "Minister Jia," as if asserting her claim on him with every sentence. "Can't you give me your message?"

"I'm afraid not. I'm sorry to disturb you." She moves towards
the door.

"Just a minute," Jia Yucun's wife says sharply, following her.
"Yes?"

"If you give me the message instead, I'll give you two silver
taels."

For a moment, Xifeng wonders whether she can use the
woman's curiosity and suspicion to raise the whole sum of
money. She decides that the few *taels* she might get from lying to
Yucun's wife are not worth the effort. "I'm sorry. My master, Mr.
Jia Lian, instructed me not to give it to anyone but Minister Jia."

"Why are you lying?" Yucun's wife cries, her face alive with suspicion. "Jia Lian is in jail. Who really sent you? One of the young ladies?"

Xifeng realizes that she is on dangerous ground. "Lady Jia sent me. She told me to say the message was from Jia Lian, because it wasn't proper for her to send to Minister Jia herself."

"What does she want?"

She decides to tell some version of the truth on the unlikely chance that Yucun's wife will help them. "Lady Jia sent me to ask for a loan. The family has fallen on hard times. My mistress remembered that Minister Jia used to visit Lord Jia in the old days, and hoped that he might help."

"You're sure you're from Lady Jia?" the woman repeats, as if she has not heard the rest of Xifeng's words. She draws closer, putting her hand on Xifeng's sleeve. "I'm sure that he was in love with one of the young ladies there. I'll give you ten *taels* if you tell me her name!"

Xifeng looks at her wonderingly. Why is she so jealous about ancient history? If only Yucun's wife had offered a hundred, or even fifty *taels*, Xifeng would have given her own name. As it is, she refuses and escapes from the house.

When she arrives home, almost sick with cold and exhaustion, the family is about to have dinner. Gratefully, she changes out of her wet clothes and sits down to the winter melon soup and steaming rice. She has just swallowed a few mouthfuls when Granny Jia says, "I've arranged a match for Ping'er. Her new husband is sending a wedding sedan tomorrow morning."

That night, she and Ping'er do not sleep in the bedroom with the others. Xifeng takes a pillow and quilt, and she and Ping'er spend their last night together huddled on the *kang* in the front room. She does not say anything at first. Ping'er is weeping silently, and Xifeng pats her shoulder. Finally, after Ping'er grows calmer, she says, with tears in her own eyes, "I tried my best to find a way to keep you. If only I had a little more time ... "

Ping'er nods and gulps, catching her breath on a sob. "It's all right. I know how hard you've tried." She sobs again, and Xifeng hands her her own handkerchief. "Sometimes even you can't fix everything."

The way Ping'er says "even you" pricks her. Once she too had believed there was almost nothing she couldn't do. How she had lorded it over others, glorying in how well she ran Rongguo. How proud she had been when she made all that money from her loans! Now, how limited, how powerless, she feels. She had not been able to save Qiaojie, and now she cannot save Ping'er.

"Did Lady Jia tell you anything about the match?"

"His surname is Jiang. He's thirty-three years old."

"Will you be his first wife, or a concubine?"

"The first wife."

"That's good." The man is old to be marrying for the first time, but she wonders whether an older husband will be gentler and more patient with Ping'er.

"The problem is," Ping'er says, "he's a tea merchant. Usually he lives in Anhui, where the tea plantations are."

"Do you mean he doesn't live in the Capital?"

"No, he comes to the Capital only once or twice a year to sell his tea." Ping'er begins to sob again. "But he decided to find a wife here, because he thought he could get someone better."

It had never occurred to Xifeng that Ping'er would be leaving the Capital. She had assumed she would at least be able to see Ping'er a few times a year. She is afraid, not for Ping'er, but for herself. How will she ever survive among the Jias without someone she can trust? In the whole great city of thousands of people, there will be no one who cares for her, no one she can turn to. Perhaps the two of them will never see each other again. A terrible fear of loneliness overcomes her. How will she struggle on alone? She realizes that even during the time that she and Ping'er were estranged, she had still drawn strength from Ping'er's presence. She begins to weep. She feels Ping'er's hand groping for hers under the covers. Their fingers interlace and they hold on to each other.

"How can I leave you?" Ping'er says. "We have always been like sisters. Even when I was a child, you took care of me. And the way you helped me take care of Qiaojie ... You couldn't have treated her better if she had been your own child."

"Perhaps things will go well for you after you are married. For all we know, he may be a kind person," Xifeng says, trying to comfort her. "Perhaps you may even have another child."

"I don't want another child."

"That's how you feel now, but perhaps you will one day. It's worse for me. I think Qiaojie was my only chance to be close to a child."

"What do you mean?"

"I don't think I'll ever be able to have a child of my own. My period is getting more irregular than ever. Sometimes I don't get it for two or three months on end."

"It's because you don't take care of yourself."

"I don't think it's that." Something is not right with her body. She feels it. She gets exhausted too easily, and her color isn't good. "Besides, I don't think Lian will ever sleep with me again."

Ping'er does not demur. She squeezes Xifeng's hands. "Yes, I'm afraid for you. He'll be so angry when he gets out of jail."

"Yes, well, it won't be for a few years yet." Xifeng tries to speak lightly. She too is afraid of what Lian will do to her when he is released.

"Will you do one thing for me?" Ping'er asks after a pause.

"Yes. What is it?"

"You'll be here, in the Capital. Will you go to see her some-times?"

Ping'er is referring to Qiaojie's grave. "Of course I will." The tears come to Xifeng's eyes again. "I would have gone even if you hadn't asked me."

"You'll burn incense, and bring offerings? I was thinking you should bring those sweet rolls with red bean stuffing. She liked those, didn't she?"

Yes, Qiaojie had eaten so little, but those rolls were one of the few things she seemed to like. "Of course."

"You'll be sure to go on the Grave Sweeping Festival?"

"I will."

"Good," Ping'er says, as if her mind has been relieved of a care. "Then every Grave Sweeping Festival I will know that you are going out to her grave, and on that one day, I'll be able to picture exactly where you are and what you are doing."

After this, Xifeng feels Ping'er's body relax against hers. They are quiet for a long time. Eventually, she sees Ping'er's eyelids start to flutter shut. In a little while, Ping'er is snoring gently. Xifeng looks at her face in the dim moonlight filtering through the window. Her eyes are still swollen and her skin is blotched with tears. The cheeks have lost their roundness and color, and there are dark hollows beneath her eyes, but still, there is a sweetness to the curve of her lips, and her breath is peaceful.

Perhaps things will not go badly for Ping'er after all. Perhaps her husband will grow fond of her, and she will have another child. Surely that will be some compensation for the loss of Qiaojie. It occurs to her that Ping'er is the lucky one—lucky to be able to escape the tyranny of Lady Jia, lucky to escape the atmosphere of disappointment and deprivation among the Jia women. How much would Xifeng herself give to be able to escape from Lian, to start again with a new husband, without a history of resentment and betrayal? How much would she give to be able to have a child?

She puts her arms around Ping'er, listening to her breathe, and lies awake until morning.

PART FIVE

Fourth Month, 1723

Parting is easy.
It's the coming together that's hard.

Li Shangyin, "Untitled Poem"

1

Baochai walks home from the marketplace with Xifeng, the weight of her laden basket bumping against her side. Now that it is spring, the vegetables are plentiful again. They have bought bunches of red-veined amaranth, tiny curled pea shoots, even a plump, golden-skinned melon to eat after dinner.

She feels the sunlight warming her hair, luxuriating in the feeling of actually being too hot. "I'm glad the winter is over. I remember how awful it was walking home from the market with the freezing wind in our faces."

Xifeng looks at her with a faint smile. Baochai notices that she is slightly out of breath. As always, Xifeng has insisted on carrying the heavier items. "Yes, the winter was hard," she says, "but there will be more winters yet before Uncle Zheng and Baoyu come home."

"Surely next winter won't be so hard. Pan will certainly be back from the south by then."

"You still haven't heard from him?"

"No, I went to ask at Jingui's last week, and she still hadn't heard anything. I don't understand what can be keeping him. She wrote to him more than five months ago." She is secretly afraid that he has gotten in trouble again, and is languishing in prison somewhere, unable to help them. Surely, if he had heard what had happened to the Jias, he would understand how much they needed him and would come home.

They walk on in silence for a few minutes. Xifeng says, "You're very patient to wait so long for Baoyu."

Baochai blushes, as she always does on the infrequent

occasions when her betrothal is mentioned. "Well, you are waiting for Lian," she says, just to deflect Xifeng's remark, which
seems to draw an embarrassing attention to her own fidelity.
The moment the words are out of her mouth she regrets them.
Of course, Xifeng must dread Lian's return.

"That's different," Xifeng says. "I'm already married to him.
I have no choice. You are only betrothed to Baoyu. There's no
reason for you to wait for him like this."

Baochai is annoyed by this attempt to revisit a topic she considered closed. "Uncle Zheng and Baoyu were sentenced for
obstruction of justice because they helped Pan. How could we
abandon them after they got in trouble helping us?"

Xifeng stares at her with an incredulous expression. "Is that
what's holding you back? What does that have to do with you?
You're a Xue, not a Jia. You might as well save yourself. When
Pan comes back, you should ask him and your mother to
arrange a new match for you."

"Don't you like Baoyu?" Baochai asks, surprised by Xifeng's
vehemence. She suspects Xifeng of some ulterior motive.
Perhaps Xifeng wants to get rid of her because she knew of
Xifeng's affair with Jia Yucun. Perhaps Xifeng does not want her
as a rival for control over the household after she marries Baoyu.

"It's not a matter of whether I like him or not," Xifeng says.
"He's going to be in jail for four more years. Besides, he wanted
to marry Lin Daiyu instead of you. Doesn't that matter to you?"

The mention of Daiyu pains her. Lying awake at night, she
often thinks of Daiyu. She tries to change the subject. "What
does it matter to you whom I marry?"

Xifeng shrugs and gives a little laugh. "I don't want you to
make a decision you'll regret."

"Why would I regret it?" Even to her own ears Baochai's
words sound hollow. She has not thought about Baoyu for
months. She tries to picture him and even has trouble conjuring

up the details of his face. Xifeng is right. Her waiting for him is just beginning.

She glances at Xifeng, again trying to fathom her motives. Xifeng has not been the same since Qiaojie's death and Ping'er's marriage more than two months ago. She has stopped arguing with Lady Jia. She no longer scolds the Two Springs when one of them is cheated at the market or burns a dish. Baochai finds her manner gentler, more approachable, than when she had ruled the roost at Rongguo. Perhaps she really is concerned about Baochai's future.

As they turn onto Drum Street, Xifeng stumbles a little, and almost drops the basket. As Baochai steadies her, she notices that Xifeng looks pale. "What is it? Don't you feel well?"

Xifeng clings to Baochai's arm, as if in need of support.

"What is it? Is something wrong?" Baochai asks again.

"It's nothing." Xifeng steadies herself and lets go of Baochai. "I just lost my balance."

"You looked as if you were about to faint. Should we send for a doctor?"

"No!" Xifeng speaks with her old sharpness. "I'm fine."

Just as they are approaching the apartment, she hears a man's voice behind her.

"Baochai!"

She turns. Pan, dressed in traveling clothes, rushes up to them.

"Pan!" She flings her arms around him. "You're back! We've been so worried about you!"

"How's Mother?"

"She's fine. Come in and see her." They rush into the apartment calling for their mother.

Mrs. Xue clings to Pan, bursting into tears. "Why didn't you answer our message? We've been so worried!"

"What message?" Pan says.

"We asked Jingui to send a message asking you to come back to the Capital."

"I didn't get any message. I suppose it came after I left Nanjing."

"Left Nanjing? Where were you?"

Pan laughs. "I went to Hangzhou, Chang'an, and Tianjin."

"Why on earth did you go to all those places?" Mrs. Xue exclaims.

"Ever since I heard the Jias were confiscated, I've been going to all their relatives by marriage, and asking them to petition the Emperor for clemency on their behalf," Pan says, beaming with pride. "I went to the Xues, and the Shis and the Wangs in Chang'an—"

Baochai almost drops her basket in surprise. It had never occurred to her that Pan was doing something to help the Jias of his own initiative.

He looks around at Lady Jia and Xifeng and the Two Springs. "I have some excellent news. I stopped by the *yamen* on the way here, and they told me the Jias have been granted an appeal!"

"What exactly does that mean?" Lady Jia cuts through the exclamations of gratitude and surprise. With Tanchun and Xichun supporting her, she moves forward from her backrest to the edge of the *kang*.

"It means there is a good chance that the sentences will be overturned, or at the least shortened."

"When will we find out?"

"In the next week or two, I should think."

Baochai sees her own surprise mirrored on her mother's face. "Pan," her mother begins, "how did you think of such a thing? I never realized that you knew ... that you thought ... "

"I knew how Uncle Zheng had helped me, so when I heard about the Jias, I went to Uncle Xue in Nanjing, and asked if he could do anything. He said he would send in a petition to the throne."

"He did?" Mrs. Xue says, startled. Baochai knows she has never gotten along with her husband's younger brother.

"I told him Baochai was engaged to Baoyu. He said he'd always been fond of Baochai, and didn't want to see such a fine girl suffer." Pan looks teasingly at Baochai. "It was my uncle who suggested that I go to the Jias' other relatives by marriage, and ask that they petition His Highness as well. I went to the Wangs first." He turns to Xifeng. "I saw your honored uncle. When I told him that Lian was in prison, he said he would write a petition right away."

Baochai notices how forced Xifeng's smile is.

Pan continues, "Then I went to the others. At first I pleaded with them, and they still wouldn't help. But as soon as I told them that Xue Bing and General Wang were already sending in petitions, they agreed to send them as well."

Of course, it makes sense to Baochai that while each individual fears to speak out alone, he is more willing to join a chorus of other powerful voices. Far more marvelous to her is Pan's transformation. He now carries himself with the easy confidence of a man well versed in the ways of the world.

She takes his hands. "Pan, I don't know what it is. You seem so different."

He smiles at her. "I feel different. You know, when Father's clerks used to try to teach me about the business, I never really paid any attention. But this time, when I was on my way south, I noticed that various medicines—rhinocerous horn, ginseng, cordyceps—were being sold at a very good price. So I spent almost all the cash I had and bought a really large quantity: several kilos of each. Then, when I got down south, I was able to sell them at a tremendous profit: three or four hundred percent! It was the first time I realized I could actually succeed at something on my own, without being told what to do." He gives a self-deprecating laugh. "You know, even though I was never good at memorizing texts, I always was pretty good at numbers." With a guilty start, Baochai realizes that although she has always been good at mathematics, it has never crossed her mind that Pan might share her talent.

"So then I started talking to Father's old clerks more about the business, and started making purchases for the Imperial Household, and keeping my own accounts. I actually found it pretty interesting."

"That's wonderful," she says. "But what about the Xias' business? Didn't Jingui want you to buy some paper and sandalwood, and bring them back up here to sell?"

At the mention of Jingui, his face seems to harden. "Actually," he says, "when I got down south, I found that the prices for those items were rather high. We wouldn't have made any profit at all bringing them back up here, so I didn't buy them."

"You've seen Jingui?" her mother asks hesitantly.

"Yes, she was the one who told me where you were living," Pan says. He says nothing more, his face still wearing the hard look. Baochai wonders what could have happened between the couple. Perhaps Pan found out something to Jingui's discredit when he went to Nanjing, or perhaps he is angry at her for not letting Baochai and Mrs. Xue live with her after the confiscation. In any case, he no longer seems to be held under Jingui's sway.

"Tell me," Lady Jia says. "Is it really true that Zheng and Baoyu and Lian will be released early? I can't believe it. Maybe we'll be able to get out of this place and move back to Rongguo ... "

"Don't outrun yourself, Granny," Pan says, laughing again. "I'll go to the *yamen* again tomorrow, and make some inquiries. And now that I'm in the Capital, I'll go to the Prince of Beijing to see if he can pull some strings. He was always good friends with Baoyu. But, based on everything that people have said, I think the chances are good they won't have to serve their full sentences. After all," he lowers his voice, "all the rival Princes are in jail, and His Highness has been on the throne for more than nine months, with no trouble anywhere in the Empire. Surely he can begin to relax . . . "

"Thank you, for everything that you have done for us." Lady Jia, with a return to her old dignity, tries to struggle off the *kang* to kowtow. "You and your sister and mother have stood by us, when everyone else abandoned us."

Pan stops her, blushing at her attempt to thank him. "That's all right. The Xues and the Jias have always been close, and Uncle Zheng saved me when I would have gone to jail." In his embarrassment, he takes refuge in teasing. He throws his arm around Baochai's shoulders and squeezes her. "Besides, I couldn't let my little sister dwindle into an old maid now, could I?"

2

Baoyu lies on the straw pallet. His face, against the dirty, scratchy sheet, is hot and dry. He alternately shakes with fever or shivers with cold. He is covered by a ragged blanket that has not been washed for as long as he has been in prison. At times he clutches it, only to fling it off when the next bout of ague descends on him. His body is crawling with lice, but he no longer bothers to scratch. The room is redolent with the stench of the chamber pot, which is emptied only once a day. Fainter than the smell of the chamber pot, but just as nauseating, is the smell of lunch—rice porridge swimming with a few dried fish—which he has not touched. As he lies there, however, his mind is far from the narrow walls of his prison cell. As always, he runs through his memories of Daiyu one by one, as if fingering a string of prayer beads. He remembers Daiyu on her first day at Rongguo in her dirty pink robe, with her strange combination of awkwardness and grace, of reticence and candor. He remembers that first dinner, when she was in an agony of blushes because she had drunk the tea for gargling. He pictures the time she had come to see him after his father beat him, and he told her about Zhu's secret life. Most often, he thinks of the time when she returned pale and spent from nursing her father in Suzhou. That was the happiest time in his life, when he had snuck into her bedroom almost every night to talk with her before she went to sleep.

Sometimes he will indulge himself by picturing every detail of her appearance: the way the hairpin holding up her bun was always slightly lopsided, the faint film of sweat on the back of her neck, the way that the soles of her shoes wore out unevenly because her feet turned out a little when she walked. Her pink fingernails, as curved and as delicate as seashells, the little frown that pulled her eyebrows together, giving her a faint look of melancholy, even when she was happy.

Sometimes he will replay one of their conversations, sifting and pondering her remarks. He will think about the time she came to see him after his face was burned. He showed her his jade for the first time, and she had made up a story about a stone coming down from the Heavens to live in the human world. When she had said the stone was from the Heavens, was she mocking him about his sense of superiority? The stone had fallen in love with a mortal girl. Did she already know then that he was in love with her? He will think about her voice, rich and low, with a slight southern accent that didn't distinguish between *n*'s and *ng*'s; about her small white teeth, which were slightly crooked, and the curve of her full lips. Lying against the rough straw pallet, he will imagine it is her body beneath his, and that he has only to open his eyes to see her face.

Sometimes he thinks he is making himself crazy living over these details from the past. But then he tells himself that reliving them is what he does to stop himself from going crazy, from giving in to lethargy and despair. What else does he have to think about in this tiny room with its high, barred window, with no brush and paper, with no books? What else does he have to focus his mind on, other than the thought that he will survive these five years, and then find her, somewhere, somehow?

He hears a key turn in the lock. His mind registers that this is an unusual occurrence, because ordinarily no one enters the cell between lunchtime and dinner, but he does not bother moving.

He hears a voice beside him. "Jia Baoyu, get up!"

He turns his head. Instead of one of the usual guards, he sees the head warden, whom he has met only a few times. "What is it?"

"What's the matter? Are you sick? Can't you get up?"

With an effort Baoyu uses his arms to push himself to a sitting position. "What is it?"

"Get your things together. You're being released today."

"Released?" he says confusedly. As the meaning of the word penetrates his murky brain, he feels a surge of hope and gladness. He tries to get to his feet but reels dizzily. "How? Why?"

The warden catches him by the arm to stop him from falling. "You've been granted an Imperial Pardon. Come along!"

Baoyu stoops to try to pick up his few items of clothes, but almost loses his balance.

"Never mind those," the warden says impatiently. "I doubt you'll want to wear them on the outside."

"You're right," says Baoyu. He goes out through the open door of the cell and staggers after the warden as quickly as he can down a series of hallways. He cannot keep up, and at one point the warden comes back to support him by the arm. They end up in some sort of office at the front of the prison. His father is there, sitting on one of the benches along the wall. Xue Pan is next to him.

"Father!" he cries.

Jia Zheng gets to his feet and hurries towards Baoyu with his arms outstretched. Although his robes are filthy and he has lost weight, he does not otherwise look unwell.

"Father, how are you?"

Jia Zheng grips Baoyu's hands. "I'm fine. But what ails you? You look terrible." He peers into Baoyu's face. "You have some sort of fever, don't you?"

"I think so. My cell was on the north side. It didn't get much sunlight, and was always cold and damp."

"We must have a doctor come as soon as possible."

"Father, what's happened? Why are we getting released?"

Jia Zheng turns to Xue Pan with a grateful smile. "Cousin Pan here has been asking our relatives to petition the throne, and it seems that His Highness has decided to grant us an Imperial Pardon, in recognition of the many years that our family has served the throne faithfully. Also, your friend the Prince of Beijing went to see him personally last week to beg for our early release."

Baoyu smiles. The Prince of Beijing has always been kind to him. He turns to Xue Pan. "I don't know how to thank you," he says, putting his hands together to make a bow.

Xue Pan catches him to stop him from kowtowing. "Please don't do that. It's nothing. After all, we're soon going to be brothers-in-law."

Pan's words strike a chill into Baoyu's heart. He had hardly thought about his betrothal in prison. It had never occurred to him that Baochai would wait five years for him to be released. He tells himself that he cannot make the same mistake as last time; he must make it perfectly clear that he will marry no one but Daiyu.

Before he can speak, however, Lian and Huan are led into the room. He is surprised by the rush of affection that he feels for them. They both embrace him, exclaiming at how ill he looks. They, by contrast, seem to be in good health despite their pallor and thinness.

And then, almost too quickly for him to absorb, their ordeal is over. The warden reads them some documents, though his head is aching too badly for him to listen properly. Their names are written down on a roster, and suddenly they are out in the streets in a wagon that Pan has hired to bring them home. Baoyu holds on to the side to steady himself, marveling at the freshness of the air and the expanses of space around him. He had lost track of time in prison, but now he senses, from the quality of the light and heat, that it is the end of spring. The sunlight is too intense for his eyes, and he shades them with his hand. Now they are approaching a busier part of town. The people on the streets strike him as belonging to a different and unfamiliar species. There are children shouting and chasing one another, peddlers standing in front of their shops hawking their wares. Their voices are too loud, just as the shapes and colors of objects seem too vivid. He sees stacks of *zongzi*, the pyramids of rice wrapped in bamboo leaves that are eaten in honor of Qu Yuan's suicide, and realizes that it must almost be the Double Fifth, the Dragon Boat Festival.

Now they are lurching down a familiar street. "Are we going to Rongguo?" he asks.

"No, it's still Imperial Property," Pan says over his shoulder. "They are renting an apartment south of Rongguo. It was rather small, so I rented the rooms next door for them as well when I got back to the Capital."

They draw into a small alley, and now the driver is pulling up the horses. As Pan helps Jia Zheng and Baoyu out of the wagon, a door bursts open and Tanchun and Xichun and Baochai and Mrs. Xue pour out to greet them. Tanchun is hugging and weeping over him and his father and Huan, while Xichun clings to Jia Lian. Baochai and Mrs. Xue embrace his father. Then Mrs. Xue turns to hug him, while Baochai gives him a formal bow, barely meeting his eye. Her coldness fills him with unease. She must still consider herself betrothed to him; that is why she treats him with such formality.

Granny Jia comes out of the apartment, supported by Xifeng. Granny embraces his father, but he cannot take his eyes off Xifeng. What has happened to her? Her complexion has taken on a strange, clay-like cast, and the whites of her eyes are a muddy yellow. She has lost so much weight that he can see the shape of her jawbone clearly. Haven't the others noticed the change in her? He looks at Lian, who is still speaking to Xichun and does not approach his wife. Surely, he thinks, Lian will take pity on her and not treat her too harshly about the loans. He takes Xifeng's hands. "Where is Qiaojie?"

A quiver runs over her sallow face. "She died last winter."

"I'm so sorry. I didn't know." He squeezes her hands, and feels her thin fingers trembling in his own. "And Ping'er?"

He realizes from her face that he has again blundered into a painful subject.

"Granny insisted that we sell her," she says.

Time had stood still for him in prison. Only now, at Xifeng's words, does he realize how much has happened in his absence, what losses and partings have rent the family. Unbidden, a line from Zhuangzi comes to him: *xuwu piaomiao, rensheng zaishi, nanmian fengliu yunsan.* "This life, this insubstantial tissue of vanity, floats like a cloud on the wind."

Now Granny is embracing him. While he feels joy at seeing his sister and cousins, he is still angry at how Granny had treated Daiyu. He submits to her putting her arms around him, and stroking his hair. Abruptly, she draws her hand away. "Good Heavens! You're crawling with lice, and your head is as hot as fire!"

"Yes, let's let Baoyu rest. He isn't well. We must call a doctor," Jia Zheng says, putting his arm around Baoyu's shoulders and supporting him into the house. Realizing how exhausted he is from the journey from prison, Baoyu allows himself to be led to the *kang*. He sinks down on some cushions, as the others begin to talk about which doctor to send for, and about bathing and getting new clothes for the prisoners.

As he looks around the unfamiliar apartment, watching everyone bustle about, he is so struck by the absence of Daiyu that he wants to cry out in pain. How can everyone else chatter and laugh, rejoicing in the return of the prisoners, without remembering those who are missing? Unable to contain himself, he says, "Does anyone know what happened to Cousin Lin after the confiscation?"

Xifeng gives a guilty start, seems about to speak, and then shuts her mouth. There is an awkward silence.

His father is the first to break it. He looks around, blinking, as if this is the first time that he notices Daiyu's absence. "I had assumed she was here with the rest of you." He looks at Lady Jia. "Where is she?"

Granny's face is inscrutable. "She disappeared from Rongguo during the confiscation. I think she must have felt we mistreated her, so she ran away the first chance she got."

Jia Zheng is shocked. "Disappeared! Where could she have run to? And anything could have happened to her during the confiscation! She could have been taken up by the soldiers as a servant, or worse! Didn't you make any sort of inquiry?"

"How could we possibly have looked for her then? We had enough to worry about—"

"Still, a young girl, alone in the Capital, without anyone to protect her," his father says, obviously distressed.

"We must do something to find her, Father," Baoyu breaks in eagerly. "We can make inquiries with the Embroidered Jackets. Probably she was mistaken for a maid and sent to some other household. We can find out where the other maids were sent and—"

"I know what happened to Daiyu," someone says quietly. Even without turning his head, he knows it is Baochai, from her calm voice, with its almost too precise articulation of consonants. He looks at her, and sees that two spots of red burn on her otherwise pale face, but her expression is as composed as always. She turns her back towards him, facing his father, as if making clear that she is addressing Jia Zheng and not Baoyu.

"What happened to her?" Jia Zheng asks.

"She went to live with Snowgoose's family."

At Baochai's words, Baoyu's heart is filled with relief, and gratitude towards Snowgoose. It was like Snowgoose, so generous beneath her brisk manner, to have made sure that Daiyu was all right.

"How do you know?" Xifeng asks Baochai.

"Snowgoose came here once, after the confiscation. She came to ask for some ginseng for Daiyu," Baochai says.

"She was ill, then?" Baoyu exclaims, at the same moment Mrs. Xue says, "Why didn't you ever tell us?"

Baochai does not speak for a moment. Then she goes on, her voice as steady as before. "She had consumption. I went to see her once in the Twelfth Month, and she was coughing terribly, and spitting up blood."

He feels his entire body grow as cold and heavy as stone. "Consumption!" he cries. Daiyu's mother had died of consumption. "Well, we must bring her here, and have the best doctors look at her. I'm sure that with the best care—"

Finally, Baochai turns and looks at him. Her face is still inscrutable, but is it possible that he hears a tiny tremor in her voice? "It's too late. I went to see her again at the end of the First Month. She was dead."

He recoils as at a physical blow. "Dead!"

"Yes. I'd given Snowgoose's brother some money. He had taken her body down south to bury her in Suzhou."

His first feeling is burning hatred for Baochai. He wants to strike her face, as cold and empty as a platter. He has always suspected that she tattled on Daiyu and made Lady Jia turn against her. Daiyu's death should be laid at her door. Only after a moment does it sink into his stricken brain that Baochai must have repented of what she had done. That was why she had paid for Daiyu's body to be buried in Suzhou.

And why does he blame Baochai? Wasn't it his own fault? He

had seduced Daiyu, sneaking into her bedroom to see her night after night. He had promised to marry her. Even though Baochai had tattled, his own actions had turned Lady Jia against Daiyu. Daiyu had probably died believing that he had abandoned and betrayed her. Can it be true that he will never have a chance to tell her how much he loved her, how not a day went by in prison that he had not dreamed of her and planned how to spend his life with her?

All his regrets will not bring her back. With a dull shudder, he sinks back down on the *kang*. He closes his eyes and feels the weight of his grief crushing his heart.

3

For all that afternoon, Xifeng has kept out of Lian's way. She knew, from the instant she saw him climbing out of the wagon, that he was still furious at her. The fact that he had not ended up serving the full sentence had not slaked his anger. She saw it in the rigidity with which he held his body, in the way he pointedly avoided meeting her eyes. He did not acknowledge her presence in any way, looking right through her as she hurried forward to greet him. She turned aside to greet Huan, hoping that in the bustle of the prisoners' homecoming his coldness would go unnoticed. All through the afternoon, in order to distract attention from the fact that he was not speaking to her, she made herself as lively and busy as possible. She had presided over the making of the dinner, laughing and joking about the menu. Pan promised to lend the Jias whatever they needed, and she bought fish and meat in honor of the prisoners' return. She bought material with which to make new clothes for the prisoners, asking everyone what colors and fabrics she should get. Then she had set out her work on the *kang* in the front room, ostentatiously rolling out the bolts of cloth, and pinning and cutting the paper patterns. Lian never even gave her a glance. She should be grateful, she told herself, that he had chosen not to humiliate her by repudiating her in front of the entire family.

Now it is evening, and she can no longer avoid facing him alone. Pan has rented the apartment next door so that the family will have more room. She and Lian, as the only married couple, have been allotted one of the bedrooms for themselves. She sits on the *kang* rapidly sewing a pair of trousers, the dread in her stomach like a lump of iron. She hears footsteps outside the door. Lian comes in.

"Look!" she says brightly, holding up the trousers. "I'll probably have them finished for you tomorrow."

He does not respond or look at her. She puts down the trousers and stands up. "What did Dr. Wang say about Baoyu?"

To her relief, he answers after a moment, still without looking in her direction. "He said it seems to be malaria. Baoyu's body seems to get hot and then cold. His spleen is enlarged and full of fire."

"But malaria can be cured, can't it?"

Lian sits down on the edge of the *kang*, and uses his toes to push off his worn and filthy shoes. He grunts. "The doctor left some medicine, but Baoyu wouldn't take it."

"Wouldn't take it? Why not?"

Lian does not answer. Momentarily distracted from her own worries, Xifeng wonders whether Baoyu is so upset by the news of Daiyu's death that he does not want to be cured. "I feel terrible about Daiyu," she says. "I should have tried harder to find out what became of her ... " Seeing that Lian is not listening, she trails off. He stands up and begins to take off his robe.

"Here, let me help you." She hurries over.

He steps away. "I can do it myself."

"Then let me help you with your socks." She kneels before his feet and strips off his dirty and holey socks. She picks up his shoes, examining the worn soles. "These are in terrible shape. I should throw them out, don't you think? I can start making you a new pair tomorrow."

He does not answer.

She picks up the robe that he has let fall on the *kang*. "We had better be careful where we put these. Are you sure you don't have lice or fleas? I have half a mind to burn everything that you're wearing. Or I suppose that we could just wash it in boiling water ... "

He still does not say anything, just strips down to his patched and stained trousers and tunic. She does not want him to get in bed wearing those clothes from prison. She hurries over to him with a vest she has borrowed from Granny, who is broad-shouldered, and one of her own looser pairs of trousers. "Here. Why don't you wear these? They're clean."

Ignoring her, he goes over to the basin of water she has heated for him. Instead of taking a proper bath, he sticks his head into the basin. He rubs a handful of soap into his wet hair, then rinses his face and head. When he dries off, he leaves streaks of dirt on the towel. She wants to ask him to wash more thoroughly, but does not dare. He goes to the window, opens it, and throws the water out into the street. He shuts and bolts the window, then goes to the *kang*, where she has laid out two sets of bedding side by side in the middle. He takes one of the sets of bedding and moves it to the farthest edge of the *kang*. Then he blows out the light.

She stands there in the darkness, listening to him climb between the quilts. She can count herself lucky, she reminds herself, that he has not yelled at her or struck her. She should just undress and go to sleep. Yet still she stands there in the darkness listening to his breathing. She knows that he is not the kind of person to relent towards her as time goes by. If she leaves matters like this, the gulf between them, their estrangement, will become permanent, immovable.

Slowly she undresses, shivering in the cool night air, laying her clothes in a neat pile on the corner of the *kang*. As her eyes adjust to the darkness, she can discern him lying there in the faint light from the window. She climbs onto the *kang* beside him, and kneels there.

"I—I wanted to tell you how sorry I am about those loans,"

she begins in a small voice. "I never thought they would get you in trouble."

For about a minute he says nothing. When he eventually speaks, it is clear from his voice that he has been lying there seething, that he can barely control his pent-up rage. "And yet, when the Embroidered Jackets were dragging me away, you didn't say a word."

"What could I have said? Even if I had told them that I made the loans, they would still have arrested you."

He sits up in bed. "Maybe you could have told the truth, and let the judge decide whether I should be convicted—"

"You would have been arrested anyway, just like Uncle Zheng and Baoyu and Huan. What good would it have done for both of us to be in jail?"

"Don't make me sick with your excuses. The truth is that you just wanted to save your own skin, and didn't give a damn if I was rotting in prison for a crime that I didn't even know anything about. I don't know how you got your hands on my chop in the first place—"

"I told you I was sorry. I used your chop because I thought it would make the loans more official. And I wouldn't have made those loans if you hadn't been so irresponsible about money in the first place—" She knows she should not bring this up, but somehow she cannot sit there listening to him without trying to defend herself.

"Money! Money! Money! It all goes back to money with you. And I should have known that you would twist it around and try to blame me!" It is turning into a repetition of an argument that they have had dozens of times before. She feels trapped, because she no longer feels like that person who used to argue with him so passionately about money. As she tries to find the words to tell him, he breaks off in frustration, letting himself flop back onto the bed. For a minute or two, he is silent.

Then he says, "And that isn't even what I'm most upset about."

He stops, and she listens to his quick, angry breathing. He seems to be struggling to get his temper under control. When he speaks again, his voice is unsteady with suppressed fury. "I suppose I should have realized that you'd use this opportunity to get rid of Ping'er."

"Get rid of her!" she cries. She sits still in the darkness, speechless for a moment. She should have expected this, she supposes. "How could you think that I wanted to get rid of her, when I loved her—"

"You were always jealous of her!"

How like him, she thinks, to be blind to the love that had revived between her and Ping'er after Qiaojie's birth. When she thinks of how she and Ping'er had struggled side by side nursing Qiaojie, she cannot bear to defend herself.

"To lose Ping'er, on top of Qiaojie . . ." Lian says, beginning to sob in the dark.

"I lost them. You didn't even care about Qiaojie." The words slip out without her intending to say them out loud.

He rises up quickly from the bed. Even in the darkness, she can see his upraised right arm.

"Go ahead and hit me," she hisses, rising up onto her knees to meet his blow. "I've always expected you to. I'm just surprised that you haven't done it before, that's all."

His arm drops. For a long time they are both motionless, only their breathing audible. It seems to her that with each breath, they exhale an invisible poison into the room, the atmosphere growing more and more toxic as the seconds tick by, so that she can hardly breathe. She feels herself grow a little lightheaded. These dizzy spells come oftener these days; she needs to take better care of herself. She does not want to live like this anymore, not after all that she has been through. She crawls closer to him on the *kang* and puts her arms around him. She can feel how tense his body is beneath her embrace.

"I don't want to fight about these things anymore." She puts her head on his shoulder. "Isn't that all in the past?"

He does not answer.

"Why don't we put our energy into working hard to help the family get back on its feet, instead of fighting?" She grabs his hands. "We can save money, start again. Maybe one day we can even have another child." In her heart she does not believe that this will happen, but she wants to conjure up a rosy vision of the future to inspire him to work with her.

He jerks himself away from her. "Don't touch me!"

She is surprised and hurt by his vehemence, and stares at him.

"I wanted to tell you something else that came out at the trial," he says. His voice is different now, casual, almost conversational. For some reason, this makes her more uneasy than when he had spoken angrily. She tries to read his expression, but it is too dark. "You know, by the end of the trial, I had almost convinced the magistrate that I really knew nothing about those loans. The obvious solution was that you had made them. But in the end, he simply couldn't understand how a woman from one of the best families, who was supposed to be sequestered in the Inner Quarters, could possibly be making loans to people all over the city. So he decided that it must have been me, after all. That's why I was convicted."

"It was the Abbess at the Water Moon Priory who helped me set up the loans," she explains quickly, licking her dry lips. "She knows everyone, and goes everywhere. She told me when someone wanted a loan and—"

He cuts her off, his tone still pleasant. "I have to admit, I wondered myself how you managed it. Then they showed me a note they had found among the loan agreements. What did it say?" He feigns absentmindedness, groping for the words.

Her heart starts to pound. Could she have been so careless as to have kept one of Yucun's notes?

"Oh, yes," Lian says, as if pleased with himself for remembering. "It said, 'I can't go another day without seeing you. Meet me at the storeroom at two.' It was unsigned, of course. But I recognized the handwriting. You see, he had written me a few little notes as well. So it wasn't hard to put two and two together. Just a few words, but they explained so much!" He laughs, as if amused by the irony.

"I was only meeting him because he was helping me out with the loans," she lies desperately.

Lian laughs again, unpleasantly. "I thought you said that the Abbess helped you make the loans."

"She did, but so did he!"

"Spare me your lies," he says. He pauses for a moment, before continuing, "Unfortunately, since there was no evidence that he had been involved in the loans, it was no use bringing it up at trial. You should be grateful to me. I didn't even say anything to Uncle. But I knew from that moment what you were."

She is silent, cold with shame and fear. It is no use trying to lie or make excuses. It is far, far worse than when it was just the loans. All she can do is sit there, with her head bowed, waiting to hear what he will do to her.

"I had decided to sue you for divorce when I got out of prison," he says. "But now that I have been released early, I'm not sure. We've been through enough scandal as it is, and it wouldn't be fair to Granny and Uncle to put them through any more."

He suddenly sounds more tired than angry. "Don't worry. I won't even tell anyone. But don't expect me to treat you like a wife."

She does not move, still kneeling there with her head bowed submissively. Inside, her thoughts are rebellious. He has never treated her like a wife, she thinks bitterly, not even at the very beginning.

"By the way," he adds, and she can tell from his voice that he is going to say something malicious, "you've heard the rumors about Jia Yucun, haven't you?"

She does not answer, knowing that he wants to rub in the fact that it was her lover who had betrayed the family.

"You really chose a good one, didn't you?" he says jeeringly. "He must really have loved you. So much that he testified against Uncle Zheng!"

His words strike her like physical blows, and she instinctively flings up her arms to ward them off. She crouches there in the dark, sick with humiliation, waiting for him to taunt her again. Fortunately, he does not say any more. She hears him lying down and turning over in the darkness. Still she crouches there, not daring to move. Eventually she hears his breathing deepen, and realizes that he is asleep. She crawls shivering across the *kang* and climbs into the bedding on the other side. She pulls the quilt over her head and wraps her arms around her body. She feels cold, so cold that she wonders whether she will ever be warm again.

4

Everyone else in the family has gone to bed. Throwing his robe on over his nightclothes, Jia Zheng rises from his bed on the *kang* in the front room and goes to the back bedroom to look in on Baoyu. The room is dark except for a small lantern casting a circle of dim light on Baoyu's head and shoulders. Since their release from prison four days earlier, the boy has refused both food and drink. He has lain all day on the *kang*, either asleep or in a stupor, Jia Zheng cannot tell. Sometimes his body draws in on itself and shivers as if he is lying on a bed of ice. At others, sweat starts out on his lip and brow, and he flings off his blankets, trying to claw open his tunic. No matter how they call his name or shake him, he does not respond. When they prop his head up to give him his medicine, he twists out of their grip, refusing to open his mouth. When Dr. Wang first came four days ago, he had predicted that Baoyu would be on his feet in a week or two. This morning, however, he had said that Baoyu's pulse was tumultuous, and his *qi* dangerously attenuated. He was dehydrated, and as a result his fevers were spiking higher and higher. If Baoyu did not begin to drink and take his medicine, Dr. Wang could not answer for the consequences.

Jia Zheng leans over his son, looking at his face. He has become so thin that his cheek- and jawbones jut through his skin. Tanchun and Xifeng had shaved him the day he got back from prison, but now the long black stubble emphasizes his waxen pallor. They washed his hair as well, but now it fans out, tangled and unkempt, across his pillow. Yet the nobility and beauty of Baoyu's face seem strangely undiminished by his illness. If anything, the broad sweep of his brow, the fine chiseling of his nose, are emphasized by his thinness. Jia Zheng listens to Baoyu's stertorous breathing, thinking what remarkable qualities his son has. Even though he did not see Baoyu for the last nine months when they were imprisoned, he had seen a good deal of him during the confiscation and trial, and felt that he had come to understand Baoyu more during that period than he had during all their previous years together. When the Embroidered Jackets had dragged them to the *yamen*, Baoyu alone had neither cried out nor protested his innocence. Other than ascertaining the nature of the charges and of the evidence, he had confined his remarks to reassuring and comforting the others. During the following weeks, he bore without complaint both his mistreatment at the hands of the jailers and police and the indignity of the trial, answering his interrogators simply and clearly. Never by word or implication did he ever suggest that Jia Zheng, by befriending Jia Yucun, was to blame for their sufferings. Jia Zheng had been used to thinking of his son as spoiled and weak. Now he understands that Baoyu was someone who needed the exigency of circumstances to make him rise to his higher self.

Baoyu stirs and turns away from Jia Zheng, pulling the blanket around himself. Jia Zheng leans over and shakes his shoulder. Baoyu does not respond. Jia Zheng shakes him, more urgently this time. He has a feeling that Baoyu's mind is only slightly below the surface of consciousness, and that if he speaks forcefully and clearly, he can penetrate the fog.

"Baoyu! Baoyu! I need you to wake up." He gently slaps Baoyu's cheeks, which are hot with fever. Baoyu's eyelids flutter.

"Baoyu, listen to me. You can't go on like this. You must take your medicine."

There is no response.

He tries again, slapping Baoyu's face a little harder. "Wake up and listen to me." He feels foolish speaking to Baoyu while he is unconscious, but he cannot let Baoyu die without trying to get through to him. "I know you're upset about Daiyu. But you can't do this. You must get better."

At the mention of Daiyu's name, as if at the incantation of a magic charm, Baoyu's eyes flutter open. Jia Zheng sees that they are bloodshot and swollen.

He bends over so his face is only a few inches from his son's. "You can hear me, can't you? You're not eating because of Daiyu, aren't you? You can't do this. You have a duty to the family—"

"I don't care," Baoyu mutters.

"You must care. What do you think will happen to everyone if you die? Our situation is still precarious. I haven't been reinstated to my old position. With all our property confiscated, the only way for us to survive is for you to pass the Exams so we have some income—" For the first time, he speaks aloud the worries that have begun to consume him since their release from prison.

Baoyu flinches, but Jia Zheng continues, "Maybe Huan can pass in a few years, but he is nowhere near ready. If you put your mind to it, you can pass next spring."

Baoyu shakes his head.

"You must. If you don't, how will we make matches for Tanchun and Xichun? How will we send Huan to school? Even Lian and Xifeng depend on you, and Granny ..."

"I can't. I can't go on."

"Why can't you?"

"Don't you understand? I destroyed Daiyu. I killed her. If not for me, she wouldn't have died."

Jia Zheng is taken aback. "You had nothing to do with it."

"But I did! Granny wouldn't have gotten so angry at her if I hadn't said that I wanted to marry her. And when she found out about my betrothal, she didn't want to see me anymore, but then I gave her the jade, and promised her I would break the betrothal ... " Baoyu sobs, almost incoherent in his distress.

Jia Zheng had not known the details, and does not want to know them. Although he feels pity for Daiyu and for Baoyu's misery, he also feels that Daiyu's death is almost a relief, a way of putting a tortuous and difficult past behind them. "You acted shamefully. But you must remember that whatever Daiyu did was her own choice."

"But I led her on, and promised her that I would marry her—"

"If she chose to believe you could marry her when you were betrothed to someone else, that was her own foolishness. And besides, you don't know that she wouldn't have died anyway, even if she had stayed here with the others. After all, Min died of consumption. She must have been infected already—"

"If she had been taken care of properly, it wouldn't have killed her! I'm sure Snowgoose's family did their best, but they're poor, and their house must have been cold and damp."

"I'm not sure things were so much better here," Jia Zheng says, looking about the shabby, dingy apartment. "After all, Qiaojie died here." When Xifeng had told him, weeping, about Qiaojie's illness and death, he had been overcome by remorse at the thought of the helpless creature suffering for his misjudgment. Tears come to his own eyes.

"Still, it was all my fault! I can't forgive myself," Baoyu cries.

"You can't forgive yourself?" Jia Zheng stares at his son's haggard face. "Do you think I don't know what it's like to have caused terrible suffering to those I love most?"

Baoyu's eyes, bright with fever and tears, gaze up at him, and Jia Zheng sees that Baoyu understands.

"You, Lian, and Huan all had to go to prison for my sake. My own mother had to live in conditions worse than a servant, and had to watch her great-granddaughter die—"

"I never blamed you for that—"

"No—but Lian and Huan and Granny have! Even when you didn't say anything, I knew I was to blame. And I feel the most guilty towards you."

"But why?"

"Don't you remember? You warned me about Jia Yucun. 'A dangerous man'—you used those very words. And I laughed at you!"

"You couldn't have known what he would turn out to be."

"You knew, and you warned me. But I didn't listen." He shakes his head, burying his face in his hands. "How could I have been so naïve? He made me feel awkward and foolish, and so I would say things about the Princes and the Court to show him how much I knew, and how little he did." He understands now how his pride had made him vulnerable to Jia Yucun. "I was a conceited fool. And all of you, the whole family, had to pay for it."

Baoyu reaches out and pats Jia Zheng's hand weakly. "Let it go, Father. It's all in the past."

Jia Zheng takes his face out of his hands and looks at his son. "Then you must let it go, also."

Baoyu's head moves restlessly on the pillow. "It's different. You had to deal with Jia Yucun in the first place, so everyone else would have the luxury of never worrying about unpleasant things. Before the confiscation, I never thought of where the fine life I had came from. It was only afterwards that I understood that you, and Xifeng, were doing all the dirty work so I could fancy myself above it all." Baoyu gives a hopeless, bitter little laugh. "So, you see, you were right about me after all. I am a useless good-for-nothing."

"But you can change." Jia Zheng grips Baoyu's hot, dry hands. "All you have to do is study and pass the Exams, and you can make up for all the trouble that you caused in the past."

"I can't make anything up." Baoyu shuts his eyes as if he is exhausted.

"Yes, you can. If you really regret what you did to Daiyu, isn't the best way to make up for it by pulling yourself together and taking the Exams? Everyone depends on you."

Baoyu does not open his eyes, but he gives a long sigh. Reading acquiescence in the sigh, Jia Zheng feels a glimmer of hope.

Suddenly, Baoyu's feverish eyes open, blazing into Jia Zheng's. "The betrothal," he rasps. "Surely I can break the betrothal. Isn't it enough that I take the Exams?"

Jia Zheng is silent. He wishes he could say yes, but then he shakes his head. "How can we break the betrothal, when Pan did so much to get us the Imperial Pardon? And now he's lending us money." He sighs, too. "I understand that it's hard for you, but look at it this way: If you can't marry Daiyu, it might as well be Baochai."

Baoyu does not speak. He bursts into a passionate storm of tears. He turns himself onto his stomach, burying his face in his hands. His whole body is racked with hacking sobs that rend the silence of the room. Jia Zheng stares at him, wondering how to comfort him. He realizes that Baoyu is sobbing like this because he is acquiescing to Jia Zheng's words. Whatever his feelings, he will not let himself die when the whole family's future depends on him. He will even marry Baochai. Wanting to act quickly in case Baoyu changes his mind, Jia Zheng hurries to the side table where there is a dose of the medicine that Xifeng had brewed earlier. He brings it to Baoyu, waiting for him to be calm enough to swallow it.

Baoyu continues to sob for a long time, until, eventually, his emotions appear to exhaust him, and he lies still. Jia Zheng waits a few minutes before bending over him and propping him up against some cushions.

"Take this." He holds the cup to Baoyu's lips.

Baoyu pulls away.

"Please, Baoyu, take it. I promise that things will look better tomorrow."

Baoyu nods, starting to cry again. But he takes the cup and begins to drink, the long unused muscles in his throat gathering and shifting as the tears pour down his face.

PART SIX

Tenth Month, 1723

Vain to imagine the warm wind
In a thousand myriad willow threads.

Wang Yisun, "Cicadas," song lyric to the
tune "Joy Reaching the Heavens"

1

"Now shut your eyes," Mrs. Xue says.

Baochai, sitting in her wedding clothes in their apartments at Jingui and Pan's house, closes her eyes and feels the soft strokes of the powder brush rapidly covering her face.

"Hold still," her mother says. "I'm going to paint your eyes."

Baochai feels her mother's finger pulling the corner of her eye, and then the tiny brush tracing her eyelid. Mrs. Xue tells her to look up at the ceiling. Then she feels the brush drawing along her lower lash line.

"Nervous?" Mrs. Xue says.

"No," Baochai replies, though her heart is fluttering like a bird's, and her palms are sweaty. She does not understand her agitation. She has thought long and hard about her decision to marry Baoyu, and her mind is made up. Why, then, this unwonted nervousness? Is it eagerness, uneasiness, or some combination of both?

Almost two months ago, Uncle Zheng had proposed to her mother that the long-awaited marriage take place, now that the one-year mourning for His Late Majesty had come to an end. Even though they originally planned that the wedding would not take place until Baoyu passed the Civil Service Exams, after everything that had happened, Jia Zheng thought it best that the match be consummated as soon as possible. Mrs. Xue had found a chance to be alone with Baochai, and had repeated Jia Zheng's proposal to her. "What do you think, Baochai?"

"What do you mean, Mother? Do you mean, when do I think the wedding should take place?"

"I mean," her mother said, with a touch of impatience, "do you want to go through with this marriage?"

Baochai gazed at her mother in surprise. "Surely you are not thinking of backing out now?"

Her mother looked at Baochai as if she were being willfully obtuse. "It's our last chance. After this, it will be too late."

"But Baoyu is back from jail. I won't have to wait four more years for him."

"That's the very reason that we can break the betrothal now. The Jias are no longer in such terrible trouble. We can back out without looking as if we are abandoning them in their darkest hour. Besides, Pan is back, and I am sure he will be happy to find you a new match."

Baochai had been silent. Her first reaction was frustration at her mother's about-face. For so many months, she had felt that she had no choice, and had struggled to resign herself to the match. Now, all of a sudden, on the verge of the wedding, she was being told that she did have a choice after all. How could she make such a choice? All the old reasons she had agreed to the match in the first place still held sway: the two families were now even more closely intertwined, and Mrs. Xue would be welcome to continue living with Baochai at the Jias'.

Her mother had looked at her with a strange expression. "The truth is," her mother said at last, "I thought *you* wanted to break the betrothal when you saw the way Baoyu reacted to Daiyu's death."

At the mention of Daiyu's name, Baochai had flinched. Baoyu's questions about Daiyu—almost the first thing he said on arriving back from prison—and his reaction to the news of Daiyu's death had at first hurt her terribly. As always, she tried to avoid the painful subject. "It doesn't have anything to do with Daiyu," she said.

"Yes, that's what I thought: Daiyu has nothing to do with

your marriage. But I thought perhaps you felt she did." Mrs. Xue had sighed, shaking her head. "You are such a reserved person, Baochai, almost secretive. I understand now that there are many things you don't tell even me, your mother. I never knew that Daiyu was sick, and that you had gone to see her. Did it ever occur to you that if I had known, I would have wanted to go see her, too?"

Baochai had shaken her head. She did not wish to explain to her mother that because she had tattled on Daiyu, she felt too ashamed to discuss Daiyu's situation with anyone.

"Given that you are so reserved," Mrs. Xue said, "I decided that I must make every effort to discuss everything with you as openly as possible. I thought that maybe you were bothered by the way Baoyu reacted to Daiyu's death. No girl would like it. But you must remember, Daiyu is dead, and far better a dead rival than one who is alive. In fact, now that he is vulnerable from her death, it is a perfect time for you to win him to yourself."

"Yes, Mother." In fact, Baochai, after the initial shock of Baoyu's reaction to Daiyu's death, had come to the same conclusions herself. Not that she hadn't been grieved by Daiyu's death, but still, she realized that it opened the possibility that Baoyu might come to love Baochai herself. And why wouldn't he, if she were as tender and gentle as she meant to be? Despite herself, she had felt the faint stirrings of hope. On top of that—and this is something that she could not admit to her mother—since Baoyu's return, she had felt her old attraction to him more strongly than ever. She wanted to be with him, even though she hated herself for her weakness. Despite his thinness and pallor, he was as handsome as before; yet he was not the same old carefree Baoyu. There was a deeper note of seriousness in his voice, and his bearing had a somber dignity. She used to watch him surreptitiously as he began to study again, sitting in a corner of the front room over his books, with a frown of intense concentration that he had never worn before.

And so, she had reassured her mother that she was not unhappy with the match. A date had been set, and, in order to observe the proper separation from her future bridegroom and in-laws, she and her mother had moved from Drum Street into the Xias' house with Pan. Pan had reassured them that they were welcome to stay as long as they liked, and had bought a few maids, so that they would not need to depend on the Xias' servants. In fact, they almost never saw Jingui, who lived in a different part of the house. Pan came to see them almost every day, and they had spent the last two months very comfortably.

"Now purse your lips," her mother says.

Baochai does so, and Mrs. Xue carefully glosses her upper lip with the thick red carmine.

"Relax your mouth."

Baochai feels her mother filling in a circle in the center of her bottom lip.

"Now for the rouge, and you'll be all ready."

Her mother uses a hairpin to scrape a tiny dab of rouge onto her palm. She softens it with the warmth of her fingers, and then spreads it across Baochai's cheeks.

"That's perfect. Now look at yourself!" Mrs. Xue hands Baochai a West Ocean mirror the size of a large platter.

Baochai stares at herself, amazed at her transformation. Gone are the plain, insignificant features that she is used to seeing. Her eyes, emphasized by the kohl, are large and dramatic beneath the delicately arched brows. Her face, already less round from the months of deprivation in Drum Street, has been given definition by the powder and rouge. Even her nose looks more finely shaped. This is a face that can make Baoyu fall in love, she thinks, with a tremulous sense of triumph. Never before has she had such a sense of her own power.

Then she hears it, the faint sound of drums and gongs perhaps two or three courtyards away.

She looks at her mother. "Am I ready?"

"There's a smudge on your chin." Mrs. Xue uses a handkerchief to dab at something. The music is coming closer and closer. Now Baochai can hear the skirling of the *suonas* as well.

"Let me straighten your hair." With a few deft movements, her mother adjusts the various ornaments.

"Now where is the veil?" Mrs. Xue says, looking around. The music grows suddenly louder as the wedding party enters the courtyard.

Mrs. Xue unfolds the veil and flings it over Baochai's head.

Now she can see nothing but the folds of red silk. She puts out her hand. Her mother catches it and leads her out into the cacophony.

It is only halfway through the wedding banquet that she notices how strangely Baoyu is acting. At first she had been too caught up in the happiness of the occasion to pay much attention. Pan was so excited that he proposed three toasts to her and Baoyu, despite Jingui's attempts to restrain him. Even her mother rose and toasted the new couple. Tanchun wrapped her long arms around Baochai, whispering that she had always hoped that Baochai would be her sister. Xifeng made Baochai blush and everyone else laugh by comparing her to the coachman's wife praised by Yan Ying, who had reproved her husband for his prideful airs. Finally, Jia Zheng had risen to toast the couple, and also to share two pieces of wonderful news: he was to be reinstated to his former post at the Ministry of Works, and

Rongguo was to be returned to the family. They would probably be able to move back before the winter. His Highness
Emperor Yongzheng seemed to be shaping up as an able admin-
istrator, and had turned his attention from purging his enemies
to reforming and reorganizing the bureaucracy.

At first Baochai had basked in the glow of everyone's praise
and congratulations, too shy to do more than glance at Baoyu,
whom she has not seen for two months. Now, during dinner,
under the cover of the general chatter, she finally takes the
opportunity to covertly observe him. He looks magnificent, his
tall, slender figure set off by his heavy wedding robes, the scarlet
of the silk bringing out the deep gloss of his black hair and the
delicacy of his complexion. During the toasts, she heard his
voice laughing and thanking everyone for their good wishes, but
now it strikes her that the last thing he looks like is a happy
bridegroom. He is nodding and smiling, but with a polite,
abstracted manner, as if he were a guest at someone else's
wedding.

She turns away, and goes back to smiling and chattering with
the others. She looks at him several times during the rest of the
evening, and each time is thrown back upon herself by his air of
remoteness. She tells herself that this is only to be expected. She
cannot expect him to be overjoyed at marrying her, so soon after
Daiyu's death. It is enough that he is making every effort to be
pleasant and polite.

Still, when she finds herself alone with him in the wedding
chamber, she feels deflated, ill at ease. All the excitement that
had buoyed her before the wedding has slipped away. The Jias
have prepared and furnished a bedroom next door to the old
Drum Street apartment as the wedding chamber. This is the
first time that she has seen it, and now she walks about admiring
the new furnishings: a dressing table with a West Ocean mirror,
a handsome desk, and a large armoire with mother-of-pearl-

inlaid doors. She pauses before the dressing table, avoiding her own reflection in the mirror, instead examining the elaborately carved rosewood frame. "This is lovely," she says brightly. "They have made such a nice room. But," she adds with a laugh, "I guess we won't be staying here for very long, after all." She smiles at him. "That's marvelous news, isn't it, that we'll be going back to Rongguo soon?"

He does not answer. Instead, he approaches the desk, where his books and papers have been arranged neatly. He looks down at them and begins to flip through a sheaf of notes.

"Surely you're not going to study tonight," she says, more sharply than she intends.

"No, no." He puts down the papers, a little guiltily, she thinks. "I was just making sure that everything was here."

"Well, I suppose I don't mind if you do study a little bit," she says, feeling embarrassed at the sharpness with which she had spoken.

"No, of course I won't study." He moves away from the desk towards the *kang*, already spread with the new satin quilt and pillows that Xifeng and the Two Springs had made for them, embroidered with a pattern of mandarin ducks. He sits down on the edge of the *kang* and begins to take off his wedding shoes.

She looks around for his slippers. "I don't know where anything is here," she says with a nervous laugh. She goes to the armoire in the corner, and finds it filled with neatly folded stacks of his and her clothing. She finds his slippers and hurries over. Instead of letting her kneel down to put them on his feet, he takes them out of her hands and puts them on himself. He takes off his vest and begins to unfasten his gown.

At the thought that he is about to undress in front of her, she is filled with a strange, fluttery panic, which she tries to hide. Reaching towards him awkwardly, she says, "Let me help you."

He waves her hands aside. "That's all right," he says pleasantly.

She feels at a loss. He is not allowing her to do a proper wife's duty. It is hard for her not to take his insistence on doing every-thing for himself as a rejection. She stands there while he takes off his gown, keeping her gaze averted. Her eyes fall on the tray of wine and snacks that has been left for them on a small *kang* table. "Do you want anything to eat or drink?"

"No, thank you. I'm fine." Wearing only a light tunic and undertrousers, he folds his clothes and puts them in the armoire. "Why don't you have something?"

Even if she had an appetite, she could hardly sit there eating and drinking while he got ready for bed himself. "Don't you want to wash?" She gestures at the basin and kettle on the stove.

He walks quickly over, before she can get there herself. He pours hot water from the kettle into the basin. Again, when she approaches to help, he waves her off. She supposes that she should begin to prepare for bed herself. She seats herself before the dressing table and begins to pluck the ornaments from her hair. She watches him in the mirror getting a towel from the armoire, and ladling cold water from the bucket to mix with the water in the basin. Slowly, she takes down her hair, and puts it into a lazy knot. She looks in the mirror. Her heavily made-up face no longer strikes her as pretty. Her eyes, drooping with the exhaustion of the long day, look garish with their lining of kohl, and her lips have been smudged from eating and drinking. Still, she feels loath to take off her makeup in front of him. She is being ridiculous, she tells herself. Of course, he has seen her without makeup hundreds of times.

"Are you ready to go to bed?" he says. He has finished wash-ing and is drying his hands on a towel.

She nods. Hastily, without looking at him, she scrubs the makeup off her face. She hears him opening the window to toss out the dirty water. Then he rinses out the basin and fills it with fresh water for her, mixing the hot and cold water and testing it with his hand. He gets her a fresh towel from the armoire. As he hands it to her with a courteous smile, she is aware of the yawning distance between them, even though she has known him for so many years.

"Thanks," she says, uncomfortably aware of her bare, blotchy face. She quickly washes her face and hands. She wonders whether she should undress, as he has, but feels paralyzed by shyness.

Probably sensing her nervousness, he offers, "Shall I blow out the lights?"

"All right."

He blows out the two lanterns near the door. Only the small lamp on the *kang* table remains.

"Ready?" he says.

"Go ahead." She is still standing awkwardly beside the basin.

He climbs onto the *kang* and blows the last light out. They are in darkness. She stands there unmoving. Then she hears him getting into bed, the rumpling of the bedclothes.

She stands there for perhaps a minute. Then, as silently as she can, she walks to the *kang* and begins to undress. She takes off her vest, fumbling with the fastenings of her gown in the dark. She folds the clothes and places them on the edge of the *kang*. She slips off her shoes and her socks. Now she is wearing only a short sleeveless tunic and loose undertrousers. She climbs onto the *kang* and crawls to the side of the bed farthest away from him. Trying to disarrange the quilt as little as possible, she slides her body underneath it and lays her head on the pillow. For a long time she lies there, trying not to make a sound, flat on her back, as far away from him as possible. Every muscle in her body is tensed, waiting and wondering what he will do. On the one hand, she is scared that he will touch her. At the same time, she is afraid that he will not come near her.

He makes no move towards her. She hears him gently expelling air through his nostrils. She begins to feel humiliated. It is not enough that her bridegroom has to humiliate her by acting silent and distant at their wedding feast. On top of that, she will lie here alone, untouched, on her wedding night. Even though she reminds herself that she must be patient and tender with Baoyu, she has not imagined that he would not even touch her. Tears fill her eyes as she stares up at the black ceiling. She lets them roll silently down the sides of her face into her hair, afraid he will notice if she wipes her eyes. The mucus is clogging her nose and filling her throat. She tries to control herself, but a single sob escapes her. She hears his head move on his pillow as he turns to look at her.

There is a silence. Then she hears him move across the bed towards her. She shrinks away, not wanting him to touch her out of pity, but his arms come around her, warm and strong. She resists a little, but then she lets him pull her against him. He holds her tightly. She feels his breath against her hair, warm and sweet. That is what she has always liked about him: he has never seemed dirty and brutish like other men. He is stroking her hair, his other arm holding her against him. He strokes her for a long time, before she begins to relax under his touch. She nestles her head into his shoulder. His touch is so gentle that it is impossible to believe that he does not feel tenderness towards her. He moves his hand from her hair, and traces her eyebrows, touches her eyelids. She begins to grow excited, and turns her body to face his. She flings her arms around him, and puts her face up to be kissed. He kisses her once on the lips, deeply, then buries his face in her neck.

Now their bodies are pressed against each other. She feels his member hard against her belly through their layers of clothing. So he is not indifferent to her, after all. Perhaps he is simply shy and self-conscious. Perhaps he had just been lying there trying to get up the courage to approach her. His fingers begin to fumble at the fastenings of her tunic. He has them open in a few seconds. Then his warm hands are on her, touching her belly, her breasts.

"Oh, Baoyu," she gasps, shaken out of her usual composure. "Oh, Baoyu."

She wants to hear his voice, she wants him to say her name. He remains silent, but lets his hands run up and down her body. Then he is fumbling with the drawstring of her trousers.

She does not resist him. Her mother had told her, years ago, what to expect. She lets him draw her trousers down over her hips. When she feels his hand touching her bare buttocks, she cannot help but flinch in panic. He withdraws his hand immediately.

At the withdrawal of his touch, she feels even more agitated. She stares at him in the darkness, unable to read his expression. She wants him to say something to encourage her, to reassure her, but he says nothing, just lying there a few inches from her.

Finally, she says, "That's all right. I don't mind."

Still, he does nothing. She begins to feel increasingly awkward about his silence. Is he trying to show her that he has the upper hand? She wants him to continue touching her. Impulsively, she takes her trousers off all the way under the quilt. She wraps her bare legs around him.

At her boldness, his constraint falls away. He puts his arms around her again, pulling her roughly against him. He rolls his weight on top of her so that she is underneath him, pressed against the *kang*. She looks up at his silhouette above her in the darkness, and pulls his head down so that he will kiss her. Instead, he buries his head in her neck again. He stays like that for a long time, his rough breath exhaling hotly onto her skin slicked with sweat. Then he parts her legs and enters her without a sound.

2

Xifeng uses the twig broom to sweep the deep snow covering the stoop. The snow is nearly a foot deep, and it is an effort to drag the heavy broom through it. She has no gloves, and the roughness of the broom's handle chafes against her bare skin. She pulls the cuffs of her sleeves past her wrists, and uses the material to pad her cold palms against the wooden handle. Again and again, until her arms are aching, she draws the broom back and pushes the growing pile of snow, until she has cleared a narrow band before the apartment. She turns back and begins to clear a second strip. Now, despite the coldness of the day, she is beginning to grow heated beneath her bulky clothes. Her panting breath forms a plume of frost in the air. Why don't any of the others come out to help her? she thinks. She supposes they are all sitting cozily on the *kang* while she struggles alone out here in the cold. Perhaps they are all in league against her. Ever since they learned of her illegal loans, everyone has treated her differently. With a gasp, she pushes the heavy pile of accumulated snow to the edge of the road. No, better that she finish the hard job herself, rather than going in and asking for help. Perhaps then they will appreciate how much she does.

She turns and begins to clear a third strip. Now she can hardly lift her burning arms. How easily she gets tired these days, not like the old days at Rongguo when she could stay up half the night with Qiaojie and be up at six thirty to serve breakfast. Just a few more paces and she'll be done. She presses down on the broom, driving it into a crack between some crooked cobblestones to scrape the snow out, and hears the click of something hard against the twigs. Something round and white rolls forward from the stroke of her broom, not snow. She stoops down and picks it up, and the instant her fingers close around its cold hardness, she knows it is Baoyu's jade. She rubs it on her skirt and holds it up. Yes, it is as familiar to her as an old friend: the size of a sparrow's egg, all streaked with creamy iridescence, showing purples and greens and blues in the winter sunlight. She almost laughs aloud from the wonder of it. How could it get here? Had it been here all along? She turns to go inside to tell everyone. Now, perhaps, the family's luck will finally change . . .

She opens her eyes, blinking. It is still dark. The night air is freezing, and she tucks her two quilts more tightly about her body. She has been dreaming, but her dream was so vivid that she could still almost feel the coldness of her fingers, the heaviness of the broom. How strange that she should be dreaming of the apartment on Drum Street when she is back in her old bedroom at Rongguo. She moves her head on the pillow, looking about her. Even though much of the furniture is gone, the shape and placement of the windows, and the height of the ceiling, with its shadowy carvings, are still familiar. And how strange that she should be dreaming of the jade, of all things. Once she had feared that the loss of the jade foretold the waning of the family fortunes, but even without it, the family fortunes are on the upswing. Jia Zheng has been reinstated, and Baoyu and Huan are both studying diligently, planning to take the Exams in the spring.

It is only her own fortunes that are declining, she thinks, staring up at the black ceiling. Lian is harsh and forbidding to her. Now that they have moved back to Rongguo, his contempt for her is clear for all to see. He refuses to sleep in the same room, and has moved back across the courtyard to where he and Ping'er lived before Qiaojie's birth. Last time he lived there it had not bothered her much. This time, she finds herself acutely self-conscious about what the others must be thinking. And she is terribly lonely, far lonelier than she has ever been. Living in the apartment that she used to share with Ping'er and Qiaojie, without even a maid to keep her company, she is haunted by memories of them: of putting her lips to Qiaojie's downy little head and drinking in her sweet, milky scent; of Ping'er combing her hair two hundred strokes every morning. And she has no work or occupation with which to push away the memories. Uncle Zheng has used his salary to buy a handful of servants; it is no longer necessary for her and the other girls to shop and cook and clean. With their southern estates gone and such simple housekeeping, there are no rents and salaries and expenditures for her to keep track of. Despite her loneliness, she is too proud to seek out Baochai or the other girls to chat. Instead she spends her day weaving or sewing in a desultory fashion, or hoping that she will feel more energetic if she takes yet another nap on the *kang*.

Her health continues to trouble her. Despite the better food and more comfortable living conditions at Rongguo, she seems to grow weaker and more languid by the day. She sleeps poorly, drifting in and out of a light doze, instead of being able to fall into a deeper, more restorative, slumber. She has no appetite, and feels so cold that she has taken to wearing two pairs of socks. More and more often, she feels sharp pains in her belly. Lian wouldn't notice even if she collapsed on the floor, but Baochai had sent for Dr. Wang. After a long examination, he had said that a mass was growing in her female organs as a result of a severe stagnation of *qi*. He prescribed turtle shell, *longkui*, and oldenlandia. When she asked him how long it would take for her to get better, he said he did not know, and some strange dread had prevented her from questioning him further. She had the prescription filled, and took it dutifully, but did not feel she was getting any stronger.

Now she feels exhaustion overtaking her, and she shuts her eyes again. She feels the half-sleeping, half-waking state, which has replaced true sleep for her, stealing over her limbs. She is cold, but is too tired to rearrange her blankets. She feels those strange phantom pains burning in her abdomen. She shifts her position, trying to make herself more comfortable, but the pains do not go away. She tries to slip into deeper sleep, but instead her mind skips uneasily over scenes from her past: her childhood with Ping'er at the Wang mansion in Chang'an, the night of Qiaojie's birth, her fights with Lady Jia at Drum Street.

She opens her eyes. The room is filled with sunlight. She has overslept. In a panic she leaps out of bed, but the sudden movement makes her dizzy. She clings to the wardrobe to steady herself, and manages to put on some clothes. Barely looking at the mirror, she twists her hair into a rough knot, and sets off across the forecourt towards Granny Jia's apartments to serve breakfast. She tries to run at first, but it makes her so dizzy that she is forced to slow to a quick walk.

As she crosses the courtyard at Lady Jia's, she hears the clink of china and the chattering voices of the family having breakfast. She steels herself for what everyone will say about her lateness, as she stops to catch her breath outside the door. Straightening her gown and drawing herself up, she passes through the door curtain. Everyone—Lady Jia, Uncle Zheng, Lian, Baoyu, Mrs. Xue, and the Two Springs—is sitting around the table eating. No one even turns their head at her entrance. Standing at the head of the table, behind Lady Jia's chair, is Baochai, in Xifeng's usual place. She has just ladled out a second serving of rice porridge for Uncle Zheng, and is now leaning over Lady Jia's plate, using chopsticks to debone a small smoked fish for her, smiling and chatting with Granny.

A surge of desolation comes over Xifeng: no one seems even to have noticed her absence. Then she is outraged: Who is

Baochai to take her place? She, Xifeng, is the senior daughter-in-law. She walks towards Baochai, expecting her to jump guiltily and yield her place. Baochai, however, comes forward to meet her, drawing her a little away from the dining table, speaking in a low voice so that the others will not overhear.

"I thought that you must not be feeling well, so I didn't send anyone to wake you," Baochai says. She looks into Xifeng's face. "No, you don't look well at all. Do you want me to send for the doctor again?"

Xifeng shakes her head.

"Are you sure? Well, at least go back and lie down. You're not needed here."

Xifeng looks at Baochai's terrible, inscrutable face. Is her concern real or feigned? Is she actually exulting in her chance to supplant Xifeng? How Xifeng both hates and fears that smooth perfection, that glossy surface off which every grief seems to slide! If only she herself were enclosed in that same porcelain armor, which nothing seems to penetrate. Instead, she has become weak, so weak. She is too weak to care what Baochai's motives are, and too weak to fight for precedence in the household anymore. Silently she turns away and goes back to her room.

3

Baochai sits in the corner of the *kang*, sewing some blinds for the still bare windows of the new apartment. When the family moved back into Rongguo, Uncle Zheng had allotted to her and Baoyu the apartments that Uncle Jing had occupied before his death. Her mother occupies a room on the other side of the courtyard. It is a large apartment, so large that even after the new furniture from her trousseau had been moved over from Drum Street, it still looked empty. The walls and shelves had been stripped bare during the confiscation, but Baochai is determined to make the place as pleasant as possible. After she had made up the deficiencies in Baoyu's wardrobe, she set herself to sewing bed hangings and a door curtain. With her mother's help, she has sewn a backrest and half a dozen pillows and bolsters, which are now scattered about the red Kashmiri rug that covers the *kang*. Once Baochai has finished the blinds, the place will look quite home-like.

Occasionally, she glances up at Baoyu, sitting at his desk across the room. In the circle of light cast by the lamp on his desk, he is totally immersed in his studies. The table is covered with books and papers. There is a blot of ink on his right middle finger. She always keeps an eye on him when he studies, so that she can attend to his needs before he can be distracted by them. She makes sure there is a cup of tea by his side, dumping it out and pouring fresh tea when it gets cold. If she notices that his ink is almost gone, she grinds more for him. If the lamp sputters, she trims the wick. He cannot afford to be distracted. The Exams are only a month away.

As always since his illness, he works with an almost preter-
natural stillness and concentration, never brushing back his hair,
never fidgeting with his papers or books. Now that he knows
the Classics backwards and forwards—she has heard him flawlessly reciting long passages from them—he is concentrating on
practice essays. He writes on every conceivable topic, likely or
unlikely, consulting thick books of commentary for added
insights, polishing his diction and tightening the rhetorical
structure. At Baochai's suggestion, he even asks his father to
read the essays and offer advice. This painstaking preparation
will enable him to face the Exams, confident that no question
will catch him unawares.

It is getting late. She puts away her sewing and takes the bedding out of the armoire, spreading it out on the *kang*. Then she
begins to fold the clothes that she had laundered for him earlier.
As she smooths out the creases in his tunics, carefully folding
them in exactly the same shape and size, she is aware of a deep
contentment. This is the life she is meant to lead: a deep and
tranquil domesticity, with Baoyu at last throwing himself into
the male world of the Exams and official life, while she excels
equally in the women's sphere of the home. She likes feeling
that she is useful, even indispensable, to Baoyu. There is not a
single practical task she does not do for him—from organizing
his papers and books and clothes to reminding him when to
wake, eat, bathe, and sleep. It is hard work, but she does it all,
with only a little help from her mother. Perhaps one day soon
they will have a maid to help. She knows that when that day
comes, she will regret relinquishing part of her responsibilities
to someone else.

As she looks at him, his sleek black hair, his angular nose, she
feels a frisson of desire. She wants to do something she has never
done before, go over and put her arms around him, or sit in his
lap, maybe even unbutton her tunic. But she quashes the

impulse. The last thing she should do is distract him from his studies. Besides, she tells herself, it is getting late and soon they will go to bed. She cannot articulate or admit to herself how much of her satisfaction in her marriage is due to her physical relations with Baoyu. Night after night since the wedding, she has only to lie in bed for a few minutes before he turns silently towards her, and begins to touch her. A few times, it is true, he seemed to have trouble getting an erection. Then he would swiftly manipulate himself under the covers, before pressing her down beneath him. Naturally, this always makes her feel a little awkward, but otherwise their sexual relations are satisfyingly regular. His desire convinces her that he is not indifferent to her, as she had first feared. He clearly wants to possess her body, and she does not believe he is someone who would want a physical relationship without caring and affection. She begins to believe that she has a power over him that he is reluctant to admit, out of pride or caution. That is why he touches her only under the cover of darkness. That is why he remains so silent during their lovemaking, as if afraid to betray his pleasure by even the faintest sound. She tells herself that Daiyu and he could have been together only a few times at the most. They simply could not have known the intimacy that Baochai now shares with him, deepening with every night they spend together. And her own feelings for Baoyu are growing as well. He is so different from the old Baoyu, who was always chattering, always distracted.

At last he rests his brush on the inkstone. He reaches out his arms, stretching and yawning. This is the usual sign that his work is done for the night, and that she can begin to help him prepare for bed. She bustles over, taking up his inkbrush and inkstone to rinse them out.

"Did you finish the Mencius?" she calls from the basin, the ink clouding the water gray.

He gestures at the paper before him. "Yes, I think this looks pretty good." He reaches his right arm behind him and massages a spot on his lower back. "I suppose I can go on to the Great Learning tomorrow."

"That's good." She dries the inkstone and the brush, and walks over to his desk to return them to their spots. He is still rubbing his back, looking down at the page in front of him and frowning as if there is a passage that still displeases him.

On an impulse, she decides to give him a hint about what she is starting to suspect. "I'm late, you know," she says, going around the desk to stand beside his chair.

He is still looking down at the essay. "Late for what?" he says absently.

She feels flustered at being forced to speak more explicitly. "I mean, I'm late," she repeats, stammering and blushing. "I mean, it's more than six weeks since my last ..." She trails off in embarrassment.

Baoyu looks up. Suddenly the atmosphere in the room is tense.

"Are you sure?" he asks, at the same moment she blurts out, wishing that she hadn't said anything, "I—I'm not really sure yet. It could be nothing, after all."

He interrupts her. "Well, if that's the case, it's wonderful news," he says. But he does not speak as if it is wonderful news. She cannot tell what he feels—she almost thinks that she sees relief in his eyes—but it certainly isn't happiness. There is an awkward silence, which he breaks by rising from his chair and walking over to the wardrobe. He begins to take off his robe, instead of letting her assist him as she usually does.

She feels like crying, as she had the first night of their marriage, before he had touched her. The confidence and contentment she thought she felt seem fragile as eggshells, so easily crushed by the strangeness of his reaction to her news. She cannot help herself. "Aren't you happy?" she blurts out.

He shrugs, not looking at her, folding his robe and putting it in the wardrobe. He turns to face her. "Why shouldn't I be happy?" he says. "A child is always a reason for joy. After all, is there anything more pure and blameless than an infant?"

He is trying to evade her by speaking in generalities. "I was talking about our child, not—not some hypothetical child," she says sharply.

He ignores her interruption. "In fact, I was just reading and thinking about that passage in Mencius about the 'heart of a newborn.'" He goes back to his desk, opens one of the books, and holds it out for her to see.

She hesitates, deliberating whether to allow herself to show any interest, to be drawn from her own point. Pinching her lips tightly together, she walks over to his desk and looks down at the page. "*Daren zhe bushi qi chizi zhi xin zhe ye,*" she reads. "'A noble man is one who does not lose the heart of a newborn.'" She looks at him impatiently. "Well, what of it?"

"What do you think it means?"

She ponders, sensing that he is testing her. "Well, he is talking about virtue, of course," she begins slowly, trying to dredge up what she remembers from long ago lessons. "He doesn't really mean the heart of an infant, literally. It's a metaphor for the purity of a sage's heart, his freedom from selfishness, and desire to help mankind, like Emperor Yao and Emperor Shun, the early sage-kings," she adds, gaining confidence.

"That's what people say, but it doesn't make sense." He shakes his head vigorously. It is the old Baoyu, animated and opinionated, that she has not seen for so long. "Think about it. Since when does a 'newborn baby' want to help mankind? That's absurd.

"So what does a newborn baby really want?" He leans forward, ticking his points off on his long fingers. "It cries when it's hungry or sick or when its diaper is wet. That's all."

"What's your point?" she says, a little tartly.

"That's what Mencius means." He shuts the book, patting its cover. "A baby *has* no desires—no ambition, or love, or greed. It is only when we get older that we learn to desire those things—"

She has no idea what he is getting at, but his remarks strike a sudden fear into her heart. "How can you put your own ideas into Mencius's mouth like that? For a thousand years, other people, far more learned than you, have devoted their entire lives to studying Mencius and figuring out what he means, and here you come along—"

She breaks off, surprised by her own vehemence. It takes her a moment to master herself sufficiently to speak with any semblance of calm. "I'm sorry. I shouldn't have said that—"

"No, you're right. I was just following my own train of thought ... "

The mutual dissatisfaction hangs palpable between them. Baoyu moves away from the desk and begins to pour hot water into the basin.

She wants desperately to bridge the distance between them. "Baoyu, you're studying too hard—"

"Studying too hard?" He smiles ironically. "Since when is it possible for you to think I am studying too hard?"

She hurries on, ignoring his jibe. "It's making us both tense, short-tempered. Why don't we do something to relax?"

"Like what?"

She answers at random. "Oh, I don't know. We could go for a walk ... Why don't we go for a walk in the Garden tomorrow if the weather is fine? It's overgrown, of course, but the fresh air will do you good—"

"No!" he says, so forcefully that she jumps. After a moment he adds in a calmer voice, "I don't want to go to the Garden."

She stares at him, but his face is expressionless. She is even more terrified than before. He begins to ladle cold water from the basin. She goes over to him and takes the ladle from his hand. Instead of ladling the water for him, she does something she has never done before. She stands close to him and tugs his hands so they are touching her body through her clothes. She lets the ladle clatter to the floor. She presses his hands flat against her body, and guides them so they travel over her belly, her hips and buttocks, her breasts. He does not resist her, his hands obedient to the pressure of hers. It is the first time that they have touched each other in the light. She seeks his eyes with her own, wanting to see the desire in them, but he keeps them fixed downwards. She takes him by the chin to tilt his face up, but still his eyes slide away from hers, so she kisses him on the lips instead, boldly, lingeringly. At first his body is rigid, but as she continues to kiss and caress him, she feels him relax. Then she leads him to the bed and for the first time they make love in the glare of the lamps.

4

The night before the Exams, Jia Zheng calls Baoyu and Huan to his study. He remembers how distraught he had been before he took the Exams so many years ago, and how he had longed for a few words of encouragement and comfort. Instead, his father had threatened to beat him if he did not pass. He had not been able to fall asleep the whole night before, and had set out in the morning slightly nauseated from exhaustion. Although he feels awkward in the role of mentor, especially after his experience with Jia Yucun, he decides he must say a few words to his sons before such a momentous occasion.

Huan comes first. The boy fidgets so much that it sets Jia Zheng's teeth on edge. He encourages Huan to keep calm and pace himself during the Exams. Having read Huan's practice essays, Jia Zheng feels that his diction is too crude and his transitions too clumsy for him to pass. Unlike Baoyu, Huan is not talented enough to master the materials for the Exams without a teacher or a tutor. After Baoyu passes and starts to make an official salary, they will be able to afford a tutor for Huan. However, since Huan has worked hard and is eager to take the Exams, Jia Zheng does not consider it right to discourage him.

After Huan has excused himself to do some last-minute cramming, Baoyu comes. "Sweeper said you wanted to see me, Father?" he says, standing just inside the door.

Jia Zheng rises from his seat. "Yes." He smiles. "Have Baochai and the girls gotten all your luggage ready?"

"I think so."

"With all the fuss they're making, you'd think you were going for three months, not three days!"

Baoyu forces a smile. He looks pale and wan, and Jia Zheng worries whether he will have the stamina to concentrate for the whole Exams. It is probably just nerves. He puts his arm around Baoyu's shoulders. "Worried?"

Baoyu shrugs, almost impatiently, his eyes on the ground.

Jia Zheng guesses he is too proud to admit that he is anxious. "You don't need to worry. You've studied hard for so many months. Just do your best." Feeling how rigid Baoyu's body is, he wonders whether he has put too much pressure on the boy. "Remember how I told you last spring, when you were sick, that everything depended on you?"

Baoyu looks up into Jia Zheng's face, his eyes strangely intent. "Of course."

"Well, things have started looking better since then, haven't they? I've been reinstated, and we're back at Rongguo. Now that you're married to Baochai, Pan has been even more generous. I want you to know"—he looks into his son's eyes— "you don't need to worry if you don't pass the first time."

Baoyu's eyes drop. "You don't really mean that, Father. You've always drummed it into my head that everything depended on my passing."

"I do mean it. I just wanted you to study hard and do your best. And now that you've done that, it doesn't matter so much if you fail. In fact—" He finds himself confessing what he has kept from his son for so many years, for fear that Baoyu would think less of him. "I failed the first time. And the second time, as well." He still feels the sting of his failure more than thirty years later, and to his amazement, tears film his eyes. He laughs sheepishly to hide them.

"Did you, Father?" Baoyu raises his eyes. Instead of the contempt Jia Zheng had half feared he would see there, Baoyu's eyes are filled with sympathy and understanding. "You never told me that."

Jia Zheng can still remember the way he had felt when the list of successful candidates was posted and his own name was not on it. He didn't want to leave his bedroom, so afraid was he of reading contempt for his failure in everyone's eyes. He had been filled with jealousy for Min, because she was so much quicker to learn than he. He had hated his schoolmaster, and his mother and father. He had been so taken up by his own despair that for once his father's scoldings and threats had no power to move or frighten him. He had felt that his whole life was over.

And yet he had picked himself up off the ground and had begun to study again. He had failed another time, it was true, but that time, one of the Examiners, a friend of his father's, had leaked the information that he had just missed the cutoff. The third time, he had passed respectably. After that he had advanced quickly, earning the respect of his colleagues and superiors, his previous failures apparently forgotten.

In a strange way, the same experience had been repeated in his arrest and imprisonment. When he had been arrested, he had thought he would never be able to hold his head up again. He had barely been able to look his prison guards in the eye for fear of what they must think of him. Again, he had been patient, and he had not only been pardoned and released, but had also returned to his former position, where his colleagues treated him with the same, if not more, respect than before. This is the wisdom that he wants to impart to Baoyu, what he has learned from the sum of his fifty-odd years, but he does not quite know how to express it.

He squeezes Baoyu's shoulders. "Everything is not won or lost in a single day. Even if you fail this year, you will pass eventually, and then you'll be surprised at how different things will look. You won't have to study all the time. You will like being an official. Some of the work is tedious, of course, but you'll also get to make decisions, even if it is over small things. And, maybe, one day, you'll have a family of your own—"

Baoyu wrenches himself violently from under Jia Zheng's arm. "I'm not interested in anything like that."

Jia Zheng had hoped time was helping Baoyu forget Daiyu. He has noticed how solicitously Baochai always treats Baoyu, and how the two of them never seem to argue, as Xifeng and Lian had, even in their newlywed days. He has allowed himself to believe that the new couple was growing together, but now he sees from the suppressed misery on Baoyu's face that he has deceived himself.

Baoyu seems to control himself with an effort. He says, after a moment, "Are you satisfied with me, Father? Have I done all you wanted?"

At this reminder that Baoyu had acted against his own wishes for the good of the family, Jia Zheng feels a pang of remorse. "Yes, of course," he says, taking Baoyu's hands. "You've done more than enough. I know that it has been hard for you—"

Baoyu pulls away, apparently uninterested in Jia Zheng's attempt to comfort him. "Then there is something I want to say to you."

"What is it?"

Baoyu draws himself up and speaks almost ceremoniously. "I would like to thank you."

"For what?" Jia Zheng says, taken aback.

"I would like to thank you for all the care that you have given me over the years, all your teaching, and patience, and concern."

This stilted little speech, after the heightened emotions of the earlier conversation, almost makes Jia Zheng laugh. "You don't need to thank me."

"But I do," says Baoyu. "If it hadn't been for you, who knows what would have become of me? As it is, I've learned little enough—"

"Hush!" Jia Zheng says, half embarrassed, half amused. "You'd better be quiet, or you'll end up making a fool of yourself!"

Baoyu stops, pulled up short, and looks discomfited. "At least let me take leave of you properly."

"Take leave of me! What next? You'll be gone for only three days—"

Before Jia Zheng can stop him, Baoyu kneels on the floor. He touches his head to Jia Zheng's feet. Jia Zheng tries to raise him up, but again and again he presses his forehead and hands to his father's shoes. For the second time that morning, Jia Zheng feels the tears sting in his eyes. This time, however, he is unable to control himself, and his tears spill over as he raises Baoyu from the floor.

5

Xifeng forces her heavy eyes open and squints at the clock. She had let herself lie down after lunch, intending to rest for ten or fifteen minutes, and here it is after four o'clock. She jerks herself upright and swings her legs off the *kang*. The sudden change of position makes her vision go black. She bends over, clutching her mouth, overcome by a sudden need to vomit. Shutting her eyes, she puts her head down, and breathes slowly and deeply to stave off the bout of nausea.

When the nausea recedes, she stands up, supporting herself against the table. Baoyu and Huan are coming home from the Exams this afternoon. The others will wonder if she is not there to greet them. The nausea rises again, but she thrusts herself from the table and stumbles towards the wardrobe. She vomits on the floor near the corner. Leaning against the door of the wardrobe, she glances down at what has come up from her stomach. There isn't much of it. She hardly eats a thing these days.

She drags herself to fetch the bucket of water. She sloshes its contents onto the vomit, and manages to sweep the mess out of the door. Then she goes to the wardrobe and lowers her pants. The cotton rag she has pinned to her underwear is soaked through with blood. After months and months of not having her period, she has started to bleed again, heavily. How long has it been? A week? Ten days? If it does not stop in a day or two, she will ask Baochai to send for the doctor again. When Baochai sent for him three weeks ago, he had said that all he could do was modify her prescription. She has taken the new prescription twice a day, but it seems no more effective than the old one.

She replaces the soiled rag with a clean one. When she pulls her trousers up, she has to stretch the waistband to its utmost, to ease it over her swollen belly. Her whole body is getting skinny, like a monkey's. Only her belly keeps growing, bigger and bigger, and is flabby to boot. She would have thought she was pregnant, except, of course, for the fact that she hasn't been touched by a man in over two years. She smooths her gown over her hips to hide her bulging belly.

On her way to the door, she catches a glimpse of herself in the dressing table mirror. Her hair is uncombed, and her makeup has been rubbed off by sleep. Without the covering of powder, her complexion is chalky. Her cheekbones and teeth, with their receding gums, seem unnaturally prominent. She drags a comb through her hair and smears two streaks of rouge onto her cheeks.

When she is crossing Lady Jia's courtyard, she notices that there are no sounds of conversation or laughter coming from the front room. Baoyu and Huan must not be home yet. Relieved, she pushes through the door curtain, crying, "Where are our successful Examination candidates?" trying to distract from her lateness with a show of gaiety.

She expects laughter, retorts. Instead, everyone in the room, Lady Jia, Baochai and Mrs. Xue, and the Two Springs, turns towards her with tense expressions, and then turn away in silent disappointment when they see it is only her.

"What's the matter?" she cries.

It is Tanchun who answers. "They really should be home by now." Her eyes shift uneasily to the clock on the wall. "The Examination papers should have been collected at noon, and then"—she counts on her fingers—"an hour to get their things together, an hour to get out of the Examination Hall, an hour to get home. That's assuming everything took much longer than it should have."

"Didn't Lian and Uncle go to meet them?" Xifeng asks.

This time Baochai answers. "Yes," she says shortly, barely opening her lips.

"Well," Xifeng says. "It's not so hard to guess what happened. There must be thousands of people there. They must be wandering around in the crowd looking for each other."

"They were supposed to meet in front of the Examination Hall," Baochai says.

"Yes, but the place is huge, and imagine how many other people have arranged to meet there, too—"

Baochai turns on her. "Do you think we're stupid? Do you think we haven't thought of that ourselves?"

Xifeng has never seen Baochai lose control of her temper like this. After a moment, she shrugs and says mildly, "Then why are you so worried?"

No one answers.

Xifeng gives a little laugh. "Baoyu's not a child who can't find his way home by himself."

Still no one replies. Xifeng looks at Baochai. She is sitting on her heels beside Lady Jia, her eyes on her lap, her fingers kneading and twisting her handkerchief. Her face is pale, but Xifeng sees blood on her bottom lip where she has bitten it raw. Xifeng climbs onto the *kang*, careful not to make herself dizzy again. Beside her, Lady Jia slouches against her backrest, with her eyes fixed on the door. Surreptitiously, Xifeng stuffs a cushion behind her back. She feels self-conscious about trying to make herself more comfortable when the others seem to be in such suspense. She feels alone, bewildered by the others' anxiety. She cannot imagine why they are acting this way, what they sense and fear that she does not. A maid comes in with tea and snacks. Baochai orders her away, although Xifeng would have liked some tea.

Half an hour drags by. She begins to slump against her cushion. She fights to keep her eyes open.

Lian bursts into the room, disheveled and out of breath. "We can't find Baoyu anywhere."

"Oh, my God!" Baochai bursts into tears.

"What about Huan?" Tanchun asks.

"We found him. He's back at the Examination Hall, looking for Baoyu with Uncle," Lian says.

Xifeng jerks herself upright. "Then what are you doing here? Go back and look for him, too!"

Ignoring her, Jia Lian climbs up on the *kang* and speaks to Baochai and Granny, his voice broken by gasps. "Uncle and I got there early, a little after noon. We stood right outside the exit. Close to about one o'clock, the candidates began to come out, one by one at first, then in little groups, and then in big crowds. Huan came out in one of the big groups, but he said he hadn't seen Baoyu. We just kept waiting, thinking he'd come out any minute.

"By three o'clock, people stopped coming out, and we still hadn't seen him." He pauses to wipe a trickle of sweat off his temple. Xifeng is surprised at how agitated he seems.

"Yes?" Baochai says. She had stopped crying as soon as he began to speak, and stares at him with her handkerchief pressed against her mouth.

"We got permission to go into the Examination Hall," Lian continues. "Sure enough, it was totally empty. We went up to the officials, and asked if anyone had seen him. At first, they said they couldn't possibly keep track of everyone who had taken the Exams. Then when we begged them to check, they went through the pile of Exams to see if he had handed anything in."

"And had he?"

"When they looked through the papers, they saw that he had been the very first, out of hundreds of candidates, to hand his Exam in. It was at the very bottom of the pile. Then one of them said that he remembered: Baoyu had actually tried to hand his paper in early, but when they told him it wasn't permitted, he had gone back to his place and got his things together, so that he was able to hand it in and leave the Examination Hall at the stroke of twelve—"

"And was it completed?" Baochai cries, leaning forward to grip Jia Lian's arm. "His Exam, I mean." Xifeng, noticing the look of unbearable suspense on Baochai's face, wonders whether she is more concerned about Baoyu's passing the Exams or his whereabouts.

"Yes. When he tried to hand it in early, they'd looked it over to see if it was done," Lian reassures her. "They said the essays looked complete.

"But the point is," he continues, "Baoyu must have been the first to leave the Examination Hall. That's why we missed him. Then we looked for him everywhere outside. We thought we were simply missing him, but then the crowds began to thin, and we still couldn't find him. That's why I came home, to see if he was here."

"Well, you can see he isn't here, can't you?" Xifeng says. "Why don't you take some servants and go back and search some more?" She has barely been able to contain her impatience during his lengthy recital.

Again, Lian ignores her. He pauses to wipe another trickle of sweat off his brow. "Then, as I was riding away from the Hall, I saw Sweeper, Baoyu's new page."

Baochai's face, already haggard, seems to lose all its color. "Without Baoyu?" she says hoarsely.

"He was alone, nearly crazy with worry and fear. He said that when they came out of the Hall, Baoyu told him to watch the luggage while he stepped away to relieve himself. Baoyu went around the corner into an alley, but then he never came back. Sweeper spent the next four hours searching for him. I think if

I hadn't bumped into him, he would never have come home, he was so afraid we would blame him for losing Baoyu—"

"It's no use looking," Baochai interrupts. "He's gone." She starts to sob again.

Xifeng stares at Baochai. Why is everyone acting so strangely? Getting so worked up because they'd missed Baoyu in a crowd. "What on earth do you mean, 'gone'? He'll show up by himself in an hour or two."

"No, he won't," Baochai says. "He's run away."

"Run away!" exclaims Xifeng, barely able to comprehend what she might mean. "From whom? From what?"

"From us. From me," Baochai weeps. She tries to control herself, pressing her handkerchief to her mouth again, but her tears continue to flow. "He said goodbye to me in such a queer way when he left, as if—as if we would never see each other again. I knew that something was wrong, but I never guessed—"

"But why on earth would he run away?" Xifeng cuts in, out of patience.

Baochai gropes for the right words. "Because he didn't care for anything anymore."

Xifeng is silent, beginning to understand. She remembers how Baoyu had wanted to marry Daiyu before the confiscation, and how distraught he had been about her death. Uncle Zheng must have strong-armed him into marrying Baochai. Now he has rebelled by running away. A part of her is envious: a woman could never escape like that. Another part of her thinks how crazy he is to run away just when he is about to achieve the success for which he has striven so long. She thinks of Yucun. Climbing the bureaucratic ladder had provided him with status and money, but not freedom. Perhaps Baoyu, with his uncanny intuitions, had realized the truth beforehand. She has never believed something as strange as the jade's appearance in Baoyu's mouth could be mere chance, just as she has felt that

Baoyu, with his quicksilver sensitivity, never seemed to belong to the Jias. Surely the jade, and Baoyu's coming and disappearance, must be part of some larger, fateful design.

"And so all the love I lavished on him, for all these years, is wasted," Lady Jia says. She speaks impassively, but Xifeng can see, at the corners of her dry, old person's eyes, two tiny tears glistening in the papery folds.

"But it wasn't wasted," Tanchun says. "He still took the Exams, and who knows but what he'll pass, and bring honor to the family."

"Honor!" Baochai cries. "What does that matter when he himself is gone?"

Xifeng looks at Baochai, struggling to understand her reactions. Despite her intelligence, Baochai has always struck Xifeng as someone who never thinks for herself, content to follow the dictates of "duty" and "filiality" unquestioningly. That was why she had married Baoyu, even though it was obvious that he was still pining for Daiyu. But today, it almost seems to Xifeng that Baochai does care for him after all. Of course, Xifeng thinks cynically, given that Baochai will be unable to remarry, it is no wonder that she is terrified that her husband appears to be deserting her at age twenty-one. She watches Baochai, pressing her handkerchief to her mouth and struggling to keep back her tears, revealing more of her emotions in this one afternoon than she has in all the five years she has lived with the Jias. It was her composure and inscrutability that has always kept Xifeng away from her. She has always suspected that Baochai knew of her affair with Yucun. While Xifeng had at first been grateful for her silence, as the years passed, Xifeng had expected Baochai to hint of her knowledge by a word or a glance. Instead, Baochai has always pretended so perfectly that nothing was amiss, that everything was exactly as it seemed, that a wall of silence had grown between them that has never been broken.

Xifeng struggles off the *kang* to her feet. "Why are we wasting time talking? Why don't we organize a search party?"

"What good do you think that will do?" Lian says unpleasantly. "Don't you think that Uncle and I have searched thoroughly?"

"But he could be anywhere. He could have bumped into a friend. He could have gotten sick and collapsed somewhere. Why don't you call together all the servants—"

"What servants?" he says nastily. "We've got only a couple of page boys and a porter. Do you really think that they'll be able to fan out all over the city?"

A wave of anger and helplessness washes over her. Even at a time like this, he cannot let an opportunity go by without trying to discredit her in front of everyone. "For Heaven's sake, surely you can make the maids go out and look for him this once—"

She feels a terrible cramping and burning in her belly. She feels as if her innards are being eaten away. It takes all her strength not to double over and clutch her stomach. She turns her face away, pressing her hand to her mouth. "I'm sorry," she manages to say. "I'm not feeling very well. I must lie down."

She staggers out the door and into the courtyard. She half hopes and half fears that someone will come after her, but as she lurches out of Granny's front gate, she hears no footsteps or concerned questions behind her. She almost runs down the path, knowing that if she does not hurry she will never have the strength to make it to her own apartments. She feels a burning sensation in her vagina, and a sudden hot gush. It reminds her of her miscarriage all those years ago, but the pain is even worse. She doubles over, and sees that the inseam of her trousers beneath her gown is stained scarlet with fresh blood. She is filled with an indescribable shame. There are drops of blood on the white pebbles that pave the path. She has to fight the impulse to try to clean them or cover them up before anyone else sees them. Instead, she forces herself to keep on walking, still doubled over. It is only about fifty yards to her apartments; and once in her own courtyard, no one will see her even if she has to crawl.

But the dizziness and nausea she felt after her nap return. Blackness fills her eyes, and she sways and almost falls. She stops walking to catch her breath. She can feel the pounding of her heart in the vessels behind her eyes. Sweat pours down her face. She stands there, blinking, propping her hands on her knees to keep herself standing. Eventually, her eyes clear. She sees that she is still standing on the path. She drags herself forward. A few steps more, a few steps more, she tells herself. She lifts her head and sees a linden sapling at the crook of the path perhaps twenty-five feet ahead. If only she can get there, she can hold on to it and rest.

The nausea and dizziness are rising as inexorably as a tide. She feels herself losing her balance, and tries to run the last five or six steps, her hands reaching out to catch the tree. But her strength has run out, and she collapses on the ground.

6

Despite Baoyu's disappearance, Baochai puts on an impassive face and sees to the arrangements for Xifeng's funeral. She would rather stay in her room waiting for news from the servants hired to look for Baoyu, especially since she is beginning to suffer from morning sickness. Now she is the only remaining daughter-in-law at Rongguo, however, and it is her duty to take care of the arrangements. Lian might help, but his hard-heartedness to Xifeng during her life has continued after her death. To Baochai's disgust, neither he nor Lady Jia even make a pretense of grieving.

And so Baochai orders a coffin and arranges for a temporary shrine to be set up in one of the courtyards, where Xifeng's body will lie in state. She sends for Buddhist monks to perform prayers for the salvation of departed souls, and Taoist priests to perform the ceremonies of purification and absolution. She orders oil, candles, paper offerings, and incense, mourning trimmings and banners for the funeral procession, and then assigns the servants to perform various tasks: keeping the lamps and incense lit on the shrine, changing the drapes, and making offerings of rice and tea before the spirit tablets.

Finally, she must entertain the female guests who come to Rongguo on visits of condolence. The Jias had been ostracized by their relatives and friends after the confiscation and their move to Drum Street. Since Jia Zheng's reinstatement and the family's return to the mansion, people have begun to pay calls on them again. Now that Baochai is a matron, she must greet and make conversation with the various wives of officials and aristocrats, most of whom she has never met before. Because Lady Jia, claiming ill health, refuses to appear, Baochai has only her mother to support her. Receiving the stream of visitors has been doubly hard for her, because she constantly imagines what the guests are whispering about her, abandoned by her husband only a few months after her wedding.

One evening during the "lying in state" period, after the paper offerings have been burnt, she goes by herself to mourn Xifeng. She walks into the silent courtyard in the dimness of dusk and throws herself on her knees beside the coffin. Without any effort, the tears begin to trickle down her face. She has been so busy with the practical arrangements that she has barely had time to feel her own emotions. No doubt this is how Xifeng had often felt.

She feels the loss of Xifeng more than she would ever have imagined. Many times during a day, when the carriage trimmings arrive badly sewn, or the servants are slow to serve dinner, or the conversation with a guest flags, she turns unthinkingly to ask Xifeng for advice or help, before realizing that she is gone. Xifeng had always worked so tirelessly and efficiently that she had made herself indispensable to everyone around her, without their realizing it. Only now that Baochai must take over her tasks does she realize how much Xifeng did. She is even more surprised at the emotional hole that Xifeng's death has left: how much Xifeng's steadiness and liveliness had kept up her own spirits, even though Baochai had never confided in or understood her. Intimidated by Xifeng's restless manner and sharp tongue, Baochai always kept her distance and distrusted her. Now, she thinks, there was no reason for distrust. When Xifeng suggested that Baochai break her betrothal with Baoyu, Baochai had suspected an ulterior motive. She sees now that Xifeng had probably spoken out of simple concern for her welfare. She remembers how disgusted and contemptuous she had been when she stumbled on Xifeng's affair. Now, having learned how it is possible for a husband to be absent even when physically present, she imagines the years of loneliness Xifeng had faced.

As she kneels, sobbing, she hears a sound behind her. It is Lady Jia, limping along with a cane. Lady Jia almost never ventures out of her apartments these days, and certainly never goes anywhere without someone to lean on. In fact, Baochai would never have supposed that she was physically capable of coming here. Hastily, she gets to her feet. There is a chair near the coffin for mourners to sit on. Baochai pulls it over for Lady Jia, and Granny sinks into it.

She is moved by the effort it must have taken Granny to come all the way to the shrine to mourn Xifeng. She must have been mistaken in believing Granny unaffected by Xifeng's death. "Have you come to make an offering?" she asks.

"I've come to see you."

Baochai is surprised. "If you wanted to see me, you could have had me come to your apartments, instead of walking all this way."

"I wanted to see you alone."

Baochai waits expectantly, but Lady Jia says nothing, staring moodily at Xifeng's coffin.

After a long silence, Baochai says, "How will we manage without Xifeng?"

Lady Jia turns to look at her. "There's no need to put on these virtuous airs with me. I should have thought you would be glad to be rid of her."

Startled by the cruelty of her words, Baochai says, "What do you mean?"

"You needn't pretend to be stupider than you are, either. Obviously it will be easier for you to manage the household without having to compete with her for control of everything."

"I—I don't want to be in control of everything," Baochai stammers.

Lady Jia stares at her, as if considering the truth of her statement. "No, I suppose not. But Xifeng did. I remember when she first came, she was so ambitious, so eager to show she was cleverer than other people. So I let her run the household, because she would have made trouble if I hadn't given her something challenging to do." Lady Jia sighs, shaking her head. "But, still, she got into trouble: those loans, and that affair with Jia Yucun, and who knows what else?"

Baochai had never dreamed that Lady Jia knew of the affair. She tries to keep her face blank, but Lady Jia sees her astonishment, and laughs.

"Yes," Lady Jia says, her eyes crinkling in malicious amusement. "I knew. Why else did he come sneaking around all the time? Making a fuss about it would have just created a big scandal. I figured out long ago that sometimes it's better not to let on how much I know." Her face darkens. "I knew that Baoyu and Daiyu were having an affair, too, before you told me."

This time, Baochai gasps and stares at her, unable to control her shock.

"Yes. When Daiyu came, I always knew there would be trouble. I sensed that there was something between the two of them, but I was willing to let it go. As long as no one knew about it, who did it hurt, after all? I thought he would get tired of her, and would stop wanting to marry her.

"But then, when you found out and came to tell me about it, I had to do something, of course. Since you were betrothed to him, out of respect for your and your mother's feelings, I couldn't ignore it anymore. Besides, you told me that he had given her the jade, which I would never have dreamed ..."

Baochai stands perfectly still. Lady Jia had known all along and had done nothing. It had truly been her own tattling that had destroyed Daiyu. She remembers how she had been buoyed by self-righteous indignation, as if it had been her duty to inform Granny of the terrible breach of social mores—whereas the truth was that Granny didn't expect anyone to adhere to those norms. Now she wonders what would have happened if she had not told. Maybe Daiyu would be happily married to Baoyu, and she, to someone else. Maybe the two of them would still be friends.

Now Granny Jia is talking about Daiyu. "She was selfish, like Min, always thinking about herself and never about her family. Parents have always chosen their children's matches, but no, she wanted to choose her husband by herself. She always had to be an exception . . . " As Lady Jia talks about Daiyu, Baochai thinks that the same could be said of Baoyu. It is the same refusal to accept the success and security that everyone else strives for that has made him run away.

Granny Jia looks Baochai in the eye. "I knew what kind of person you were when you told me what she and Baoyu were up to. You didn't shirk your duty. You weren't hampered by sentimental ideas. That was why I chose you to marry Baoyu years ago. You're like me, and I wanted you, not Xifeng or Daiyu, to run the family after I'm gone."

Baochai wants to resist Lady Jia's words, but a part of her has to admit that they are true. She compares Xifeng and Granny. She had been used to thinking of Xifeng as hard and cold-hearted, because of her treatment of the servants, but, looking back, she sees that Xifeng had risked herself for the sake of the three people that she loved, Jia Yucun, Qiaojie, and Ping'er. In contrast, Lady Jia claimed to dote on, at various times, Xifeng, Baoyu, and Baochai. In reality, Lady Jia had favored each person only as long as he or she was useful to the family. She pampered Baoyu because he was likely to pass the Exams. Her kindness to Xifeng lasted as long as Xifeng did an exemplary job of running the household; Granny was the first to suggest getting Lian a second wife when Xifeng didn't bear a son. Granny chose Baochai as a match for Baoyu because of the Xues' wealth and power, and because she thought Baochai would be able to succeed her as matriarch. For all her little gifts and compliments, Lady Jia is cold, swayed only by pragmatism and never by personal feeling. While her interests always focused on the advancement of the family, she understood that what was best for the family also ensured her own comfort and security.

As for Baochai, does she really resemble Lady Jia? She had considered Daiyu her closest friend, but then, unlike Xifeng, she had betrayed her friendship in order to make sure her own marriage would prosper. She had married Baoyu knowing that he loved another woman. Perhaps Granny is right. Perhaps she is Lady Jia's true heir after all. Her eyes fall on her belly, already growing round beneath the waist of her gown, and she thinks of Baoyu. Perhaps, she thinks bitterly, she is simply the victim of unrequited love, marrying Baoyu because she loved him even though he did not return her feelings. That makes her more foolish than either Daiyu or Xifeng.

7

Baochai sits on the *kang* in the room that she had shared with Baoyu, exhausted by the day's trip to the family burial grounds for Xifeng's interment. A tiny, half-finished vest lies in her lap, but she feels too tired and dispirited to work on it.

She hears the sound of quick steps outside the door curtain and Jia Zheng comes in. Knowing that he would never burst in on her like this unless there was news, she jumps up, crying, "You've heard something about Baoyu?"

"Yes. How did you know?"

She sees how somber his face is, and feels a spasm of panic. "He's dead, isn't he?"

"No, no!" Jia Zheng shakes his head reassuringly. "Why would you think that? In fact, it's good news."

"What is it?"

"The Examination results were posted today—"

"Did he pass?"

"Yes—"

"Thank Heaven!" She clasps her hands together. For a moment, her pain over his disappearance recedes in a feeling of triumph and relief.

"In fact," Uncle Zheng continues, "he passed at the top of the lists." He smiles. "Third out of three hundred and sixty candidates, no less. Huan didn't pass, but I hardly expected him to."

"That's wonderful!" Baochai can hardly believe it. At last Baoyu has shown how exceptional and talented he really is. At last he has made some return for all the care and love that the family has given him. "Third! It's marvelous!"

It strikes her that Uncle Zheng still looks grave, despite the wonderful news. "What's the matter? Aren't you happy?"

"You're forgetting that we still haven't found him yet."

She laughs. "Of course, he will come back and show himself now, when he finds out that he's actually passed at the top of the lists!"

Jia Zheng looks at her a little strangely. "Do you really think he is suddenly going to pop out and reveal himself, like a child playing hide-and-seek? The reason that all our inquiries have yielded nothing is that he does not want to be found."

"But surely now that he's proven to everyone how talented he is, now that he's achieved everything he worked so hard for, he will come back! He has only to reappear, and then he'll probably get a high position, and everyone's respect, and ... "

Uncle Zheng's mouth twists into a bitter smile. "You act as if Baoyu were like other people."

She is surprised, and irritated, by Uncle Zheng's pessimism. "Well, I think all people, even Baoyu, want to succeed rather than fail, and want praise rather than blame, no matter what airs they put on."

"Then why didn't he study before? He must have known he was clever enough to pass without much difficulty."

She shrugs. "He was too lazy, I suppose."

"Then what made him stop being lazy? What made him want to study so hard in the end?"

For some reason, Uncle Zheng's persistent questioning brings tears to her eyes. She blinks them away, pondering the question, trying to fathom Baoyu's motivations. "I'm not really sure," she says at last. "I thought he was growing out of those strange, childish ways of his. I thought that being in prison changed him. When he saw how desperate the family was after the confiscation, I suppose he realized he couldn't shirk his duty anymore."

"That was part of it, I think. But in reality he was deceiving us, and he was the same old Baoyu. Don't you see? He wouldn't study hard when he had everything to gain by it, not even when I beat him for it." Uncle Zheng shakes his head, as if still trying to make sense of it himself. "No, I think he studied hard at the end only because he knew he was leaving, and wanted to make it up to us somehow. That was Baoyu: he would never act out of pragmatism, only out of sentimentality, feelings—"

"You mean you think he had decided to leave long ago?" she says, shocked.

"Yes."

She cannot speak for pain. Her mind rushes back to her time with Baoyu. Could it be that their sexual life, which she took as a sign of intimacy, was simply his attempt to do his duty by impregnating her before he left? Did he marry her always knowing that he would leave? She feels a surge of anger such as she has never felt before. Didn't he realize how terrible it would be for her? Did he think she had no feelings? At the same time, she feels so humiliated that she resolves not to tell anyone, not even her mother, what Uncle Zheng had said. She manages to speak with composure until Uncle Zheng leaves. When her mother comes in, she has regained enough control of herself to act as if she is delighted by Baoyu's Examination results.

PART SEVEN

Third Month, 1736

The ornamented zither, for no reason, has fifty
    strings.
Each string, each fret, recalls a glorious year.
Master Zhuang in his morning dream, entranced
    by a butterfly,
Emperor Wang gave his heart, full of spring, to
    a cuckoo.
Vast ocean, bright moon, the pearls shed tears.
At Lantian, sun warmed, the jade breathes mist.
This feeling, if I could wait, would become a
    fleeting memory.
Only, at the time, I was already overcome.

Li Shangyin, "The Ornamented Zither"

1

Baochai settles herself at the head of the breakfast table in Lady Jia's old chair as the rest of the family takes their seats. Standing behind her, Lian's wife Autumn ladles out the rice porridge, while Huan's wife, Hushi, passes around the steaming bowls. The group gathered around the breakfast table is just as numerous and bustling as it was in the old days when she was growing up at Rongguo. However, looking around the table as she picks up her chopsticks, she is struck by how different the faces are. Her father-in-law, Uncle Zheng, sitting to her left, looks roughly the same as before, only his hair has grown more grizzled, and his paunch more pronounced. But the lower end of the table, where Daiyu and the Two Springs used to sit, is now occupied by Lian and Huan and their children, attended by a gaggle of nannies and wet nurses. Jia Zheng had arranged Huan's match to Hushi eight years ago, after Huan passed the Exams. Now they have two childen, a boy and a girl. A year after Xifeng's death, Lian had found her former maid Autumn in the service of the Countess of Xiping. He had bought her back as a concubine, and elevated her to principal wife after she had given birth to a daughter and two sons.

Now Lian says, smiling at Baochai across the table, "Cousin, we were wondering if we could hire another nanny for the boys. Taking care of them is wearing Autumn out."

"Of course," Baochai says. "Should I increase your allowance by two *taels* a month?"

"That should be plenty," Lian says gratefully.

Autumn cuts in, "Make sure you give it to me, not Lian.

Every copper he gets his hands on, he spends on gambling and drinking."

Lian turns on his wife. "Will you be quiet?"

"Why should I? I'm only telling the truth."

"Oh, so I'm the only one who gambles? What about you?"

The two of them often engage in this kind of wrangling, undeterred by the presence of others. Baochai is always embarrassed by it, not only because of their evident discord, but also because of the private details each blurts about the other. Strangely, despite their bickering, they seem a closely united couple. Lian is more affectionate to Autumn than he had been to either Xifeng or Ping'er; and, as far as Baochai knows, he has never mentioned getting another concubine.

Probably in order to change the subject, Jia Zheng turns to Baochai. "Didn't you say that Tanchun was coming to visit today?"

"No," Baochai says. "She had planned to, but her daughter isn't feeling well. She sent a message that she would come tomorrow afternoon."

"Good. I'll come back from the Ministry early to see her," Jia Zheng says, rising to go.

"Tomorrow?" Huan says, rising also. "I'll try to be back early, too."

Since Lady Jia's death two years ago, all the petty rivalries that once divided the household have dissipated, and Tanchun and Huan now treat each other with affection. Perhaps Baoyu's disappearance also made Tanchun more appreciative of her only remaining brother. Baochai has always been grateful for the fact that Tanchun lives close enough to visit frequently. When the time had come for Uncle Zheng to make a match for Tanchun, he had refused an advantageous offer from a Chang'an official in favor of a more modest proposal from a Capital family. Granny Jia had resisted strenuously, but Baochai had supposed that he did not wish to be parted from his only daughter.

"Is Xichun coming from the Priory too?" Uncle Zheng asks.

"She said that she would come when the Abbess could spare her, but I don't know when that will be."

At the mention of Xichun, Baochai sees Lian frown. Xichun had begged for years to be allowed to shave her head and take the vows of a Buddhist nun. Although Uncle Zheng put off making a match for her for nearly seven years, he had consented to her becoming a nun only last year, when Lady Jia was no longer alive to oppose it. Xichun had given away all her possessions and moved out to the Water Moon Priory. To Baochai, she seems quite content, but Lian has never become reconciled to his half sister's choice.

Uncle Zheng and Huan gather up their papers as they prepare to set off for their Ministries. Huan, in particular, straightens his official's robes and shuffles his papers with an air of importance. Watching them, Baochai is filled with pride. Two generations of Jias in the Civil Service! she thinks triumphantly. How proud Uncle Zheng must be to attend Court accompanied by his son! No one can say that the Jia family is not thriving now. It occurs to her that if Baoyu had only come back, there would have been three Jia men in the bureaucracy. The thought makes her feel faintly wistful, but it does not otherwise pain her. Baoyu has been gone so long that he scarcely seems real to her.

While Hushi says goodbye to Huan, Baochai goes to her father-in-law.

"How about your mother? Is Mrs. Xue coming today?" Uncle Zheng asks.

"No, she said that she'd come tomorrow when Tanchun comes," Baochai answers. This is the greatest source of sadness in her life: that after everything they have been through together, her mother has elected to live with Pan. There is a good reason for her mother's decision, Baochai knows. For two years Jingui had not become pregnant, and Pan had bought a concubine. Eventually, Jingui gave birth to a daughter, while the concubine had two sons, who were now six and five. Neither Jingui nor the concubine had paid the least attention to the children, and none of the servants were able to keep them from running wild. Finally, Pan asked Mrs. Xue to come to his house to help teach the children properly. Her mother had been reluctant to leave Baochai. Still, it had been obvious that it made sense for her to go to Pan's. Her grandchildren needed her there, while there was little for her to do at Rongguo. Baochai misses her mother terribly. She comes to visit, often with Pan, once or twice a week, but still, it is not the same as living with her.

She notices a worn spot on Uncle Zheng's sleeve. "This robe is getting a little shabby. I'd better make you a new one."

"That's all right."

"It's looking a little overcast. Don't forget to take your umbrella."

In the absence of Baoyu, or a child of her own, he is the only one left for her to fuss over.

After breakfast is cleared, Baochai always spends two hours teaching her two elder nephews to read from the *Three-Word Classic*. With one boy on either side of her, she draws her index finger beneath the characters, and reads the endless series of rhyming three-word aphorisms. *"If you don't teach, then nature becomes weak. When teaching the way, concentration is key ... '"* Lian's son only pretends to listen, playing with the colorful tassel that she uses as a bookmark. Huan's son is slightly more attentive, and can recognize a few of the more common characters.

Sometimes when she is teaching them, she imagines what it

would be like to have her own child at her knee. She had miscarried in the seventh month of her pregnancy. Her son—for she had been able to tell that it would have been a boy—would have been twelve years old by now. She pictures what he would be like: with Baoyu's grace and handsome features, and her own steadiness and patience. When she lost the baby, she had felt that her life was over, and that, with neither husband nor child, there was no source of either happiness or hope left to her. But then Granny had had a stroke and needed to be waited on hand and foot. Tanchun had been betrothed, and the details of her trousseau and wedding needed to be arranged. The demands of running the household had dried her tears and forced her out of bed. They had saved her from despair and given purpose to her life.

After the boys' lessons, she usually has an hour or two to herself before lunch. She makes her way towards the Garden with her sewing basket. Taking the small path that runs around the foot of the mountain, she walks to the lake. Several years after Baoyu's disappearance, after they had given up hope of his ever returning, Jia Zheng had hired gardeners to clear out the long-neglected Garden. Even though it seemed an extravagance, Baochai was glad. As long as the Garden was overrun by brambles and thistles, she felt cut off from that period of her girlhood, as if it were a path she could no longer take, even in memory. Now, although the old apartment she shared with Daiyu had long ago fallen into disrepair, peach and plum blossoms arch like fluffy clouds over the walk along the shore.

She comes to the nine-angled bridge, and walks out to the pavilion in the middle of the lake. It is a windy day, and she settles herself in a sheltered corner to sew. She is embroidering a pillowcase for her father-in-law. She sews slowly, placing each stitch precisely, enjoying the long, swooping glide of the thread through the fabric. After a few minutes, she is distracted by the sound of laughing and shouting. She puts down her sewing and goes to the railing of the pavilion. Freed from their lessons, the children are standing on the shore near the rose pergola flying kites. There is a scarlet crab, a "beautiful lady," and a greenish-gold centipede. A butterfly, caught in an updraft, soars high into the air. She is pierced, quite suddenly, with longing for Daiyu.

Epilogue

In the glare of the noon sun a tall monk in ragged robes goes from stall to stall begging for his lunch. Working his way through the crowds of customers, he presents his begging bowl, worn smooth by long use, with his head bowed. Most of the vendors turn him away. One even calls him a lazy good-for-nothing and knocks the bowl out of his hands. He bends and picks it up, his expression unchanged.

One of the vendors gives him half a bowl of rice and a few cubes of scorched tofu. As he throws himself down to eat in the shadow of a wall, he sees two stone lions at the far end of the street. A scurry of memory, like a mouse in the ceiling. He forces himself to look down, wiping his hands on his robe. Without raising his eyes, he blows on his food and uses his fingers to push it into his mouth. For years he has wandered as randomly as a leaf borne on the wind, never knowing the direction he travels, or the names of the cities he passes through.

Nearby, two small boys are playing a game of marbles. Sunlight falls on a round stone, catching a milky gleam. He puts his hand to where the jade used to rest against the base of his throat, and all of a sudden he is back at Rongguo. He remembers waking each morning to the sound of dripping, the neroli-scented oil being dribbled by a maid into the basin in which he would wash his face and hands. He remembers the long still afternoon naps lying beside his mother, the slide of satin against his cheek as he burrowed his face into her back. He is sitting beside Zhu as the tutor drones on about the

"Golden Mean," watching the flies blunder against the gauze windows. From outside he could hear the shrill, piping voices of the Two Springs, and couldn't stop fidgeting. He would be almost mad with joy when he could finally run outside to join them.

What has become of them, his sister and cousin, with whom he had spent his childhood? Are they married now, with children? And his father—even if Granny must be dead, surely his father is still alive. As for Baochai—she had been pregnant when he left. Perhaps even now he has a son himself. How old would he be, eleven or twelve? His heart begins to beat faster. He could walk down the street to the triple gates. He wouldn't identify himself, could simply watch and perhaps ask the lackeys at the gate for news. He rises to his feet.

He does not move, looking down at the boys' game. The old regret, which he has tried to run away from for twelve years, wrings his heart with its old bitterness. He, who loved Daiyu, had been responsible for her death and suffering. He had destroyed the one person on earth who understood and loved him. It had been that thought which had driven him from home, goading him on through the driving spring rains. Her name had been on his lips when he flung himself down at dusk, so exhausted that, even in those first days, he had been able to sleep soundly on stone doorsteps. In the morning, even before he opened his eyes, he was aware of the weight of sadness crushing his breast. Each day he had dragged that weight farther and farther, until he came to regions where people spoke with accents he could barely understand.

He cannot go back. To go back would be to confront the enormity of his crime, the emptiness of life without her. He picks up his begging bowl and continues on his way.

A gleam of white catches Daiyu's eye at the jeweler's stall. She is holding her younger son, Adou, and a basket filled with vegetables hangs from her arm. Still, she can't help stopping to take a look. There it is, lying in a silk-lined box, Baoyu's jade, or something very like it. She tells her older daughter, Shushu, to take the baby, and picks the stone up. It lies in her hand, the size and shape of a sparrow's egg, with the suppressed, milky radiance of a sunlit cloud.

It can't really be the jade. After all, how could it have made its way all the way down here to Suzhou from the Capital? Still, she does not want to put it down, and stands looking at it far too long, so long that Adou gets restless and starts to whimper. It comes back to her, that terrible year when both her parents died and she went to live at Rongguo with her mother's relatives. She sees her adolescent self, both awkward and defiant, her nerves so raw that she was offended by trivialities. She was so lonely and needy after the death of her parents that she had fallen a little in love with both her cousins, Baochai as well as Baoyu.

The jeweler breaks in on her reverie. "Forty *taels*," he says. "Take it or leave it."

She jumps, and puts the jade down. "No, thank you," she says. She takes the baby from her daughter, and they weave their way through the market stalls towards home, but still, her mind is filled with the past. Even though it was so many years ago, her anger at Baoyu has not quite died. Had he really loved her? Had he just been pretending? She asks herself the questions, but they no longer seem urgent. She adjusts the basket on her shoulder, tells Shushu not to stray too far from her in the busy streets.

Their way home takes them near the banks of the Grand Canal. She lets Shushu run ahead. The girl skips along the shore, shouting and laughing, as she points out a snapping turtle or the silver flash of a fish. The water glints lazily in the sunlight, so powerful beneath its deceptively silken surface. She can never pass the canal without thinking how it had saved her life. That final week in Flowers Street, two weeks after Baochai's visit, she had become so ill that she hadn't been able to keep food or water down for three days.

Snowgoose had purchased material for her burial clothes, but Zhen Shiyin had yelled at his sister. "No!" He had gone to the *kang* and sat beside Daiyu, taking her hand in his. "I heard you say when your cousin was here that you would like to see Suzhou again."

"Yes," she had whispered through her parched throat.

"Then why don't we go? You were never sick like this down there. Perhaps the climate, the air, is better for you."

"How can we go?" she had said, starting to cry from sheer weakness. "I can't even get out of bed."

"We'll take a barge and I'll carry you."

"I'll never make it."

"Yes, you will. I'll take care of you."

"It's so far, and we don't have the money."

"Yes, we do." He had taken something out of his sleeve. With a rush of gratitude, she had seen that it was Baochai's pendant.

That very afternoon, Shiyin had arranged to sell the forge and booked two seats on a barge. He had carried her off the dock onto the boat, with their modest luggage slung over his back. She remembers lying there on the deck, wrapped up in blankets, looking up at the cold, distant sky. The first week, she couldn't do anything but shiver in Shiyin's arms. She shuddered with dry heaves from the rocking of the boat. But once they passed Yangzhou, it seemed that with every mile south, some of the ice gripping her chest loosened its hold. She began to eat and drink again. When the barge rounded the giant gorge to the north of Wuxi, she sat up against Shiyin's shoulders and saw the lights of the city. In Suzhou, she had walked off the boat, leaning on Shiyin's arm.

The first years were hard. She and Shiyin had used the money remaining from Baochai's pendant to get married. She hardly remembers anything about the wedding. Instead, what she remembers about the beginning of her love for Shiyin was a moment when their hands met on the deck of the boat. They had always touched each other a great deal, because he had nursed her for so long, but this touch was different, their fingers intertwining under the cover of a blanket. Of course, she could never have embarked on this journey with him if she had not already loved and trusted him. Looking back, she can't help contrasting her violent infatuation with Baoyu with her love for Shiyin, growing as naturally and imperceptibly as the moss that springs to life in the cracks between stones.

After they were married, they moved in with an old neighbor on Bottle-Gourd Street, sharing the single room with six other people. Shiyin worked long hours as a journeyman in someone else's blacksmith shop, and she struggled to regain her health. Then something happened that gave them new hope and strength. Snowgoose's mistress in the Capital, the Princess of Nan'an, had decided she was too old to be a maid, and had married her off. Her new husband was a merchant who did most of his business in the south. The third year after Daiyu and Shiyin had left the Capital, Snowgoose and her husband arrived in Suzhou. By the time that she and Shiyin could finally afford their own place, Snowgoose and her husband had moved in just down the street.

The path veers away from the canal now. There is one last hill to climb before they reach home. She tells Shushu to put the frog she has caught back in the water. As she waits for her daughter to catch up, she tries to picture what Baoyu and Baochai are doing. Surely Baoyu has risen high in the Civil Service by now. Who knows, perhaps he is in the Ministry of Works like his father? She imagines Baochai watching over their children as they play in the Garden. She imagines girls, plump and placid like their mother, and boys, tall and well-grown like their father. The picture makes her smile.

Shushu comes panting up the hill behind her, her face flushed from running. She sees that Daiyu is struggling with the baby's weight, and takes Adou into her own arms. She puts him up on her shoulders, and he starts to giggle and babble.

"Why were you looking at that jade so long?" Shushu asks. She reminds Daiyu of herself as a child, with her serious eyebrows and thin face. "Was that the jade? Was that Uncle Baoyu's jade?"

Daiyu stares at her. She has forgotten that once, when Shushu was restless and couldn't fall asleep, she had told her daughter the story of the boy who was born with the jade in his mouth. She smiles and ruffles Shushu's hair. "No." She shakes her head. "It looked like it, but I don't think it was."

"Tell me again how you went to live with the Jias in the Capital—" Shushu begins, then cuts herself off. "Listen! There's Daddy's hammer!"

Daiyu hears it too, the sound of Shiyin's hammer striking the forge. She listens to the silver notes, steady and pure.

Shushu sets off with Adou bouncing and giggling on her shoulders. Daiyu labors after them the last few steps of the slope. She gasps for breath—her lungs have never fully regained their strength after her illness. There is only one more block to home. She thinks about seeing Shiyin, and begins to run.

A Note on the Text

Aficionados of the original novel may well be appalled by how I have shuffled, truncated, and eliminated both characters and plotlines of the original to create a cohesive and more compact work. At the same time, many of my changes have been guided by an attempt to be faithful to the novel's deeper meaning and context:

(A) While Cao's original ending has been lost, the *Zhiyan zhai*, "Red Inkstone Commentary," interlinear notes believed to have been written by one of Cao's family members on an early manuscript, gives several clues to how Cao intended to conclude the novel. The "Red Inkstone Commentary" seems to suggest, for instance, that Baoyu is imprisoned and that Wang Xifeng recovers the lost jade while sweeping snow in the original ending. I have included these incidents in *The Red Chamber*, although they do not appear in the existing ending by Gao E.

(B) In the original novel Zhen Shiyin and Jia Yucun are somewhat minor characters who make only intermittent appearances. However, their names are highly significant, being paired puns for "The truth remains hidden" and "The false words remain." In *The Red Chamber* I use the names to contrast a faithful lover, Zhen Shiyin, with a false one, Jia Yucun.

(C) Although history records that Cao Xueqin's family, on whom the novel is based, did indeed suffer from demotions and confiscations following the accession of Emperor Yongzheng, the existing novel is carefully apolitical, appearing as it did during "Qianlong's Literary Inquisition," a period during which numerous writers were killed for supposedly seditious passages in their work. Indeed, some scholars believe that the original ending of the novel may have been suppressed because it contained passages that might have offended the Emperor. In *The Red Chamber*, I have reintroduced a fictionalized political subplot concerning the confiscation and Yongzheng's succession based loosely on the experience of Cao Xueqin's family.

While I have attempted to base my descriptions of food, clothing, architecture, holidays, etc., on the actual text, there are many times that I depart from historical accuracy in the interests of narrative fluency. One of my most drastic deviations from accuracy is the elimination of a large number of servants. For instance, in chapter 3 of the original novel, we learn that Daiyu, like Baoyu and the other girls in the household, is to be attended by five nannies, two body servants, and five or six maids for housekeeping. However, the presence of so many servants would have made it difficult for me to stage the private interactions that are so important to the development of the relationships between the characters.

A note on footbinding: While aristocratic Han Chinese women continued to bind their feet during the Qing dynasty, Manchu women did not. I follow David Hawkes, the eminent translator of the novel, in believing that the Jia women, as Bondservants with strong cultural connections to the Manchus, did not bind their feet, and thus could enjoy such activities as walks in the Garden and kite flying.

Acknowledgments

My deepest gratitude goes to Leo and Somiya, the sun and the moon, for daily joy and inspiration; and to Dad, Janet, and Stanley, for their love and strength.

Many thanks to Elyse Cheney, Sarah Rainone, and Jordan Pavlin, whose insight helped me realize my vision, especially to Elyse, for being so uncompromising about the quality of the book. Thanks also to Leslie Levine and Hannah Elnan for unfailing patience and professionalism throughout the process. To Sarah Stoll, Qiusha Ma, Sarah Kovner, Howard Huang, and Bill Petersen for years of friendship and support; to Jen Shults and Martha Ferrazza, for making Oberlin feel like home; and to Ben Howe for keeping me afloat with his encouragement and advice when I was sinking. To Andrew Plaks and Yu-Kung Kao for sharing with me their love and knowledge of Chinese literature. To Oberlin College for travel funds and the use of its library. For invaluable assistance and advice at various stages of the draft, I thank Gillian MacKenzie, Claire Messud, Ursula Hegi, Murad Kalam, Tom Downey, Mingmei Yip, Elizabeth Elrod, Sonja Boos, Jeff Bartos, Gary Lowitt, Shannon Jones, Oliver Schirokauer, and Laura Bentz. Thanks also to Dr. Peter E. Schwartz for helping me get a second chance, and to Dr. Shohreh Shahabi, Dr. Mert Ozan Bahtiyar, and the nurses on 9W in Yale – New Haven Hospital for being there in the silent watches of the night.

Although I worked from Cao Xueqin's original text, the debt I owe to David Hawkes and John Minford's translation *The Story of the Stone* (London: Penguin, 1973) is immense. In particular, David Hawkes's monumental work in contextualizing the novel, in finding English equivalents for difficult terms, and in shaping and interpreting the novel in the process of translation, has been a never-ending source of inspiration.

The translations of Tanchun's and Baochai's lantern riddles in II.4 and Daiyu's lantern riddle in II.5 are taken from *The Story of the Stone*, as well as the definition of a "bamboo wife." In addition, the translations of the inscription in the reception hall in I.12, and of the line from Zhuangzi in V.2 are also from *The Story of the Stone*.

These passages also borrow language from Hawkes and Minford's translation: the use of the term "career worm" and the description of the jade in I.11; the description of Baoyu's clothes in I.4 and of his apartment in I.11; the legal terminology used for Pan's case in I.6 and I.7; Silver's words in I.14; the description of Pan's gifts in II.2; the saying about the "beast of a thousand legs" in II.3; the description of the lanterns in II.4; the medical diagnoses in II.5 and II.8; Baochai's remarks on Silver's death in III.4; Baochai and Baoyu's discussion of the "heart of an infant" in VI.3; and the description of preparations for Xifeng's funeral in VI.6.

The translations of the poems at the beginnings of sections are my own, as is the translation of the quote from Mencius in I.5.

About the Author

After studying classics at Harvard and law at Yale, Pauline Chen completed a doctorate in Chinese literature at Princeton University. She has taught Chinese literature, language, and film at the University of Minnesota and Oberlin College. She is the author of *Peiling and the Chicken-Fried Christmas*, a novel for young readers, and lives in Ohio with her two children.

About the Artist

Jiang Guofang is a contemporary Chinese artist best known for his *Forbidden City* series of oil paintings, to which *Spring Dream in the Still of the Palace*, the image on this cover, belongs. He graduated from the Central Academy of Fine Arts in Beijing, and has taught both there and at the Central Academy of Drama. He has held solo exhibitions at the Palace Museum in Beijing, the Palazzo Venezia in Rome, the Berlin Arts Center, and in Hong Kong, Athens, and Treviso, Italy.